THE ULVERSCROFT FOUNDATION
(registered UK charity number 264873)

was established in 1972 to provide funds for research, diagnosis and treatment of eye diseases. Examples of major projects funded by the Ulverscroft Foundation are:-

- The Children's Eye Unit at Moorfelds Eye Hospital, London
- The Ulverscroft Children's Eye Unit at Great Ormond Street Hospital for Sick Children
- Funding research into eye diseases and treatment at the Department of Ophthalmology, University of Leicester
- The Ulverscroft Vision Research Group, Institute of Child Health
- Twin operating theatres at the Western Ophthalmic Hospital, London
- The Chair of Ophthalmology at the Royal Australian College of Ophthalmologists

You can help further the work of the Foundation by making a donation or leaving a legacy. Every contribution is gratefully received. If you would like to help support the Foundation or require further information, please contact:

THE ULVERSCROFT FOUNDATION
The Green, Bradgate Road, Anstey
Leicester LE7 7FU, England
Tel: (0116) 236 4325

website: www.ulverscroft-foundation.org.uk

HER HEART'S CHOICE

Lou Channer wants a life outside of North Devon, somewhere she's never left. She yearns to contribute to the war effort and takes a job as a clerk in the Royal Canadian Naval Yard in Plymouth, lodging with other girls from the depot who take her under their wing.

When Lou catches the eye of local wheeler-dealer Harry, who dazzles her with nights about town, she finally feels like one of the girls. And when Lieutenant Douglas Ross asks her out, Lou can't believe her luck — or decide who to give her heart to.

But during war, tragedy is always just around the corner, and when Lou's depot is burgled, she's suddenly the primary suspect — and her whole future is on the line.

ROSIE MEDDON

◆

HER HEART'S CHOICE

Complete and Unabridged

MAGNA
Leicester

First published in Great Britain in 2021

First Ulverscroft Edition
published 2021

A catalogue record for this book is available from the British Library.

ISBN 978–0–7505–4854–0

Published by
Ulverscroft Limited
Anstey, Leicestershire

Printed and bound in Great Britain by
TJ Books Ltd., Padstow, Cornwall

This book is printed on acid-free paper

For Merle

For Merle

Woodicombe House, Devon

June 1940

Chapter 1

Itchy Feet

'I'm sorry, love, but no, I don't think that's a good idea at all.'

'But Dad—'

'I wasn't convinced last time you suggested it, and I'm minded no differently now.'

Dragging her forefinger through the dust on her father's workbench, Lou Channer sighed with frustration. It was always the same. Every time she mentioned getting a job, Dad came up with a dozen or more reasons why she shouldn't. To make matters worse, his objections weren't even genuine; he was just being old-fashioned.

Well, this time, she wasn't going to be deterred. This time she was going to remain calm, stick to the approach she had spent hours rehearsing in her head and remind herself not to start whining about things being unfair. Whining was guaranteed to make him cross.

With that thought uppermost, she wandered across to his sawing horse, brushed the wood shavings from the top and perched on the end.

'But why not?' she asked. 'What was the point you paying for me to do that secretarial course if you were *never* going to let me go out and get a job?'

Setting down his chisel and wiping his hands down the front of his overalls, Luke Channer gave a weary shake of his head. 'Things are different now, love. There's a war on—'

'Even more reason for me to do something to help out

3

then, wouldn't you say?'

'—and with the way things are headed, almost anywhere could be a target. But at least here, with us being so far from anywhere important, we'll be safer than most.' 'But *last* time there was a war on,' Lou said, already struggling to keep her tone respectful, 'Mum left Woodicombe to go and work for Aunt Naomi, *right in the middle of London. And* the two of you were already married. *And* things back then were far harder and more frowned-upon than they are nowadays — or so you're forever telling us — but you never told *her* she couldn't do it.'

'I didn't, no, but only because last time around, the idea that the Germans could come over and drop bombs on London was unthinkable. Had I known—'

'You would have forbidden her?'

''Course I would have.'

'Like you're forbidding *me*?'

In response to her challenge, Luke sighed. 'Look, love, you know I can't *forbid* you to do *anything* any more — not since you turned twenty-one. But that doesn't mean I can't say I'd prefer you stayed at home, where I can see to it that you don't come to harm. Besides, what's the rush? Isn't there enough to keep you busy here, helping Mum and Nanny Edith? And what happened to that idea you had to help out Mrs Foster and Miss Nurse with the evacuees? I thought you liked littl'uns.'

'Actually,' Lou said, picturing the dozen grubby and lice-ridden children who'd been evacuated from St Ursula's in Paddington, to the vicarage at Woodicombe Cross, 'I've since discovered that I *don't* like them. I certainly don't like those at Mrs Foster's. They snatch everything… and they're greedy and foul-mouthed. And they refuse to do as they're told.'

4

When her father grinned, and his eyes creased up at the corners, she couldn't help smiling back.

'Good practice for when you have children of your own, I should have thought.'

'Happen I don't want children of my own.' Now she was just being silly. Act like a child and she would never win him over.

'Anyway,' he ignored her remark to continue, 'you've *got* a job, keeping the books for Browns. It's why I made you that desk and got you that typewriter you kept on about — so you could type up their invoices, do their accounts and what-not.'

'I *know*,' Lou said, her exasperation perilously close to boiling over. 'But the work is dull. And because Mr Brown brings the books *here* each week, it doesn't feel like proper work at all. Worse still, since the whole lot only takes me a couple of hours, the amount I get paid is barely enough to keep me in kirby grips.'

'Well, if it's money you need—'

'No, Dad, can't you see?' By her sides, her frustration was curling her hands into fists. 'This isn't about *money*. It's about—'

'Look, love,' her father interjected, 'what's brought all this on again, eh? Is it that business with young Esme? Is that what's got you so restless?'

She sighed. Poor Esme. There she was, just two days from marrying the rather lovely Richard Trevannion, son of a Member of Parliament and who had a job doing something hush-hush in the War Office, when wallop! Out of the blue, Aunt Naomi had broken the news that she and Captain Colborne were not Esme's real parents: Esme, it turned out, was actually the daughter of an East End railway labourer and his illegitimately born wife, Bertha, the latter a half-sister to Naomi through her seri-

5

ally philandering father, Hugh Russell. Hardly surprising then, that after that bombshell, not only had her poor cousin felt unable to go ahead with the wedding, she had decided to run off and make a fresh start where no one knew anything about her. Of course, with the way things were working out *here*, she, Lou, now regretted not going with her. Now that it was too late, she could see that Esme had been right: together, they could have gone anywhere, done anything. At the moment of Esme suggesting it, though, all she had been able to see were the risks. And on that score Dad was right: the upset *had* left her feeling unsettled. But admitting that would only give him more ammunition to use against her. And he had enough of that already.

'No, Dad,' she said, looking up to find him watching her. 'It's not that. I'd be lying to say what happened to Esme didn't make me stop and think. But that's not why I want to do this. I want to feel *useful*. Hopeful, even. I want to get out and make new friends, see new things.'

And it was true. For some long time now she'd been wanting to strike out and make something of herself. And while she might have missed the opportunity to start afresh with Esme, it didn't mean she couldn't pull herself together and do *something* with her life. Thanks to this war, women were taking on all sorts of jobs. No longer was a woman's only choice to stay at home, waiting to be married and start a family: women these days were earning their own money, contributing to the war effort by filling the jobs vacated by their serving menfolk. And, if the recruitment adverts plastered everywhere were to be believed, they were having fun doing it. And fun was something she craved almost more than a bit of independence and some money in her pocket.

6

'Well,' Luke Channer picked up again, 'if your mind's set on getting a job, then all I can do is prevail upon you to be sensible and pick something out of harm's way.'

'But Dad —' Wait… he was giving in? He was going to cease raising objections and let her go out to work? Because, if he was, she should act before he changed his mind. 'I will,' she said quickly, avoiding looking at him directly. 'You have my word. I won't do nothing foolish.'

With a rueful shake of his head, her father pushed himself away from his workbench and came limping towards her. When he then reached to give her a hug, her nostrils filled with the smell of sawdust and Brylcreem — aromas that triggered memories of being hoisted high upon his shoulders while he lolloped about the garden pretending to be a wild horse. The only difference now was that those curly locks to which she had once clung for dear life, screaming with a mixture of terror and delight, were turning from the russet and bronze of youth to the silver and ash of middle age.

'Something tells me you and your mother have already talked about this anyway,' he said, his hand on her shoulder, his expression one of resignation.

'Actually,' she replied, still astonished by the fact that he had relented, 'I came to talk to *you* first.'

'So, for once, the two of you didn't gang up on me?'

She grinned. 'Me and Mum? Gang up on *you*, Dad? Never.'

'Serious, though, Lou. Please have a care not to go upsetting your mother. That business up in London with young Esme has really knocked her for six, especially coming on the back of your brother Vic joining up… and now young Arthur saying he's minded to do the same.'

7

''Course,' she said, leaning across to kiss his cheek and then turn promptly for the door. 'I always *try* not to upset *anyone*. I know better than to burn my bridges.'

'I should hope you do,' he called after her, 'because the timber and the nails to repair them is hard come by these days. And there's only so much magic I can work to mend the things you children keep breaking...'

Stepping outside into the warm June sunshine, Lou couldn't stop grinning. Dear Dad. Never in her wildest dreams had she expected him to be so quick to concede. But, now that he had, she mustn't waste time: she must go straight in and ask Mum for help. Best to strike while—

'Back safe from London, then.'

With a start, she looked up. Scrunching across the gravel towards her was Freddie Paddon. Bother. She did hope he hadn't come to ask her to go out with him, because all of a sudden she had a lot on her plate: thoughts to get straight in her head; ideas to come up with; Mum to ask for help in actually finding a job.

'Yes,' she nevertheless answered him brightly. 'We got back Sunday teatime.'

Waiting until she drew level, he turned about and fell into step beside her. 'I knocked at the kitchen porch first. Your ma said you were out here.'

She smiled back at him. With his wispy fair hair, pale blue-grey eyes, and the sunlight picking out the line of freckles across the bridge of his nose, he didn't look a day older than when they used to sit next to each other at school.

'I was in the workshop talking to Dad.' She saw no reason to explain why — not until she was more certain of how the business of finding a job would work out.

'Bet you're glad to be out of London.'

Again, she smiled. 'You know what they say — no place

like home.'

Just lately, though, it couldn't feel less true. After the vibrancy of Clarence Square, Woodicombe felt drab and lifeless and so horribly old-fashioned. According to Mum, in the days before the *last* war, the Russells used to come and stay here for the whole of the summer, Grandmamma Pamela filling the house with guests, and hosting magnificent parties with music and dancing and entertainments and feasts. Looking about at the neglected state of the place these days, it was hard to imagine.

'Good weddin'?' Freddie went on to enquire.

Unable to face raking over the details yet again, she nodded. 'Fine, thank you.'

'Good.'

'So, what brings you up here this bright morning?' Something about his manner told her he'd come to do more than just pass the time of day.

'I've got something to tell you. Something real important.'

Poor Freddie. He was a nice enough lad — clean, polite, not one to take liberties. Not so long ago she might even have settled for marrying him — better the devil you knew and all that — but, just lately, the prospect had lost any glimmer of appeal. Mrs Frederick Paddon: the name alone conjured aprons and headscarves, a washing line pegged with nappies, a pram clogging up the hallway, and the real Mrs Paddon constantly popping in with unsolicited advice about everything from whooping cough and nappy rash to sore nipples. Lou Paddon. Hardly a name to cause someone to mistake her for a film star, no matter the care she took with her appearance. Bad enough that she had her mother's dull brown hair and ordinary features but add to that the name Mrs Freddie Paddon and no one would be in the least surprised to learn she was the wife of a man who worked as a joiner in his father's cabinet-making business. Paddon *& Son* as Freddie always took great pains to stress, as though the prospect of him one day taking over from his father would make her swoon. No, while she'd hate to be accused of snobbery, she really was hoping for something more.

Feeling the sun starting to burn her arms, and anxious to get back inside to talk to her mother, she glanced to his face. 'Important, you say?'

Waiting for him to reply, she folded her arms. Then, realising how the resulting stance made her look like the housewife she was desperate not to become, she lowered them to her sides.

'I've joined up.'

He'd *joined up*? He was *going away*? In a bid to conceal a mixture of surprise and relief, she smiled. 'Well done!'

'Royal Navy, 'course.'

''Course,' she said, nodding encouragingly.

'Well ... I were a Sea Scout, weren't I?'

With a vague recollection of him turning up one summer in a uniform of navy-blue jersey and matching shorts, she continued to nod. 'But didn't you tell me you were in a reserved occupation — that being a carpenter and joiner meant you wouldn't have to serve?'

'It's true. I don't *have* to. But I *want* to. I want to do my bit, like Pa did in the last war.'

'Yes. Yes, of course you do.' Doing the right thing was Freddie through and through. 'So, when do you go and... start ... or whatever?'

Pushing a hand inside his jacket, he pulled out an envelope, from within which he extracted a piece of paper and held it up for her to see. Across the top were printed the words *National Service Acts. Enlistment Notice.* Hand-

10

written in the box underneath were his name and address.
Turning it back, he read aloud.

'*Dear Sir,*

In accordance with the National Service Acts, you are called upon for service in the Royal Navy and are required to present yourself on Monday 10th June between 9am and twelve noon at —'

Monday the tenth of June? He would be going as soon as Monday? 'Golly,' she said. 'That's awful quick.'

Refolding the document carefully along its crease, Freddie slid it back into the envelope and then pushed the whole thing back into his pocket. 'It is. But I'm ready. Well, almost.'

Behind her ribs, a gentle ache set in. Freddie was going in the navy, and she was surprised by how much she suddenly minded. 'So ...'

'Any road,' he said, his expression straightening as he took a step towards her. 'Since I *am* going, and since there ain't much time afore I do, I thought to come up and see you to... well, to ask if you'd...' Swallowing down a gulp, Lou fought to conceal a sudden panic at Freddie's words. '...wait for me...'

Oh, dear. Just as she'd feared. 'Um...'

'I know we've not been courting proper... the blame for which rests entirely with me for never quite managing to pluck up the courage to ask you... but we *have* walked out a time or two. And if it weren't for me joining up, then some day now I'd be setting that situation to rights. In fact, I suppose that's what I'm doing now, asking you to stay true to me until I can come back and court you in the manner you deserve.'

11

When, flushed of face, he tailed off and stood staring back at her, all she could think was that her mouth suddenly felt as dry as sandpaper. What on earth did she say? Here she was, viewing his imminent departure as an opportunity to distance herself from him and yet what *he* wanted was precisely the opposite: he wanted her to wait for him.

Feeling her face burning, she stared down at her feet. 'Gosh,' she said, still floundering for a response. 'I wasn't expecting *that*.'

'See, once I'm away at sea,' he went on, 'doing my duty and whatnot, I shan't want to be a-worrying about things back home. So, although I'm not a forward sort — well, you seen that well enough — and I shouldn't want to push you, I *should* prefer to go off knowing we've come to an understanding… so that I can be out there, doing my bit, with something to look forward to when I get back.'

Clearly, Lou reflected, the poor lad had been stewing over this for some time; his declaration almost certainly the longest speech he'd ever made. So, what did she do? Did she suggest that they wait and see how they both felt when he came back? Did she say that, given the uncertainty of war, might it not be better that he didn't feel bound to her — the chance of girls in foreign ports and all that? Did she announce that she had plans of her own and couldn't possibly know where she would even be when he came back? Or did she just say that she'd never really thought of him as a sweetheart, thus bringing to an end the chance of his misunderstanding persisting? Surely, all things considered, that would be the fairest.

'Freddie —'

'Heck, Lou. I've gone about this all wrong, haven't I? I've put you on the spot, thought only about what *I* want.'

Meeting his look, she gave a light shake of her head. 'No, Freddie, it's not that. I can quite see why you would

12

ask. Joining up is a big step. A brave step.' *Careful not to overdo it.*

'I don't *feel* brave. Truth be told, Lou, I'm more than a bit scared, you know, of all that might happen. But that's no reason not to go an' do my bit, is it? But what *would* help is knowing that you're … well, that you'll be here when I get back …'

Oh dear. What on earth did she say?

'If you'd like me to write to you while you're away… keep our friendship going along…'

Instantly, his expression relaxed. 'Would you do that? Would you write to me? Oh, Lou, you're the best. You won't believe how long I've sweated over asking you. Wish I'd thought to bring my Brownie now, then I could have took your picture and had it to carry with me. Happen you could get Mr Channer to take one. Then you could send it to me. There's an address for writing to ships at sea, you know.'

Rueing that she had failed to make herself clear, Lou did her best to smile. 'I'll see what I can do.'

'Oh, thanks ever so, Lou. You wouldn't believe the relief I feel to know this is settled. Thank you. Thank you!'

When he then lunged towards her and wrapped her in a bear hug of an embrace, her smile finally slipped. 'No,' she said softly, it being far too late now to clarify what she had actually meant by *keep their friendship going.* 'I daresay I can't.'

★ ★ ★

'Ah, there you are, love.'

'Yes, Mum. I just went out to —'

'Did Freddie catch you? I told him you were out there

13

somewhere.'

'He did, yes.' Probably best to say nothing of why he'd come to see her. Mum was fond of Freddie. And, given that she was about to seek her help in finding a job, it might be better not to put the notion of wedding bells into her mind.

'Oh, and here, the postman brought you this.'

Wondering who on earth would be writing to *her*, Lou watched her mother pull from the pocket of her housecoat a small ivory-coloured envelope. Accepting it, she studied the handwriting. It was neat and precise, and the postmark — once she managed to make it out — said London SW19. London? Then it could really only be from Esme.

Wandering along the hallway, she ducked into the drawing room where, in keeping with almost every other room, the furniture and knick-knacks stood swathed in dust covers. This morning, with the weather fine, at least the French doors had been thrown wide to rid it of the smell of disuse.

Perching on the arm of the nearest chair, she slid her forefinger under the flap of the envelope and pulled out a single sheet of notepaper. And yes, it was from Esme.

Dear Lou,

Quite by chance, I have found perfectly acceptable lodgings with a pleasant widow, whose cooking (I hadn't realised until now that meat was rationed on a shillings and pence basis!) is plain but wholesome.

How typical that Esme should know so little about rationing! But honestly, was that really the first thing she'd thought to tell her? Of more use would surely have been

14

to describe the house and this widow — was she young? Old? Wealthy? And how had she found her? For goodness sake, Essie, what was the place like?! Everyone was out of their minds with worry about her disappearance and yet here she was writing about the price of meat?

With a vexed sigh, Lou read on.

Please do not be offended that I have chosen not to furnish you with my address, but, for the present at least, I have no wish to be 'found'. I am sure you will understand.

Please apologise on my behalf to Aunt Kate for the wasted trip to London for you both. And please do not worry about me. I am perfectly fine and will write again should my circumstances change.

I trust that you are well and do not think too badly of me, with all my love, Esme.

Well, if her cousin had intended this strange little letter to act as reassurance, she had missed the mark by a mile: in typical Esme fashion it raised more questions than it answered. She made no mention of how long she intended to stay in these *perfectly acceptable lodgings*, nor did she say what she thought to do to support herself. She had her own money of course, but surely not enough to just ... well, to just what? She gave not the slightest clue.

Refolding the sheet of paper, Lou slipped it back into its envelope. At least her cousin had thought to write. And, since she hadn't mentioned Richard, or returning to Clarence Square and the Colbornes, at least she appeared to be sticking to her guns about needing to work out who she was and what she wanted to do next — was showing the courage of her convictions. That she didn't wish to be found also showed a determination to do this at her own speed and in her own way. Well, good for her.

15

Getting to her feet, Lou exhaled heavily. Everyone, it seemed, knew what they wanted. Her brother Vic had joined up; her brother Arthur had begun talking of doing the same. Cousin Esme was following her heart — even if she didn't know where it was taking her. Even Freddie knew what *he* wanted. So, since she had no desire to be left in their wakes, now was the time to muster some of the decisiveness and determination being shown by everyone else around here and go after her *own* dream. After all, if they were all doing it, it couldn't be *that* hard, could it?

★ ★ ★

'Goodness. Hello, Arthur, love. What are you doing, home at this hour?'

Following the line of her mother's eyes across to where, in the corridor, her younger brother was pulling off his cycle clips, Lou frowned. Yes, why *was* her brother home so early? Too much to hope he'd been given the sack.

'It's Wednesday, Mum. Half-day.'

Bother. So it was. And just when she'd got Mum to sit down in the servants' parlour with her for a moment, too. She'd spent ages yesterday planning how to approach Mum about this and now, here was Arthur to get in the way.

'Lord, 'course it is,' Kate Channer remarked with a dismayed shake of her head. 'Being away those few days last week has completely thrown me. Don't know whether I'm on foot or on horseback at the moment.'

'Not surprised, Mum,' Arthur said, tugging off his jacket and running a hand through his sandy-coloured hair. 'I mean, what a waste of time that was, the two of you traipsing all the way up to London for some fancy wedding and then it didn't happen.'

Beneath the table, Lou clenched her fists. How dare her brother make light of what had happened to their cousin! If it wasn't for the fact that she needed Mum's help, she would march over there and take a swing at him for showing such disrespect.

'Oh, shut up, you clot,' she rounded on him anyway. 'You've not the least idea what you're talking about.'

'No need to go taking it out on *me*,' her brother parried. '*I* didn't jilt nobody at the altar.'

'For your information,' she responded through gritted teeth, '*no one* jilted *anyone* at the altar. And so I'll ask you to keep your nose out of it.' Of course, really, she should just ignore him. But where her brothers were concerned — and Arthur in particular — that was easier said than done.

'For pity's sake, you two, lay off one another,' their mother chose that moment to plead.

'Sorry, Mum.'

To Lou, her brother sounded anything *but* sorry. But then ever since he'd turned fifteen and talked his way into a job as a trainee mechanic down at Brown's Quality Motors, he'd become such a cocky little devil. Still some way off eighteen, he was already talking about joining up. But not to do as their brother, Vic, had done and follow their father into the army. Oh, no. Arthur was going in the navy. *All the nice girls love a sailor.* Strutting about, whistling that same tune all the time. Driving everyone mad with it, he was. Well, from now on, she wouldn't let him rattle her. He could do what he wanted with his life. She had plans of her own to see to.

'Any dinner left?' Arthur asked. 'I could eat a horse.'

'Nanny Edith has left you a plate on a pan on the range,' Kate replied. 'But just make sure to clean thoroughly under your fingernails before you sit down to eat it.'

17

'Yes, Ma.'

'And lay a proper place at the table. I don't want to come through and find you leant against the sink, shovelling it off the plate with a spoon.'

'No, Ma. I'll lay a place.'

'Good lad. Off you go, then.' Turning her attention back into the room, Kate gave Lou a warm smile. 'Now, where were we, love?'

Telling herself to forget about Arthur, Lou smiled back. The trick now that he was home — with his habit of continually asking Mum to find or do something for him — was to keep her mother's mind on the Situations Vacant long enough for them to spot something for which she might reasonably apply. 'We were looking here,' she said, pointing her finger at a column on the page entitled 'Administration & Clerical'.

'So we were. Look, love,' Kate said, her tone neutral, 'are you sure you wouldn't be just as happy with the Women's Voluntary Service? It's real popular now. Lots of women are joining—'

'Mum, you know how hopeless I am at knitting.'

'Silly,' Kate said, reaching across to pat Lou's hand. 'It's not just knitting—'

'And I'm even more useless at tea and sympathy—'

'Reverend Gilbert's wife runs the local branch now. I saw her in the Post Office only last week.'

Inwardly, Lou groaned. 'No thank you, Mum. I'm sure the ladies of the WVS do a fine job. Most likely more than fine. But what I want is to be properly employed.'

Her mother's response came with a resigned sigh. 'Well, a good number of these vacancies would be no good for you anyway. Take this one for instance: *mature lady required for typing and filing work*. And look, here's a part-time position but it's down at the chandlery, and that's too far for you to cycle even through the summer.'

Lou stared down at the advertisement. The work sounded ideal, and stipulated only that a *young and presentable lady, aged 21—30,* was required. But Mum was right. She would have to take two different buses to get there, which would mean that after paying the fares from a wage for just twenty hours a week, it wouldn't be worth going.

'But where *am* I going to be able to get to?' she moaned, despondency dampening the enthusiasm she'd felt when her mother had agreed to help her look through the vacancies in the local newspaper.

'I'm sure I don't know, love.'

'There's nothing in the village...'

'No. Though I see Hearn's the butcher has a sign in *his* window.'

When Lou turned, ready to call her Mum soft, it was to see that she was grinning, the glint in her eye lifting years from her appearance. Like Dad, she too was showing the first signs of middle age.

'Something tells me it's not a typist or a secretary he's after,' she said, grinning back.

'No. Though his lad must surely have been exempt, he's gone and joined up anyway.'

'Hm. You don't happen to know anyone who's had a secretary go and join up, do you?' Already, this was beginning to feel like a lost cause — and just when she'd got Dad on her side, too.

''Fraid not, love. But there's no need to give up just yet. Let's keep looking down the rest of these adverts. There's plenty here to be going on with.'

With that, from the mass of small print, a darker headline caught Lou's eye.

Office, Stockroom & General
Warehouse Hands Required

Plymouth. MOD requires women for full-time civilian positions.

Excellent Rates of Pay. Lodgings Available. Must be single, aged 18—25 and physically fit. Clerical or stockroom experience preferred.

Apply in the first instance to:

'Look, Mum,' she said, hardly daring to breathe in case the opportunity staring back at her disappeared before her eyes. 'I could do *this*. I know how to do clerical work — accounts and filing and the like.'

Beside her, her mother bent lower over the page. 'But it's in Plymouth, love. How the devil would you get all the way down there?'

This, Lou knew, was where she was going to have to be clever; sound too gung-ho and her mother would come up with all manner of reasons why it wasn't even worth her applying. Act calmly, on the other hand...

Tucking a loose strand of hair behind her ear and trying to ignore the excited thudding of her heart, she drew a breath. 'Well, I haven't thought that far yet. But look, it says that lodgings are available. So, I suppose that means they expect you to go and live nearby. Well, they must do, otherwise why advertise all the way up here in the *North Devon Crier*? No one could travel all the way from here to Plymouth every day.'

'Leave home, do you mean?'

Feeling her mother looking sideways at her, Lou

fixedher gaze on the far wall. 'I have to go *some* time, Mum.'

'Well, yes, I know that. 'Course I do. But I always thought that wouldn't be until you were wed.'

Through Lou's mind went the words *what, like Esme, you mean?* Best not to voice them, though. 'Well, yes,' she said. 'And until this war started up, *I* thought that, too. But how many times have you told me stories about when the last war was on, and what you did to help out, and how, for much of that time, it was as though you and Dad hadn't got married at all?'

The unexpected lack of a comeback from her mother made Lou relax a little. It was crafty to bring up the last war; Mum was forever saying that in many respects, it had been the making of her. Well, now, perhaps this war could be the making of *her*, too.

'Well ...'

'Look, why don't I just write a letter of application?' she said. 'If I have a go at setting down what I know how to do — about Brown's and that, you could look it over for me and then I could type it up all nicely. Happen they'll take one glance at it and write back to say I don't have the right experience. But, even if they do turn me down, at least I will have tried. And you do always say there's no harm in trying.'

She had her mother there. *At least have a go*, or *at least try it*, were phrases Kate used a lot.

'And you're certain you want to do this? You're not letting yourself be swayed by what happened to Esme?' her mother asked. 'After all, just because *she* threw everything up in the air and went off in search of... well, I don't rightly know what it is she's gone looking for, doesn't mean you have to.'

'No, Mum,' Lou said carefully. 'I won't deny that Esme

21

running away like that did make me stop and think. But it's got nothing to do with me wanting to get a job.'

'Very well, then,' her mother said. 'If you're sure. But just don't expect me to explain it to your father if they write and say they want you to go and be interviewed. That task will be down to you and you alone.'

Leaning across from her chair, Lou wrapped her mother in an awkward hug. 'Thanks, Mum. What's that thing you always say? Nothing ventured, nothing gained?'

'Hm. I'm still not telling your father for you.'

'No need for you to go a-worrying about *Dad*,' Lou said, grinning broadly. 'I've a feeling he won't be as surprised as you think.'

In that moment, Lou felt brighter than she had in ages. Though she might have led her parents to believe otherwise, a part of her knew that it *was* Esme's bravery spurring her to do this — inspiring her to get away from this musty house and her stifled existence within it. So, yes, she could say with all certainty that she *was* sure: the time had finally come to show the world there was more to Lou Channer than met the eye.

★ ★ ★

Well, don't you look the business.

With her father's remark from first thing coming to mind, Lou smoothed a hand down the front of her navy-blue box-pleat skirt. While her outfit might not be fancy, she was pleased with the way she had put it together. Yes, her checked jacket was older than she would have liked and wasn't the best match for the slender cut of her skirt but, by taking it off and putting it over her arm, she didn't think it looked out of place. And, by virtue of a good soaking in a bowl of soda crystals dissolved in warm water, her plain old white blouse had come up surprisingly bright, too. All told, she thought she looked purposeful, which was surely what any interviewer would expect from a candidate for a clerical position.

Growing steadily more nervous, she pushed back the cuff of her blouse and peered at her wristwatch. Ten minutes to twelve. She'd been sat on this wooden bench for quarter of an hour. No wonder her bottom was numb. *Better to be there in good time*, her mother had said when they'd been studying the railway timetable. *Best not to arrive flustered and sticky*. Sticky. Discreetly, she tried to sniff her armpit. Miracle of miracles, she still smelled relatively fragrant. She did wish she could powder her nose, though. Not that she'd brought her compact. Fresh-faced and healthy was a better look than red-lipped and tarty, her mother had said when she'd asked her about applying a little foundation and lipstick. At the time, she'd been disappointed by her mother's view that make-up was inappropriate, but, with hindsight, Mum had probably been right. When it came to that sort of thing, she usually was.

Mortified to hear her stomach rumbling from hunger, she shifted her weight. A sleepless night and an attack of butterflies first thing had meant that at six o'clock this morning, all she'd been able to manage were a couple of mouthfuls of cornflakes. Then, once she had been ready to leave, Dad had driven her to Barnstaple, from where her train had taken an hour to reach Exeter St David's. There, she'd had to cross the platform and wait for a second train for a journey of another hour. Eventually, arriving in Plymouth, she had found her way to the Employment Exchange, grateful for the instructions sent with the letter inviting her for interview. And this was where she had been sitting, trying not to fidget, ever since.

With nothing to do but try to remain calm, she took

another look along the corridor. On both sides were wooden doors, each with a small pane of glass, above which was a number. She wondered into which of the many rooms she would be going, and how many people would interview her. In an attempt to prepare for this moment, she had sat with her mother and tried to imagine the sorts of questions she might be asked but, since neither of them had ever been interviewed for a job before, they had only been able to guess. In her handbag, Lou had a letter of reference, kindly written for her by Mr Brown, along with her examination certificate from school and the documents showing her shorthand and typing speeds. If they wanted to see anything more than that, she would be stuck.

'Miss Louise Channer.'

Hearing her name, she shot to her feet. Halfway along the corridor stood an older woman in a plain grey suit.

'Yes,' she said, starting towards her. 'I am she.' The women beckoned. 'Come in. Take a seat.'

'Thank you.' Opting to place her jacket on the back of the wooden chair, Lou sat down. The room was small with a tiny window high up on one of the walls. The overhead light was bright, the desk in front of which she found herself bearing a folder, the cover of which lay opened back to display her letter of application. Heavens, this was it. She really was doing this.

'Miss Louise Channer of Woodicombe House.' Sensing that it was a statement rather than a question, Lou nevertheless nodded. 'Yes.'

'Aged twenty-one.'

Again, she nodded. 'Yes.'

'Unmarried.'

'Yes.'

24

'Very well, Miss Channer, my name is Mrs Spears and it is my job to recruit civilian workers for the Canadian Royal Naval Depot recently set up within Devonport dockyard. Should you be successful in obtaining a position, the depot would become your place of employment. You would work nine hours per day, between eight in the morning and six at night, with a thirty-minute break for lunch and two fifteen-minute tea breaks. You might also be asked to work on Saturday mornings from eight until twelve, for which an additional payment at overtime rate would become due. Now, I see from your letter of application that you are qualified in typing and shorthand.'

'I am, yes.' Unfastening the clasp of her bag, Lou withdrew the envelope containing her certificates. 'I've brought these.'

She watched Mrs Spears take out the documents and spread them out on the desk in front of her. 'Your level of attainment would seem satisfactory. And I see from your letter that you are currently employed in an administrative capacity.'

Realising that her mouth suddenly felt parched, Lou forced a swallow. 'Yes. I keep customer accounts, type invoices and letters... that sort of thing.' With that, she remembered Mr Brown's reference. 'I have this letter from my employer.' There really was no need, she decided, to do herself down by mentioning the rather low-key nature of her employment, nor the fact that she performed her duties sat at a homemade desk in a disused butler's pantry.

'Just the ticket. When could you start?'

The directness of Mrs Spears' question caught her unawares. Was she being offered the job?

'Um...'

'What period of notice must you give to your current employer?'

25

Period of notice? Frantically, she tried to think. 'A week,' she said, hoping it a likely amount of time.

Mrs Spears turned to examine a calendar on the wall behind the desk.

'So, if I were to suggest that you report for duty on… shall we say, Monday the seventeenth of June, that would be acceptable to you?' Evidently seeing that she was having difficulties working it out, Mrs Spears unhooked the calendar and laid it in on the desk. 'Today is the seventh. You would need to go home and give your notice today, leaving you one clear week to work your notice to… Brown's Quality Motors… and report to the dockyard on the following Monday.'

It was then Lou realised that she'd given no thought whatsoever to what would happen in the unlikely event that she was actually offered the job, even less, how she would react. With the squares on the calendar seeming to have little bearing to real life, she forced herself to think. One more week at home; one week to get herself sorted out. 'I think that would be all right,' she said, hoping that her voice wasn't trembling as much as it sounded in her head.

'Good. Well then Miss Channer, I should like to offer you the position of junior clerical assistant. I doubt you will be required to use your shorthand, though you might like to keep it in good order by practising from time to time, but you will be typing, keeping records, filing and so on. You will work in an office within the depot, details of which I will forward to you by letter.'

'Will I get a uniform?' Lou thought to ask, her mind already on the matter of which of her few belongings she would need to pack.

'Uniforms are supplied for storekeeper positions only. For your particular duties, a skirt and blouse will suffice,

26

and flat shoes are preferred. You will, however, be entitled to put in for an apron, once you join. By all accounts, the warehouse is a dusty place.'

An apron. Oh well. 'Thank you.'

'And I assume from your home address that you will require lodgings.'

Golly, yes. She'd almost overlooked the small matter of where she would live. 'I will, yes.'

Flicking open a spiral-bound notebook, Mrs Spears peered at several of the pages until evidently arriving at the information she sought. 'Here,' she said, writing an address on a piece of paper and handing it to her. 'Jubilee Street. Number eleven. The landlady is Mrs Hannacott. She has several of our girls there already. I've seen the place for myself. It's comfortable enough and less than ten minutes' walk from the dockyard. You'll share a twin room, breakfast and dinner included, the rent for which will be stopped weekly from your wages. There's a canteen in the yard for lunches. You will be paid on Fridays and no doubt be pleased to learn there's no week-in-hand.'

Not entirely sure what was meant by week-in-hand, Lou confined herself to nodding. As it was, her head was already swimming. 'Thank you,' she eventually managed.

'I will inform Mrs Hannacott you will be arriving on the afternoon of Sunday the sixteenth.'

Moments later, walking back out into the bright sunshine, Lou stood for a moment, dazzled and uncertain. Had she really just got herself a job? A proper job with a proper wage, paid every Friday? And somewhere to live, too? Had it really been that straightforward? Golly. What on earth were Mum and Dad going to say?

Realising she was standing in the middle of the pavement with people skirting to either side of her, she turned back in the direction from whence she had come an hour

27

or so earlier. Heavens. She had only gone and got herself a job!

Grinning with delight, she glanced at her wristwatch: plenty of time before the departure of the train she'd planned to catch, and so she would find a cafe. She would use the coppers Dad had given her to buy herself a bite to eat somewhere. Oh, if only she knew where Esme was! She would love to be able to tell her that she'd got a job.

Crikey. After so long thinking it would never happen, she was about to become an independent woman. And she really couldn't wait.

Chapter 2

A New Start

'I hope you don't snore.'

It was late on Sunday afternoon and Lou had arrived at the lodgings in Jubilee Street tired, grubby and anxious, her three-hour journey providing more than enough time for her to have second thoughts about her undertaking. It was too late now, though, because here she was, peering into a room containing two narrow beds, a modestly sized wardrobe and a matching chest of drawers. Under the bay window, at which greying net curtains were flapping in the breeze, stood a wooden clothes horse draped with stockings and smalls.

'I don't snore, no,' she replied now to the young woman who was stood, hands on hips, appraising her appearance. 'Least, no one's ever said I do.'

'Jean Rudd,' the room's occupant said, extending a hand and moving towards her.

'Lou Channer. Pleased to meet you.'

'Likewise, I'm sure. Well, that's yours,' Jean said, gesturing to the closest of the two beds, 'along with the bottom three drawers, the right-hand side of the wardrobe and the right-hand side of the shelf.' It was only when Lou stepped properly through the door that she saw a washbasin, above it a mirror and short wooden shelf, the left-hand side of which was crammed with cosmetics. 'Though you might not think so to look at the place,' Jean went on, 'having the only room with a basin makes us the chosen ones. Oh, and the bathroom's at the end of the landing, the lav out in the yard.'

'How many girls live here?' Lou asked, the weight of her suitcase pulling at her shoulder. For some reason, she couldn't bring herself to put it down — as though the act of doing so would confirm her decision to stay, when she wasn't altogether sure yet that she would.

'Seven now you're here. Four up in the big room in the attic, the two of us, and Queenie on her own next door. *On* the subject of Queenie, a word to the wise. She's the self-appointed bathroom monitor. Expect a rap on the door if you overstay your time.'

To Lou's mind, Jean didn't look as though she was joking. 'Duly warned,' she said and tried to raise a smile. 'If you walk smartish, it's eight minutes from here to the dockyard gates and another two or three to where your lot clock-in.' *Your lot?* Was this Jean woman not one of them, then? 'Breakfast — if you're the sort to bother with it — is quarter past seven, supper, half six. Front door is locked each night at half ten. We're not supposed to have keys but, if you keep up the act and moan about the inconvenience of having to be in so early, I'll lend you mine to get one cut. There's a place in the yard that'll do it for you. Oh, and we're not allowed to smoke up here, only downstairs. So at least have the sense to hang out the window if you're gasping.'

Despite having never smoked, Lou nodded. ''Course.' 'Well, come on in then. Get yourself settled. Sunday nights it's just tea and cake at five o'clock, on account of us having had Sunday dinner.'

Finding this confident young woman unnerving, Lou moved further into the room and put her case on the little stool at the end of her bed. 'Have you lived here long?' she asked, pressing the locks to her case and watching them pop undone. From the woman's accent, she got the impression she hailed from London. She certainly wasn't from anywhere in Devon.

'Coming up on four months,' Jean replied, flopping onto her own bed. 'I work in Wages. I keep the sick records and help make up the pay packets. In our section there's me an' another girl who does three days a week. We work in a pokey little hole of a place between the cash office and Personnel. The men call us *The Money*. The work's deadly dull but the pay's not too bad... and there's the odd perk, too, once you know your way around. And you get your pick of the fellers, always assuming you're looking.'

Lifting from her suitcase a couple of blouses, miraculously still crease-free, Lou went to the wardrobe and opened the right-hand of the two doors. From the rail inside hung three empty hangers. She should have thought to bring some from home.

'I'm not, not really,' she said, starting to hang two blouses on one hanger and opting to sound vague. 'Looking, I mean.'

'Got a chap back home then?'

She turned back to her case. 'There's one who wants to be... but...'

'You're not keen.'

Unused to discussing her private affairs with people she'd only just met, Lou shook her head. 'Not especially.'

'Where are you from?' Jean went on to enquire.

'Woodicombe — a little place no one has ever heard of, near Westward Quay.' She supposed that sharing a room would get easier. She supposed that eventually, this grown-up woman would cease to make her feel like a schoolgirl.

'I could tell you weren't from around here.'

'And you?' she plucked up the courage to ask. 'Where are you from?'

31

With a yawn, her roommate leant back against her headboard. 'I grew up in South London, but my family's back down here now, back where they all came from in Gran and Grandad's day, worse luck.'

That was why her accent sounded like Grandpa Hugh's, then, Lou thought.

Lifting out and re-folding her underwear, she glanced across at her roommate's reclined form. Jean wasn't overly tall, but she was eye-wateringly curvy. Close-fitting navy-blue slacks accentuated wide hips and a neat little waist, while the buttons of her flowery short-sleeved blouse strained across her chest. And her dark, pin-curled hair was glossy and perfectly in place. How did she manage to keep it looking so clean this far into the week? And how did she keep her nails so neat — and painted, too!

'And do *you* have a… man?'

With a groan, Jean rolled her eyes. '*A* man? Yes. *The* man? Let's say I'm undecided. Enjoying finding out, though. Anyway, you might want to get a move on. Tea's in ten minutes.'

Moments later, her unpacking finished and her hands washed, Lou followed Jean down the stairs and through to a room beyond the small kitchen. In it were a sideboard, a dresser, and an oblong table around which were crammed eight hard-back chairs. Covered with a red and white checked oilcloth and set with tea plates, knives, and cups and saucers, it looked cramped but homely.

'Everything all right, lover?' the landlady, Mrs Hannacott, enquired as she came through from the kitchen carrying a plate piled with a dozen dumpy scones.

Lou smiled. 'Yes, thank you. Everything's fine.'

'Anywhere you like then,' Mrs Hannacott went on, evidently noticing her hesitation. 'Jean, go through an' fetch the pot for me, would you? There's a love.'

Despite Mrs Hannacott's instruction to sit down, Lou continued to prevaricate. As a newcomer, it felt wrong to choose just any chair when the others might have a favourite place.

As it happened, when Jean returned bearing an over-sized Brown Betty, the other girls drifted in behind her and, from what she could see, sat wherever the mood took them.

'Ladies,' Jean said as the last of them wandered in. Setting down the teapot, she covered it with a knitted cosy. 'Meet Lou Channer. She's joining your lot, Liddy.'

'Lucky you,' a girl with red hair pinned high on her head piped up.

'Yeah, how come she gets the Canadians?' her fair-haired neighbour wanted to know.

Pulling out the chair at the end of the table, Jean sat down. 'Lou, meet Jess, Winnie—' By turns, the redhead and the girl next to her nodded. '—Nora, Liddy and Victoria or, as everyone calls her, Queenie.'

Depositing a jar with a handwritten label proclaiming *Glad's Rhubarb Jam May '40*, the woman *everyone calls Queenie*, reached to shake Lou's hand. 'Pleased to meet you. And for the record, not *everyone* calls me Queenie —just this lot.'

Accepting Queenie's hand, Lou thought the rather plain-looking woman seemed surprisingly old to still be lodging somewhere like this — possibly even as much as thirty. 'How do you do,' she replied.

'For God's sake sit down, then,' Jean urged. 'Unless you're not stopping.'

Picking the nearest of the two empty chairs, Lou sat between Jean and Queenie while, reaching between them, Mrs Hannacott deposited a plate stacked with slices of bread. Spread with what Lou assumed to be margarine,

33

they were cut so thin they could pass for lace.

'Marmite. Tongue. Jam. Tuck in, all of you. There's water on the boil to top up the pot.'

When their landlady returned to the kitchen, half a dozen hands shot towards the bread.

'Whatever you do, don't wait,' Jean turned to her to say, 'or you'll go hungry. We might none of us have an appetite for breakfast in the mornings, but we make up for it later on. Here, take some of this. What d'you want on it?'

Helping herself to two slices of bread from the plate Jean offered towards her, Lou glanced about the table. 'Tongue, please, if there's enough to go around.'

'There's a slice each,' Mrs Hannacott called from the kitchen.

'Mustard?' Jess asked, lifting a small earthenware pot and waving it in her direction.

Lou declined. She'd never liked mustard — not since trying some off her father's plate one day when she'd been about five; she could clearly recall thinking her mouth had been set on fire.

'So, Lou,' one of the other girls asked. 'Where d'you come from then?'

Not surprisingly, the question was just the first of many. How old was she? Was this her first job? Her first time living away from home? Did she have a feller? It was the shake of her head to that last question that seemed to bring their interest in her to a close, the conversation switching to an interrogation of the fair-haired Winnie, and whether a lad called Robbie Smith had plucked up the courage to ask her out yet. For Lou, the cessation of their interest in her came as a relief; she preferred to sit and listen, the titbits revealed by each of the girls telling her something of their characters: Jess seemed lively and quite shameless; Winnie was giggly and easily embarrassed. The girl called Nora rarely spoke and when she did it was only to answer a question, never to ask one herself. Liddy, the girl with whom she was apparently to be working, appeared unassuming and like someone with whom she might actually become friends.

With the plate of bread and marge devoured, the girls started on the scones, Winnie having no qualms about helping herself to two. Lou, though, found hers dry and rather heavy — not a patch on Nanny Edith's. But then she supposed it was probably more difficult to get the ingredients with which to make them here. At Woodicombe, eggs, butter and milk were plentiful, and Nanny Edith was able to bake much as she always had. With flour not being on the ration — not yet, anyway — it was only getting the sugar that caused a problem. And the family never wanted for meat — as long as it was rabbit or mutton.

The table stripped of food, the girls began to drift away, only Queenie staying behind to talk to Mrs Hannacott in the kitchen and help with the washing up. About to make her own way back upstairs, Lou remembered promising to telephone home to let them know she'd arrived. And so, popping up to fetch her purse, she went back downstairs to where, on the wall just inside the front door, there was a telephone.

Lifting the handset from the cradle she pressed it to her ear, the traces of fragrance left upon it by the previous user smelling like Coty's L'Aimant. Hearing the purring tone on the line, she inserted her pennies and dialled the operator.

The telephone at home was answered surprisingly quickly.

'Woodicombe 213.'

Mum!

Hastily, she pressed button A and heard her coins drop. 'Mum, it's me.'

'Hello, love. You got there all right then.'

At the sound of her mother's voice, she smiled. 'I did, yes.'

'How were the trains?'

'Not too bad.'

'And the place is up to scratch?'

'It is. I share a room with a—' She had been going to say 'a girl' but, with a picture of Jean coming to mind, hesitated. On the other hand, she didn't want to give Mum reason to worry by calling her a woman. '—with a girl called Jean.' No need, either, for her mother to know her roommate hailed from London. 'There's seven of us lodging here, and one them works in the place I'll be. She said I can walk down with her.'

'That's nice of her.'

'It is, yes.'

'Well, look, love, don't go using up all your precious pennies. It's good of you to let us know you arrived safe. Happen you'll telephone next weekend and tell us how you get on.'

Lou swallowed hard. She hadn't expected the sound of her mother's voice to make her feel so wobbly. 'Yes. All right. I'll do that. Bye then, Mum. Love to Dad.'

'Bye, love.'

★ ★ ★

That night, unable to settle in the strange little bed with its hard mattress and flat pillow, Lou wasn't surprised to find she couldn't sleep. Through her thoughts kept running the realisation that, whenever she'd pictured coming here to do this job, she'd hadn't appreciated just how much her life would change. Number eleven, Jubilee Street, had been just an address on a piece of paper — a means to an end to taking up the job she'd been offered — not the place she would have to make her home. Now that she was actually here, she felt like a fish out of water, unsure what to make of anything.

One thing she had been intrigued to learn, was that working for *the Canadians* meant you were much envied. Asking why that was, Jess had told her it was because *the Canadians* made the local lads seem even more like the graceless Janners they truly were. Unfortunately, Jess had gone on to point out, *the Canadians* were not allowed to *get serious* about local girls.

It was at that point Lou realised that pretty much the only thing her fellow lodgers talked about was boys — or, rather, men — and that, when it came to discussing the attributes of the latest 'hottie' or 'cutie', they didn't hold back, their language rather more direct than anything she was used to. They were also quick to notice how easy it was to make her blush.

Hearing Jean breathing softly in the next bed, she reached out to try and find her wristwatch. It wasn't difficult; the room was nowhere near as dark as where she slept at home; here, the landing light bulb seemed to be left on all night, allowing a triangle-shape of light to seep under the door. In addition, since the room faced onto the street, she could hear every noise made by any-one passing underneath; there might be a blackout, but an awful lot of people still seemed to be going about as normal.

Angling the face of her watch and seeing from the luminous hands that it was half-past midnight, Lou sighed. Was she *never* going to get to sleep? The last thing she needed was to start her first day at work too tired to concentrate.

Eventually, though, sleep did come. And she knew this because, seemingly only moments later, she was startled awake by a terrific blast from a steam hooter.

'Evans Foundry,' Jean mumbled, pulling her pillow over her head. 'Six o'clock. Go back to sleep.'

If only, Lou thought. But, with all the commotion going on outside, there was little chance of that. Somewhere close by, a couple of dogs that had started yapping, causing someone to repeatedly yell at them to *shut up*; what sounded like machinery somewhere was making a low grumbling noise; someone's tiny baby wouldn't stop crying.

But it wasn't just the ruckus outside that had her on full alert: today was her first day at her new job and the only thing from which she could take comfort was that she had Liddy to walk in with. According to Jean, the dockyard was a sprawling place, several miles long, with women few and far between. Too late now, though, to wonder whether she'd made a mistake: now she was here, all she could do was remind herself that this was what she had so badly wanted — to forge her own path as Esme was doing.

Not in the least reassured by the thought, and with her restlessness turning to agitation, she pushed back the eiderdown, folded back the sheet and swung her feet down to the floor. Reaching for the underthings she had left ready on the stool at the foot of her bed, and then crossing to the shelf above the basin for her wash bag — the brand new one, printed with sprigs of violets, that Mum had given her as a going away present — Lou crept towards the door, carefully turned the handle and stepped out onto the landing. Just as she had hoped, no one else was about.

In the bathroom, she hung her underwear from the hook on the back of the door, put her wash bag on the stool and stared into the mirror above the basin. At least she didn't look as tired as she had feared, even if she did look pale. Turning on the tap, she waited for the water to grow warm and then pressed the plug into the hole. Then she stripped off her nightdress and had a good wash. Last night, she'd had a bath but, not wanting to appear pushy, had waited until last, the result being that the water had been barely lukewarm. Already, she thought, as she scrubbed her neck with her flannel, it was plain that if she was ever to feel at ease here, she was going to have to be a good deal more assertive; if she was constantly afraid of putting a foot wrong, she would never settle.

And so, hearing the hall clock strike the half hour, and with her hair now pinned, she crept back into the bedroom, pulled on her clothes and went downstairs.

From the kitchen she heard the whistle of a kettle.

'Mornin', lovely,' Mrs Hannacott greeted her. 'You're about bright and early. Attack of the abdabs — first day and all that?'

Lou smiled. 'A bit. See, I'm not really sure what to expect.'

'Nobody ever was on their first day, love. The rest of them were the same — and don't let them tell you otherwise. But you'll settle to it soon enough. Mark my words, come Friday, you'll wonder what on earth reason there was to be so jittery.'

Again, Lou smiled. 'I do hope so.'

'Look, why not pop a couple of those slices of bread under the grill and I'll make us a pot of tea. Most of the others don't come down until the last minute… and then they fly about, getting in each other's way. You should hear the cursing that goes on. Enough to make even my

Alfie blush, it would have been.'

Reaching for the bread, Lou stole a glance at her land-lady's face. With her hair in curlers under a hairnet, there was nothing to conceal the considerable creases to forehead. But, while her lips were thin and almost disapproving, her eyes were bright — definitely someone who didn't miss a trick.

'Shall I lay the table?' she asked, feeling a bit of a fraud to be simply standing there while the grill got hot.

'If you like, love. Just set two places and one for yourself if you've a mind to sit down. There's only ever the two of them as bothers. *Try getting up ten minutes earlier* I tell the rest of them. But do they listen? What do you think? Any rate, cutlery in the top drawer, plates in the dresser. Marmalade in the pantry, margarine in the butter dish. Milk on the doorstep, assuming he's been. Getting later and later, that lad.'

Mrs Hannacott turned out to be right about breakfast. Only Queenie and the girl called Nora sat at the table. After that, Liddy darted in, grabbed a piece of toast and then stood there just long enough to smear margarine over it and bite off a corner before dashing back out again.

Next to appear was Winnie. Holding her dressing gown about her slight frame with one hand, with her other, she poured herself a cup of tea. 'Mornin' Mrs H.'

'You going to have something to eat?' Mrs Hannacott enquired of her.

Her curls still in pins, Winnie shook her head. 'No, ta. I'll make do with a fag on the way down.'

After Winnie, came the red-headed Jess. 'Ooh, good, the toast's still warm,' she said, grabbing a piece of it and then, eschewing the oily block of margarine, dabbing it with a spoonful of jam. 'Nora, lend us some of your acetone, will you? I've got to get this nail varnish off before I go in and I've used all mine. I'll lend you some back next pay day.'

'You wait until they get a bit older,' Mrs Hannacott remarked over her shoulder to Lou, as Jess ran back along the hallway and bounded up the stairs. 'Ten years' time and all you get for eating like that is a bad case of indigestion.'

With that, Liddy reappeared. 'Ready?' she poked her head around the doorframe to look across at Lou and ask.

Raising a smile, Lou nodded. *Ready or not*, she thought, following Liddy out through the front door, *here goes*.

* * *

It wasn't at all what she had been expecting. The building to which Liddy took Lou was at the top of the yard, some distance from the actual docks and the ships or — as she had gathered from Liddy they were more properly called — *the vessels*. Surrounded by other similar sheds painted the identical shade of battleship grey, the entrance to the warehouse they were now approaching had double-height doors that slid aside on rails, presumably, Lou decided, feeling her spirits sinking, to allow access for lorries to unload goods. As they drew nearer still, and she could see inside, she noticed wooden racks stacked with boxes, cartons and crates.

Following Liddy in, she glanced about. Just inside the doors, a section of the larger space had been partitioned off to form two offices, one at ground floor level, the other, above it, accessed by a metal staircase. The lower of the two rooms had a rickety-looking door alongside what appeared to be a sliding glass hatch. At the sight of it, her heart sank further. As a place of work, this was going to be about as appealing as Pa's joinery workshop in the stables at home: dim, dusty and, come December, decidedly draughty.

41

'Well, this is you, then,' Liddy said, pushing open the door to the office and reaching in to switch on the light. 'Might as well go in and take a shufti. Miss Blatchford will be along any minute.'

'Miss Blatchford?'

'Geraldine Blatchford. Our supervisor. Red hot on rules but won't hear a word said against us just because we're girls. It's why we like her.'

'And is that her office up there?' Lou asked, gesturing to the room up the flight of stairs and noticing as she did so that perched on one of the rafters above it was a pair of pigeons.

Liddy shook her head. 'No, she works across the yard with the top brass. No one uses that room up there, which is handy for us because when it's raining, we can pop up there for our tea breaks. See, when it's wet, they open the refreshments caravan just along the way there. Saves us the walk to the canteen, and the getting soaked through for the sake of a cuppa and a drag. Oh, look, here's Flossie.'

Turning over her shoulder, Lou saw that coming towards them was a gangly young woman of about eighteen dressed in the same sort of overalls as Liddy. Wearing clumpy work boots, and with all but a few wisps of pale hair hidden beneath a turban of navy fabric printed with sprays of blossom, she looked like a girl from a Ministry of Labour poster — the sort that urged women to join the war effort.

As the girl came ambling towards them, Lou noticed how her eyebrows were plucked into fine arches, and that her mouth was painted the shade of pillar box red that was all the rage these days.

'New girl?' the young woman came to a halt and addressed her remark to Liddy.

'Lou Channer. She's stopping with us in Jubilee

42

Street. Come to do the clerical.'

'Flossie Pascoe,' the girl introduced herself with a nod. 'I live with me Gran up the road. So, you're in the office then.'

'Yes,' Lou said, wondering how someone so slight could be suited to the type of duties required in a warehouse. Despite the lipstick, this close up she didn't even look to be eighteen.

'Well, best get on,' Flossie said. 'Don't want to be stood around gassing when Miss Blatchford gets here. See you at tea break.'

Lou raised a smile. With this girl Flossie seeming as friendly Liddy, perhaps this might not be so bad after all.

'Ah, Miss Channer.' Hearing her name, Lou swivelled about. Approaching was a young woman in a navy-blue suit. 'You're punctual. Well done. I can't abide poor time-keeping.'

'Good morning,' Lou replied. This, then, must be her supervisor.

'Geraldine Blatchford.'

When the two shook hands, Lou wished her palms weren't so clammy — not a good first impression! Not that she could help it; she always felt sticky when she was nervous. 'How do you do.'

'Very well, thank you. And very pleased to see *you*. Even just standing there you look more capable than the last girl the labour exchange sent. Couldn't add up to save her life. Least sign of difficulty she burst into tears. But I can tell already that *you've* got some grit.'

Grit? Her? It wasn't the description most people would use. 'My parents say I'm stubborn.' Oh, good Lord, would she *never* remember that being nervous made her prattle? 'Much the same has been said of me,' Miss Blatchford said drily, 'which I choose to take as a compliment since,

43

to my mind, stubbornness is merely another name for tenacity. Well, come on, then, in you come. Let's see what you're made of.'

To her relief, Lou found that Liddy was right; Miss Blatchford's manner might be brisk, but she wasn't unreasonable. Indeed, after two hours of instruction, Lou felt she had grasped the basics of the system of requisitions and invoices, how to enter them into the various sections of the many ledgers and how to tally the stock. From what she could see, everything from toilet paper — supplied in units of a gross — to Royal Crown Canadian Whisky — crated, by the dozen — came through this store en route to its destination, usually a vessel, every movement of it followed by a piece of paper of one sort or another.

'Yes, I see,' she said to each instruction. Occasionally, 'I understand.'

And the time flew. When Miss Blatchford paused her tuition to suggest Lou might like to go with Liddy and Flossie to the canteen for their tea break, Lou couldn't believe it was already ten o'clock.

'See what I mean about her being fair,' Liddy said as they navigated their way across railway tracks and between various buildings to the canteen.

Concerned that left to her own devices she would never find her way back again, and casting about anxiously for landmarks she might commit to memory, Lou agreed. 'Yes. She seems nice. Patient.'

Eventually, at the end of a long brick building that put Lou in mind of the old workhouse in Westward Quay, Flossie led the way in through a low door. Following her down a couple of steps, Lou found herself in a space resembling a school hall, furnished at the far end with long wooden trestles and benches, while, closer to, were set out a dozen or so Formica-topped tables with

44

matching chairs.

'If you sit down there at one of the benches,' Liddy said as they settled a while later with their teas at one of the small tables, 'you risk having some great lump of a welder plonking himself down next to you and trying to chat you up.'

The thought of a man she didn't know trying to draw her into conversation made Lou squirm. She'd be mortified if that happened to her. 'But they don't come and sit up this end?' she decided to check.

'There's no official rule says they can't,' Liddy explained, 'but they don't like these spindly little chairs. Since they were put out here, us girls get nowhere near so much pestering.'

'Doesn't stop the half-wits whistlin' or shoutin' obscenities, though,' Flossie observed, sliding the metal ashtray across the table to where Liddy was lighting up.

'Mostly they do it in the hope of seeing us blush,' Liddy went on, exhaling a stream of smoke. 'Or to get a rise out of us.'

'Best thing is to ignore them,' Flossie advised. 'Most of them are wed anyway and just doing it for the sport, to look big in front of their mates.'

All of a sudden, the shoots of confidence Lou had begun to feel under Miss Blatchford's instruction felt rather less certain. Having never been anywhere like this before, she'd had no reason to consider the wider ramifications of working in a place where nearly all the other workers were men. All she could do now was hope that coming here didn't turn out to be a mistake. Having found the work within her abilities to actually do, it would be a shame to have to give it up for reasons over which she had no control.

'Mind you,' Liddy piped up, 'if you've got to work in the dockyard, our little depot is by far and away the best place to do it. Truly. Ask anyone. The Canadians have such nice manners. It's the locals you have to watch out for, 'specially with you being new in.'

'But, like I said,' Flossie picked up again, evidently reading the concern on Lou's face, 'just ignore them. And if anyone tries to take liberties, tell Miss Blatchford. She don't stand for no nonsense.'

Stubbing out the end of her cigarette, Liddy pushed back her chair and got to her feet. 'Come on then,' she said, 'if we don't want to spend forever in the queue for the lavs, best get a move on.'

Back at the depot, the first of the day's deliveries had arrived. For Lou, the timing was fortunate since it meant she had to bury concerns about men taking liberties and concentrate instead on what she had to do.

'Mornin', Derry,' Flossie greeted the elderly man leaning against the bonnet of a grey truck.

'O'right, maid?'

Clearly, he was a regular.

'First thing,' Miss Blatchford said, appearing from the office, 'is to get the delivery note from the driver. And then check that the consignment is actually for us. You'd be surprised the number of times a driver turns up here when he's supposed to be somewhere else.'

Catching her eye, the elderly Derry sent her a wink.

'Yes,' Lou said, examining the top of the docket he handed her and reading from it their details.

The speed with which Liddy and Flossie then set about unloading the lorry took Lou by surprise, the way they called out the items for to her to check to the delivery note reminding her of when she was small, and she would play bingo with her brothers and Nanny Edith. At the time, she had been so much quicker than all of them.

'Dettol, ten boxes,' Liddy called. 'Ammonia, six.

Ronuk lino polish, four.'

'Bronco, four gross,' Flossie yelled.

'Well done,' Miss Blatchford said when, with the lorry empty, Lou checked down the note for discrepancies, stamped all three copies 'Received', wrote the date and signed her name across the stamp. 'Top copy in the tray for Accounts, middle copy for your ledger, bottom copy back to the driver. That sounds like another lorry reversing up, so, set the papers aside for now and let's see what's coming in next.'

'Ovaltine, large, six dozen.'

'Beefex, four dozen.'

'Ideal Milk, eight dozen.'

'Do the deliveries always come straight in one after the other?' Lou asked when the second lorry eventually pulled away.

Miss Blatchford shook her head. 'There's no telling. Usually the girls get a breather between them. But, while they're getting it all put away on the racks, you need to start writing up the ledgers.'

At twelve-thirty, Miss Blatchford announced that it was time for lunch — or, as the other two called it, dinner. And when the three of them traipsed back to the canteen, Lou was surprised to find a choice of two hot dishes, followed by a pudding and a cup of tea, all at no charge. Having chosen minced lamb with triangles of fried bread and tinned peas over oxtail stew with dumplings and carrots, she was just leaning across to take a bowl of spotted dick when, from behind her, an arm reached over her shoulder for the same thing and a man's groin pressed hard into the small of her back. Astonished at what she could feel through her clothing, she froze.

It was Liddy who leapt to her rescue. 'Lenny Grant, get off her right this instant.' With the offender's weight moving away, Lou exhaled with relief. 'Unless you want trouble, that is. Only I'm more than happy to report you to our supervisor. I've done so afore, as well you know.'

'Whassit to you?' a man's voice hissed. 'For all you know, it's just what the maid likes. I don't hear *her* making a fuss.'

'You're taking advantage of the fact she's new in,' Liddy called after him as he stalked away, her voice deliberately loud. 'But take it from me, try it again and you'll regret it.'

'Thank you,' Lou whispered, deciding not to turn around and look at this Lenny Grant fellow, her hand shaking as she put the bowl of pudding on her tray. In truth, after that little episode, she no longer really fancied it.

'Next time one of them tries something like that, just step back and stand on his foot, or kick his shin if you can. Then just move on.'

'I'll try and remember.' She did wish her hands would stop trembling; she was in danger of slopping her tea.

'Told you, didn't I?' Flossie said, putting her tray on an empty table, pulling a chair from underneath and nodding across to where, in the thick of the benches, a roar of laughter had just erupted. 'Because you're new, they think you won't dare stand up for yourself.'

'But eventually they get fed up,' Liddy said 'and move on to the next poor soul. In the main they're harmless. But if one of them does overstep the mark, don't be afraid to go straight to Miss Blatchford.'

But what, precisely, Lou wondered, still prickling with embarrassment, constituted overstepping the mark? The likes of this Lenny Grant clearly knew to stop short of doing anything he couldn't pass off as accidental or, as she'd once overheard Arthur telling Vic, as *just a bit of fun*.

'Surprising what you can get away with,' Arthur had

said to his brother after getting a job one summer at one of the holiday parks in Westward Quay. 'Pick the right girl... and if you're clever, you can cop a quick feel of her behind and then pass it off as just an accident. Most of them wouldn't dream of making a complaint for fear of having their parents put the fetters on. Besides, it's only a bit of fun.'

At the time, she had simply smiled, thinking that sort of behaviour typical of Arthur. But now, with the boot on the other foot, she realised that for the poor girl in question it was no fun at all.

Determining to heed the advice of her colleagues, she picked up her knife and fork and started upon her lunch. Questionable men aside, she was rather encouraged by her first morning's work. Shame, then, to let a little bit of unpleasantness from one dumb oaf take the edge off it.

★ ★ ★

'Not so nervous today, then?'

It was the following morning and, beneath the sign decreeing *No Smoking,* Liddy was stubbing out the end of her cigarette with the toe of her work boot.

'Not now I know what to expect, no,' Lou said. And it was true: this morning, she'd awoken from a much better night's sleep to find she was quite looking forward to going to work. She'd even managed something that could pass for a proper breakfast: two whole slices of toast and a cup of tea. *Someone's got more of an appetite this morning,* Mrs Hannacott had remarked.

'Good for you,' Liddy said now, adjusting her cap over her long plait of hair and sauntering ahead of her through the doors into the warehouse.

Later, it turned out that Miss Blatchford was pleased

49

with her, as well.

'Very neat,' she said when she came to inspect Lou's entries in the ledgers. 'Just make sure to record every single item, both coming in and going out. Otherwise, at the end of the week, you won't tally. And trust me, you don't want to be the one holding up everyone knocking off on a Friday afternoon.'

Later still, in the canteen for their morning tea break, and seated at what she now surmised was their usual table, Lou smiled to herself. Not only was everything going to be all right, but she had a feeling Mum would be proud of her — Dad, too, if she could but get him to admit it.

'Have you always lived around here?' she asked, watching Flossie dunk a Digestive into her tea and recalling her mentioning living with her Gran.

Flossie nodded. 'Plymouth to my bones.' Lou liked the way Flossie pronounced it *Plymuff*. 'Dad's family, mind, the Pascoes, they were from Saltash, only crossing over to Devon when he was ten. He's been gone five years or more now though.'

'Oh. I'm sorry,' Lou said. 'I didn't know.'

Flossie shrugged. 'He got pneumonia. It shouldn't have killed him — he was only forty-five — but he was gassed in the last war and ever since then was under the doctor for a bad chest. He kept telling them it was the gas what done it to him, and that he should be getting the proper pension for it, but nobody listened. Anyway, my brother, John, is ten years older 'n me and so, when Dad died, and John got wed, Mum went to live with *him* and I went to live with Gran, who was willing to have me till I turned eighteen.'

'But you're still there,' Lou surmised.

Leaning across the table, Flossie lowered her voice. ''Cos I'm not eighteen yet...'

Then no wonder she looked young! 'But I thought—'

50

'Not my fault no one bothered to check, is it?'

Lou smiled. 'Well, I'm sorry for what happened to your family —'

'No need. But thanks anyway. What about you?'

By comparison, Lou felt her own background, although dull, was going to sound rather privileged; better, perhaps, not to mention that her family lived in a country mansion owned by her Grandpa Hugh, whose own home was a vast place in a smart square in Kensington. 'I live with my mum and dad and two brothers,' she said flatly. 'Oh, and Nanny Edith, Mum's mum. My brother Vic's gone in the Devonshires, my brother Arthur is waiting to turn eighteen and go in the navy.'

'And what about you?' Flossie asked. 'Got a feller?'

She shook her head. Why was everyone obsessed with men? 'No.'

'Plenty of choice around here,' Flossie went on. 'Though perhaps not so much if you're fussy.'

'Come on, then,' Liddy said, getting to her feet. 'Best be getting back to it.'

Liddy, Lou decided, she would have to find out about another day. Picking up her cup and saucer and following her across to the crockery hatch, something in the girl's manner suggested that she, too, had an interesting background. In fact, of all the lodgers at Jubilee Street, she suspected that little Lou Channer was the only one who hadn't. Despite actually being here in *Demport* — as pretty much everyone except Jean seemed to pronounce it — and having a job in the dockyard, she still couldn't believe she had finally escaped that stifled existence to embark upon a proper life. Harder still to believe was the fact that, already, it showed all the signs of turning out really rather well...

★ ★ ★

51

'Ah, here she is, Lieutenant Ross.'

It was a few days later and, returning to the depot after lunch, Lou found Miss Blatchford standing with a man in military uniform. It was, she realised, the first time she'd come across one of *the Canadians*. And she could see now what the others meant. What a smart man.

'Good afternoon, Miss Blatchford,' she said.

'Lieutenant Ross, may I introduce to you Miss Channer. She joined us on Monday as the new clerk of stores. And very capable she's turning out to be, too.'

'How do you do, Miss Channer,' the lieutenant said, his hand extended towards her in greeting.

Hastily wiping her palm down the side of her skirt, Lou reached to shake it. 'How do you do.' His grasp was firm, his fingers large and warm.

'Lieutenant Ross is responsible for everything that happens within this section, from the moment the goods arrive, until the moment they are accepted onto their intended vessel.'

'That's right,' the lieutenant agreed. 'So, it's me who comes down here every Friday to check the ledgers, tally the stocks and commit my reputation to everything being shipshape.'

Check the ledgers? Miss Blatchford had said nothing about that. Still, if she was doing her job properly, then presumably she had nothing to fear. Miss Blatchford looked them over each day anyway.

'Nice, him, ain't he?' Flossie said when the lieutenant and Miss Blatchford wandered away to inspect 'the cage' — the enclosed corner of the warehouse where high-value goods were locked away for safe keeping. 'Tall. Lean but not scrawny. Broad shoulders. Nice head of hair.'

'And those blue eyes,' Liddy whispered, arriving alongside her. 'And don't get me started on that voice of his. Just my type, that one. More's the pity—'

'Hush up,' Flossie hissed, 'they're coming back around.'

'Nice to meet you, Miss Channer,' Lieutenant Ross called to her as he strode past. 'Keep up the good work.'

Once he was out of earshot, Liddy sent Lou a grin. '*Keep up the good work.*'

'Didn't sound nothin' like him,' Flossie dismissed her remark before turning to go back inside.

Honestly, Lou thought, the two of them were as bad as Winnie and Jess — obsessed with the opposite sex, the lot of them. To be fair, though, she thought, heading back towards her dingy little office, without Liddy and Flossie, the place wouldn't be nearly as enjoyable, the hours spent in this draughty shed of a building little more than one long blur of deliveries and collections, ledgers and dockets. She should count herself lucky to live and work among so many girls of her own age, girls who, in time, might well come to feel like the sisters she'd never had. Never in her wildest dreams — even as recently as her trip to London for Esme's wedding — could she have imagined that after just one week in a new job she would have made so many friends. Granted, their worldliness sometimes made her feel horribly naïve but, without them, settling in would have been twice as hard, not to mention twice as unenlightening and twice as dull! So, good fortune all round, really.

* * *

'Feels good, don't it?'

Walking back up the hill to Jubilee Street, Lou nodded.

Liddy wasn't wrong. The elation she'd felt at signing for her first pay packet had taken her by surprise. *Pleasantly* by surprise.

'It does,' she agreed. 'Makes the toiling worthwhile.'

'Saturday mornings, some us go into the town — you know, to have a look about and get a few things. You can come with us if you like.'

Pleased that Liddy should think to extend the invitation, Lou smiled. 'Thank you. Might take you up on that — even if only to see how to get there… and to find out what's what.'

Making a trip into Plymouth — somewhere she'd only glimpsed on the day of her interview — sounded like fun, and something else to tell her Mum about. In fact, after supper was finished, and still buoyed by the gratifying sum in her little brown envelope, she gathered together some coins and went down to the hallway to telephone home.

Unsurprisingly, it was her mother who answered.

'I thought it would be you, love. How are you? All well, I hope.'

'Fine, Mum,' she replied, surprised at how nice it was to hear her mother's voice; these last two or three days, she'd barely given Woodicombe a thought. 'I've just been paid. My first proper pay packet. Can't really believe it.'

'Have you now?' Somehow, she could tell that Mum was smiling. 'So, you like it there then?'

She didn't hesitate. 'I do. First day or two were a bit nervy —'

'Bound to be. I still remember the day I left here for London. Thought I'd never stop shaking. Nice people, are they?'

'Miss Blatchford — she's my supervisor — is very fair and…' She stopped short of saying *stands up for us* in case her mother should read too much into it and start to worry. '...and says I've made a promising start. She said my handwriting is very neat and that I seem very thorough.'

'Well, of course. That's because you are.'

'So, how's Dad?'

'He's fine.'

'Any word from Vic?'

'A few lines the other day. He seems cheerful enough. Says he's got some good pals.'

'Did he say where he is?'

'He didn't, no. But, reading between the lines, your dad thinks he's over on the North Sea coast somewhere. Somewhere like Lincolnshire. Long old way, that's for sure.'

'And Arthur?' For a moment, her mother didn't reply. 'Mum?'

'Arthur's ... gone, love.'

Gone? How could he be *gone?*

'Gone where, Mum?'

'Said he couldn't wait about to turn eighteen, and so he's took himself off to go in the merchant navy. Left us a note saying he was going up to Cardiff with a friend — Cardiff, of all places — to join a ship.'

'When was this?' Lou asked, on the one hand surprised, on the other not in the least. Arthur had been restless ever since Vic had left.

'When I went in to wake him up on Monday morning, I found two notes on his bed... one for us and the other for Ronnie at the garage.'

Unsure what to say, Lou held off replying. The likelihood was that Arthur had been spurred into going by her own departure. Stupid boy. 'And no word since?'

'None.'

Guessing at how her mother must be feeling, Lou exhaled heavily. 'Oh, Mum, I'm so sorry.'

'Nothing for *you* to be sorry about, love. We're just cross he felt the need to go about it in secret. Like your dad said, if he'd told us, we could have helped him go about it proper — not all underhand and in a rush. Now we don't even know which ship he's gone on.'

Never had Lou so badly wanted to put her arm around her mum's shoulders. Never — until now — had she been unable to do so.

'Well,' she said, determining not to cry, 'he's not a bad lad. So, I expect once he settles... and once he gets the chance, he'll write. Maybe even telephone. You know what he's like. Act first think later.'

'Your dad said much the same.'

'Well, sorry, Mum, but there's the pips and those were my last coppers.'

'All right, love.'

'But I'll call you in a few days — see if there's any news.'

'All right, love. Thanks for thinking of us. Look after yourself.'

'You too. Love to Dad.'

'Bye, love.'

'Bye, Mum.'

Reaching to place the receiver back on the cradle, Lou let out a long sigh. How thoughtless of Arthur to go off like that. Did he not care for Mum's feelings? Did he not stop to think how worried she would be? No, he'd known *exactly* how she would feel but had decided to go anyway, had decided he could do without the bother of having Mum pleading with him to just wait a while longer to do it properly. Only ever put himself first, that one.

Turning to go upstairs, the shine taken right off her week, she caught sight of Jean in the front parlour, the door open just wide enough for her to discern that she was gesturing as though in exasperation. Curious to see

56

who she was with, she crept across the hall and peered between the door and its frame. Word among the others was she was *seeing an older man*.

'And why should I be bothered what *you* think?' Well, the voice was definitely a man's. And he didn't sound happy. 'What's it to do with you?'

'When you bring trouble for my Mum,' she heard Jean say, her tone short, 'you *make* it my business.' To Lou's mind, it didn't seem the sort of conversation she'd be having with her feller — especially if he was older.

'Trouble? What trouble do *I* bring?'

'Look, if it was just me, I wouldn't give a hoot *what* you do. For all I care you can go an' jump off the pier in a pair of concrete boots. All I ever ask is that you leave Mum out of it.'

Preferring not to be caught eavesdropping, Lou turned away. Jean's business was none of hers. But, barely had she put one foot on the bottom stair, when the parlour door swung open and through it came a dark-haired man who looked to be in his late twenties.

'Well, hello, there,' he said. '*You're* a new one.'

From behind him, Jean appeared, the look she sent Lou one of displeasure. 'Take no notice of him. He's leaving.'

Unsure what to do for the best, Lou stayed where she was.

'Come on, now, Jeanie, where's yer manners? Ain't you going to introduce us?'

Her despair seemingly continuing, Jean shook her head. 'Harry, this is Lou Channer. She shares my room. Lou, this is my stepbrother, Harry Hinds. There. Happy now?'

Since it felt only polite to accord a member of Jean's family a proper greeting, Lou stepped back down from the staircase. 'How do you do.'

Accepting her hand, Harry raised it to his lips. 'Delighted to make your acquaintance, Lou Channer.'

Her cheeks burning from embarrassment, she bowed her head.

'Lord, spare us,' she heard Jean mutter. 'Come on, then, Harry. You said you had somewhere to be.'

'Hold on, hold on,' Harry replied. 'No rush.' Despite the fact that he was addressing Jean, when Lou looked up it was to find his eyes meeting her own. Then, to her mortification, she was left to stand and flush even hotter as they slowly wandered the length of her body before eventually returning to her face. Thinking she might as well have been stood there stark naked, she was relieved when he at least let go of her hand. 'You know me,' he said, still not turning back to his stepsister. '*Never part on a cross word*, ain't that what your ma's forever saying?'

Jean rolled her eyes. 'What of it?'

'Well, you know I don't like it when you and I have a falling out, 'specially not over something of nothing. So, how about you let me make it up to you?'

This time Jean's sigh was one of utter exasperation. 'And how the devil d'you propose doing that, Harry Hinds? By taking yourself back off to Lewisham and never coming back?'

'Now, now, Jeanie. No need to go taking that tone. I'm offering to make it up to you.'

'Huh.'

'Come on, let me take you dancing. Both of you go and get your glad rags on. Couple of drinks ... quick turn on the floor...'

'What, down the pier?' Jean said. 'No thanks.'

'Nah. Not the pier on a Friday. Too many sailors. No, I was thinking more up the Empire.'

'No thanks,' Jean said shortly. 'I'm off out later anyway.'

Still Harry held Lou's gaze. 'I've told you before, Jeanie. That Paul's no good for you. His eyes are too close together. Something shifty about him.'

'Happen it's not Paul I'm seeing tonight,' Jean replied. Her tone reminded Lou of when she, herself, had an argument with Arthur and he got all snide with her. Stupid Arthur.

'What do you say, Lou? You up for some dancing?'

Was it possible to flush any redder, Lou wondered, feeling her forehead growing sticky? If Jean had been going, then she might have said yes — *might* have — and gone along too. But she couldn't possibly go alone with this man; he had to be at least seven or eight years older than her, maybe more. Besides, for all his captivating charm, she knew nothing about him.

'I don't think I—'

'Come on,' Harry said. This time when he went to reach for her hand, she was quick to draw it behind her back. 'It's nice up the Empire. Classy. Not rammed with Janners and skates getting into drunken brawls over the prettiest girls.'

She smiled apologetically. 'Sorry, but I don't think—'

'She *said no*, Harry,' Jean came to her aid, 'so leave off. Go home… or wherever it is you were headed.'

Unconcerned by her tone, Harry shrugged. 'Fair enough. Be seein' you, then, Jeanie. And I'll definitely be seeing *you*, Lou Channer.'

When he went out through the front door and closed it smartly behind him, Lou was left to stand and listen to him whistling gaily as he made his way along the street. Golly, how she wished her heart would stop racing: it was beating so fast she wouldn't be surprised if Jean could hear it.

'Don't let him fool you,' Jean said matter-of-factly as

she brushed past on her way up the stairs. 'All Brylcreem and flannel, that one. 'Course,' she added, looking back over her shoulder, 'for all I know, that's just your type.'

Having a 'type' was something the girls talked about a lot, Lou thought as she followed Jean up the stairs, her legs trembling beneath her. *He's not my type. Ooh, he's just your type*. Until now, those had been the conversations from which she had shied away, having never known enough men — certainly not in the way the others meant — to understand what was meant by a 'type', let alone to know with any certainty what hers was. Besides, Jean was bound to be dismissive of Harry — in the same way that she, herself, was often quick to dismiss Arthur — because they were related. Albeit in Jean and Harry's case, *sort of* related.

For her own part, she found Harry striking — rather sure of himself, yes, but, unlike some men, with good reason. While not overly tall, his broad shoulders lent him a certain presence and enabled him to carry off that suit — that *expensive-looking* suit. The confident way he stood there suggested he knew how to look after himself, too. And his immaculate grooming showed that he took pride in his appearance.

Perhaps, then, *her type* was a man who wasn't just arresting to look at, but who made no apologies for going after what he wanted, who didn't beat about the bush. How would she know? How would she ever know if she didn't… well, if she didn't at least go on a few dates and attempt to find out? If the point of escaping Woodicombe had been to see something of the rest of the world, and if she was serious about discovering more about life and men, then with Jean and the other girls on hand to steer her right, could there really be any safer place to start her quest than with the confident and good-looking Harry Hinds …?

Chapter 3

Harry

'Well, how do I look?'

'You look …' Not used to giving fashion advice — certainly not to someone who always looked so effortlessly stylish — Lou studied Jean's appearance and thought for a moment. Since she was hoping to pry from her some information about Harry, she could do worse than resort to flattery.

'Only, I don't much go in for skirts,' Jean went on. 'My ankles are too fat.'

Instinctively, Lou looked down. 'Oh, I wouldn't say that.' Truth was, Jean's ankles really weren't that bad. 'I think you look very… smart. The slim cut of your skirt really flatters your hips and your waist.'

There. Simply by listening to the other girls discussing these things, she had learned that it was quite easy to appear informed; you just had to sound confident.

'Thanks.'

It was Saturday evening. And, in their bedroom at Mrs Hannacott's, Lou had been watching Jean get ready to go out.

Kicking off her shoes and flopping onto her bed, she glanced again to her roommate. 'Where are you going?' she asked, her aim being to keep her chatting.

'Paul's taking me to this restaurant he's been harping on about, and fancy places aren't something I normally go in for.'

'But I thought you told your brother you weren't

61

seeing Paul any more.'

'I think you'll find I said the person I was talking about *might not* be Paul,' Jean replied. 'And I only said *that* because I don't like the way he always presumes to know everything.'

'Mm.'

'And he's not my brother. He's my *step*brother. And to save you asking, his mum died when he was about ten. And *my* mum couldn't marry my Dad because he was killed in Flanders before I was even born — didn't even know he'd got her pregnant. So, left in the lurch, she went to live with her sister, my Aunty Glad, and got a job on a barrow down the market. That's where she met George — Harry's dad.'

Well there was some useful information — and she hadn't even had to ask for it, either. 'Oh, I see.'

'Mum's mum and dad, my Gran and Grandad, had a grocer's shop over in Stonehouse. When Grandad died, about ten years ago now, he left Mum the shop. So, George upped sticks and brought me and Mum and Harry down here to take it on. Says it's the best thing he ever did.'

'And what does Harry do?' Ordinarily, she wouldn't pry into other people's families but, since yesterday evening, she'd been surprised to find her thoughts keep returning to Harry Hinds — to his dapper appearance and confident manner. She'd fallen asleep thinking about him, woken up thinking about him and, through being preoccupied with him, had somehow spent the three hours wandering around the shops in the centre of town with Liddy, Jess and Winnie, in a sort of a daze.

'Supposedly, he works for George. But in truth he does just enough to be useful and pay his way while actually doing very little at all.'

'Oh.' Much like Arthur then.

'Could talk an Arab into buying sand, that one, which is why I said to you to watch out for his flannel.'

'Mm.'

'Anyway, these or these?' Jean asked, holding up two pairs of shoes. 'And for heaven's sake don't say *neither*.'

'Those,' Lou replied, pointing to the pair of peep-toe courts in Jean's left hand. 'Better with that skirt.'

See, she said to herself, it was just a case of using common sense and sounding sufficiently decisive.

'Thanks.'

'Well, I hope you have a nice evening.'

'Yeah. And I'll try not to wake you up when I come in.'

Lou shrugged. 'Don't worry. I'm so exhausted I doubt I'll hear you anyway.'

Once Jean had left, and stuck to know what to do with herself, Lou got up and went to the window. Lifting the nets, she looked left and right along the street, the sight of a young lad in cadet's uniform giving her an idea: she would write to Freddie. She had said she would keep him up to date with her news. So, she would write and tell him about her new job, and about her lodgings and her new friends.

Oddly, though, having found her pad and pen, she struggled to get going; was her news the sort Freddie would want to read? How would he feel to learn from her very first letter that she had embarked upon a new life? He did tend to be sensitive. On the other hand, if she didn't tell him about her job and all that went with it, what was she going to write?

Tapping her pen on her teeth, she stared down at what she'd written so far.

Dear Freddie.

I hope this letter finds you well.

Clearly, this was going to need more thought. Perhaps she would try again tomorrow.

Screwing the lid back on her pen and closing her pad, she exhaled heavily. Perhaps, instead of writing to Freddie, she would wash her hair. Granted, it was a day early, but what else was she going to do?

'Lou? You up there, love?'

Thinking she heard Mrs Hannacott calling, she opened the door and leant out.

'Yes?'

'Visitor for you.'

A visitor? Who the devil would be calling on *her*? She didn't know anyone.

Nevertheless, slipping her feet back into her shoes, straightening her skirt and tugging the collar of her blouse into place, she started down the stairs.

Halfway down, though, she stopped in her tracks. *Harry?*

'Hello, Lou.'

'Um...' *Harry? To see her? But why?* 'I'm afraid you've just missed Jean.' Christ. How pathetic must she sound!

'I know.'

He knew? Then why was he here?

'But I could give her a message if you'd like.'

'It's not *Jean* I've come to see.' Feeling as though she might pass out from nerves, she fastened her fingers around the newel post. Harry Hinds had come to see *her*? To *see her*? 'See, I figured if Jeanie weren't here, then I might get a different answer when I ask you again to come

64

out with me.'

He was asking her out? On a date? Now what did she do? 'Um...'

'Forget about Jeanie,' he said, moving to the bottom of the stairs. 'You don't need her permission. This ain't nothing to do with her. So, Lou Channer, how about you let me take you out for a drink?'

'Not tonight,' she said, her mouth seeming to work of its own accord. 'Nor tomorrow.'

'Monday then,' he said gently. 'I could call for you around... half seven?'

Unable to believe what she was doing, she nodded. 'Yes. All right.'

She saw him smile.

'Good. Well, then. Monday it is. Half seven.'

'And Jean?' she asked.

'Up to you,' he said, turning towards the door and opening the latch. 'But I wouldn't have thought there was any need for her to know, would you?'

'No,' she said, wary of going to see him out in case he tried to kiss her. 'Not really.'

After all, she told herself, watching as he pulled the door closed behind him, they were only going for a drink. Once he found out how dull she was, he was unlikely to want to see her again anyway. Then she would have risked causing a fuss with Jean for nothing. Besides, he wasn't even Jean's proper brother. And they *were* both adults, free to do as they pleased. So, no, she would keep this momentous occurrence to herself.

In something of a light-headed muddle, she turned to go back upstairs. Golly. What an unlikely turn of events! Barely had she got settled in and she'd been asked on a date. Who would have thought it? Apparently, that old saying was true: fortune really did favour the brave.

★ ★ ★

'Well aren't you the picture.'

Just as she had known she would, Lou blushed. 'Thank you.'

'Here, mind your frock and I'll help you up.'

It was Monday evening and, as arranged, on the dot of half past seven, Harry Hinds had arrived to take Lou on their date. And she was so nervous that she was trembling. Ever since agreeing to go out with him, she had been unable to settle to anything. She had spent most of Sunday in a private panic about what to wear and rueing that, while in town on Saturday, she hadn't had the sense to treat herself to a new skirt. As she hadn't, she was having to make do with one of the only two dresses she had brought from home — a simply-cut cotton affair of wide peach and blue stripes on a white background. Mum had run it up for her from a pattern they'd seen in a shop in Barnstaple and she loved it. The freshness of the fabric gave a lift to her rather nondescript colouring and made her feel summery. It wasn't the most sophisticated of outfits, she knew that, but at least she didn't feel frumpy.

Panic had set in again when she'd had to get ready. Thankfully, once they'd all finished eating supper, Jean had announced that she was going to see her mum. A stroke of good fortune, it had saved her facing an inquisition into where she was going and with whom. Harry might have appeared untroubled by the prospect of Jean finding out but, for her part, Lou had been desperately hoping that she wouldn't. It wasn't just Jean, though: she didn't really want *any* of the girls knowing. If nothing else, she could do without all the nudging and winking that was bound to ensue.

With her wristwatch showing seven o'clock, she'd had a quick wash, pulled on her dress, tidied her hair and applied the lightest coat of lipstick. Although tempted to apply some mascara, she'd decided against it; the little brush that went with her palette was ancient and, no matter how wet she made the block, made no difference whatsoever to the appearance of her lashes. Even on the odd occasion when it did give them some colour, it always seemed to dry in clumps. Next weekend, she would treat herself to a new one. And to one of those eyeliner pencils Jean used. Mind you, she'd have to get some tips from her on how to apply it; it looked like a tricky thing to get right. At least her lipstick was reasonably new; at her mother's suggestion, she'd bought a shade of coral rather than the scarlet colour currently all the rage. She still coveted crimson lips for the way they alluded to screen siren rather than girl next door, and were rather more sexy than safe. Not that she wanted to be sexy; if Jean was anything to go by, it looked like hard work. There also seemed to be a fine line between sexy and what her Mum would term 'fast', the thought of accidentally being taken for the latter making her shudder.

Anyway, since she'd been ready far too early, she'd gone to wait by the window in the front parlour in order to see Harry arrive. With no idea where he was taking her — other than *for a drink* — she'd been surprised to see a van drawing up. In a shiny dark green colour with fancy cream writing on the side, it looked new. *Hinds' the Grocers*, it said. Harry Hinds. Thinking about it now, his name made him sound like one of the gangsters in the comic books her brothers used to read. It was a thought that made her giggle.

'I thought we'd go up The Lamb & Lantern,' Harry said now, having handed her up into the passenger seat and then gone around to get in beside her. 'You ever been up there?'

Having never heard of the place, she shook her head. 'I've only been in Plymouth a week.' Then, lest he thought her a country bumpkin, she added, 'So I've not had chance to get out and about much yet.'

'I think you'll like it,' he said, and with which she heard the van's engine clattering to life. 'It's got a beer garden at the back and from the front there's a view out over the sea. Course, it's quiet these days — too far to walk and beyond most people's petrol ration. But I don't mind a bit of peace and quiet now and again. Besides, I know the landlady.'

While Harry's attention was taken with negotiating the junction at the top of Jubilee Street, Lou found herself drawn to looking at his hands. Resting on the steering wheel they looked manly, one of his fingers bearing a signet ring with a dark red stone. His nails were blunt, and clean, too. She glanced at his face; his complexion was the same olive-colour as his hands. Perhaps he was naturally dark-skinned. After all, it was early in the year to have seen much sun yet.

While he continued to concentrate on driving, she made a discreet study of his clothing — a dark grey suit with double-breasted jacket, wide trousers with turn-ups and a starched white handkerchief in his top pocket. Beneath his trilby hat his hair looked almost black, his eyebrows and pencil thin moustache the same. In fact, the word that kept coming to mind was *foreign*. But then, perhaps, in part, he was.

As he guided the van across the main road and up the hill on the other side, he glanced across at her. Flushing, she directed her eyes back out through the windscreen.

The road they were on now was narrow, the houses a raggle-taggle collection of cottages with tumbledown outbuildings and rambling gardens.

'All right?' he asked. To Lou's mind, his accent was similar to Jean's and marked him out as being from London.

She nodded. 'Fine, thank you.'

'So, what do you think of *Plymuff*, then?'

At his imitation of the way the girls pronounced it, she smiled. 'Haven't seen much of it yet. I went into town with Liddy on Saturday morning and it seemed very... busy.'

Beyond the next corner, the countryside ahead of them opened out, the lane crossing an area of ragged heathland.

'Go on the tram to Woolworth's, did you?'

'We did, yes. Jess wanted to buy some make-up.'

'Quite a girl, young Jess. Filthy laugh.'

The way he said it made Lou wonder whether he'd taken *her* out, too — or had at least tried to. For some reason, the thought of him doing so made her squirm.

'Mm,' seemed the best way to reply.

After a while, when the van had chugged up a long incline, Harry brought it to a halt at the side of the road and slid back his window. 'Too misty today,' he said, as into the van came the tang of salty air. 'Shame. See, on a good day, you can look right out over Rame Head — that's on the other side of the river there. I'll bring you back another day and show you. I'll take you over Rame Head one day too. Maybe on a Sunday afternoon. Right up the top, there's a little church. We'll take a picnic.'

When Harry closed the window and revved the engine to pull away, Lou didn't know whether to feel flattered or alarmed. They hadn't even arrived at the public house and yet, already, he was talking about seeing her again and the places he would take her. Was a date with a man you didn't know supposed to go along this fast? Having never met anyone like him — and having certainly never been out with anyone even remotely similar — she had no idea. Perhaps, tomorrow, she could ask one of the girls. No need to mention that it was Harry she'd been out with; if she was clever, she could just sort of steer the conversation around to dating in general. Given that all most of them talked about was men, they were unlikely to suspect anything.

Hearing the van's engine slowing, she looked out of the window. They were pulling onto a scrappy hardstanding in front of a low stone building with a thatched roof. At intervals along the front of it hung baskets planted with what she guessed were petunias in clashing shades of purple and scarlet and pink.

'It's pretty,' was all she could think to say about it.

Having secured the handbrake and climbed out, Harry came around to her side, opened the door and helped her down.

'Old coaching inn,' he said. 'Shall we?' Taking his arm, she walked beside him to the porch where they ducked underneath the low overhang and went in through the door. The smell that greeted them a stale mixture of ale and woodsmoke. Once inside, Lou glanced about: low beamed ceilings stained brown from the fire; wooden floorboards with wormholes; dark wooden tables with wheelback chairs. Adorning the walls were faded water-colour prints in gilt frames along with horse brasses and wall lights with tatty red lampshades. Remembering him mentioning a garden, she hoped they were going out there. 'Come on through,' he turned to say as though reading her thoughts. 'It's warm enough to sit outside for a bit.'

The little courtyard, like the pub itself, was empty. She supposed it was down to it being a Monday night, when few people went out anyway.

'This is nice,' she said, hoping that it was. Having never been in the garden of a public house before, she had no yardstick against which to measure it.

'Go an' find somewhere to sit. Shan't be long.'

Looking about, she chose a bench in the far corner, away from the door, where she could sit with her back to the stone wall and see anyone coming out. Glad she'd thought at the last minute to bring her cardigan, she buttoned it across her chest; while the evening wasn't cold, it wasn't particularly warm, either. Besides, she would rather put up with a cool breeze than sit in that dark and dingy little bar. Her father would have a fit if he knew she'd been in such a place.

Moments later, Harry returned with what looked like a half of ale in one hand and something red in a wine glass in the other. Only then did she realise he hadn't asked her what she wanted to drink.

'Thank you,' she said when he put the glass on the table in front of her.

'Port and lemon,' he said. 'Ladies' drink.'

She stared down at it. Port. Golly. She didn't think she'd ever tasted that — couldn't recall there ever being any in the house. But, something about the fact that he had picked it for her made her feel special.

When Harry raised his glass, she picked up her own. And when he clinked the edge of hers with his, she smiled. Clearly, he didn't know that clinking glasses was bad form: you raised your glass but never touched anyone else's with it. Lots of people didn't know that, even some who should.

Unable to put it off any longer, she took a sip of her

drink and put the glass back on the table. To her surprise, the contents were sweet and tasted of berries... or was it plums? It was fruity, anyway. At least, it was until it went down her throat where it took on something of a heat — but in a nice, grown-up sort of a way. In an attempt to place the taste, she took another sip.

'Nice,' she said, staring into the glass.

'You've had it before, though?' His look was somewhere between amusement and disbelief.

She nodded. 'But not in a while. I'd forgotten the taste of it.' It was only a tiny lie. And it wasn't as though he could prove otherwise.

'So, Lou Channer, what brought you down from the wilds of North Devon to the grime of Plymouth?'

'Work,' she said. Regretting then how that might make her sound dull, she took another rather larger sip of her drink. To her surprise, the effect seemed to strike instantly at the centre of her forehead. 'And for the chance to get away from *the wilds of North Devon*.'

Bringing his elbows to rest upon the table, he leant towards her. 'Yeah? And is it all you thought it would be?'

She raised her glass and drank some more. It made her feel warm and fuzzy. 'Too soon to say.'

From there, he went on to ask her about her family, and she replied by telling him about her brothers, and about her recent trip to London for the wedding of her cousin, although stopped short of including the fact that it hadn't gone ahead. Then she told him how her mum and dad had grown up together.

'Childhood sweethearts,' he said with the sort of tone that made her wonder whether he was mocking them. Knowing so little about him made it difficult to decide.

'And what about *your* family?' she was surprised to hear herself ask.

72

'Nothing worth telling that Jeanie won't have already told you. George married her mum, who was then left her father's grocer's shop. We moved down here a couple of years after I left school since George fancied taking on the running of it. Little goldmine, it turned out to be.'

'And you work for him,' she ventured.

'I work for myself, Lou. Only fools and paupers work for someone else. See, I've always meant to make money... and now, this war's gonna make that happen.'

He said it with such conviction that she didn't know how to answer. 'Do you have any brothers and sisters?' she asked instead.

'Brother. Eight years older than me. Didn't come down here with us. Wanted to stay up in London. Last I heard he'd got three kids. But that was a while back. There might be four or five by now. Anyway,' he said, draining his glass, 'you finishing that?'

She shook her head. There was hardly any left anyway. 'No, thank you.'

'Well, look, I know it's still early, but I've got somewhere to be later. So, I'll drop you home, go on and do this bit of business and pick you up Thursday, same time.'

She liked the way he took charge. It was manly. It also meant she wasn't faced with having to decide for herself, with the attendant risk of appearing dim.

'Yes, thank you,' she said, it seeming only polite. 'I'd like that.'

'Good. But for now, then, Lou Channer, let's get you home.'

★   ★   ★

It felt good to have a secret. Walking to work the following morning, knowing that not only had she been on a date

73

with Harry but that she'd done so without anyone finding out, felt to Lou like a significant achievement — one that she wasn't yet ready to have picked over by all and sundry. For now, at least until she knew whether anything was going to come of it, she wanted to keep Harry a secret. She might only have been lodging in Jubilee Street for just over a week but she had quickly come to realise that, in this particular house, there was very little privacy; not only did everyone know your business, they took it is as read that over supper every night, you would fill them in on the latest developments. As a case in point, last night, Winnie had let slip that she'd bumped into Robbie Smith on her way to the newsagent's for some fags and immediately the rest of them, led by Jess, had demanded to know what had happened and why she hadn't said anything. Had he been alone? Had he asked her out? What had he been buying? *What had he been buying? That's* what they wanted to know? Still, Lou supposed, a certain smugness coming over her, that's what you got for fancying a *boy* instead of a man.

This morning, though, it was beginning to dawn on her that dating a man wasn't for the fainthearted. As last night had shown, a proper man didn't expect you to be impressed by being taken out in a van, nor by being bought a port and lemon. Nor, presumably, did he expect your sole topic of conversation to be the filing systems of the Royal Canadian Navy. No, going out with a man like Harry Hinds was going to require a certain sort of behaviour, a certain maturity — was going to need her to act as though she'd done it all before. Given that she hadn't, all she could foresee was pitfalls. Yes, sadly, she was going to need help, the sort of help she was more likely to get from Jean than — with that, she glanced to Liddy, walking beside her — Liddy or any of the others.

And therein lay her other difficulty: when she did tell Jean about Harry, she couldn't be sure how she was going to react. While it had been easy to keep it from her thus far, she couldn't imagine it remaining so. When Harry had dropped her off last night, Jean had still been out. But the odds of being able to continue creeping around behind her roommate's back were low. And the last thing she needed was Jean finding out by accident; for their friendship to stand any chance, she, Lou, had to be the one to tell her.

The other problem she foresaw was the matter of clothes or, rather, her lack thereof. She had a smartish skirt for work and another that could be pressed into service if need be. She had a couple of blouses to wear with them and a jacket. She had a couple of other garments that could pass muster for wear at the weekends. But what she didn't have was anything to wear out — certainly not to the sort of places Harry might take her. Last night he'd mentioned walking up a hill to see the view and have a picnic, which would need slacks... or perhaps even shorts. Jess had a pair of baby blue ones with turn ups that she wore with a flowery blouse and a fancy belt. Perhaps she could ask Jess where she'd got them and then hope to find them in a different colour so that it didn't look as though she was copying her. And then she supposed that at some stage, Harry would want to take her dancing. Lord, a whole separate nightmare in the making! She'd never been to a dance before, least, not one held somewhere other than a village hall, where you were only required to shuffle about with members of your own family.

'You all right?'

In response to Liddy's question, she looked up, stunned to find they had walked all the way down the hill, across the road and through the gates into the dockyard without her noticing a single step of it.

'Sorry,' she said, shaking her head as though in dismay. 'I was miles away.'

'You can say that again. Might as well have been talking to a lamppost for all the sense I got out of you these last five minutes.'

Arriving at the entrance to the store, Lou reached to Liddy's shoulder and gave it a squeeze.

'Yes. Sorry.'

'Well you'd best buck up. Miss Blatchford can spot a slacker a mile off.'

'Warning heeded,' she replied. 'Thanks.'

'See you at tea break then.'

'All right. And Liddy?'

'Yep?'

'Will you be going into town again on Saturday?'

'Usually do. Unless it's pouring with rain.'

'Only, I might have enough money this week to buy a skirt. Maybe even a dress… and I was wondering if you could tell me the best place to look for things like that.'

Liddy shrugged. 'Tell me later what you're after and I'll see where I can think of.'

Lou smiled. 'Thanks, Liddy. See you later.'

★　★　★

'Hey, dolly daydream.'

Suddenly aware that someone was talking to her, Lou looked up. She was sitting with Flossie and Lou at their usual table in the canteen, oblivious — again — to the topic under discussion and with her tea growing cold in front of her.

'Sorry,' she apologised to Flossie.

'You sickening for something?'

'Or some*one*,' Liddy chipped in.

'Ooh, one of our lovely Canadians?'

'Well I doubt it's Lenny Grant or any of his ilk.'

'Only, if it's one of the Canadians, she's got to join the queue. You and me were here first.'

Determining not to get flustered, and raising a smile, Lou shook her head. 'No,' she said. 'I'm not trying to jump the queue for a Canadian. It's just that I didn't sleep well last night and can't seem to get going this morning.' As it happened, it wasn't a lie.

'Better not let Miss Blatchford catch you daydreaming.'

'Told her that once already this morning,' Liddy remarked.

'She can spot a slacker a mile off.'

'Told her that, too,' Liddy added.

Yes, Lou thought, she really must pull herself together. At this rate, they would guess what was on her mind long before she was anywhere near ready to tell them.

'So, what's this I hear about you going on a shopping spree?' Flossie changed tack to ask. 'Wages burning a hole in your pocket already?'

Was absolutely *nothing* private?

'I wouldn't call it a spree,' she said. 'It's just that now I've got a bit of money, I can get a thing or two to wear.'

'Gran's been buying cotton poplin and flannel by the bale. Reckons clothes and material for sheets will be going on the ration. Says she's not going to risk being caught short.'

'They'd ration clothes?' Liddy remarked. 'Can't see how that would work. I mean, what would they do? Same as they did with margarine: you know, take over the garment factories and dress us all the same?'

When Flossie burst into laughter, Lou smiled. It did seem a ridiculous notion but, if there was even the remotest chance of not being able to buy things to wear,

77

it made even more sense to stock up now.

'Well, Gran seems to think it's more than likely,' Flossie remarked.

'Then maybe I should replace my second-best slacks,' Liddy mused. 'Anyway,' she said, turning to Lou, 'assuming you don't have enough money to shop in Spooner's or Dingle's, then Marianne's, round behind the market, isn't bad for skirts and whatnot.'

'Ooh, yes,' Flossie joined in, 'or Maison French just up from Dingle's. Last week I noticed they had shirt dresses in one window and bathing suits in the other.'

'Saturday morning, then,' Liddy said. 'And we'll stop for a tea and a pasty in Drake's.'

That was that settled then, Lou reflected as the three of them made their way back to the warehouse. And, on the plus side, she would have someone to tell her whether or not an outfit looked all right — even if she couldn't tell them why she wanted to buy it in the first place. In the meantime, for Thursday evening's trip back to The Lamb & Lantern, she would have to stick with the dress she'd worn last night, and hope Harry didn't think too badly of her for it.

* * *

'Jeanie at home tonight then?'

Accepting Harry's hand up into the van, Lou nodded. 'Just up there,' she whispered, gesturing with her head towards the window above the front parlour.

'So, you thought to wait for me outside. Good girl. No sense inviting a fuss, is there?'

Earlier, when she'd decided to come out and wait on the doorstep, she'd fretted for a while that Harry might think she was doing it because she was ashamed to be seen with him; seemingly, she had worried for nothing. Seemingly, he was in no rush for Jean to find out either. 'That's what I thought, too.'

'Nicer night for it,' he said, climbing into the driver's seat and starting the engine.

'Yes.' Her sneaking about over — she had changed into her dress in the bathroom and come straight downstairs afterwards — she could now look forward to being out with him. Even knowing where they were going made her feel less anxious than the other night.

'Should be a better view... if you're up for a little walk.'

Watching him steer the van along the lane, she smiled. 'That sounds nice.'

'Good. Good. We'll have a little drink, take a stroll and be back down here before the blackout. Where will you tell Jeanie you've been?'

In that moment, Lou couldn't decide whether he was asking because he didn't trust her to lie or because he did. In a way, she hoped it was the latter. 'I'll only say anything if she asks. And then... I'll just be vague.'

'I see you've got that pretty frock on again,' he changed the subject to remark.

She wasn't sure how to respond. While it was comforting to know he liked it, she would rather not admit to having only two dresses, the second, with its white Peter Pan collar, being nowhere near womanly enough to wear on a date. 'Well...'

'I'm glad.'

Still she didn't know how to reply. 'Oh.'

'I like the way it buttons down the front.'

He liked buttons? Then she should try to remember that when she went shopping on Saturday. Flossie had said one of the stores in town had shirt dresses in the window;

79

they would have buttons. Maybe she could look at some of those.

'So, how's work?' he asked.

Ahead of them now was the stretch of road that opened up over the heathland. It was reassuring to recognise where they were.

'Good,' she said.

'Getting the hang of it? Finding your way around?'

'Little by little. I'm only a junior clerk, and I only enter dockets in ledgers, but I quite like it.'

'Good for you.'

He was right about it being a nicer evening, she thought as she looked out through the little windscreen, The Lamb & Lantern coming into view up ahead.

'You go on through to the garden,' he said when they had pulled up outside and he was helping her down. 'I just need a word with Ivy.' In response to her blank look, he added, 'The landlady.'

She smiled. 'All right. I'll go on through.'

Out in the courtyard, she chose the same bench and rickety table as the other night and sat down. Through the cotton of her dress she could feel warmth from the wood.

The little garden, she noticed, looking around in the better light, could do with some attention: there were weeds growing up through the cinder path and sprouting from between the stones of the wall; down near the back door, the tubs of petunias looked to be gasping for water. Grandpa Channer would have had it all sorted in a trice. Dear old Grandpa Channer; though it must be ten years since he'd passed on, she still missed him.

'Sorry about that.' Coming towards her with a drink in each hand, Harry was smiling. 'Mind if I take off my jacket,' he said as he put their glasses on the table.

'No, 'course not. It's very warm against this wall.'

His jacket removed and his tie loosened, he sat down next to her. Inwardly, she smiled. Last time, he'd sat opposite.

'Cheers.'

She raised the glass he'd put in front of her. Port and lemon again. She didn't mind; it didn't seem as strong as some of the drinks from which, at the occasional family party, she'd stolen sips.

'Cheers.' She still couldn't help cringing when he clinked her glass though. Aunt Naomi would have a fit.

'So, Lou, lovely Lou. You're settled in down here now then?'

Having taken a sip of her drink, she put the glass back on the table. It felt a bit soon to say for certain; hard though it was to believe, she hadn't even been there two weeks yet. Heavens. Who would have thought so much could happen in less than a fortnight? It certainly wouldn't have done in Woodicombe.

'I think so.'

'Not homesick?'

She laughed. 'Definitely not homesick, no.' It wasn't strictly true; she was beginning to miss Mum terribly but there was no need for him to know that. She was trying to sound grown-up.

'No chap at home I should be on the lookout for? Nobody who asked you to be their sweetheart?'

Telling herself that Freddie didn't count, she shook her head. 'No chap.'

As though considering her reply, he nodded slowly. 'Good, good.'

Then, just in case she'd led him to thinking she'd never had a boyfriend at all, she said, 'There was one for a while. But he's gone in the navy and I didn't like him enough to wait.'

'Your drink all right?' he changed the subject to ask.

Thinking to pick it up and take another sip, she nodded. 'Nice, thank you.'

'Knock it back then and I'll get us another. Or something different if you'd like.'

Something different? Since she had no idea what that might be, she shook her head. 'No, another of these is fine, thank you.' The truth was, she didn't really want another of anything. This first one was already giving her a fuzzy head. Nevertheless, she took a gulp of the contents and then pushed the glass towards him. The good thing about it, she decided, angling her head back to take in the warmth of the sun, was that it made her forget her nerves — made her feel relaxed.

'There you go,' he said, returning moments later to put an identical drink in an identical glass down in front of her. 'We'll drink these... and then since I'm a man of my word, we'll wander along and see that view I promised you.'

'Yes,' she said, wondering briefly at his obsession with the view, 'I'd like that.' Living on the coast at Woodicombe, she rather took sea views for granted. But, tonight, for his benefit, she would act impressed, won over. After all, he *had* brought her all the way up here again just so she could see it.

'Well then,' he said after a while longer, 'finish it off and we'll make tracks.'

Not wanting to appear ungrateful by leaving most of her drink, she picked up the glass, stared at the contents and then took a long slug. Feeling him watching her do so, she swallowed it, put the glass to her lips for a second time and drained the contents. Unavoidably, she shuddered.

'Done,' she said, reaching for her handbag.

Getting up from the bench, he held a hand towards her and, feeling unsteady on her feet, she took it. Just the effects of guzzling down that last lot, she told herself. Get walking along and she'd be fine.

'Night, Ivy,' he called as they went through the pub towards the front door.

From somewhere unseen, a woman's voice called back. 'Night, Harry.'

'All right?' he asked as they set off in the opposite direction from his van, the view ahead of them opening up to reveal a shaft of sunlight meeting the water of Plymouth Sound in a pool of liquid silver.

'It's ... lovely,' she said. And it was, too. Below them spread the whole of the city and the curves of the river as it made its way down from the moors and out to sea.

'Cornwall,' he said, pointing away to the right. 'And over there,' he went on, pointing to the left, 'beyond that headland, is South Devon. Tell you what—' Letting go of her hand, he turned back. 'Stay there. I'll just nip back and fetch something.'

Wondering what he was up to, but too slow of thought to ask, she simply stood where she was, her bag over her shoulder, her arms folded about her waist, a smile on her lips. Who would have thought it, little Lou Channer out on another proper date and not with a boy but with an actual man? A good-looking and charming one. A good-looking and charming one who liked her enough to bring her all the way up here so that she could see the view — and buy her two port and lemons while he was at it.

Feeling an arm about her waist, she turned sharply. 'Oh. You're back.'

'Just remembered,' he said panting lightly, 'I had a rug in the van. Come on, let's go a down here and find somewhere to put it down. Then we can sit and ... admire

83

the view.'

The view again. She must remember to tell him about the view at home, the one from the beacon down over Westward Quay. If he liked views, he'd love that one.

The grass, as they made their way down the hillside, was deep and, worried about turning an ankle, she held tightly onto his arm. 'I don't... like this,' she said, the greenery ahead of them unexpectedly blurring.

'It's all right,' he said softly. 'We're almost there now.'

'We are?'

'Keep a tight hold of my arm. Not far, then we can have a sit down.'

When he drew to a halt, she looked around. 'Here?'

'Here.'

'But won't those bushes... be in the way of seeing the...?'

'Shush,' he said, landing a brief kiss on her mouth. 'Are you all right to stand there a moment while I—' But, without waiting for her to reply, he had let go of her arm and was shaking out the rug. 'There, sit yourself down. You'll feel better. Come on.'

Feeling his hands on her waist, she let him guide her down to the ground. He was right. She definitely felt better now that she was no longer standing up.

'But the view...' she said, gesturing vaguely to the gorse bushes in front of them.

'Is just fine from here,' he said, reaching behind the knot of his tie to undo his collar.

It was then she noticed that he was in his shirtsleeves. 'You've lost ... your jacket.'

'Didn't need it,' he said, settling beside her. 'Put it in the van.'

'Oh.' Well, that made sense. 'It is a bit... warm.'

'So, what we'll do,' he said, 'is put your handbag over

84

here …' Away to her left, she could make out that he was moving something. '… so that you can just lay back. That way you'll be out of the sun.' When he took a gentle hold of her shoulders and eased her backwards, she let him. Then, feeling the ground safely beneath her back, she closed her eyes. 'Better?'

'Better,' she agreed. And it was. Down here, and especially with her eyes shut, things didn't feel nearly so wobbly.

'Told you it would be.'

'Mm.' He really was quite thoughtful.

'Still a bit warm?'

In as much as she could, she nodded. 'Mm.'

'Tell you what, let's try taking your mind off it.' With that, seemingly from nowhere his mouth was on hers, the tip of his tongue pushing apart her lips. In her shock, she stiffened. 'Relax,' he paused briefly to whisper. 'I promise you you'll like it.'

When he tried again, she let him, the feel of his hot tongue exploring her mouth less off-putting than she would have expected. But when, without warning, he pulled away, her instinct was to worry that she'd done something wrong. 'You've … stopped,' she said, desperate for reassurance that it wasn't her fault.

'Only while I undo your dress,' he whispered. 'You do want me to, don't you. Only, we have come all the way up here…'

With his fingers setting about her buttons, she realised that he wasn't so much asking her as telling her. *You do want me to, don't you.* Feeling somehow detached from what was going on, she closed her eyes. 'Yes,' she said breathily, anxious that he shouldn't think badly of her. *We've come all the way up here.*

Aware that she could feel more of the breeze on her

skin, she opened her eyes, everything in her line of sight swaying from side to side.

'All right?'

'I think so.'

Having started to push her slip up her thighs, he stopped. 'You think so.'

'No, no,' she rushed to assure him. 'I'm… fine.'

Realising he was taking her at her word, she felt his fingers behind the waistband of her knickers and then felt them being dragged down over her hips.

'You still all right?' he looked back at her to ask.

If she let him down now, he might not be pleased. He certainly wouldn't want to take her out again. Besides, deep inside her was an urge — a sort of compulsion to let him keep going. 'Yes,' she said. 'Yes.'

It was over disappointingly quickly. There was a brief moment of discomfort, when she did her best to contain a gasp and then, just as she was thinking it might not be so bad, he groaned and slumped on top of her, his head coming to rest heavily in the crook of her shoulder, the rhythm of his breathing leading her to wonder whether he had fallen asleep. Trapped under his weight and having no clue as to the done thing in the circumstances, she simply resigned herself to laying there until he stirred. But really, that was it? That was *doing it*? Perhaps, being a bit tipsy from the drink, she had missed something. Oh, dear God, what if she had missed something?

In the event, a moment later he raised himself up, the expression on his face an odd little half smile. 'Here,' he said, offering her his hand, 'sit up. Let's make you decent.' It wasn't until he was nimbly doing up her frock that his words from earlier came back to her. *I like the way it buttons down the front.* How could she have missed what he'd meant by that — missed that his aim all along had been to bring her back up here, buy her a couple of drinks and then take her into the undergrowth and do it with her? And all the while, she'd been merrily thinking that when he'd talked about it being a nice evening to see the view, he'd meant just that. How on earth could she have been so slow-witted? How could she not have realised that dating a proper man like Harry Hinds would come with certain... obligations? Only someone whose sole experience of men amounted to holding hands with Freddie Paddon could possibly have been so naïve. Thankfully, she seemed to have got away without making a *complete* fool of herself.

Her clothing back in order, he helped her to her feet.

'You know what this means now, don't you, Lou Channer?' Taking her hands in his, he gave them a squeeze. With no intention of saying that she had no idea what he was talking about, she simply stared back at him. 'This means you're mine now. You're my girl. *I* look after *you*, and *you* don't look at anyone else.' Trying to digest what he was saying while a dozen hammers were pounding away in her head, she settled for giving him a single nod. 'You understand that, don't you?'

You're mine now. 'I ... understand.'

'In which case,' he said, letting go of her hands, reaching into the pocket of his trousers and pulling out a brown leather wallet, 'take this and buy yourself something smart. Saturday night I'm taking you to a club.' When all she did was stare, transfixed, at the wad of ten-shilling notes he was holding towards her, he gave a wry grin. 'All right then, you little minx.' Re-opening his wallet, he pulled out several more notes. 'Get yourself a pair of shoes as well. Something with heels. Can't have people thinking Harry Hinds doesn't know how to treat his girl proper, now can we?'

'You went out with him then.'

Unable to believe she'd slept through until Jean's alarm had rung at seven o'clock, Lou squinted across to where her roommate was moving about at the washbasin. God, she felt tired. If she didn't lift her head off the pillow and get up right this minute, she was in danger of going back to sleep.

To avoid that happening, she hauled herself upright, pushed back the eiderdown and forced herself out of bed. As for Jean, well, she would admit to nothing until it was plain whether she actually knew anything or was just hazarding a guess.

'What?' Rounding the end of the bed, she stumbled over the corner of the rug.

'You went out with Harry.'

On the other hand, why was she bothered what Jean thought? Harry had said she was his girl now, which had to mean he didn't mind who knew it, his stepsister included. 'How did you know?' God, how she wished her head would stop pounding.

'Heard the van pull up. Looked out and saw you getting in.'

Then the cat was out of the bag; she now had Jean's disapproval to contend with as well as a thick head to try to overcome. 'Sorry,' she said, deciding it the best way to avoid an argument. She really didn't need the day to get off on a sour note. 'I should have told you.'

From the corner of her eye, she saw Jean shrug.

'Nothing to do with me. All I'll say is the same as I did last time. Harry Hinds is fickle. Let him take you out, let him spend his money on you... if that's what you want. But for Christ's sake look out for yourself.

88

And when it all ends in tears, don't say I didn't warn you.'

Pulling her slip down over her underwear and then crossing to the wardrobe for her skirt and blouse, Lou sighed. Jean was entitled to think what she wanted about her stepbrother, but when Harry was with *her*, he was different: she was his girl; he would look after her. He'd said so last night. Little point trying to convince Jean of that though.

'Fair enough,' she said, pulling her skirt up over her hips and reaching to fasten the waistband. Pausing to run her finger around the rim of the button she grinned. *I like the way it buttons down the front.* Good job she *hadn't* realised what he'd meant by that because she would have insisted that he bring her straight home. And then she would have missed out on this feeling of confidence she seemed to have this morning — this new womanliness. And a sort of pride at recalling what they'd done. Nor would she suddenly have felt so *knowing*. In fact, after the events of last night, she understood now what was behind Jean's assuredness, what it was that put that wiggle in her walk. Ooh, and there was another thing: *get yourself some heels*, Harry had said. Well, she would. And then she would practise walking in them until she could make her hips sway like Jean's did.

'Are you done at the basin?' she asked, glancing across to where Jean was at that moment rolling a stocking up her leg.

'Yeah. While you're there, in the top of my wash bag you'll see some Alka-Seltzer. Drop two of them into a glass of water, wait for them to dissolve, then drink it down.'

With a frown, Lou leant across the basin to examine her reflection in the mirror. Was it so obvious? Sadly, it was, although it was probably the speed with which she was

89

moving — or lack thereof — that had given her away first. 'Thank you. I'll get some and replace them.'

'Port's the very devil for a hangover, especially mixed with lemonade. Next time tell him you want a gin and orange, or a vodka and lime. Clear drinks — them without no colour, I mean — don't make you feel nearly so bad.'

'Thank you,' she said again, deciding she'd rather not ask how Jean knew what drink Harry had bought for her. 'I'll remember that.' She hadn't the least clue whether she would like either of those two drinks but, if it meant never having to wake up with her head feeling like it did this morning, then she was more than happy to give them a go.

* * *

Thank goodness tomorrow was Saturday: no squinting at scrawled delivery notes and no having to concentrate on writing legibly in the tiny columns of the stock ledgers. And sleep, Lou thought, fighting off a yawn; this evening she could have an early night followed by a lie-in. And she was going to need it, too, because, tomorrow night, Harry was taking her to a club and the last thing he'd expect would be to have to leave early because she couldn't stay awake.

'Oy, dozy. You coming or what?'

Turning sharply over her shoulder, Lou saw Flossie leaning in the doorway to the warehouse, her head cocked in enquiry. Carefully setting her ink pen on the blotter, she glanced in disbelief to the time. Already ten o'clock and so little done! Who knew that two port and lemons would make it so hard to think straight?

''Course,' she said. 'I'll just get my bag.'

Unhooking the strap of her handbag from the coat peg

and popping it over her shoulder, she paused for a moment to gather her thoughts. All she could think about this morning was what she'd done with Harry last night — and how hard it was proving to act as though she hadn't — especially when all she really wanted to do was drop hints to the others. Of course, she would do no such thing, and not just because she doubted that either Liddy or Flossie would understand something so adult. No, she could do without having them think her fast. Because she wasn't. Although… was she? She had done it with a man on just their second date, and out on a hillside, to boot. No, of course she wasn't fast. Look at her; fast women didn't look like she did. If anything, they looked more like Jean. Besides, Harry was a real catch; doing it with him came with the territory.

Flushing uncomfortably nevertheless, she left her office to find Flossie waiting with Liddy at the bottom of the loading ramp.

'If I were you,' Liddy said, thrusting her hands into the pockets of her overalls and watching her approach, 'I'd skip the tea this morning and have coffee.'

'And I'd put a couple of spoonfuls of sugar in it,' added Flossie, 'to give you some go.'

Setting off beside them, Lou chose to merely smile. Was it possible that Jean had already said something to Liddy about Harry? Or had these two, noticing that she looked rather drawn this morning, simply decided to fish for details? Remembering what her Mum always said about it usually being the little things that gave you away, she determined to remain tight-lipped. 'I don't really like coffee.'

'You don't have to *like* it,' Liddy remarked, going ahead of her through the door into the canteen, 'you just need to drink some to perk you up.'

'And by heaven could you do with some perking,' Flossie agreed.

Beside them, Lou gave a resigned sigh. 'Very well. I do feel sluggish. I'll try it.'

'And in return for the tip, you can tell us where you went last night,' Liddy said. Indeed, a minute or so later, with the three of them seated at their table, it became clear to Lou that Liddy wasn't going to let the matter drop. 'So?' her friend pressed, offering her cup to her lips to test the temperature of her tea. 'Where were you?'

'More to the point, who with?' Flossie whispered. 'You better not have landed one of the Canadians because that wouldn't be fair. There is a queue, you know.'

In a way, Lou thought, a Canadian would be easier to explain. 'If you must know,' she said wearily, certain they would wheedle it out of her at some point anyway, 'I went out with Harry.'

'Jean's Harry? You do know he kept asking Jess to go out with him, don't you?'

She hadn't known for sure about Jess, no, but she *had* noticed how he had smiled that time he'd mentioned her name. Unsure how it felt to have her suspicions confirmed, she took a sip of her coffee. It tasted horrible and bitter and wasn't even terribly warm, and she wished she hadn't let them talk her into trying it. Still, if it did as they suggested and perked her up, it would be worth it.

But what to say to them about Harry?

'I didn't know that, no —'

'Went out with him just the once. *Not her type,* was what she said afterwards.'

The only way she was going to be able to stop squirming, Lou reflected, was by telling these two enough to satisfy their curiosity. 'But then I don't see how Harry going out Jess is any of my business. All I did was go for a drink with him. I should imagine he's been out with a lot of girls, just as I've... had boyfriends before.' It was only a white lie. And it wasn't as though they could prove any differently.

'So, when are you seeing him again?'

She shook her head in dismay: nosy pair. 'Who said I am?'

'No one,' Flossie retorted, leaning across the table towards her and grinning. 'But you are, aren't you?'

With some reluctance, Lou nodded. 'Tomorrow. But please don't go telling everyone else. I'm only telling the pair of you because we work together and because you've been kind and helped me settle in.'

'Won't say a word to a soul,' Flossie said. 'Cross my heart and hope to die.'

'Same as her,' Liddy agreed, albeit rather less convincingly. 'Oh, and I'm not going into town tomorrow now,' she went on. 'I know I said I was, but my brother's got a weekend pass and so I'm going to see him instead.'

'That's all right,' Lou said. 'I'll go on my own. There's only a couple of things I need. I'm sure I'll find my way around.'

For Lou, the rest of the day was to prove a trial. Not long after returning from her tea break, she knocked over a bottle of ink, making a mess that took her ages to clear up. Then two deliveries arrived in quick succession and, with her head still pounding, she was slow checking the goods to the dockets as the other two called them out, causing one of the drivers to *curse the day they ever allowed women into the dockyard* and Flossie and Liddy to moan at her for making them late for lunch.

But worse was to come. Halfway through the afternoon, Lieutenant Ross arrived to carry out his weekly tally of the ledgers to his records — except that the totals didn't tally at all.

'You'd better find out where you've gone wrong pretty quick,' Flossie said when the lieutenant had left her alone to 'take another look'. 'Because on the way home on Fridays I gets cod an' chips for me an' Gran. And I like to be there before the queue snakes halfway down Gas Street.'

'How much are you out by?' Liddy rather more helpfully wanted to know.

Lou gave a weary sigh. She wished she knew. 'He didn't say.'

'Dammit. If we knew how much you were wrong, we might be able to narrow down where to look. Are you over or under?'

'Over or under?' Still troubled by her thick head, not to mention a mounting sense of panic, Lou didn't even understand Liddy's question.

'Are you looking for something not in the ledger or for something you've entered twice?'

It seemed as much as Lou could do to fight back tears. '*I don't know.*'

'Then I think I'd best go an' fetch Miss Blatchford,' Liddy said, rolling her shirtsleeves back down to her wrists and buttoning her cuffs. 'I'll tell her we think it's a bit mean, with you still in your first proper week on your own, not to even give you a clue where to start looking.'

Less than ten minutes later, as good as her word, Liddy was back with Miss Blatchford, the latter bearing an oversized ring binder.

'Your tally is out by quite a lot,' she announced matter-of-factly as she set the massive binder down on the desk. 'So, I imagine you've missed an entire page from a docket. It's easily done.'

All Lou could think, as she sat alongside Miss Blatchford comparing delivery notes from one set to another, was that the girls had been right about this woman; she was patient and fair, which only made her feel all the worse for having let her down.

'I'm sorry about this,' she said as they sat turning the pages in their binders.

'Don't worry. It might be the first time you've gone wrong, but I doubt it will be your last. That it's taken a whole week for you to come a cropper is actually a jolly good show —'

'Here!' Lou suddenly exclaimed, spotting that one of this morning's deliveries only had two of the supposed three pages. 'You were right. I'm missing a whole page.'

From there, Lou knew that her error was easily remedied, the missing page even turning up on the floor beneath her desk.

'I'll leave you to it then,' Miss Blatchford said. 'And I'll suggest to Lieutenant Ross that he comes back in half an hour. And next time, try looking on the floor first...'

'I will,' Lou replied, her relief immeasurable. 'And thank you.'

Walking up the hill to Jubilee Street that evening, Lou made herself a vow. No matter how things turned out with Harry — the control for which she guessed rested with him anyway — she would never again allow going out with him, or, indeed, anyone else, to distract her from her work. Had she known that all it would take to muddle her head was two port and lemons, she would never have gulped down that second one — indeed, would have declined the offer to start with. Not that she recalled having any say in the matter. Anyway, Harry might have announced that he would look after her, but she still needed to earn a wage, and this job was so much better than most she could have ended up doing. So, from now on, and seeing as she had no desire to give up her newfound freedom and go back to living at Woodicombe, she would see to it that she did nothing that might cause her to lose it.

Chapter 4

Harry's Girl

Shopping, when you had money in your pocket, was fun. It was even better, Lou decided, when you were on your own because the shop assistants paid you more attention. They'd certainly taken notice when she'd mentioned that what she was looking for *today* — as though there might shortly be future occasions — was a smart skirt and blouse for daytime wear and a dress more suitable for evenings out. As a result, the trail of garments brought for her approval was never ending. So caught up in the excitement did she become that it was only when trying to decide between two skirts — and wondering whether she might buy them both — that she even stopped to enquire of the prices.

It was Saturday morning and, having taken the tram into town, Lou had found her way to the dress shop called Marianne's, where, for the last half an hour, she had been in the little fitting room with the assistant — Myrtle, daughter of the proprietress, no less — helping her to narrow down the choice of garments.

'Red really does seem to be madam's colour,' the mannequin-like young woman assured an uncertain Lou. 'Which is fortunate because it's so popular right now — everyone wanting to lift their spirits and seem patriotic.'

With that in mind, Lou finally settled upon a scarlet linen skirt, admiring the way the panel of pin tucks skimmed over her tummy and how the box pleats at the knee flicked about when she walked. To go with it, she went with Myrtle's other recommendation of a short-sleeved cotton blouse with tiny sprigs of wild strawberries printed upon a cream background. Worn together, Myrtle assured her, the two looked summery and yet would lose nothing of the overall effect by being teamed with a cardigan or jacket for a cooler day, and with which, as if by magic, a soft cream cardigan had been produced. It had been as much as Lou could do not to actually sigh with delight.

When it came to choosing a dress, Lou knew she was even deeper in uncharted territory, momentarily rueing she hadn't accepted Esme's offer that she keep the shocking pink Schiaparelli creation she'd borrowed from her on that fateful evening of the family party in Clarence Square. All well and good with hindsight, she reminded herself, but, at the time, she had been completely unable to imagine an occasion that would warrant the wearing of it. She doubted it would have been right for Plymouth anyway.

'For what type of event is madam buying?' Myrtle had enquired.

'My boyfriend is taking me to a club.' *My boyfriend.* What a joy to be able to say such a thing!

'Something in rayon would suit best then,' Myrtle had said. 'Perhaps... yes, one of our new lines, one that hasn't even gone on display yet.'

And now, as a result, here she was, back in Jubilee Street, standing in the room she shared with Jean, regretting that there was no full-length mirror in which to admire herself and hoping the dress looked as nice as she remembered it in the shop. And yes, Mum *would* be surprised at her choice of colour, having only recently pointed out that red really didn't suit her. Well, Myrtle thought it perfect on her, suggesting that anything more

98

sedate would quickly be lost in the atmosphere of a club — a venue that Mum would surely know nothing about.

Exhaling a long sigh, she smoothed her hands down over her hips. The fabric was slinky and clung lightly to her shape. With short puffed sleeves, and a sweetheart neckline — the very latest style from America, Myrtle had said — the bodice had a row of tiny buttons that ran down the centre as far as the waistline. The hem of the skirt sat just below her knees and she loved the way it swished about her legs when she moved. It was her first really grown-up frock.

The problem was, while she was more than capable of pinning up her hair, when it came to applying make-up she was rather less confident. And this dress definitely needed her to wear make-up.

'What is it you want help with?' Jean replied to Lou's tentative approach a while later.

'I've bought some eyeliner,' she said. 'But I'm not sure how to get the shape like you do. The assistant said it was easy but … well …'

'Look,' Jean said, taking the eyeliner from her and getting up from where she had been sprawled on the bed reading the agony aunt column of the latest *Woman's Own*, 'all you want is a thin line immediately behind your top lashes. Close your eyes. I'll do it for you.'

'Would you?'

'Well isn't that why you asked?'

She smiled. 'Actually —'

'Look,' Jean said, growing impatient. 'Do you want me to do it for you or not?'

'Yes please.'

'Then close your eyes and hold still.'

A line traced across each of her lids, Lou went to

look in the mirror, unprepared for the effect upon her appearance. 'Golly.'

'Is that what you wanted?'

'Perfect,' she breathed.

'There's a knack to it. You just have to practise.'

'I will,' she said, unable to believe the difference the two fine black lines had made to her eyes. For a start, they seemed so much larger.

'And do your mascara slowly,' Jean warned. 'Far better to apply three coats than too much in one go and end up with it all going clumpy. And for heaven's sake use water on the block. Don't spit on it. What colour have you got for your lips?'

Crossing to the bed, Lou ferreted about among the wrappings from her shopping trip. 'This one,' she said, holding up the little gold tube for Jean to see.

Taking it from her, Jean squinted at the tiny label. 'Forever Red. Matte finish. Good. Put plenty on. That dress is going to need it.'

Lipstick applied, all that remained was for Lou to put on her new shoes. She'd never had anything like them before and was hoping desperately they wouldn't pinch her toes or rub her heels. Made from black leather, the heels were chunky, the sides of the shoe open, the strap over the top almost as high as her ankle. Oh, and they had peep toes. *Shoes for dancing in*, the assistant in the shoe department of Dingle's had said.

As she stood now, angling Jean's hand mirror to try and see as much of her appearance as possible — a pointless exercise, really — she wished Esme could see her. Equally, she was relieved that Mum and Dad couldn't. She felt so different: womanly; confident; sexy, even.

And Harry, when he rapped on the door less than five minutes later, clearly thought the same.

100

'Well look at you,' he said, his eyes wandering the length of her body and then back up again. Leaning across, he kissed her cheek. 'Got something for you in the van.'

The 'something' turned out to be a bluey-green box with gold embossing. Taking a moment to realise what it was, she gasped. 'Perfume.'

'French,' he said, her astonishment seeming to amuse him, 'though don't ask me to say the name of it.'

Je Reviens. Worth. Paris. She wasn't about to pronounce it, either. But real perfume? She didn't know what to say.

With a quick glance to his face, she carefully opened the little flap at the top of the box and reached inside. The bottle that slid out from the inner sleeve was of blue fluted glass with an ornate stopper. It looked expensive — very expensive.

'Thank you,' she breathed. 'Thank you so much.'

Grinning back at her, he tapped a finger on his cheek.

In response, she leant across and kissed him. 'You know how you're supposed to put it on, don't you?' When she shook her head, he took the bottle from her and twisted out the stopper. 'Come here.' When she slid across the seat towards him, he dabbed the bottom of the stopper on her neck, just behind her ear. 'You put it where you get warm,' he said, dabbing some on the other side of her neck. 'Show me your wrists.' When she offered up her arms, he applied some on the insides. 'One dab does the whole lot. More than that and it'll be too strong. But,' he said, wafting it under his nose, 'since it would be a shame to waste what's left on the stopper, how about we put it somewhere else you get warm.' With that, he slid a finger into the neckline of her dress, held it away from her body and then dabbed the stopper at the base of her chest. 'There.'

Blushing vividly, she bowed her head. 'Thank you.'

'Put it back in the box for now and you can leave it in the van while we're in the club.'

Accepting back the stopper, she held it to her nose and inhaled. What a heavenly scent: grown-up and sophisticated; cool and flowery and yet warm and spicy, too. Unexpectedly it triggered a memory of being small and going to see Grandpa Channer working in the spring border: lilac, hyacinths, violets. But then there was also Nanny Edith's baking — vanilla, definitely — smells from home that made it feel even further away.

'Thank you,' she said again as he started the engine. 'It's lovely.'

'Then just make sure to wear it for me,' was all he said as they pulled away up the hill.

★ ★ ★

It wasn't what she had been expecting. When Harry had said he was taking her to a club, the picture in her mind had been of a dancehall or ballroom, neither somewhere she knew much about but which she had always imagined to be high-ceilinged and brightly lit. This little place, called 'Ruby's', accessed down a flight of grubby stairs from the street and then through an anonymous wooden door and a heavy red curtain, felt like somebody's basement — small and cramped, a spot-lit stage to the rear, a bar along the left hand wall, tables and chairs on the main floor and little booths along the wall to the right. There was a dance floor, it was true, but it seemed almost an afterthought — a small area left clear of tables where a handful of couples could dance something fairly sedate. If she was honest, it was all a bit … tawdry and disappointing. Still, it was Saturday night and she was in a club with a man who'd not only given her money to buy a dress and shoes but had presented her with a bottle of French perfume. Discreetly, she raised a hand as though to check her hair, in reality to catch a waft of *Je Reviens*. She must try to find out what it meant in English.

Making their way across to one of the little booths seemed to Lou to take forever. At almost every table they passed, Harry knew someone who wanted to say hello, shake his hand or remind him or ask him about something, their conversations seemingly picking up where they had only recently left off. While she supposed she shouldn't be surprised — Harry Hinds was clearly someone with a lot of friends — she noticed he didn't introduce her to any of them. As she stood waiting half a step behind him, her hand firmly in his grasp, one or two of the men — mainly older and with physiques that had seen better days — made no effort to conceal that they were looking her up and down. Few of them were with women, she noticed, those wives or girlfriends who *were* there wearing expressions that looked hard and disinterested, their red lips as often as not fastened about a cigarette.

'Right then,' Harry said, eventually moving away from one particularly lengthy conversation, 'we'll get a booth and a drink.' Handing her onto a leather banquette, he scanned the room, signalled to a man in a waiter's apron and then slid in beside her.

'Port and lemon for the lady,' he said as the chap drew near.

'Actually,' she said, recalling Jean's suggestion, 'could I have a gin and orange?'

'Course you can,' he said, unbothered. 'Gin and orange and a Johnnie Walker.'

'You have a lot of friends,' she remarked once they were on their own.

'I wouldn't call most of them friends.' In his palm was a gold-coloured lighter that he repeatedly turned, first one way and then back again. 'They're more business acquaintances. And you know what they say about mixing business and pleasure.'

Actually, she didn't know but, thankfully, the need to say so was avoided by the arrival of their drinks. Seeing the orange colour of hers in the glass, she relaxed a little; with a bit of luck, the gin would be barely noticeable. *Shop girl's drink*, she suddenly remembered overhearing Aunt Naomi once say of the concoction. Well, she was a dockyard girl now. What would Naomi Colborne make of that?

Her drink, she was grateful to discover when she took her first sip, although seeming to contain a good measure of something bitter — presumably the gin — tasted predominantly of orange squash. Perhaps, the fact that it wasn't as sweet as the port and lemon the other night would make her less tempted to drink it too quickly. If she was to avoid a repeat of that evil hangover, she had to make this one last as long as possible.

'So,' Harry said after a moment or two of silence between them, 'where did you get the dress?'

'A little shop called Marianne's.'

'Round behind the market.'

That he knew it came as no surprise. 'Yes. One of the girls told me about it.'

'I know the owner, Marian. Some years back, when her husband died, she gathered up anything of his with any value, sold it and sunk the proceeds into that place. She thought *Marianne's* sounded more upmarket than Marian's. Does Myrtle still work there?'

She stared down at her hands. Don't say he'd been out with *her*, as well? 'Yes, she helped me choose.'

'She did well. Looks good on you.'

104

'Thank you.'

'If you want another one, drop it in to Eli Ackermann's a few doors down. Pick a fabric from his sample books and he'll run one up in it for you. Be ready in a couple of days. Tell him Harry Hinds sent you and he'll do it for little more than the cost of the cloth.'

'Really?'

'God's honest. The stuff Eli's girls turn out is good quality, too. His garments sell in Spooner's and the like for ten times what they cost him to run up.'

'Gosh. Then I'll go and see him,' she said, almost salivating at the thought of a second dress for a fraction of the price of this one.

'Just one of the perks of going out with Harry Hinds.'

'Thank you.'

With that, she heard someone tinkling the keys of a piano and, when she looked across to the little stage, it was to see a group of musicians — exceedingly good-looking Black musicians — taking up their instruments. Along with the pianist, there was a drummer, a man with a trumpet, another with a trombone and a saxophonist. A jazz band: golly, she'd never heard jazz music played live before.

'You sit here and listen while I go and have a quick word with someone,' Harry said, leaning towards her to be heard. 'I'll get another gin and orange sent over.'

Quickly, she shook her head. 'No, it's all right, thank you, I haven't finished this one yet.'

'Fair enough.'

As Harry set about weaving his way between the tables towards the bar, a hush descended and, from the stage, the drummer could be heard counting the players in.

'A-one, a-two, a-one, two, three, four...'

With the trumpeter blasting out the opening bars of music, several couples rushed to the tiny dance floor.

105

Unable to help it, Lou tapped her foot to the beat and watched as they started to dance. And when a willowy Black woman appeared from the back of the stage and moved to the microphone, Lou's ribs reverberated with the roar of approval that went up as she started to sing.

Feeling a tingle of excitement run down her spine, she'd tried to take everything in. She felt so grown-up sitting there, watching a jazz band play, a proper drink in front of her on the table, her boyfriend pleased with the way she looked. She supposed this was how it must be for Esme when she went out with Richard. Well, when she *used* to go out with Richard. And possibly how it was for Jean and her chap, Paul. It certainly wasn't how it had been for Mum and Dad. Neither, for all their swagger, would Vic or Arthur ever be likely to take a girl somewhere like this. Her only wish now was that she could dance. She supposed she could always go about learning — not that this was the style of dancing one went to a little old lady to be taught, as one would to learn to waltz or do the quickstep. Perhaps Jean would know somewhere. She knew most things. It would certainly be better than asking Harry; how much nicer to just surprise him one day by being able to join in. She could do it as a mark of her gratitude for all he kept doing for her.

As one upbeat number rolled into the next, she continued to watch, the dancers on the floor showing no signs of flagging — despite the flamboyance of some of their moves — the foreheads of the musicians quickly starting to glisten under the spotlights.

'Good, aren't they?'

She slid further along the banquette. Harry was back.

'Very,' she raised her voice to reply. 'Do they have a name?'

'The Eighth Notes. I'll get you another drink.'

106

When he started to look about for a waiter, she caught hold of his arm. The taste of the gin and orange was growing on her and the thought of another one was tempting. But fresh in her mind was her vow about avoiding a hangover and keeping her job.

'No thank you,' she said. Tomorrow might be Sunday, but she needed to get into the habit of refusing more than one drink.

'Dance, then,' he said. 'They always play a slow one just before they go off for a break.'

Since he already had hold of her hand and was helping her to her feet, there was little point objecting.

With the band playing the opening notes of a more sedate number, and some of the couples heading back to their tables, spaces opened up on the dance floor. And with Harry putting a hand in the small of her back and holding her close against him, she was relieved to find she didn't have to think about where to put her feet. She supposed it was easy to dance with a man who knew how to lead his partner. Nevertheless, for a moment, she was acutely aware of just how close he was holding her — especially given that they were in public — even if their surroundings were now in almost complete darkness. Through the thin fabric of her dress she could feel the warmth of his body, the buckle on his belt, even the buttons on his shirt. Against her cheek his stubble felt scratchy. This close to, she could smell his hair oil, and faint but sour traces of perspiration. Against her like this he felt purposeful, unfamiliar, exotic. Manly.

With that, she felt the touch of his lips at the base of her neck and hoped he didn't feel the shudder it sent through her. Dangerous. That was how it felt to be out with Harry Hinds, his world foreign to her, his ways unpredictable.

When the music drew to a close, they joined the

107

couples around them in polite applause.

'That was nice,' she said, turning back to him.

'And time to get you home.'

Home? Already? But it probably wasn't even half past ten yet. Disappointed by his suggestion, she nevertheless managed a smile. 'All right.'

'The blackout makes it tricky enough as it is, without being on the roads when all the drunks are staggering home.'

'Yes. Of course.' Not even a mention of him taking her somewhere more private? After he'd got her feeling all... urgent... she'd been rather hoping he would want to go somewhere and kiss her like he did that evening up on the hillside. Tonight, without too much drink inside her, and with her first time out of the way, she might enjoy it more. Would it be wrong to try and put the idea into his head? While she really wanted to please him, to hang onto him, she didn't want to appear *too* forward.

'We'll come here again,' he said, noticing but mis-reading her disappointment.

Bother. Already his mind was on other things. Never mind; no need to rush it. Doubtless there would be other nights for that sort of thing. 'I'd like that,' she said.

'Next Friday.'

'Next Friday,' she repeated, following him out through the curtain at the exit and trotting behind him up the stairs, his hand firmly around her own.

'And don't forget what I said about going to see Eli Ackermann,' he added when they reached the van and he was assisting her in.

'I won't. I'll go next Saturday.'

After that, she quickly came to see what he meant about driving in the blackout. Despite the bases of the lampposts and the fronts of cars being daubed with white paint, supposedly to make them stand out, the lack of street lighting and the shutters fitted on the headlights of motor vehicles made it almost impossible to see more than a couple of feet ahead, such that, as Harry edged the van along the road, she found herself curling her fingers around the front of the seat.

Eventually, arriving in Jubilee Street, he pulled up a few houses short of number eleven and turned off the engine.

'Shame I won't see what's under this nice dress tonight,' he said, sliding along the seat towards her, pushing back the silky material of it and running his hand up her thigh. When his lips then started to explore her throat, it was as much as she could do not to groan. 'Maybe one evening in the week,' he whispered into the hollow at the base of her neck, 'it'll be warm enough for us to take the rug somewhere. I know a nice spot or two.'

Realising how rapidly she was breathing, she nodded into the darkness. 'Yes …'

'Come on then, let's get you indoors before one of these nosy neighbours comes out and bangs on the side of the van.'

When he pulled away and slid back across to open his door, forcing herself to swallow down her disappointment, she pushed her dress back down her legs. Sometimes, it was as though he had a dozen things on his mind, among which she only ranked about halfway.

On the doorstep to number eleven, he glanced quickly about and then drew her close. 'Kiss your Harry goodnight then and I'll pick you up half seven on Wednesday. Start of next week I've got a bit of business on. But Wednesday, we'll go for a drink. I know a place you'll like.'

She nodded. Clearly, when it came to going out with

this man, she still had a lot to learn. But, presumably, she couldn't be doing too badly, or he wouldn't keep wanting to see her. And since he was just about everything she had always hoped for in a boyfriend — good-looking, generous, mature — it was down to her to see it stayed that way.

* * *

Jean had been right: gin and orange *didn't* give you a hangover. At least, sticking to drinking just one of them didn't.

It was Sunday morning and Lou had woken to the sound of rain against the window, a glance to her watch telling her that it was seven-thirty. In comparison to how she'd felt after those port and lemons, her head this morning felt surprisingly clear.

Unable to discern any sounds from the bathroom, and noticing that Jean was still asleep, she tiptoed across to fetch her wash bag from the shelf above the basin, gathered her underwear from the foot of her bed, and crept from the room.

A little while later, washed, and wrapped in her dressing gown, she went downstairs in the hope of finding Mrs H making tea.

She was in luck.

'Mornin', lovely,' her landlady greeted her. 'Did you see there's a message on the board for you?'

Puzzled, Lou looked along the hallway towards the telephone. 'For me?'

'Nora took it, around half-nine last night I should think.'

Who would telephone *her*, Lou wondered? The only people to whom she'd given this number were her

110

parents. With a frown, she went along the hallway and, pulling the slip of paper from the board, squinted at Nora's spidery writing.

Lou. Your father telephoned. Please call him <u>*urgently*</u>. *N.*

Noticing how Nora had underlined the word 'urgently', she frowned even harder. Then she glanced to her wrist-watch. For a Sunday morning it was still early, but Dad would have been up for ages. She wandered back to the kitchen.

'It's from my father,' she said.

'Bad news?'

She shrugged. 'I don't know.'

'Want to borrow a couple of coppers?'

'Would you mind? I'd rather not risk waking Jean. I'll pay you back later.'

When Mrs Hannacott gave her the coins, Lou went to the telephone, lifted the receiver and pressed the first of them into the slot.

'Dad? It's Lou.'

'No need to say *it's Lou*, love. I know your voice.'

'Sorry. I've just got your message. You rang last night.'

'I did, yes.'

To Lou, her father's voice sounded flat. 'Dad, is everything all right?'

'Last night, love, we got word that one of the ships sunk in the Atlantic yesterday was Arthur's.'

Feeling her heart thudding, Lou sank onto the stool beneath the telephone. Arthur's ship? Sunk? 'I didn't think we knew which one he'd joined ...'

'He wrote. Sent a note the day he set sail, it just took a while for it to get here.'

'So ...'

111

'There's been no official word yet. No one I've managed to speak to so far will confirm either way ... won't even tell me whether there's survivors or not ...'

Survivors *or not*? Arthur's ship might or might not have been sunk? And he might or might not have survived? Good God, no wonder Dad sounded so solemn.

Gripping the edge of the stool, she tried to think of something to say. 'So ... what happens now?'

'We've to wait for news.'

'Well,' she said, her voice trembling and her eyes filling with tears, 'no news is good news, right? Besides, you know Arthur, born under a lucky star, that one.'

'Your mum's distraught. Didn't sleep a wink all night.'

'No, I suppose not.' In a way, she was glad now that she *hadn't* seen his message last night because *she* wouldn't have slept for worrying either.

'She was waiting for you to call.'

'Waiting for *me* to call?' What did Dad think *she* could have said or done to help her mother sleep?

'Where were you, Lou?'

Feeling her insides twisting with guilt, she searched for an explanation that wouldn't land her in trouble. Saying that she was at a jazz club with a man wouldn't help in the least. Even saying she was out with friends wouldn't be much better.

'One of the girls at work had a birthday. We all went out for fish and chips.'

'At nine o'clock at night?'

'Well, no, of course not. Afterwards, we went up to a place near The Hoe for a while to listen to a band playing ... and then we all ... came home.' Good heavens. It sounded lame even to her ears.

'Hm. Well, anyway, when can you come home?'

112

Hearing the pips, she pressed another of Mrs Hannacott's coins into the slot. 'Sorry, Dad, the pips went. What did you say?'

'I asked when you can come home. Mum needs you.'

Poor, poor Mum. She must be beyond distraught. And yes, ordinarily, she would be there to comfort her. But she wasn't. She wasn't even just up the road and able to pop in and see her. But then what help would she be to her anyway? As Dad had just said, all they could do now was wait for news.

'Dad, I'm not sure how me coming home is going to help. I can't magic up news of Arthur any more than you can. Besides, I might not be able to leave work ...' And that was another thing: leave the depot? For an unknown length of time? Even if Miss Blatchford allowed her to take compassionate leave, it would only be for a few days at best. Need any more than that and she would have to leave the dockyard altogether. And if she did that, if she left Plymouth, Harry wouldn't trail all the way up to North Devon to keep seeing her. He would find himself someone else. Yes, she argued with herself, but, on the other hand, Mum needed her.

'But I don't know what to do with her, Lou. These last twelve hours she hasn't stopped crying.'

'And I'm sorry for that, Dad,' she said, trying really hard not to let him hear that she, too, was on the verge of tears. 'When I put down the phone in a minute, no doubt *I* shall be upset too. But I really do think that for the moment, the best thing would be for me to wait here and telephone each day to see what you've heard. And if you think it won't make things worse, then next time, I'll talk to Mum myself.'

At the other end of the line there was only silence until Luke Channer said, 'Well, I don't mind admitting to being

113

disappointed in you, Lou. Once upon a time, if I'd said your Mum was upset, you'd have been back here like a shot.'

'And if I didn't have a job here, Dad, I still would be now.' Don't snap at him, she reminded herself; Dad was clearly worried out of his mind. 'Look,' she said, rather more softly, 'why don't I just wait for a day or two? By then, happen I won't need to come at all. Happen we'll have had word that Arthur's fine.'

'Hm.'

'Anyway, Dad, I'm sorry but that's the pips again and I don't have any more coppers. Please give Mum a kiss from me and tell her I'll call again soon.'

Having said goodbye and replaced the receiver on its cradle, she stood for a moment to wipe away tears. Neither of the choices open to her — go home and wait with Mum for news or stay put and keep her job — came without costs. And so, if, by tomorrow, there was still no word of Arthur, what was she going to do — her duty to her parents or her duty by her employer?

'Here, love,' Mrs Hannacott said, coming along the hall with a cup and saucer held towards Lou. 'Bad news from home, was it?'

Accepting the cup of tea from her, Lou nodded. 'Yes,' she said, proper tears now beginning to roll down her cheeks. 'And there's nothing we can do but wait.'

* * *

There was still no news. Thirty-six hours later, and after an entire day of not being able to think straight at work, Lou had telephoned Woodicombe to learn from her father that he had called the doctor out to her mother and that, having taken one of the tablets he'd given her, she was

114

now asleep. In a way, the fact that she couldn't speak to her came as a relief, since, despite a whole day spent anticipating their conversation, she had failed to come up with anything to say that might offer her mother any comfort whatsoever. As far as she could see, the words to do that didn't exist.

Sadly, the following evening, her telephone conversation with her father followed an almost identical course.

'Any news?' she'd asked, her tone deliberately hopeful.

'None, love, no.'

'And Mum?'

'Much the same.'

'Can I speak to her?'

''Fraid not. She's asleep.'

'Then will you tell her I called and give her my love?'

'Of course.'

The night after that was Wednesday. And, having pushed aside thoughts of Arthur, and of Mum and Dad, and got ready to go out with Harry, Lou was now watching from the parlour window, waiting to see him draw up in the van, a tiny but insistent part of her wondering why she had chosen not to mention him to her parents. Yes, he was older than her — although by precisely how much, she didn't know — six or seven years, maybe? — and they might not like that. And, yes, compared to anyone she'd known before, he was rather... worldly, especially when judged against the young men from around Woodicombe. But he was also clean and thoughtful and charming. And generous to a fault. Mum, she couldn't help thinking, would understand what she saw in him. She would also immediately mark him down as a bit of a smooth talker. And she wouldn't be entirely wrong; Harry certainly had all the patter. The problem

115

would be Dad. Dad would take an instant dislike to him, and no amount of assuring him that Harry looked after her would change his mind. Oil and water, those two would be.

Lowering herself onto the arm of a chair, she let out a weary sigh. Well, what her parents thought of him couldn't be helped. When it came to choosing the man she wanted to go out with, she was old enough to make up her own mind. Besides, the sheer distance between her and her parents made it unlikely they would ever meet him anyway. Perhaps, then, notwithstanding the matter of Arthur still being missing, she could be forgiven for not mentioning him, no matter how much part of her might secretly want to.

Lifting aside the net curtain, she peered down the street. Then, with a frown, she turned to the clock on the mantel: ten to eight. *Pick you up at half-seven* he'd said. So, where was he? Since it was unlike him to be late, at what point did she start to worry?

With that, she heard the sound of an engine. Yanking aside the curtains, she let out a sigh of relief. He was here.

'I was beginning to think something had happened to you,' she said as he helped her up into the van. The way he banged the door shut behind her made her wish she hadn't. On his face, as he walked around to the driver's side, was a deep frown. 'Silly of me,' she added as he climbed in, fearing she had somehow spoken out of turn.

Without acknowledging her remark, he pressed down on the clutch and put the van into gear. Only when they had reached the bottom of the hill and turned onto the main road did he say, 'I've got some people to see.'

Beside him, she tried not to sound surprised. 'Oh.'

'Won't take long.'

'All right.'

116

After several minutes sat in silence, Harry clearly preoccupied, she not wanting to risk upsetting him with idle chat, they pulled up on a cobbled side street alongside a brick warehouse. From the little she could work out from the route they'd taken to get there, they had to be somewhere between The Hoe and the quays around Sutton Harbour. In the air, was a strong smell of fish.

'Stay here,' he said, stuffing the key into his pocket. 'And don't get out of the van. I won't be long.'

Unsettled, she nevertheless nodded. She didn't like the idea of being left alone in this deserted street. 'All right.'

Evidently spotting her concerned expression, he gave an irritated shake of his head. 'If something frightens you, press on this bit here and sound the horn.'

Not wanting him to become any more exasperated with her, she nodded purposefully. 'Press there. All right. But I'm sure I won't need to.'

With that, he got out, closed the door and stood for a moment looking up and down the empty street. Then he buttoned his jacket, adjusted his trilby and strode back in the direction from whence they'd come. Despite wanting to see where he went, she forced herself not to turn around and look, suspecting that if he thought she was watching him he would be cross. He didn't strike her as the sort of man to discuss business with a woman anyway — few men ever did — and something about his manner tonight suggested it would be unwise to test his patience. So, she would do as he said. She would sit here and wait. And, when he came back, she would resist the urge to ask what he'd been up to or say anything to upset him.

Though it quickly started to feel like an eternity, he was gone less than fifteen minutes — something she knew from glancing discreetly at her wristwatch as he suddenly opened the door and peered in.

'All right?'

She nodded. At the same time, from behind them came the sounds of the rear door being opened and something being loaded into the back. *He's just going about his business,* she reminded herself, resisting the urge to turn around and look. *It's nothing to do with you.*

When the door slammed shut and Harry reappeared, she smiled at him. 'You weren't gone long at all.'

'I'd hoped not to have to drag you all the way out here,' he said, his mood noticeably lighter. 'But when some feller tells me he'll deliver by Wednesday and takes half from me up front on that basis, he should know to keep his word. Let things like that slide, and people will think Harry Hinds is a pushover. No, I told George I'd get him what he wanted. And no one makes me look bad to my old man.'

The warmth of her smile when she nodded her understanding was down to her relief that all was well.

'No,' she said.

'Anyway,' he went on, reaching into his pocket, 'I've got something for you. Call it an apology for leaving you sitting out here.'

The flat little packet he handed across to her was wrapped in crackly cellophane.

'Stockings!' she gushed.

'French ones,' he pointed out. 'Might not be able to get you any more as classy as those, so try an' make 'em last. Even before Jerry marched in to occupy the place, factories in France were spinning the silk for stockings into parachutes instead. Look at the tops,' he said, pointing across to the drawing on the packet. 'Little bows.'

In the gloomy half-light, she stared down at the drawing. An impossibly long-legged woman was hitching up her slip to reveal that at the top of each seam was a little bow. 'They're lovely,' she breathed. *See,* she thought, relieved to have him back to his usual chirpy self, she *knew* it hadn't been on account of her that he'd been grumpy. He hadn't, as she'd started to fear, gone off her; these stockings were proof of that.

When she looked across at him, he tapped a finger on his cheek. 'Kiss for Harry?' Sliding across the seat towards him, she planted her lips where he had indicated. 'Maybe keep them to wear under that nice red dress of yours,' he said, reaching to put the van in gear. 'Friday night I'll take you to Ruby's again. You liked it there.'

'I liked the music,' she said. 'I just wish I knew how to dance to it.'

'I'll get Desmond to show you.'

'Desmond?'

'Manages the musicians. Used to play in a big band himself once. Think he's given all that up now, though.'

What she'd been hoping to have him say was that *he'd* teach her. Still, never mind. To be able to dance at all would be something. And if she was doing it with his blessing then at least there could be no reason for him to object.

'Right then,' he said, breaking into her thoughts, 'I'll take you home. We'll have that drink tomorrow night now instead. I'll need to see to a thing or two first, but I'll pick you up at eight.'

Go home already? But they hadn't *been* anywhere yet. Even so, it might be best not to let him see her disappointment. 'Yes. All right. Eight o'clock. I'll be ready.'

''Course you will. Because you're Harry's girl, and Harry looks after his girl, doesn't he?'

'Yes, Harry,' she said, smiling back at him. 'You do.'

★ ★ ★

The Royal William was busy. Unusually, for a public house, the saloon bar and lounge were up a flight of stairs, meaning that the windows had magnificent views out over the Sound.

'Gin and orange?' Harry said as he led Lou across to a small table and chairs in the corner farthest from the bar.

Although tempted to try a vodka and lime — the sound of it suggesting it would be exotic — she decided not to chance it. 'Yes please.'

'Be right back.'

Turning to take in the view, Lou allowed herself a sigh of relief. This evening, he had arrived on the dot of eight. He had greeted her with a kiss and complimented the way she looked — which just went to show how far away his mind had been the previous night because she was wearing precisely the same outfit! On the drive here, he had enquired how she was getting on at her job. Was it busy? How many people worked in the depot? What did she think of the Canadians?

'All the other girls fancy them like mad,' she had replied to that last question. 'They claim they've got lovely manners.'

Yes, the evening had got off to a much better start.

But, no sooner had he returned to their table with their drinks, than a man came across. Nodding apologetically in her direction, he addressed himself to Harry.

'Sorry to interrupt, Harry.' With his shirtsleeves rolled up above his elbows, he struck Lou as someone who worked there. 'But young Austin's in the saloon bar. Says he needs a word … something about his uncle and that thing out Mutley way —'

Lou's heart sank. More business. It had to be.

120

'Tell him I'll be through in a minute,' Harry said. 'Tell him I'm having a drink with my girl.' Reaching across the table, he jiggled Lou's hand. 'He can wait till I've finished my drink. But don't let him leave till I've spoken to him.' As Lou was quickly to discover, though, to Harry, *finishing his drink* meant downing what remained of it in one go. 'Want me to get you another?'

She shook her head. 'No thanks.'

'Five minutes. Promise,' he said, getting to his feet and then bending to kiss her cheek. 'You'll be all right here. I'll tell Peggy behind the bar to keep an eye on you.' And, with that, he wove his way between the other tables and out through the door.

Watching him go, Lou exhaled heavily, Nanny Edith's expression about being too quick to count your chickens coming to mind; in thinking the evening had got off to a better start, she might have been premature.

After a quarter of an hour or so, the woman Harry referred to as Peggy came around collecting empty glasses. Stopping to pick up Harry's, she met Lou's look. 'Known him long, have you?'

'Couple of weeks,' Lou replied, unsure whether, in Harry terms, that constituted 'long'.

'We don't see him down here as much as we did once upon a time. Few years back, he was in here pretty much every other day. When he stopped coming, I assumed there must have been a falling out. He ain't a bad lad, though.'

Lou raised a smile. 'No.'

'Just always on the go. Always on the lookout for the next big thing. *It's not what you know, Peggy*, he used to say to me, *it's who*. It's why he keeps up with so many folks, I suppose. Anyway, just give me a wave if you want another,'

Peggy said, gesturing to Lou's glass.

'Thank you. I'll do that.'

'Lovely blouse, by the way,' Peggy said, gesturing towards her with the empties. 'Real summery.'

'Thank you.'

To Lou's mind, Peggy was the type Mum would call *the salt of the earth* — no airs, no graces, but who would walk a mile out of her way to help if she thought you were in trouble.

'Want me to go and fetch 'im?' she asked on her next visit to Lou's table, at least a half an hour later.

'No, please don't,' Lou replied. 'He'd only be cross.'

'I don't know where his manners are,' Peggy grumbled. 'Brings you out and then leaves you to sit here all on your own without a soul to talk to. If he was one of mine, I'd give 'im a clip round the ear. He's not too old. Might knock the thoughtlessness out of him.'

The thought of Peggy boxing Harry's ears made Lou laugh. 'I'd like to see that.'

But it wasn't funny any more. In fact, it hadn't been from the outset. All this talk from him about *Harry looks after his girl* and yet, when it came down to it, he thought nothing of leaving her in the corner of the lounge bar of a public house with nothing she could do about it. Talk about a puzzle. How could one man be so both so thought*ful* and yet so thought*less* at almost the same time? Were all men like it? She doubted Freddie Paddon would have been. Poor, dear Freddie.

Eventually, more than half an hour after that, the door flew open and bowling through it came Harry, his hands raised as though he was merely the victim of a hold up in the traffic.

'Lou, Lou, my lovely Lou. Forgive me, forgive me.' Arriving alongside her, he crouched down.

Grateful, more than anything, that he had finally returned, she couldn't help it; despite having determined not to mention the length of his absence, the words just fell from her.

'You've been gone so long.' At least they came out in a plaintive tone rather than an accusatory one. The last thing she needed was for him to think her critical of him.

'I know, I know,' he said, reaching for her hand and stroking the back of it. 'It was business. You understand that, don't you.'

She felt herself nodding. Perhaps if she knew something of the nature of this 'business' he kept on about then she *would* understand. But everything was always so secretive. And a secretive man had secrets to hide, or so Nanny Edith always maintained. Although what *she* knew about men was anybody's guess.

'Yes, but Harry —'

'I'll get you another drink.'

'No,' she said, wearily shaking her head. 'Please, I don't need another one.'

'Lou, I'll make this up to you,' he added, getting to his feet and raising her hand so that she had no choice but to get up from her seat. 'We'll go to Ruby's. And I'll see Desmond about teaching you them dance steps you want to do. Tomorrow, we'll go tomorrow. Wear that nice dress. I'll pick you up at eight.'

As they made their way across the lounge to the door, Lou caught sight of Peggy putting away glasses behind the bar. When she sent her a faint smile, Peggy's response was to raise an eyebrow.

'Night, love.'

'Goodnight, Peggy.'

On the drive home, neither of them spoke much

until Harry turned the van into Jubilee Street and, as usual, parked a few doors short of number eleven. It was, Lou noticed, looking up through the window, barely even dark. Midsummer evenings were so lovely and long, and there was even talk that next year, through the introduction of something called 'double summertime', twilight would be even later. But this particular evening felt to have been entirely wasted.

'You do forgive your Harry, don't you,' he said, silencing the engine and turning towards her.

She nodded. 'I do, yes.' What choice did she have? If she *didn't* forgive him, he would stop seeing her. And whereas *he* would easily find someone else to go out with, *she* would be left with no one. And it wasn't as though he was cheating on her with another girl; as he always made sure she understood, it was business.

'Only, it's business, Lou.'

See.

'Business, yes.'

'Tomorrow night we'll have some fun at Ruby's.'

Without being asked, she leant across and kissed his cheek. 'Goodnight, Harry.'

When she then let herself in through the front door, somewhere close by a blackbird was warbling its evening lament. It was a sound that transported her to dusk at Woodicombe, when the garden would be heady with the fragrance of honeysuckle and jasmine, when the air would be balmy — the sea breezes having dropped with the setting of the sun — and the skies would be turning to shades of rose pink, amber and peach, the waves down in the cove lapping silently onto the sands. Rather different to the brick and tarmac of *Demport*.

Still, she thought, slipping off her shoes and starting up the stairs, tomorrow she could wear her gorgeous red dress with those beautiful stockings. And Harry was going to get someone called Desmond to teach her how to dance. And where, in Woodicombe, no matter how romantic the evenings, could she be doing *that* on a Friday night?

Chapter 5

Harry's Girl II

Was it wrong of her to hope — just this once — that tonight, Harry *didn't* actually turn up on time? Only, this evening, everything about getting ready seemed to be taking so much longer: her hair had taken ages to pin; her eyeliner had smudged so badly that she'd had to remove it with cold cream and start again. And one of her earrings had gone missing. And now, at five minutes to eight, the stockings were still in their packet and she couldn't find a clean handkerchief anywhere. And she mustn't forget to put on some of Harry's *Je Reviens*. Tonight, he was going to *make it up to her* for yesterday, and she wanted everything about her appearance to be just right — including the way she smelled.

'Have you seen my perfume?' she said to Jean, also getting ready to go out.

'It's here,' Jean said, turning back from the mirror above the washbasin to hand it to her.

'Thanks.'

'Where's he taking you tonight?'

'Ruby's.'

'Hm. Not bad, as places go.' From the tone of Jean's response, Lou detected reluctant approval.

'What about you? Where are you going?'

'Paul's taking me to the Gaumont Palace to see *The Dark Eyes of London*.'

Dabbing behind her ears with the stopper of her scent, Lou shrugged. 'Haven't heard of it.'

'It's new. Came out just before Christmas. It's a horror film about a scientist who murders people to get their insurance money. It's rated 'H', so it must be quite grisly.'

Perching on the end of her bed, Lou opened the packet of stockings. 'H?'

'For 'horrific'. Unsuitable for anyone under the age of sixteen.'

'Heavens,' she said, rolling one of the stockings up her leg. 'And you like that sort of thing?'

'Me? I love a bit of blood and gore. Besides, pretending to be frightened makes sitting in the back row worthwhile, if you know what I mean.'

'My seams straight?' Lou asked, getting to her feet and raising the hemline of her skirt for Jean to check.

'Fine.'

'Lou? You up there?'

The voice calling to her from downstairs was Winnie's. Bother. Harry must have arrived. Typical that tonight, when she wasn't ready, he should be on time. 'Coming,' she called.

'Telephone for you.'

Oh. Not Harry then.

'Who is it?' she yelled back. Perhaps, if Harry had realised he was going to be late, he'd decided to call and tell her.

'A man,' Winnie poked her head around the door to say before continuing on her way back up to her room.

'God, Winnie,' Lou mumbled, scampering down the stairs. 'What man?' Arriving breathless at the telephone, she grabbed the receiver from the shelf. 'Hullo?'

'Lou? It's Dad.'

Christ! She'd forgotten to ring and see if there was any news about Arthur. Reaching to the wall, she tried to quell a dizzying surge of guilt. 'Dad. Hello.'

'You didn't call.'

Now what did she say?

'Is there news, then?'

'No.'

'He's still not found?'

'No, Lou. He isn't.'

Golly her father sounded displeased with her! Hardly surprising: she'd completely forgotten she'd said she'd call. How awful was that? 'We still don't know either way?'

'Couple of days ago, I telephoned Captain Colborne in the hope he might be able find out what was going on. This afternoon, he called me back. He said that since there were so many ships lost that day, the details are being kept out of the newspapers... and so he shouldn't really be telling me... but Arthur's ship *was* one of those sunk. He also said that, so far at least, his name's not on the list of survivors... but then neither is he on the list of bodies recovered...'

She wished she didn't feel sick; she also wished she wasn't all dressed up and ready to go out. It felt completely wrong. But Harry would be here any minute. 'So... that's good news, isn't it?'

'Well, there's still close on fifty hands not accounted for. Some of them might have been picked up by other vessels, but Captain Colborne says the ship was torpedoed by a U-boat... and warned me that U-boat captains aren't known for showing mercy to stranded crews. Needless to say, I haven't passed that on to Mum.'

Lou swallowed hard. After that sort of revelation, it was nigh on impossible to sound optimistic. 'How *is* Mum?'

'How do you *think* she is, Lou? If you'd telephoned like you said you were going to, you wouldn't have to ask. And if you were actually *here*, you'd know first-hand.'

In a way, she deserved that. But, on the other hand...

'Dad, I'm sorry. I'm sorry for you and I'm sorry for Mum. And I'm sorry about Arthur. But I can't magic up news of him — good *or* bad. Trust me, I wish I could. I feel awful about the whole thing. Dreadful. But please don't make me feel even worse by keep asking me to come home when I can't...'

'Lou, love—'

'Look, Dad, how about I telephone Sunday and speak to Mum then? When would be the best time for me to try?'

'Well... sometimes, around about nine, I manage to persuade her to get up for an hour or two...'

She glanced to her wristwatch. Ten past eight. How ironic that tonight she should be grateful to Harry for being late! 'All right. I'll try sometime after nine o'clock. And Dad... I truly am sorry. I'd do anything to make this not have happened. You know that. But all the while there is no news, I, for one, choose to believe there is still hope. I simply can't think about it any other way.'

'No, love. Me neither.'

'All right then, well, I'll telephone Sunday.'

'Yes, love. Goodnight then. Sleep tight.'

'Goodnight Dad.'

As she replaced the receiver, she found herself fighting to hold back tears. God, her father would be so disappointed if he could see her all got up and waiting to be picked up by a man and taken to a club while her youngest brother was missing at sea. Thought about like that, she didn't feel particularly good about it herself. In fact, every time she thought about Mum crying, she felt utterly torn. But, realistically, what could *she* do about Arthur being missing? She, too, was devastated by the possibility that he had been lost. And she feared for how Mum would *ever* get over it if he was. But, surely, for the living, life had to go on — at least, it did until there was some actual news.

Weighed by guilt, she let out a sigh. The trouble was, if she gave in to her very real terror about Arthur's fate and became upset, she suspected it wouldn't go down well with Harry. After all, why would *he* want to spend his evenings with someone weeping over her missing brother? He wouldn't. So, no, she must keep a lid pressed firmly upon her fears, not only to sound strong for Mum and Dad but because, if she was to hold onto her job and her boyfriend, then she must find a way to carry on as normal. She didn't feel proud to be thinking like it, but such was her situation. Besides, if the worst news did come, she would go straight to Miss Blatchford and ask for some leave to go home. But, in the meantime, she would do her best to stay strong.

Her earlier enthusiasm about going out now well and truly dampened, she went back upstairs and checked in her handbag for her purse and her door key.

'Everything all right?' Jean looked across at her to ask.

With a long sigh, she shook her head. 'Not really. A few days back, my brother's ship was torpedoed. He was in the middle of the Atlantic … and we're still waiting for word as to whether he survived.'

Immediately, Jean's expression changed. 'Christ, Lou. Why didn't you say?'

'I suppose because there's nothing anyone can do. We've just got to wait until … well, until there's word either way.'

Heading towards the door, her jacket over her arm and her bag over her shoulder, Jean reached for Lou's hand. 'Lord, what a worry. I'll cross my fingers for you for good news.'

'Thank you.'

When Jean had left, Lou cast about the room for her shoes, slipped her feet into them and then went to the little mirror to check her appearance. Deciding she looked rather lacking in colour — and not in a *pale and interesting* way, either — she reached into her bag for her little tube of Forever Red lipstick and, remembering what Jean had said last time about this dress needing a good amount of it, applied an extra coat. Concerned then that she had overdone it, and that she now resembled a clown, she blotted some of it away. Then she went downstairs to wait in the parlour, hoping it wouldn't be too long before Harry arrived.

An hour or so back, when she'd first started getting ready to go out, the prospect of an evening at Ruby's had filled her with excitement. Having Harry promise to *make things up to her* felt nice. She'd even put on her new rayon brassiere and matching panties, in their (apparently) fashionable shade of peachy pink. If Mum could see her finished appearance, she would disapprove of the amount of make-up she was wearing. She would probably also still insist that red didn't suit her unremarkable colouring. And Dad, well, Dad would ask her what on earth she thought she looked like and tell her to go and change into a nice skirt and jumper. But it wasn't *their* approval she was after — they had no comprehension of how a young working woman these days liked to dress — no, the effort was for Harry, who had very clear ideas about how he liked her to look. Besides, she liked feeling as womanly as this, even if she hadn't yet developed Jean's level of confidence for carrying it off in public.

Lowering herself into the chair by the window, she looked across at the clock: five-and-twenty minutes past eight; clearly, he'd got held up again. Well, there was no sense fretting about it. There was a war on. Some men, like Vic and Freddie, chose to do their bit by going to serve; Harry helped to keep people fed by getting his father's customers what they needed. It was, as he was forever telling her, *business*.

The next time she checked the clock, it was ten to nine. Then it was ten past. Getting up from the chair, she went out into the hall and lifted the receiver to the telephone. No, it wasn't broken; she could hear the dial tone. Worst thing would be for him to be trying to get through only for one of the other girls not to have put the receiver properly back on its cradle. It had happened before.

Returning to the parlour, she twitched aside the nets. Any minute now, Mrs Hannacott would be in to secure the blackout. Any minute now, it wouldn't be worth going out.

Trying to ignore her growing frustration — along with an equal measure of panic — she sat down again. Though it probably couldn't be helped, she didn't mind admitting to being disappointed. Once it had become apparent that he wasn't going to be here by eight o'clock, could he not have telephoned? Had she known in advance that he was held up somewhere, she wouldn't have minded nearly as much.

Unable to bear the thought of Mrs Hannacott coming in to do the windows and finding her still waiting to go out, she got up, checked along the hallway and crept back upstairs. Then, closing the bedroom door behind her, she put down her handbag, eased off her shoes and sat wearily on the side of the bed.

Seeing from her wristwatch that it was now half past nine, she slowly unbuttoned the bodice of her dress, stood up, eased it off over her head and went to the wardrobe to fetch its hanger.

With that, there was a tap at the door. Opening it, she found Nora.

'Harry's downstairs. I shoved him in the parlour so Mrs H don't see him ... but you'll have to be quiet, the two of you.'

Unsure quite what Nora thought they were planning to get up to, and cross that Harry should arrive the moment she'd started to get undressed, she decided the best thing to do was pull on her dressing gown and then go down and tell him to wait while she got ready again.

'Thanks, Nora,' she whispered back, closing the door and lifting her dressing gown from the hook on the back of it. Then, not wanting to risk ruining her brand-new stockings, she pushed her feet back into her shoes. Yes, she must look frightfully odd, but she was only going to be a minute at most.

'Lou, Lou,' he greeted her as she went in through the door to the parlour. The windows having been blacked out, a lamp on the sideboard was attempting to fill the room with a yellowy light. Taking in her appearance, his expression changed. 'What's the matter? Are you unwell?'

Stopping a pace or two short of him, she shook her head. What she wanted to do was tell him he was late — more than an hour and a half late — but, despite the depth of her disappointment, she knew better than to risk making him cross. Besides, she knew what his excuse would be: *it's business.*

Instead, feeling far too weary to risk incurring his displeasure, she gave in to her need to talk about something else.

'My brother's missing.'

He frowned. 'Missing?'

'His ship was sunk by a torpedo in the North Atlantic and there's been no word of him since. We don't know

133

whether he was drowned or picked up... or taken prisoner ... or ... or what.'

Almost before she started to cry, Harry had his arms around her, holding her tightly against him.

'When was this?' he asked into her hair. 'How long ago?'

'A few days,' she said, sniffing. 'Earlier this week. But Dad just rang to tell me there's still no news.' Through her dressing gown, she felt his hand stroking down her back.

'Why didn't you tell me before?'

It was a good question. But there was no way she could explain the need she felt to keep him, and her life here in Devonport, separate from her family. She didn't even understand it herself; all she knew was that it felt vital that the two didn't mix.

'You seemed to have a lot on your mind,' she said flatly.

Removing his hands from her back, he cupped her face. 'Lou Channer,' he whispered, 'I've told you, you're my girl. And what does Harry Hinds do for his girl?'

She found herself looking straight into his eyes. They really were the most even of browns: no flecks; no blotches; no hint whatsoever of any other colours. In anyone else, she would say they were honest eyes. 'He looks after his girl.'

'That's right. So, you go back upstairs, put on that nice dress, and I'll take you to Ruby's.'

The thing that struck her most in that moment was that he'd made no mention whatsoever of his extremely late arrival. Did he not know the time?

'Would you mind if we didn't?' She said it softly in the hope that if he thought she was tired, he would be less likely to press her.

'If you don't want to go out,' he began, lowering his hands and unfastening the belt of her robe. 'Then I'll make

134

it up to you here. Come on, take this off.'

He meant to undress her here, in the parlour, with Mrs Hannacott sitting out the back listening to the wireless and at least three of the girls upstairs? In her dismay, she tugged the front of her dressing gown back across her body. 'Harry...'

'Come on,' he said. 'Let me see those pretty things you're wearing. That *is* why you put them on. For me.' She forced a swallow. She *had* put them on for him, yes, but that was before— 'Then let me see them.' Unfastening her fingers from where they were gripping the edges of her dressing gown, he lowered her hands to her sides.

'But Harry ...' She might not know much about men but, in that moment, she knew from his eyes that he wasn't going to relent. And so, deciding it would be best not to argue, she took off her robe and reached to put it over the back of the armchair.

'You do *want* me to make it up to you.'

Well she certainly didn't want to get on his bad side. ''Course I do.'

When he went to the sideboard and switched off the lamp, she stayed where she was, breathing rapidly, wondering precisely what he was going to do. He wasn't going to do it to her on Mrs Hannacott's sofa, was he? Please, oh please, tell her he wasn't.

In the event, he guided her back to the wall and did it there, leaning against her, the dado rail pressing into the small of her back.

'We'll go to Ruby's tomorrow,' he said afterwards, and with which she heard him zipping up his flies. 'I'll pick you up at eight. I'm sorry about your brother. I hope he turns up.'

With that, she felt his lips brush her cheek, heard the door open and close, and then, out in the road, the sound of the engine starting and the van pulling away.

For a while afterwards, she didn't move, there being something about the enveloping darkness that meant she didn't have to try and make sense of what had just happened. Having got her first time out of the way, she'd be hoping that this time around there would be rather more to it. After the way he'd got her all worked up the other night, she'd been looking forward to it — had pictured him holding her close and kissing her, had expected something altogether more... well, more romantic.

Starting to shiver from cold, she let out a weary sigh. Then, deeply disappointed, she rearranged her underwear, tied her dressing gown tightly back about her, peered out into the hallway and crept back upstairs.

Thank God Jean was out, she thought as she went to the window and stood looking down into the street. While, on the one hand, Jean was probably the best person with whom to share her confusion, and from whom she could seek help in making sense of it all, she would never do so. *Don't say I didn't warn you*, she'd said that day. But she was the only other person in this house who had — at least, she *assumed* she had — the sort of relationship with a man that qualified her to help. Despite all their bravado and their banter, none of the others, especially not Liddy or Winnie, would have the faintest notion of how complicated things became once you let a man have sex with you.

Too tired now to think straight, she pulled down the blackout blind and then felt her way back across to the little table alongside her bed and switched on the lamp. Then she went back and drew the curtains.

At the mirror, she stared in displeasure at her smudged lipstick and the dark tracks where her tears had carried

136

mascara down her cheeks. No wonder Harry had switched off the light to have sex with her; she looked a mess. Tomorrow, no matter how she felt, she would have to make sure she looked just right — dress on, hair in place, a smile on her lips.

Having wiped her face clean of make-up, brushed her teeth and removed the pins from her hair, she got into bed and switched out the light. She did wish she had someone to talk to: at this precise moment, all she could think was that when it came to Harry, she must be doing something wrong. Every time he sensed her hesitating over something, he was quick to remind her that she was his girl, and that he looked after his girl. But what did he mean by that? What did he mean by either of those things? He turned up late; he left her to sit, alone, in the van in a deserted street; he all-but abandoned her in the lounge bar of a public house, and then, in a rather half-hearted show of contrition, he promised to make it up to her. But if he really felt bad about putting business ahead of her — if he truly liked her — then why didn't he treat her better? It could only be because, as his girl, she was failing him, falling short of some or other mark. Her mum would probably know; she'd often said that when she'd been courted by Dad, many was the occasion she'd been exasperated with him. She imagined that Esme would know where she was going wrong, too. After all, Esme had been on the verge of getting married and had talked a lot about *just knowing* that Richard was right for her. Unfortunately, apart from having that strange address for her in London — and the nature of her concerns not being something she could put in a letter — she didn't know where Esme was.

No, sadly, how to be a proper girl for Harry Hinds was something she was going to have to fathom for herself.

And if she was serious about it, then she really ought to try and get it straight in her mind before he took her to Ruby's tomorrow night — always assuming, of course, that he was as good as his word and turned up at a more sensible hour ...

★ ★ ★

It was a good sign. Saturday evening and, as promised, he was here — and on time, too.

With the clock on the mantel of number eleven Jubilee Street chiming eight, Lou watched as Harry brought the van to a halt alongside the kerb. On her way to letting herself out of the front door, she allowed herself a sigh of relief.

'Got something for you,' he said, coming across the pavement, giving her a kiss and then helping her into the van. 'Here.' Settling beside her, he withdrew from his jacket a slender brown box, its lid embossed with swirly gold writing. 'Go on then,' he said when all she did was stare down at it. 'For Gawd's sake open it.'

Noticing how his expectant grin made him look like a little boy, she smiled and eased off the lid, what she saw inside making her gasp. Pinned to a layer of dark-coloured velvet was a bracelet: five ornate shell-shaped links, each one embedded with two-dozen or more tiny white stones.

'It's ...' But momentarily she was lost for words.

'Here,' he said, taking the box back from her, 'I'll put it on for you. Real fine with that dress, this is going to look.'

When she held out her wrist, he put the bracelet around it and fastened the tiny clasp. When she tilted her arm to admire it, the tiny stones twinkled in the light.

'It's beautiful,' she whispered. And it was. She'd never

seen anything like it. Well, no, that wasn't strictly true: Esme wore things like this all the time and thought nothing of it. But for certain Mum had never had anything so glamorous.

'You gonna give your Harry —'

This time, she didn't need him to tell her; leaning across, she kissed him, deliberately avoiding his cheek and landing her lips on his mouth instead. To her delight, she didn't even blush.

'Thank you, Harry. It's beautiful.'

'Then let's go and show it off.'

'Yes. Let's.'

This was more like it, she thought, looking out through the window and wanting to hug herself as he drove up the hill towards the junction. Clearly, neglecting her this last week had been playing on his conscience. Well, starting now, *she* had amends to make, as well. Last night, it dawned on her that she needed to be less timid and in awe of him and rather more like Jean. Harry Hinds wanted a woman, not a girl. And so, although it wasn't going to come naturally to her, that's how she would endeavour to behave.

To that end, as they walked from the van towards Ruby's, she felt the stirrings of excitement. Here they were, back at this smoky, poorly lit, noisy little dive of a place... and she couldn't be happier! This, she thought, this was precisely the sort of experience she'd left home to come in search of and precisely the sort of place she would never have known about had she stayed in Woodicombe.

With Harry greeting the doorman, she raised her wrist and angled it against the light. She knew, of course, that the stones weren't diamonds, but it didn't matter; it was the sparkliest thing she had ever owned. Did the shop sell matching earrings, she wondered? She couldn't really ask

Harry lest he thought she was angling to be bought a pair. No, but she *could* look at the name on the box, find the shop and take a look for herself. Pound to a penny, it was in the centre of Plymouth.

'We'll sit over there,' Harry said as they went in through the door at the bottom of the flight of steps.

'All right.'

'Gin and orange,' he said, handing her into the little booth.

'Lovely.' *See*, she told herself, watching him summon one of the staff, sounding confident and assured was easy. It was all in the tone of your voice.

Their drinks ordered, Harry sat down beside her. 'You look lovely. Smashing.'

Pleased by the compliment, she opted for nonchalance. 'Thank you.'

'Any news about your brother?'

She shook her head. 'Not since last night, no.' No need to admit that, since she hadn't rung home today, she didn't actually know. She must remember she'd said she'd ring tomorrow.

'No news is good news.'

'That's what *I* said.'

Seeing the bracelet on her wrist, he reached across and traced his finger along the links. 'You know why I gave you this, don't you?' Realising she could easily be horribly wrong, she chose not to answer. 'Because for all the saying that you're my girl and that I look after you, I didn't. You got bad news, but I didn't know because I wasn't there when I'd said I would be.'

Was this contrition? From Harry Hinds? Goodness, there was a turn up.

'Well, I didn't actually —'

'I mean, business has to come first, you know that. But

140

you shouldn't never be able to say I neglect you. And if ever I do it again, remind me whose girl you are.'

Seeing the waiter bringing their drinks, she leant closer and kissed him. 'Might have to hold you to that.'

'I mean it.'

As they clinked gasses, she noticed someone approaching their table. A chap of about seventeen or eighteen, he was clutching what looked to be a rather battered biscuit tin.

'Hello, Sam,' Harry greeted the lad.

'All right, Harry?'

'What can I do for you, Sam?'

'Ronnie sent me over.' At the mention of the name Ronnie, Lou saw Harry's attention flick towards the bar. 'I'm not doing business tonight, Sam. I'm with my girl.'

She smiled. At the beginning, the idea of being known as 'Harry's girl' rather than 'Lou' had felt odd, but now it was growing on her. *Hello, I'm Harry's girl.*

''S'not business, Harry,' the lad said. 'We've got up a Spitfire Fund. Ronnie saw it in the paper. Said if we got customers to put cash in a collection, we could try to get enough for a whole aeroplane. He said if we do, they'll let us call it Ruby's.'

'And how much does Ronnie think we should all put in?' Harry reached into his jacket and asked.

''S'up to you, Harry. But Mr Donovan put in *two pounds.*'

Lou saw Harry raise an eyebrow; he wouldn't want to be outdone, especially not in front of her.

'And how much do one of these Spitfires cost, then?'

'Ronnie says five thousand pounds.'

'Then perhaps,' Harry said, peeling banknote after banknote from the roll he'd pulled from his pocket, 'I should just donate that whole amount and be done with.'

141

He was joking, of course, Lou thought. Well, she *assumed* he was. One by one, he dropped five one-pound notes into Sam's tin. 'Then I could tell them to name it *My Lovely Louise.*'

So much for acting confidently, Lou thought, feeling herself blushing fiercely.

'Cor, thanks, Harry. Wait till I tell Ronnie how much you put in!'

'Young Sam,' Harry said as the lad walked away, 'is Ronnie's sister's boy. Poor kid doesn't play with a full deck, so Ronnie gets him to do odd jobs about the place to keep him occupied.'

Lou smiled. 'And Ronnie is...?'

'I didn't introduce you last time?'

She shook her head. 'No, Harry, you didn't.'

'Could have sworn I did. Any road, Ronnie owns this place but it's his wife, Ruby, what runs it. Leave it to Ronnie and he'd drink all the profits, either that or bankrupt the place by letting all his friends drink for free.'

'Ah.'

'Ronnie and I do the odd bit of business.'

'Mm.' In an ideal world, this would be her opportunity to ask Harry more about the precise nature of this *business* he kept on about. But there was a difference between being more confident and overstepping the mark.

Taking a sip of her drink and placing the glass back on the table, she gave a little sigh. She could see that, tonight, things between them were going to be all right. The Harry she'd been so taken by that first afternoon was back — sparky but smooth. Straight talking. Generous. It was down to her now to be play her part in keeping him that way.

'You hungry?' he turned without preamble to ask.

142

As it happened, she did feel peckish. 'A little, per-haps.'

''Round the corner,' he said, starting to get to his feet and reaching for her hand, 'Ronnie's sister's got a little place that does a pie and mash. We'll pop in there for something and then come back here after. I'll get Ronnie to keep the booth for us.'

Well there was a surprise. 'Sounds just right.'

Ronnie's sister's little pie and mash place turned out to be called *The Corner Pie Shop*. And all it served was 'pie of the day' with mashed potato and gravy.

'It's rabbit, Harry,' the girl behind the counter said without him even needing to ask. 'And yes, for the second time this week. Even Ronnie can't get his hands on much else at the moment.'

'Two then, please, Vera.'

Their meals paid for, Harry pointed towards a table against the window.

'Rabbit pie reminds me of home,' Lou said when Harry pulled out one of the wooden chairs for her and she sat down.

'Yeah?'

'Nanny Edith simmers the rabbit joints with bacon and apple and cider.'

'Not sure this one will have bacon in it,' he said, wiping the side of his hand across the table to remove the grains of salt left by a previous occupant. 'But it might have cider.'

Their pies arrived surprisingly quickly. Brought to them on heavily scarred china plates with chipped rims, they smelled heavenly.

'I didn't realise I was this hungry,' she said, cutting into the crisp golden pastry. From the corner of her eye, she watched Harry slice his knife straight through the middle of his and then, into the pool of gravy that spilled from inside, slide the mound of mashed potato. From the way he did it, she suspected it was a habit.

The pie turned out to be easily the nicest thing she'd eaten since leaving home. The suet pastry was light, the gravy inside thick and tasty, the rabbit tender. Clearly, Ronnie's sister knew what she was doing.

'That's better,' Harry said, his pie devoured. 'All it needs now is —'

'Crust for you, Harry.' Arriving at their table, Vera, from behind the counter, put down a tea plate with the end of a loaf cut in two.

'— some bread to mop up the last of this gravy.' Unable to help herself, Lou laughed. 'What?' he said, one of the pieces of bread poised for action.

'Nothing,' she said, smiling back and watching him wipe it around the plate.

'No point wasting it. Want the other bit?' When she shook her head, he picked up the second piece of bread and did the same. His plate, when he'd finished with it, almost didn't need washing up.

'I enjoyed that,' she said when they were walking, her arm through his, back around the corner to the club.

'My second home, that place,' he remarked. It was, she realised, the first time he'd made mention of anything personal. She had always assumed he lived with his dad — George, as he called him — and Jean's mum, but he'd never actually said.

After the relative quiet of the little cafe and the calm of the dimpsey, going back down into the clamour of Ruby's felt like a rude interruption to a gentle evening. In their absence, the band had started to play, and the dance floor was heaving with bobbing heads.

Arriving back at their booth, Harry pushed aside the little 'Reserved' notice and, as they sat down, Lou noticed

144

one or two couples nearby glance up at them.

'I'll get you a drink,' Harry said above the music. 'Two ticks.'

Watching him weave his way towards the bar, Lou hoped he was right about the 'two ticks'; she hoped he wasn't going to get distracted by someone or something, and that the evening would continue to be as lovely as it had been so far. Tonight, rather than spend most of her time slightly in awe of the fact that he was taking her out — and more than a little scared of showing herself up as naïve and unworldly — she was actually enjoying herself. Harry was calmer, more attentive. She was more confident. They had the makings of a good couple, a couple others envied.

'There you go.'

She needn't have worried about him disappearing; in no time at all he was back with a gin and orange.

'Thank you.' Fortunately, she hadn't drunk all of the one he'd bought her earlier. And anyway, with some food in her stomach, and no need to get up for work in the morning, there was probably little harm in enjoying a second.

Without even sitting down, Harry drained his whisky. 'Back in a minute,' he said, depositing the empty glass on the table.

Now where was he off to? She did hope she hadn't been too quick to count her chickens. Ooh, perhaps he'd gone to find that Desmond fellow he'd mentioned — the one he'd said would teach her to dance. Yes, that could be it.

When he returned a few minutes later, though, over his arm he seemed to have a woman's coat.

'What have you —'

'Stand up,' he said. He was grinning like a small boy. 'Come on, stand up. I've got you something.'

He'd got her something else …?

'Where are we going?'

'We're not *going* anywhere. I just thought you'd like one of these. It's fox fur. A *stole*, that's what you women call these things, ain't it?'

When she got to her feet, he wrapped it around her shoulders, the shape of it fitting them perfectly.

'Harry ...' she breathed, genuinely lost for words.

'Ronnie got them off a warehouse. They was supposed to be going to a department store up west but ... well ... with the war on, seems there's not much call. He's got a dozen of them proper fox-shaped ones with the head still on as well, you know, all teeth and beady eyes, but I didn't think you'd like that. This is just the pelts put together to make it look like one big fur.'

'Harry,' she tried again to express her gratitude. 'It's so ...'

'Classy.'

She nodded. 'Makes me feel like a film star.'

'Makes you look like one, Lou Channer.'

Heavens. Closing her eyes and savouring the feel of the fur tickling her neck, she hugged her shoulders. How she wished she'd had all of these lovely things for Esme's wedding. Perhaps then she wouldn't have felt so out of place.

'It's very lovely.'

'Then just make sure you wear it for me.'

'I will. Always. I love it.'

'Show your Harry how much then.'

When she looked back at him, he was standing with his cheek angled towards her. Deliberately ignoring it, she once again kissed him on the lips instead.

'Thank you, Harry. It's perfect.' This, she thought, turning in a circle and still hugging herself, was the sort of treatment she could get used to. At this rate she would soon be a match for Esme, and all nice things she had — not to mention the nightlife she saw.

'Want me to have them put it in the cloakroom?'

She didn't hesitate. 'No chance. I want to wear it.'

'Might get a bit warm.'

'I don't care. I'm not taking it off.'

'Fair enough,' he said, clearly amused. 'I just need to pop back and see Ronnie a mo. Won't be long.' He glanced to her glass. 'I'll get you another drink.'

In that moment, she didn't even care that he was leaving her there to go back and see Ronnie. In that moment, she could forgive him anything. First an expensive bracelet. Then the unexpected treat of proper pie and mash. Now this gorgeous stole. A stole! *He'd bought her a fox-fur stole.* If she couldn't find the words to tell him how pampered she felt, she could at least put up with him going to talk to Ronnie.

With the waiter bringing the drink Harry had ordered for her, she motioned to him to wait while she downed the last of her previous one and then gave him the empty glass. Who would have believed it? There she was, just a few short weeks back, rueing that life at Woodicombe was so deathly dull, her greatest concern that of how to avoid becoming inextricably tied to poor old Freddie, and now look at her! Here she was, in a nightclub, drinking gin and orange, wearing an expensive bracelet and a fox-fur stole while listening to a jazz band.

Settling back into the curved part of the banquette, she sighed contentedly. Jean was wrong about Harry. Deep down, he was caring and thoughtful — a bit unreliable, yes, but that was only because until now, no one had given him reason to be otherwise. But now that he had her, Lou Channer, as his girl, he was bound to become more considerate. After all, he wouldn't want to risk losing

147

someone he thought this much of, would he?

Thank goodness now, that when she'd felt sorry for Freddie that afternoon she hadn't caved to his plea and vowed to be true to him because, weighed against life as *Harry's girl*, the poor boy wouldn't have stood a chance.

★ ★ ★

What on earth ...?

Opening her eyes and blinking into the darkness, Lou tried to work out what was going on. Then it came to her: that wailing sound was the air raid siren! Despite the glowing green hands on her alarm clock showing that she had been in bed less than half an hour, she now had to get up again.

'Jean, Lou, wake up! Air raid!' It was, Lou eventually realised, Queenie calling from the landing.

Praying that when she'd come stumbling in, she'd remembered to pull down the blackout blind, Lou felt about and clicked on the lamp. Squinting in the brightness towards the window, she saw then that Jean wasn't even home yet.

To the thud of feet coming down the stairs from the attic, she hauled herself out of bed, reached to the back of the door for her dressing gown, felt in the pocket to check that her torch was still there, and then wrestled her robe on top of her nightie.

Shoes, she thought, glancing about. To go down to the shelter she needed shoes. With the wailing of the siren making it hard to think, she spotted them lying where she had kicked them off, went to retrieve them and pushed them onto her feet. Golly, she was tired. Dragging her eiderdown off her bed and starting towards the door, she then remembered the lamp. Pressing the little button on her torch, she switched it on, went back to extinguish the light and then finally headed downstairs, turning off the lights on the landing and in the hallway as she went.

'Come on!' she heard Jess urging from beyond the back door. 'Jerry could be here any minute.'

Bundling her eiderdown under her arm in order to avoid dragging it through the dirt, Lou turned to close the back door. 'Coming,' she hissed.

The entrance to the Anderson shelter in the garden to number eleven involved negotiating five rickety wooden steps set into the earth. Once inside, if anyone slightly shorter than average height was prepared to cock her head to one side, she was just about able to stand up. Nora and Queenie, on the other hand, both of them enviably tall, had to stoop.

'My shelter takes eight,' Mrs Hannacott had proudly informed Lou on the day she had arrived. But, on the only other occasion — not much more than a week back — when she'd had to go down there for the first time, Lou had thought her landlady's assessment optimistic; eight adults would make for a very snug fit indeed.

'Mrs H ain't here,' Winnie said, evidently seeing Nora making a silent headcount. 'Gone over her sister's at Stonehouse. Said she'll be back in time to do Sunday dinner.'

'Assuming Jerry leaves her a house to cook it in,' Jess said dourly.

'And Jean?' Nora asked.

Dumping her eiderdown on the bench between Queenie and Jess, Lou shrugged. 'Not home yet.'

Having reached up to fasten the wooden door and then unfurl the blanket that would protect them from shards of timber in the event of a blast, Winnie turned back to face

149

them. 'Do you think it's for real this time?'

No one answered her.

Her eiderdown arranged on the bench, Lou sat down. And then, removing her shoes — and regretting having had to wear her lovely new ones down here in the dust — she tucked them beneath the bench. Copying what she had seen the others do last time, she then drew up her legs and wrapped her eiderdown about her to form a sort of a cocoon. She did hope the raid wasn't going to go on for long; after a lovely evening at Ruby's, she was exhausted, and the prospect of not being able to go to sleep any time soon was already making her grumpy.

With the shelter falling silent, she glanced about. To her left, Queenie was reading a book, the cover of which she couldn't see but the print of which looked miniscule. How could she see to read in such dim light? And why would she want to? To her right, Jess was sitting cocooned like the rest of them. On the bench opposite, Nora, by the door, looked tense, Winnie in the middle looked frightened and, leaning against the corner, Liddy had her eyes shut as though trying to get back to sleep. In the dingy light, their complexions all looked grey.

For a while, Lou simply sat waiting, her ears trained for the first sound of aircraft. But, with the warning siren having fallen silent, there was nothing to be heard from anywhere. Even the neighbours' dogs were quiet. Perhaps, she thought, giving in to a yawn, they somehow sensed it wise not to bark.

Five minutes of waiting turned into ten, ten to twenty. Nothing happened. Although a couple of the girls had their eyes closed, she doubted they were asleep. For her own part, although still drowsy from the effect of three gin and oranges — yes, she was acquiring quite the taste for them — her senses were still too alert to allow her

150

to sleep. And she suspected it was the same for the others, too — although minus the gin and orange. What a super evening it had turned out to be! Other than stopping for the odd chat with someone, and the fifteen minutes or so spent with Ronnie, Harry had been his most attentive ever. And as if the bracelet hadn't been apology enough for the other night, seemingly on the spur of the moment, he had bought her a fox-fur stole. Perhaps, when the air raid siren had gone off, she should have grabbed *that* rather than her dressing gown and worn it down here: that would have got them talking. She would never do that though — wasn't one to rub her good fortune in the faces of others — she'd been brought up differently to that. *No one likes a show-off*, Mum had always told the three of them when they were small.

'I wish if they were coming, they'd hurry up and get on with it,' Jess suddenly moaned.

'Me too,' Winnie agreed. 'I can't hardly keep my eyes open.'

'Then close them,' Nora suggested.

'Can't. Don't want to fall asleep down here. There's spiders.'

'Then lump it like the rest of us,' Nora replied, surprisingly sharply for her.

'How about a game?'

Jess's suggestion met with puzzled stares.

'A game?'

'Two Truths and a Lie.'

Opposite Lou, Winnie perked up. 'Ooh, good idea.'

'Go on, then,' Nora said with a sigh. 'It might at least stop me wondering what's going on up there.'

'You in, Lid?' Jess asked.

In the corner, Liddy opened an eye. 'Might as well. It's not like I'll be able to sleep if you lot start guffawing anyway.'

'You?'

For Lou, it was time to admit she didn't know what
it was they were proposing. 'I've never played,' she said,
hoping she wasn't about to get roped into something she
was going to regret.

'It's easy,' Winnie piped up, brushing the hair from
her eyes and pulling herself and her little cocoon more
upright. 'We each take a turn of telling the others three
things about ourselves, two of which are true and one of
which isn't. The others have to guess which of the things
is the lie.'

'The secret,' Jess chipped in, 'is to make all of the things
sound equally believable — either all similarly dotty or all
similarly dull.'

Lou smiled. It sounded harmless enough. 'All right. I'll
play.'

'You go first,' Winnie said to Jess. 'It was your idea.'

Jess nodded her agreement. Then, having paused for a
moment to think, she said, 'I once pushed my brother
in a river and then had to go in and get him out because
I thought he was drowning. When I was six, I got pneumonia and nearly died. My middle name is Flora.'

'Those could *all* be true,' Nora said.

'She has got a brother,' Winnie remarked.

'And getting pneumonia as a child can be serious,'
Liddy chipped in. 'What do *you* think, Lou?'

For a moment, Lou didn't answer. 'I think,' she said,
knowing to be careful, 'she would definitely have been
the sort of girl to push her brother into a river. Who
wouldn't? I also think she might panic and worry about
getting into trouble and go in and get him out. The pneumonia? Strikes me as the sort of calamity that might befall
anyone. But I don't think she looks like a Flora.'

152

Seemingly surprised that she should be able to put together such a rational case so quickly, the others nodded.

'That's what I think, too.'

'So, *you're* saying,' Jess addressed her remark to Winnie, 'that my middle name isn't Flora.'

'I am.'

'You're right. It's Rose. Your turn.'

'Really it should be Lou's turn,' Winnie said. 'She was the one to say it first.'

'No, it's all right, you go next,' Lou said, anxious to give herself time to work out what to say when her turn did come.

Winnie grinned. 'Very well. When I was ten, my cousin gave me my first cigarette, which I smoked halfway down and then threw up over his shoes. When I was eight, I took off my knickers for a bet and gave them to a boy in my class to hoist up the flagpole in the school playground. Apart from when I was baptised, I've never been in a church.'

To Lou's mind, it was Winnie's last revelation that felt the least likely. Everyone went to church; they were made to by their parents. Conversely, given the amount Winnie smoked, she could believe she had done so from an early age. And the story about the knickers sounded so fantastical it *had* to be true. But she wasn't going to say anything yet because she still had no idea what to disclose when her own turn came.

Around her, the discussion about Winnie's statements became lively.

'This bet,' Jess said.

'The one about my knickers?'

'Well how many *other* bets did you make in the school playground when you were eight?'

153

'Perhaps I shouldn't say.'

In the end, noticing that Lou hadn't said anything, they turned in her direction.

'I can't believe she's never been in a church,' she replied to their looks.

'And yet you do believe she'd take off her knickers for a bet?'

To her left, Lou heard Queenie grunt her disapproval. In the end, and after much bawdy discussion, it was three to one for the bet about the knickers being the lie.

'Wrong!' Winnie replied.

'Tell me it's not the church thing,' Liddy pleaded, tears of laughter running down her cheeks.

'Nope. That's also true. I've never been.'

'*The cigarette?*'

Winnie nodded. 'Of course it was the cigarette. I never tried one until I was at least thirteen.'

The merriment dying down, Liddy said, 'So who goes next? Nobody won.'

Just as Lou feared, Winnie proposed it should be her. 'She did guess it right last time.'

Still unprepared, Lou felt her heart speed up. What on earth could she disclose without genuinely giving too much away? And then it came to her, each of her ideas feeling as unlikely as it was credible.

'Until I turned twenty-one, my parents never let me wear lipstick. The house my family live in has more than twenty rooms. Two days before I was due to get married, I jilted my fiancé and ran away.'

Her statements, delivered with the straightest of faces, met with such silence that she was left wondering whether she had done it wrong.

Eventually, though, Liddy spoke up. 'She *might* have jilted someone. Could be why she came *here*. After all, which one of us didn't come here to get away from something at home.'

To Lou, the atmosphere in the shelter felt suddenly sombre and she wished she had picked more light-hearted anecdotes. There must have been *some* funny or mischievous things she'd done, growing up with her brothers.

'No,' Winnie said. 'I don't see her being fresh from jilting someone. Put it this way, *if* she ever did, it wasn't recent. I mean, think about it, she's been mighty quick to take up with Harry.'

'Winnie!'

In response to Nora's scolding, Winnie merely shrugged. 'I only say it how I see it.'

'It's all right,' Lou said. 'Harry and I are no secret.'

'Don't know what you see in him,' said Jess matter-of-factly. 'Only needed to go out with him the once to know he wasn't *my* type. He's a tad too fresh for one thing.'

'Fresh?' Nora looked up to ask.

Wrapped in her eiderdown, Lou squirmed. She might have known this would happen.

'You know, hands everywhere. After the quickest route into your underwear.'

'The lipstick thing,' Winnie said, her tone that of someone anxious to move the conversation along.

'Lipstick,' she said, grateful nevertheless for Winnie's intervention. 'What of it?'

'Well, how old are you now?'

'Twenty-one.'

'Then one of those two things *can't* be true,' Jess pronounced. 'Your parents were happy for you to get wed but not for you to wear lipstick?'

'Good point,' Winnie agreed.

'An' *I* reckon she *might* live in a big house,' Liddy joined in. 'I seem to remember she once mentioned something about stables...'

For a while longer, the conversation went back and forth, none of them knowing enough about her to reach a firm conclusion either way. In the end, it was the sound of the All Clear that forced Winnie to say, 'Well, I don't reckon she jilted no one, no matter how long ago.'

Slipping her shoes back on and getting to her feet, Lou grinned. 'You're right. It was my cousin in London who, just last month, jilted her fiancé and left without a word to anyone. Well,' she added, 'to anyone other than me.'

'Sounds like a belter of a story for next time we're stuck down here,' Jess remarked, gesturing Lou ahead of her up the steps.

'Happen it is,' Lou agreed. Anything, she thought, to divert interest away from her and Harry. There might indeed be no harm in her *taking up with him*, as Winnie had described it, but she had no desire to be grilled on the details. On the other hand, she would quite like to put them right about him — explain that he wasn't the sort of man they thought he was. Well, not entirely. The trouble was that even by just talking about him, she ran the risk of letting slip details that should remain private. Details that *had* to remain private if they weren't to think badly of her. Besides, some aspects of Harry's behaviour *would* be hard to defend; he *was* a bit unreliable. But he was also generous and exciting.

Well, she thought, trudging back up the stairs to her bedroom, at the end of the day, what did it matter what they all thought of him; she was the one he had picked to be his girl; she was the one being bought lovely gifts; she was the one he had chosen to turn into a woman while they were all still very much girls. And it was because they *were* still *girls*, and knew so little about who he really was, that they had him all wrong ...

Chapter 6

Trouble Brewing

The last week had simply flown. Just as Miss Blatchford had warned, at the depot, things had become even busier. Not only were there more lorries and vans making deliveries every day, but many more goods were now being requisitioned and taken for loading onto vessels. There was even talk of another girl being taken on to help Liddy and Flossie in the warehouse.

For her part, Lou discovered that being fully occupied during the day made her look forward to those evenings she got to spend at home, evenings when she didn't have to get dressed up to go out with Harry. Only now did she appreciate just how much work was needed to look nice for a boyfriend who took you out as many as four nights a week. Her so-called 'free nights' were easily swallowed up with attending to tasks such as shaving her legs, plucking her eyebrows, filing and painting her nails — a skill with which, truth be told, she was still getting to grips — and washing her hair, this last chore something she now felt it necessary to tackle twice a week, despite the shortage of decent shampoo and the time it took to pin it and wait for it to dry. In fact, such was the effort involved in looking nice that she couldn't have seen Harry any more frequently had she wanted to.

This particular evening being Friday, Harry was picking her up to take her for a drink at a pub called The Smugglers' Moon. *You'll like it*, he'd said the other night, as he so often did of these places. *It's on the water.* She'd assumed he didn't mean literally.

Sitting on the bedroom floor, fanning at her newly painted toenails — something else that felt necessary now she owned a pair of peep-toe shoes — she glanced to the clock. Thankfully, there was a while yet before he would be here. She had to hand it to him, since that unfortunate episode last Friday, when he'd let her down by not turning up until after nine-thirty, he'd arrived when he'd said he would, hadn't abandoned her part way through the evening — well, not for more than a couple of minutes in order to *have a quick chat with someone* — and had been unfailingly charming.

Arriving later at The Smuggler's Moon, Lou found it to be a quaint but rather precarious building at the top end of an old fishing quay.

'Imagine all this in its heyday,' Harry said, his left hand keeping a tight hold of her own, his right hand gesturing along the quayside. Given the narrow and uneven nature of the cobbled alleys, they'd left the van at the top of the hill and walked down, a feat that had immediately proved tricky in her high heels, hence Harry's firm grasp on her hand.

'Were there really smugglers?' she asked, taking in the sign hanging above the door, the crescent moon having been made to look deliberately eerie by being painted half-obscured behind a wisp of cloud.

Laughing, he reached to push open the door. 'There still are. Mind your step.'

The rickety entrance gave directly onto a room with an uneven flagstone floor, an inglenook fireplace, a small bar with a hinged flap for access and a half a dozen rustic tables and chairs. Despite the fire being unlit, the room smelled strongly of woodsmoke. With Harry in his smart suit and she in her red skirt and strawberry-print blouse, she couldn't help feeling they were overdressed, not to mention, in her case, overly made-up. The pair of them must look, she thought, like the holidaying Londoners who ventured into The Ship at Anchor in Westward Quay in search of an authentic West Country experience with which to regale their friends at home — in fact, not unlike how Harry would look if he turned up there. Still, on the way in, she'd spotted that outside, under the bow window, was a bench; perhaps she could suggest they take their drinks out there.

As was so often the case when they entered somewhere like this, Harry was welcomed like an old friend.

'Good to see you, Norrie. How you keeping?' he greeted the chap behind the bar.

'Can't complain, Harry, can't complain. You?'

He also seemed to know the rotund and florid-faced man seated on a stool in the corner.

'Evening, Perce.'

''Ow do, 'arry.'

Though it wasn't unusual for Harry's acquaintances to look her up and down, sometimes even leer, it was rare for any of them to go so far as to acknowledge her. It wasn't so much that she was invisible to them but rather that she was of no consequence. Not that it mattered to *her*. By now, she was used to it, would be surprised if they behaved any differently. Besides, sometimes, they didn't look particularly savoury, Norrie and Perce being cases in point.

'Johnnie Walker and a gin and orange, if you would, Norrie.'

'I'll bring them over,' the man called Norrie replied and nodded towards the seat in the bay window.

'We won't stop long,' Harry whispered in her ear as he handed her across to the cushioned bench. 'I've got the

159

rug in the back of the van, and up the hill there's a nice little spot. After this, we'll mosey on up there and... watch the sun set.' Pleased to discover they weren't to spend the entire evening there, Lou sat down. 'You got them silky knickers on?'

She despaired of him, she really did. 'I might have.'

'Good girl.'

'On the 'ouse,' the barman said, arriving with their drinks and putting them down in front of them.

Concerned that he might have overheard what they'd been discussing, Lou blushed. Thankfully, it was something she did far less nowadays.

'You're a good man, Norrie Chubb.' Picking up his glass, Harry turned and raised it in her direction. 'Cheers.'

She returned the gesture. 'Cheers.'

Having taken a slug of his drink, Harry put his glass back on the table and looked around. 'Just imagine if these walls could talk.'

Putting down her own glass, Lou tried to hide her astonishment. Harry Hinds entertaining fanciful thoughts? Whatever next?

'Happen they could tell a tale or two,' she agreed. 'You know, supposedly, there are tunnels running under the creek from here to the other side. Apparently, smugglers would bring in their bounty over yonder, where the excise men weren't expecting, and then their partners in crime would roll the barrels back through the tunnels to be picked up from here. No way to know if it's true, of course.'

'Well —' But, just as she was about to remark that old rumours usually had their roots in fact, the door opened and in came a couple of men. Instantly, Harry was on his feet.

'Harry Hinds,' one of them greeted him.

160

She exhaled a sigh of disappointment. Just when they were holding a proper conversation, someone he knew turned up — and most likely not by chance, either. Still, he'd made clear his plans for later on, meaning he was unlikely to want to get stuck here for too long.

'Bit off your manor, ain't it?' she heard the second of the men say.

With the three of them falling into conversation and heading towards the bar, Lou tried to bury her disappointment by turning to look out through the bow window. The general dirtiness of the quays aside, this was quite a charming spot. Not romantic in the traditional sense but, as Harry had said, evocative of rugged seamen, secret assignations, and derring-do on the high seas.

In a bid to occupy herself further, she got up from the window seat and went out onto the cobbled quayside, where the odour of woodsmoke was replaced by the tang of salt, and brine-soaked ropes and tar. Continuing to the edge of the dock, she simply stood for a moment looking across the narrow inlet to the piers and the yards on the other side. Below her, the tide was lapping rhythmically while, overhead, a couple of herring gulls were wheeling like performers on a trapeze, their forms silhouetted against the late evening sun.

Grateful for the warmth of her cardigan, she turned over her shoulder towards the pub; reflections from the sinking sunlight upon the window glass, though, meant she could see nothing of what was going on inside.

Folding her arms against the breeze, she wandered further along the quay but, with the adjacent buildings shuttered and barred for the night, the whole place felt forlorn and slightly eerie. No wonder they had been the only customers in the pub; situated this far from a road, it was an establishment unlikely to attract passing trade.

161

Walking a little further, she smiled; Harry did take her to some of the oddest places. But it was better than going nowhere at all. And, to be truthful, she would miss it now if he didn't.

A little further along, a boatman was rowing two passengers across the short stretch of water between two jetties, the slow stroke of his oars barely disturbing the surface of the pool-like dock. On that far side, the land rose quite steeply to what looked to be a castle or a fort, beyond which she supposed was The Hoe.

Shivering now, she turned to start back. With any luck, Harry would be done talking and have other things on his mind.

Back inside, though, she found him sat at the bar with the two men who had arrived earlier and a third, who must have come through from the back. Although her return caused all four to swivel in her direction, not even Harry acknowledged her. Clearly, they were not, as she had hoped, finished with their business. Well, if she had to continue to wait, she would do so on the bench under the window.

After what felt to be twenty minutes or more of sitting outside, and beginning to grow properly cold, she turned to peer through the window. To her dismay, the four of them hadn't moved. That Harry should so easily have reverted to old habits was disappointing, but remembering what he'd said to her about not letting him neglect her ever again, she got up, straightened her skirt and went back in.

The sound of her progress across the flagstones brought the conversation at the bar to a close. Too late to change course, she saw Harry's shoulders sag.

'Gin and orange, if you wouldn't mind, Norrie,' she heard him say.

Trying to think how to avoid making the situation worse, she remained where she was, teetering with one foot in front of the other.

'One gin and orange. Sure.'

The drink arriving in front of him, Harry got down from his stool, picked up the glass, turned and came towards her. Drawing level, he grasped her arm, his fingers pressing into her flesh, and led her back to the window seat.

'Sit there,' he said, putting the drink on the table and guiding her onto the seat.

'But I thought you wanted us to watch the sun set.'

'When I'm done here. Now stay there and drink this. If you finish it, get another. Get as many as you want but stay put.'

'It's just that the other day, you said to tell you if you were neglecting me...'

Even as she was saying it, she realised her mistake, the expression with which he looked back at her one of intense displeasure.

'But clearly *not* when I'm doing business. Now *sit down*. I shan't be much longer.'

When he turned and walked away, she hung her head. If he hadn't meant what he'd said about reminding him not to neglect her, he shouldn't have said it. Now look what she'd done. She'd made him so cross he'd talked to her through gritted teeth.

Feeling humiliated, she rubbed her arm, still able to feel where his fingers had dug into her flesh. Sometimes, it was as though there were two people inside Harry Hinds, it never being clear which one of them she was going to get.

Across the room, the sound of movement made her raise her head to see what was happening; as a group, the men were getting to their feet, the three including

Harry following the fourth through the flap of the bar and out through the door behind it. Now where were they going? And how long would they be gone? She looked at her watch. He'd said he wouldn't be much longer. But how long was that? What, by most people's understanding constituted 'not long'? For how long would any woman sit there, the only person in a public house on a Plymouth quayside? Weighed by a mixture of helplessness and despair, she sighed. Ten minutes. Given that he'd already ignored her for the best part of an hour, she would give him ten more minutes.

In the event, she gave him fifteen, at which point it was even tempting to give him another fifteen. But, if she did that, wasn't she saying to him that she didn't matter? That he could neglect her without consequence? Didn't it let him keep buying her things and making it up to her without having to actually change his ways? Wasn't she worth more than that?

Disappointment turning to anger, she got up and went to where Norrie was perched on a stool against the bar, reading a newspaper. He didn't look up.

'I wouldn't disturb them, love.'

'I don't intend to,' she said. 'But when he comes out, please tell him I've gone home.'

'Gone home. Right you are, lover.'

'And that I do not wish him, at whatever time he deigns to be done here, to turn up on my doorstep because he'll be wasting a trip. I shan't see him.'

'I'll be sure an' tell him. Where're you headed for?'

'Close by Devonport dockyard.'

'Best way at this time of night is to get old Wilf to row you across the other side and then you'll want to walk up to The Hoe and get a tram.'

'Thank you,' she said, realising she'd overlooked how

she was actually going to get home.

Once outside, having eventually succeeded in attracting his attention, the man called Wilf was reluctant to take her. 'Just mooring up for the night, miss.'

In her desperation to gain a head start on Harry — who would have to walk all the way up to the van and then drive back around to The Hoe — she got out her purse and peered in at the coins. A faded sign on the wall stated that the fare one way was 2d.

'I'll pay you sixpence. One way. To cover the cost of you having to come back again empty.'

She watched him take in her clothes and shoes. 'Have a care on them steps then.'

Once assisted out on the other side, and with no clear path up the hill — just a track worn into the grass — she followed her nose, it quickly becoming apparent that her shoes were entirely unsuited to the steep and uneven terrain, the thin little straps across the top digging into her flesh, the backs rubbing her heels. With no choice but to keep going, though, she hobbled to the top of the slope, where she stood, panting, while she tried to get her bearings. In the fading light, she was relieved to see that across The Hoe was the tram stop. And thank goodness for that, because the heel on her right shoe felt to have come loose and the back of her left foot was bleeding.

At the tram stop, she had to ask several people which of the routes went towards the dockyard before finding someone who knew. At least, she thought, boarding the tram when it arrived and trying to ignore the gawking of a peculiar little man chewing a toffee on the seat opposite, she might now be home and indoors before Harry got to Jubilee Street. No matter what he said when he turned up, which, in a fit of pique, he surely would, she was not going to talk to him. He had to understand that she was no longer prepared to be treated like a doormat.

After a while, through the window of the tram she caught sight of the dockyard gates, where she got off, and, wincing with almost every step, limped back up the hill to number eleven.

Letting herself in, and grateful to discover that Jean was out, she eased off her shoes, peeled off her laddered stockings and examined her feet. Rubbed raw, that was the state of her heels.

Fetching the little enamel bowl that she and Jean used to wash their smalls, she limped to the bathroom and filled it with warm water. Before she could apply a dressing to the wounds, she would soak them. To that end, stripping off her skirt and blouse, and wrapping herself in her dressing gown, she sat on the stool with her feet in the bowl of water. For a number of reasons, tomorrow was going to be agony. But at least she didn't have to go to work. As for Harry, well, he could either stew in his own outrage or else he could come back tomorrow, when he'd had the chance — as her mother would say — to reflect upon his behaviour. Regrettably, that wasn't the sort of thing Harry Hinds was likely to do.

Eventually, switching off the lamp and climbing into bed, she gave in to tears. Surely, having a boyfriend wasn't supposed to make you feel so... but so what? Exasperated? Frustrated? Humiliated? If Mum knew how he treated her she would tell her to forget him. She would say that no man, no matter how many expensive gifts he gave her, should make her feel worthless. And, loath though she was to admit it, worthless was how she was beginning to feel. But she *liked* Harry. She liked that he was different to anyone she had ever known — confident. Mature. Thrilling, even. Everything poor Freddie would never have been.

Dear Freddie. She did hope he was all right. She'd promised to write to him but never had. To be honest, until recently — and only then because she'd used him as an unfavourable comparison to Harry — she'd forgotten all about him. Perhaps tomorrow she should try again to drop him a line or two; there was no need to sound overly gushing, just let him know about her work. Yes. Then she might not feel so bad about ignoring him.

The other thing she really must do tomorrow was telephone her mother. How badly must she be taking the situation with Arthur if all she did was stay in bed, crying all day? She would also ask Miss Blatchford for some leave — even just a single day added onto a weekend would be time enough to get the train home for a night or two. As she had said to her father, she couldn't magic up news about Arthur — but she *could* go home and comfort her mother. And perhaps Dad, too. She could share their burden. It might also bring her some comfort of her own.

Relieved by the idea, she exhaled heavily. Yes, in the midst of all her other upset, it sounded like a plan.

★ ★ ★

'I've said I'm sorry, Lou.'

'I know.'

'And I am. But I've told you before, it's business.'

'I know.'

It was Saturday morning and, just after ten o'clock, Winnie had come up to announce that Harry was downstairs. On learning of his arrival, Lou's first thought had been to ask Winnie to relay the message that she didn't want to see him, the only thing stopping her being the prospect of the other girls newsing behind her back about who had dumped who. On top of everything else right now, being the subject of their gossip was something she could do without.

And so, having arrived in the parlour and deliberately chosen to sit in one of the chairs — rather than on the settee where he might sit next to her — she was now staring down at the rug, waiting to see what he had to say for himself. So far, she had heard nothing new.

'Look,' he said. Obediently, she looked up. This morning, minus both his hat and his tie, and with his shirt collar undone and his sleeves rolled up above his elbows, he looked unfinished. Ordinary. A bit scruffy, even. The problem was, it could so easily be part of an act to elicit her sympathy. She wouldn't put it past him. 'You liked the bracelet, didn't you.'

And that was another thing: he never asked her a question so much as delivered a statement, usually in a tone that made it difficult for her to disagree.

'I did. It's beautiful.'

'And the fox fur... and the perfume. You liked the perfume.'

'I've liked everything you've given me,' she said flatly. There was no point lying. He would see through a lie in an instant. 'You're always very generous.'

'Well, then you need to understand how it's me doing the business you don't like that gets all the things you do.'

Still nothing new. 'I know that too.'

Getting to his feet, he came to crouch in front of her. He didn't, she was relieved to notice, reach to take her hands. Having him touch her would weaken her resolve even further, and it was shaky enough as it was.

'Look, Lou, some men work by sitting on their arses in a cushy office all day. Others build ships or drive a tram or... or grow spuds. Me, I graft on the streets. I'm not complaining. I get by on my wits and reap the rewards of my own efforts. But it ain't the sort of work that can be done between the hours of eight and six. I have to meet people, haggle, grease palms, whatever it takes to do the deal and get the stuff people want. Stuff people don't mind paying for. And I make no apology for being good at it.' With a shrug of his shoulders, he sat back on his haunches. 'But then you seen that already.'

Trying to avoid meeting his look, she pressed her lips together. Nothing he'd said was untrue. The problem was, neither did it change anything.

'I know all of that,' she said, finally meeting his look. 'But you being so busy doesn't leave no room for *me*—'

At this, she saw him frown.

'*Room* for you?'

'Whenever we're out together,' she began, knowing she had to avoid sounding accusatory, 'you're doing business. And though I know *why* you're doing it, it's of no help to me when I'm sat there, on my own, without a soul to talk to save the odd barmaid who takes pity on me. Sometimes, apart from the drink in front of me, and for all I actually see of you, I might as well have stayed home.'

'So ... what are you saying ...?' Finally, an actual question from him. There was irony. 'That you don't want to be Harry's girl no more?' *Two questions in a row? Heavens.* 'Because if that's not what you want...'

What she wanted, she realised then, was likely impossible: she still wanted to be his girl, of course she did, just not with things between them remaining as they were now. She would gladly — well, reasonably gladly — forgo the lavish gifts in exchange for a more normal relationship. But how to explain that to him? She couldn't expect him to change, least of all for her. He was who he was, which was pretty much what he'd just said.

Weary beyond belief, she let out a long sigh. There was no denying he was a decent catch. A man like Harry would be hard to let go. She was even quite fond of the streak of arrogance he had about him. It was, in part, what had probably drawn her to him in the first place. But what it seemed to boil down to was that she could have Harry as he was — warts and all — or else finish with him and find someone more… normal; someone who would arrive at her door once a week, shoes shined, neck washed, modest amount of wages in his pocket and, in front of her at least, mind his manners and show her some respect. Come Fridays, he would take her to the pictures, buy her an ice in the interval, tentatively take her hand on the walk home and then hope for a goodnight kiss when he delivered her safely back to her doorstep. And, after a couple of weeks of his diligent courting, she would be bored out of her brains with him and itching for something more. After all, if that was all she'd wanted, she could have saved herself the anguish of moving all the way across the county by staying at Woodicombe, surrounded by familiarity and comforts, never once having to wonder what her parents would think of her dress or her make-up or the man who arrived in a grocer's van to take her to a smoky club.

But none of that was of any help to her now.

'I do want to be Harry's girl …'

His expression didn't change. There wasn't even a flicker of relief. 'But?'

'But maybe it would be better, for both of us… if I didn't see you quite so often.'

When she paused to choose her next words, he stared at her, his expression one of incredulity. 'You want to be Harry's girl but not so often.'

Put like that, she had to admit it did sound ridiculous. 'What I mean is, if I saw you twice a week, say, instead of every other night, then maybe I wouldn't get in the way of your business so much. You wouldn't have to worry about leaving me alone while you...'

From the way he was shaking his head, she knew she'd made a mistake.

Seemingly exasperated, he got to his feet. 'This ain't something I can just switch on and off, Lou. If you don't want to see me so often then I got to think your heart ain't in it. What would you do on the nights when you didn't see me? Go out with Jess and Winnie? Is that what you're angling for? To go out with the girls, up the pier to dance with sailors and—'

'No, 'course not!' *Don't raise your voice. Don't make him cross.* 'No,' she said more carefully. 'On the nights I didn't see you, I'd do what I do now. Stay in, read, keep my beauty routines up together... You'd be amazed the time it takes to —'

'Lou, Lou, stop. Can't you see, that's not how this works. My mistake, I suppose, for thinking you knew what you were getting into, that you were grown-up enough for something less juvenile —'

'I ... am.' She mustn't let lose him. She must *not* lose him. 'I just don't want to feel as though I'm a burden on you.'

Unfortunately, he still looked cross. Worse than that, she was pretty certain she was going to cry.

'If and when you become a burden, I'll tell you. *I'll* tell *you.*'

Stop crying, she remonstrated with herself. *Do you want to confirm his opinion that you're not properly grown-up? Stop it.* 'Please don't think ... I'm ungrateful ...'

'When you carry on like this, Lou, I don't know

what other conclusion to come to. Put yourself in my shoes.'

'Sorry.'

'Look,' he said, reaching for her hands and pulling her to her feet beside him. 'I've got somewhere to be. And you need to go and... freshen up. So, how about we pretend none of this ever happened — chalk it up to you being over-tired. Don't feel too badly, I've known other women get like this from time to time. So, how about, if I'm prepared to overlook how you ran off last night, and how that made me look in front of people, you'll swear to me you'll think long and hard about what it is you really want and then promise me we won't be going through this nonsense again *next* month. Because I really don't have time for this.'

Oh, thank goodness. He was going to forgive her. It was her lucky day.

She nodded. 'I don't need to think about it. I know.'

'Think about it anyway,' he said. 'Think about what it would mean to walk away from being Harry's girl.'

'I will. Yes.'

'Right.' Glancing about and seeing the clock, he grimaced. 'Now, I need to be going. I *had* been going to take you out for supper tonight, but I shan't now. Saturday or not, I'll give you your night at home.'

I'll give you your night at home. He managed to make it sound like punishment.

'Will I see you tomorrow?'

Decisively, 'No. But if I can make time, I'll pop over Monday evening.'

'All right.' Christ, she was going to have the devil's own job to make it up to him now. And it was all her own fault.

'Not many men would give you a second chance. You know that, don't you.'

172

Now she could barely see for tears. 'I do. Yes.'

'Kiss for Harry then.'

''Course.'

When he offered her his cheek, she kissed it. But going through her mind was the idea of suggesting that if he didn't have to rush off right this minute, and if they were really quiet, might there not be something else he would like to do with her first? She was pretty certain Mrs Hannacott had gone over to her sister's, and she knew for a fact that Liddy, Winnie and Jess had just gone into town. But, when it came to saying the words, she found she couldn't. She couldn't risk making yet another mistake. No, for a while to come, she was going to have to do only as he asked — and do it as though commanded to walk on eggshells while about it.

Turning away from her, he left the room and went straight out of the front door onto the pavement. Unsure what to do for the best, she scurried after him.

When he reached the van, he called back to where she was stood in the doorway, breathing rapidly. 'Think about what I said.'

Forced to stand and watch as he drove away without so much as a wave, she gave in and cried. What had she done? What *had* she done? What she had *done* was ruin everything. Fortunately — unbelievably, given her stupidity — he seemed prepared to give her another chance a chance she absolutely must *not* waste, and one for which, when she saw him on Monday, she must take every opportunity to show her gratitude.

* * *

Watching Liddy drive her forklift machine, Lou smiled. It seemed such a fun thing to be able to do that she longed to have a go at it for herself. Liddy might swear about it sometimes, calling it 'a beast of a thing' to manoeuvre through the narrow aisles of the warehouse but, to Lou, Liddy always looked to be enjoying herself. Sadly, it was expressly forbidden for anyone other than Liddy, who had been taught how to operate it by one the Canadians, to set foot on it.

'Done,' Liddy said, bringing the thing to a halt inside the entrance doors. 'Another day's toil over.' Stepping off the driver's platform, she tugged off her leather gauntlets.

'I'm done, too,' Lou said, leaning in the doorway to her little office. 'While you've been putting it all away, I've got the ledgers written up.'

'You mean,' Flossie said, coming to join them, 'that for once, we're all three of us straight? On top of everything with time still left in the day?'

'It would seem so.'

Beside her, Liddy delved into her pocket and pulled out a packet of Woodbines and, when Flossie declined her offer of one, proceeded to light up.

'Can't stand them ones,' Flossie observed.

Liddy grinned. 'Me neither. But there's a ruddy war on.'

There's a ruddy war on was now an everyday expression, Lou reflected as she watched Liddy exhaling twin streams of grey smoke. Just lately it excused everything from shortages of foodstuffs to the increasingly shoddy quality of the things you could actually still get. And the war hadn't even been going a year yet. *It'll get worse, too*, Miss Blatchford had warned them only the other day. It was a prospect, she remembered thinking at the time, they could all do without.

At the sound of a motor pulling up outside, Liddy let out a long groan and pushed herself away from the

174

wall. 'Well ain't that just typical,' she said, dropping her cigarette to the floor and stubbing it out with the toe of her boot. 'We're just about to knock off and another load turns up.'

'It's all right,' Flossie announced, having gone to peer beyond the doors, 'it's only Harry.'

The news made Lou stiffen. Harry? Here? Now what did she do? He'd never seen her in work clothes and with nothing but the remains of a smear of lipstick on her face.

'Afternoon, ladies.'

Too late to remedy the situation, she realised she'd have to rely on a warm smile alone. And so, forcing herself to swallow down her panic, she turned slowly about.

'Hello.' Oh, dear Lord, now she'd sounded like a ten-year-old.

From the corner of her eye, she noticed Liddy and Flossie slipping away.

'Found myself passing right by the gate and so I thought, I know what: I'll drop in and see Lou.'

Beginning to breathe more easily, she went towards him, the kiss they exchanged a chaste one.

In the meantime, opening the passenger's door of the van was a man not unlike Harry to look at — similar sort of age, same dark colouring — but not so close that they would be mistaken for brothers.

'My pal, Charlie,' Harry explained, gesturing over his shoulder. 'Helps me out from time to time. You know, with the heavy stuff.' When Charlie raised a hand in greeting, Lou nodded back. 'So,' Harry went on, 'this is where you work.'

She nodded. 'Yes.'

'Just the three of you for all this?' When he gestured into the warehouse, she turned to look.

'Just us. If it's a box or a crate or a barrel, Liddy and

175

Flossie take care of it. If it's a piece of paper, that's down to me.'

'Crikey, Lou. The way you spoke of it, I didn't realise it was this big. Got a lot of goods, these Canadians.'

Unable to recall having ever mentioned anything about the scale of the operation, she frowned. Of more concern, though, was why he was here in the first place. At least he seemed in a good mood — albeit somewhat distracted. But then given how annoyed he'd been with her about Friday night, perhaps she was just on high alert. Not helping was the knowledge that, somewhere close by, Liddy and Flossie would be eavesdropping.

'We have to close up in a minute.' In saying so, she hoped he would get on and explain why he was there. Had he come to tell her he was going to take her out tonight or to tell her that he wasn't?

He glanced to his wristwatch. 'Ten to six.'

'Yes. We finish at six. Assuming everything's in and away.'

Charlie, she noticed, was now standing in the entrance, hands in pockets, looking around. 'Who drives the fork-lift?' he asked.

'Liddy.' There was something about him she didn't like.

'A girl on a forklift, eh? Wouldn't mind seeing that.'

Now she liked him even less.

'Look, I'd best get on,' she said, still wishing Harry would come out with it — whatever 'it' was. 'Miss Blatch-ford will be by in a minute and I can't afford to look as though I'm standing around gassing.'

'She's your supervisor woman?'

'She is.'

'All right. Well, wouldn't want to get you into trouble with the boss.'

'No.' And *still* he hadn't said why he'd come.

176

'Pick you up from here tomorrow. I'll take you for a fish and chip supper.'

From here? Straight from work? 'But I won't have time to change—'

''S'only fish and chips.' With a shrug, he turned towards to the van. 'Six o'clock.'

Sauntering back across the ramp, Charlie turned to give her a wave. 'Good to meet you, Lou.'

As she stood watching them get into the van and then drive away, Liddy came to stand next to her. 'Date tonight, then?'

Lou shook her head. 'Tomorrow.'

'Come on, then, let's head home.'

'Yes,' she said with a frown. 'Let's.'

★ ★ ★

'Lou? You up there? Telephone for you.'

It was after supper that same evening, and Lou had been standing staring into the wardrobe, trying to work out which of her skirts and blouses she might reasonably take to change into before Harry arrived tomorrow to take her out. She daren't risk wearing something smarter to start with in case an accident befell it. Twice already she'd had to darn her navy-blue skirt: once from snagging it on one of the racks in the warehouse; once from catching it on a splinter on her desk. If anything like that happened to her scarlet one, she'd be distraught.

'Coming,' she called back to the voice at the bottom of the stairs, no nearer a decision.

Arriving at the telephone, she picked up the receiver. 'Hullo?'

'Lou, love, it's your dad.'

She froze. Arthur. It had to be. Dear God, please let

177

him be calling to tell her something good!

'Dad, yes, hello.'

'Lou, I'm afraid there's been some bad news.' With a gasp, she sank onto the stool. 'Freddie's been killed.' *Freddie?* 'There was a bombing raid on Portsmouth. They struck the base where he was training. Friday night, apparently. Mr Paddon telephoned. Thought we should know, seeing how you and Freddie were close.'

Close. Hm. 'Dad. I don't know what to say. That's…'

'Thing is, love, that same day a letter arrived for you. It's postmarked Portsmouth and your Mum recognised the handwriting as being his. I'd offer to open it—'

'No,' she cut in. No, it was better they didn't read him lamenting the lack of any word from her.

'— or I could send it on. Unless you're planning on coming back soon, and then I could just keep it safe here for you.'

'Yes,' she said, 'keep it safe for me.' Having Dad hold onto it served two purposes: firstly, it would reassure him that she was trying to arrange leave to go home and see them; secondly, it gave her one fewer thing to have to deal with right now.

'All right, love.'

'Any news of Arthur?'

'Captain Colborne is still trying to find out the names of survivors picked up by the Germans. They're supposed to send a list to our government — the Germans, that is. But he said there's usually a delay in it arriving and that so far there's been no word.'

'Well at least he's trying,' she said. As comments went, it wasn't much help. Given the rather hopeless circumstances, she could think of nothing better.

'He is, yes.'

'It also means there's still hope.'

178

'Yes, love. And we're clinging on to it.'

'All right, well, give my love to Mum.'

'Will do. And I'm real sorry about Freddie.'

'Yes, Dad. Me too.'

Replacing the receiver, she stood for a moment, too ashamed to even move. It was nothing short of wicked to let her parents think Freddie had been dear to her. She *had* liked him. He had been gentle and kind and genuinely taken with her. She was sorry he had been killed. Truly sorry. But here she was, using the news of his death to distract from failure on her own part — like her failure to telephone home often enough to keep abreast of news of her brother, or to find out about Mum and how she was going along. And then there was the fact that in letting her father think there had been something proper between her and Freddie, she was diverting attention from the relationship she really had — with a man they almost certainly wouldn't like.

Well, while it was too late to make it up to Freddie himself, she could at least write to his parents and express her sorrow for their loss. In fact, yes, she would do it now. Then she would see if Mrs H had any stamps to spare and drop it in the post box on her way to work in the morning. If nothing else, it might take the edge off her guilt.

To that end, rummaging in the drawer of her bedside table, she pulled out her writing things. Sitting heavily on the side of her bed, she unscrewed the cap of her fountain pen and tried to think. Best keep the letter brief. There was no need to gush. She would say only that— Lowering her eyes to write her address at the top of the page, she gasped.

Dear Freddie.

I hope this letter finds you well.

There, in her handwriting, was the beginning of the letter she had started some weeks back, a letter she had been unable to continue to write because the choice between telling him she was seeing someone else, or otherwise concealing the fact and continuing to lead him on, had been beyond her, both options feeling duplicitous. Even reading those words now rekindled that same sickly sense of treachery.

With a low groan, she put down her pen. Dear God, how had she become so heartless? What was it going to take for her to stop thinking so much about herself and start thinking about other people — her family included? Carry on like this, and she would end up at a point where not only would her parents want nothing to do with Harry, they would want nothing to do with her, either. And for that, she would only have herself to blame.

* * *

Charlie? Why was *he* here again?

When Harry drew up at the entrance to the warehouse at ten minutes before six the following afternoon, Lou was dismayed to see his pal Charlie grinning out of the window at her. Clearly, she had been mistaken to assume that in offering her a fish and chip supper, Harry had meant just the two of them.

Still in her work apron, she went towards them, wondering how to broach the subject without making herself look a fool.

'We're dropping Charlie off on the way,' Harry said as he came across to greet her, mercifully doing away with the need for her to ask.

When he then slid his arm around her waist and kissed her on the lips, she felt her whole body soften: her old Harry was back.

'All right,' she said, smiling warmly. 'But you're a bit early. We've still got to pack up for the night and I need to get changed.'

'Don't fuss too much,' he said, lowering his arm. 'It's such a warm night I thought we might sit up on The Hoe and eat them.'

'Sounds nice,' she said. And it did.

'I see he's got his sidekick again,' Liddy remarked drily as Lou went back inside.

'Mm. Real odd bod, that one,' she replied, glancing back to where Charlie was now standing in the entrance staring up at the racks. 'Apparently we're dropping him off on the way.'

'Right.'

'Look,' she said, 'why don't you and Flossie go on home. It's five to. No one will turn up now. I'll close up once I've got changed.'

Opening the door to the cleaning cupboard and reaching to put her broom inside, Liddy nodded. 'Yeah. All right. We'll head off.'

'Enjoy your supper,' Flossie said, winking at her as she brushed past.

'Thanks. And I'll see you tomorrow.'

Once back in her office, Lou closed the door and slid shut the panel of the little service hatch. Then, taking off her apron, she hung it from the hook, unbuttoned her blouse and slipped off her skirt. It was a pity she couldn't have a wash, but it wasn't as though they were going anywhere fancy; they were only going to sit on the grass, eating fish and chips from newspaper, which, in any event, was by far the best way.

With that there was a tap at the door.

'You decent?'

'No,' she called back. 'Five minutes. Maybe less.' Golly, he was impatient! Still, if his rather more effusive greeting just now was anything to go by, he was back to being pleased to see her. And that could only be a good thing.

Carefully folding her skirt and slipping it into her shopping bag, she laid her red one on the desk and smoothed a hand over it: not too badly crumpled.

With that, the click of the door latch made her turn sharply over her shoulder.

'Perfect timing, by the look of it.'

'Harry!' Mortified that he should come in while she was undressed, she quickly wrapped her arms quickly across her brassiere. 'You can't be in here.'

Taking no notice, he moved around the desk towards her. 'Why not? Ain't as though I haven't seen you in your skimpies before.'

'I know,' she whispered, glancing over his shoulder as he put his arms around her and drew her close, swaying her from side to side as though they were dancing. Of all the times! 'But this is my place of *work*. If anyone comes in and sees you, it'll be bad enough that you're in here, let alone that I'm barely dressed.'

'It's all right,' he said, 'if anyone's coming, Charlie will start whistling. It's a signal we have.'

'Seriously,' she hissed, 'it's me that'll get the sack.'

'So… you wouldn't want me to do this, then?' Sliding her bra strap off her shoulder, he then reached behind her back for the fastener.

Despite feeling a familiar stab of urgency, she pulled sharply away. 'No!'

With a hapless grin, he shrugged. 'Shame.'

182

'So you say.'

'All these bits of paper then,' he went on, reaching across her desk and pulling a sheet from the tray labelled 'In'. 'This your work?'

'It is.' Relieved that he was occupied for a moment, she tidied her underwear. 'Those are requisition dockets waiting to be entered into the ledgers.'

'Requisitions for goods.'

'Uh-huh.'

His interest eventually seeming to wane, he dropped it back into the tray.

'You *sure* you wouldn't like to slip out of those things and see if we can't put this desk to better use?'

'Quite sure.'

'Might be fun.'

'It might, yes,' she said, reaching for her blouse and, in her rush to feel less exposed, ignoring the buttons and pulling it hastily over her head. 'But please, just go and wait outside. I promise I won't be long.'

In a gesture of defeat, he held up his hands. 'All right, all right. Not my fault I can't resist you ...'

When he went out and closed the door behind him, she sighed with relief. While it was hugely comforting to know she was back in his good books, when it came to this job, she couldn't afford to be careless. Lose this work, she thought, buttoning the waist of her skirt at the same time as slipping her feet back into her shoes, and she'd be in it good and proper.

With a quick glance about to make sure she hadn't left anything lying around, Lou switched off the light and then went out to tug the door to the loading bay the last couple of feet along its rail.

Standing by the passenger door to the van, Charlie bowed deeply and gestured to her to get in.

'You must be important if you're in charge of locking up,' he said, climbing in beside her.

She hoped it wasn't far to wherever they were dropping him off. Something about him made her flesh creep. Unfortunately, he was Harry's friend and so she needed to at least *appear* respectful.

'Me? I'm about the least important person in the whole dockyard,' she said. 'I just close the door. Someone from the office comes down to lock it later.'

Beside her he grunted.

'Still busy in there?' Harry asked, acknowledging the guard at the entrance who raised the barrier and signalled them to drive out.

'Now more than ever,' she said. 'Non-stop comings and goings from first thing till last.'

'Drop me on the corner if you like, Harry,' Charlie offered into the conversation as they approached the end of Union Street. 'I've a mind to pop into Monty's for a swift half.'

With Charlie getting out, no longer having to sit squashed up against him, Lou finally relaxed.

'Sorry about him,' Harry said as he put the van into gear and pulled away from the kerb.

In the name of conversation, she asked, 'Have you known him long?'

'Couple of years.'

'Oh.' The topic of Charlie exhausted, she took to looking out at the people making their way home. Since Harry seemed in no rush to mention the events of Friday night — nor his visit to her on Saturday morning and his instruction to her to think about what she wanted — she wouldn't raise them either. Hopefully, it was an upset now consigned to the past. 'Where are we going?' she asked instead.

184

'Place on the pier. Always get a good rock an' chips up there.'

And so that was what they did, Harry taking the blanket under his arm on the way there, she taking it on the way back so that he could carry their parcels of food, the smell of beef dripping and the tang of vinegar making her feel ravenous.

Several minutes later, seated alongside him on the rug and licking the grease from her fingers, she couldn't help smiling. Moments like this were all she needed — just the two of them, doing something simple. The other places he took her to were nice, but there was something about the gentle warmth of the evening sun, the light briny breeze and Harry in a good mood that made her forget Arthur and Freddie, and Mum and Dad, and meant that she didn't have to fear him *just popping over for a word with someone* and then being gone for the rest of the night. This, she thought, catching his eye and smiling, was what she'd always imagined courting would be like.

'Lovely,' she said, scrunching the greasy newspaper into a ball. 'So lovely, I could eat it all over again.'

'Get you some more if you want.'

Bursting into laughter, she shook her head. 'My *mind* could eat it all over again but I'm not sure my *stomach* could.'

'And we wouldn't want them panties of yours splitting at the seams.'

Laughing even harder, she lunged at him, only to be left wriggling when he caught hold of her arms, and then proceeded to grip them tighter the harder she tried to get away. And then he was kissing her, and she was kissing him back. And she didn't care how many of the old couples sitting on the benches might be shaking their heads in disapproval. Her warm and happy Harry was back. And all this without him having yet seen — or even knowing about — the slinky new black dress she'd asked Eli Ackerman to run up for her, and the new black cami slip he'd recommended she have made to wear beneath it. With Eli's suggested tweaks to the design, it was going to look fabulous with her fox-fur stole.

Yes, she thought, sighing happily, her insides aching from laughing so hard, this was her reward for learning her lesson; this was how it was supposed to be. And she would do everything she could to keep it that way.

* * *

'Seriously?'

Lou nodded slowly. 'Sorry, Floss, but according to your count, the warehouse is light. So, though I know you've already checked twice, could I ask you to go back and count them again? *Please?*'

It was now Friday morning — the day when Lou had to tally her ledgers not only to the totals held by Accounts, but to the actual stock in the warehouse as well. Thankfully, having lost a docket that week back at the beginning, when the totals in her ledger were out by a mile, she'd been spot on every Friday since. This morning, though, she had three discrepancies that no amount of re-checking seemed about to remedy. And the longer she puzzled over the situation, the more she began to think that it wasn't just because she had a thick head from last night.

Last night. What unexpected fun that had been! Remembering it fondly, she smiled. Harry had taken her to a new place he'd claimed to want to go and see — a recently opened club called The Starlight Lounge. Unsurprisingly, it transpired that he knew the owner and so, equally unsurprisingly, he'd spent a couple of hours talking business with him. As it happened, Lou hadn't minded in the least because the owner's girlfriend — a long-limbed blonde who went by the unlikely name of Cherry, and who was one day going to become an actress had taken a shine to her and proceeded to mix various cocktails that she *simply must try.* One or two of them, even by Cherry's own admission, had been truly terrible. 'Maybe I misread the instructions,' she'd collapsed into fits of giggles to confess.

But one or two of her concoctions had been really delicious. And — it turned out this morning — rather strong. The Bloody Mary had been nice, the one called Singapore Sling too potent. Her favourite, though, had been the one whose name neither of them had been able to pronounce but that on the list behind the bar had read 'Daiquiri': white rum, sugar, lime juice — or, in their case, and given that there was *a ruddy war on,* lime cordial. Remembering the bemused expression on Harry's face when he'd eventually come to find her, giggling madly, made her smile even now.

Unfortunately, of all the mornings to have a hangover, today was not the one she would have chosen.

'Nope,' Flossie said, reappearing in the doorway a couple of minutes later, her hands raised in a gesture of regret. ''Fraid I can't make the totals come to any different. There's still only four of each.'

'Of all three things?' Lou checked.

''Fraid so.'

'Creamola, Camp Coffee and Wrigley's gum are definitely all two cartons short?'

'According to you.'

'And they couldn't have been put in the wrong place — by accident, I mean.' Even *she* knew that was clutching at straws now.

'Since we've tallied everything else, no, we would have seen them, wouldn't we?'

Flossie was right. If she said they weren't there, then they weren't there.

'All right,' she said. 'Then there's only one thing for it. I'll have to go and tell Miss Blatchford.'

'She's not in today. Remember? She told us yesterday her fiancé's got embarkation leave.'

Damn. Now she would have to admit the discrepancy to Miss Blatchford's superior. And that was the Canadian lieutenant who came each week to sign the ledger. From the little she saw of him he always seemed nice enough, but how would he react to news that they had stock missing — six boxes of it? She could only pray it wasn't significant enough of a loss to get her the sack, not when she was just getting everything else in her life on an even keel.

She didn't have to wait long to find out. Shortly after the three of them returned from their dinner break, Lieutenant Ross arrived, ring binder under his arm, whistling something catchy as he strode in through the door.

Seeing him coming towards her, Lou drew a breath and got to her feet.

'Lieutenant Ross, good afternoon.'

'Good afternoon to you, Miss Channer. And how are you today?'

'Actually,' she said, deciding to get it over and done with, 'I'm … concerned.'

Putting the binder down on her desk, he looked straight at her. 'Concerned? That doesn't sound good.'

How, she wondered, in all the previous weeks, had she never noticed the depth of the colour of his eyes — the most unusual of blues. Turquoise. 'Um, no,' she said. 'You see … we can't account for six units of stock.' There. At least she'd told him. *And* she'd managed to avoid using words like 'missing' and 'lost'.

'You've double-checked?'

She nodded. 'Quadruple checked, if there's such a thing.'

'Show me where.'

Opening her ledger at the page she'd marked with a scrap of paper, she ran her finger down the columns, stopping to point out the goods in question.

'The odd thing is,' she decided to try to help matters along by explaining, 'none of those items have been received in this week, nor, from what we can see, have any of them been despatched. So, I don't see how they can be wrong. The stock should be identical to last week.'

She glanced to his face but, unfamiliar with his usual expression, could read nothing from it. At least he hadn't flown into a rage.

'Show me where on the racks they should be.'

Going ahead of him out into the warehouse, she led him to the first location, where he stood looking at the various cartons.

'It's a puzzle, sir,' Flossie said, with which Liddy kicked her ankle.

'You run a neat operation, Miss Knight.'

'Thank you, sir,' Liddy replied. 'We do our best.'

When he turned and headed back to the office, with a quick glance to Liddy and Flossie, Lou followed. Now she would find out what he proposed to do.

Rather casually, Lou thought, he opened the binder he'd brought with him and flicked through what she recognised as the week's despatch notes. Finding nothing of interest, he closed the cover.

'Tell me, Miss Channer, do you like working here?'

She felt her cheeks flush. *Here it comes*. 'Very much, sir.'

'I don't mind saying it's both unusual and encouraging to come across a warehouse on this scale being run by just three young women. Present conundrum aside, you do a good job.'

She risked a look to those turquoise eyes. 'Thank you, sir.'

'Always clean and shipshape.'

'We try our best, sir.' But what if their best wasn't good enough for the Canadian Royal Navy?

'So, on this occasion, I recommend we put this down to a clerical goof up. Note it against the items in question as a balancing error and we'll start afresh on Monday. Nothing I ever see here gives cause for concern and the value of the missing items is, frankly, negligible. So, how does that sound?'

It was only then she realised she'd been holding her breath. 'Very fair, sir.'

'An acceptable solution, given the amount of time the three of you have no doubt already spent on trying to resolve it?'

She nodded. 'Yes, sir. But we'll keep an eye out in case they turn up. Which I hope they do.'

When he smiled, she smiled back. Heavens, he really was quite handsome — if blue eyes and a gentle manner was your type.

Getting up from where he had been perched on the corner of her desk, he picked up his binder. 'Good stuff. Carry on, Miss Channer.' In disbelief that they weren't to be reprimanded in some way, she followed him out of the door. 'Good afternoon, ladies.'

The moment he was gone, Liddy and Flossie bounded towards her. 'Well?'

Still astonished that he should so easily have accepted

190

the situation, she shook her head. 'He said to put it down to a clerical something-or-other — I don't rightly recall the exact word he used — and to show it in the ledger as a balancing error.'

'So, we're not in trouble?' Flossie asked.

'On the contrary. He praised the way we run the place.'

'And so he should,' Liddy remarked. 'We do a damn fine job.'

'Clean and shipshape, was how he described it.'

'Well then,' Liddy picked up again, doing a little jig, 'make way, Friday, Saturday and Sunday here we come!'

'Yes,' Lou agreed, still hardly daring to believe how reasonable Lieutenant Ross had been. With that worry lifted, she could look forward to Harry's face when he saw her in the black dress Eli Ackerman was going to have ready for her to collect in the morning. She was rather hoping he would be speechless.

The only thing she needed now was news that Arthur had turned up alive and well; then, everything would finally have come together. This new life of hers would be perfect.

Chapter 7

Lieutenant Ross

Well, that hadn't lasted long. Harry was back to his old ways. Here she was, dressed to the nines, hair pinned, face made up, and yet still, within ten minutes of arriving here, he'd gone goodness-only-knew-where with someone into whom, supposedly quite by chance, he'd just *happened to stumble*. By her reckoning, that had been almost an hour ago and she hadn't had sight of him since. *Happened to stumble*, my foot. There wasn't a grain of chance about it. She hadn't believed *that* for a moment. But she also knew better than to make a fuss — after all, look how that had turned out for her last time. No, thank you, she could do without another episode like that.

Looking around the bar, Lou sighed. Tonight, he'd brought her to the Duke of Cornwall Hotel, where, he'd told her, there would be a dance. Except that there wasn't. He'd got the wrong night. Unperturbed, he'd suggested they stay for a drink anyway. And so, here she was, all on her own again. Sometimes, she wondered why she bothered. How could he be all cosy with her one moment and then completely ignore her the next? Surely that wasn't normal? Surely, if you liked someone enough to date them, then you actually wanted to spend time with them, not treat them as something to be got out and given a quick airing from time to time?

'Would you like another, ma'am?'

Unsure whether she was the 'ma'am' in question, Lou looked up to find an immaculately liveried young barman awaiting her reply. If Harry insisted on abandoning her, then at least this place was a notch up on most of his haunts.

'Yes,' she said decisively. 'Another vodka and lime, please.'

'With ice?'

'Yes please.'

'Very well, madam.'

When the waiter left to attend to her order, she let out yet another sigh. This might be a classier place than most, the clientele certainly wealthier, but that didn't stop the men staring at her — even those who arrived with a female companion on their arm. Perhaps they thought she was a *lady of the night*, to borrow her mother's polite phrase for what her father would call a tart. *Her mother*. Golly, she really must telephone her.

'Thank you,' she said when the waiter returned with her drink.

Actually, she thought, picking it up and taking a sip, perhaps, sat here on this little velvet sofa, she did look as though she was available for business. This dress *had* turned out to be a bit on the racy side — not what she had intended when she'd taken her beloved scarlet one to Eli Ackerman to have a copy made up. With hindsight, perhaps she shouldn't have gone with his suggested enhancements — *a little nip in here, a fraction off there*. Harry liked it, though. He'd said it made her look like a starlet from a Hollywood movie, and then he'd slapped her behind and said he couldn't wait to see what she was wearing underneath. At that moment, she'd giggled. But now she just felt slightly uncomfortable. And conspicuous. She also felt slightly queasy, which could be her own fault for skipping supper on account of being concerned about getting into the dress to start with. It was certainly a closer fit than her scarlet one.

Eventually, with no word as to where he'd been, Harry reappeared. As usual after such an absence, he looked pleased with himself.

'Want another?' he asked, rubbing his hands together and motioning with his head towards her glass.

She shook her head. 'No, thank you. I doubt I shall finish this one.'

'Turns out the dances are on Wednesday and Saturday,' he said. 'Not Tuesdays.'

She nodded. 'Oh.'

'So, I'll get you home.'

Straightening her fox fur on her shoulders, she got to her feet. 'All right.'

'And we'll come back for the dance another time.'

'Yes.'

Slipping an arm about her waist, he steered her towards the door. 'And we'll save exploring beneath this dress for another night, too.'

'All right.'

But it wasn't all right, she thought as they went out through the foyer and onto the street. And it was becoming less *all right* as time went on. But as for what she was going to do about it, she hadn't the least idea.

★ ★ ★

'Sorry to interrupt.'

From where she had been poring over her ledger at work the following morning, Lou shot upright. 'Lieutenant Ross. Sir.'

What was *he* doing back here? It was Wednesday; they weren't due to reconcile the stock for another couple of days yet. Unless, given last week's discrepancy, he was

194

proposing to carry out a spot check — catch them out if they were involved in any wrongdoing. It was what she would do, if she were in charge.

'Yes. Good morning, Miss Channer. Sorry to drop in unannounced.'

Standing behind her desk, Lou put down her pen. From his manner, she deduced that whatever his reason for coming, it was causing him some discomfort. Well, the three of them had nothing to hide. He would find no misconduct here.

'How may I help you?' she asked, anxious to allay her fears, nonetheless.

Placing his cap on her desk, and then adjusting the position of it to align perfectly with the edge, he turned and closed the door. Oh dear. This was worse than she'd thought. When a superior closed the door, you were generally in trouble.

'Well, please, forgive the suddenness of this… but I was wondering whether you would like to come for a drink with me? One evening, I mean.'

What? He was asking her to go out for a drink with him? *Her?*

'Yes.'

'You would?'

'I would, yes.'

What the hell did she think she was she doing?

'I wanted to ask you the other day, but the moment wasn't quite… well, appropriate. Besides, I thought I should check first that you were, as I thought, *Miss* Channer and not *Mrs.*'

'No,' she said, aware that the width of her smile might be making her look simple. 'I'm definitely Miss.'

'Great. Well, good. Thank you. How about… Friday? Or is that too soon?'

195

She shook her head. Was she really doing this? 'Friday, yes.'

'I'll wangle some transport and pick you up.'

She nodded. Golly, all of a sudden it was hard to breathe. 'All right.'

'When I come by on Friday morning to sign the ledgers, you can give me your address.'

'Yes.'

'Well, see you Friday, then.'

'Yes,' she said again, watching as he reached for his cap, put it on his head, adjusted the angle of it and went out through the door.

What on earth had she just done? Lieutenant Ross had asked her to go for a drink with him and she had said yes. She hadn't even hesitated, not for a second. Well, clearly, she couldn't go through with it. She couldn't actually go out with him. For a start, it was rare for Harry not to take her out on a Friday. Perhaps she could ask Lieutenant Ross to pick another night. Like... Monday. Yes, Harry rarely took her out on a Monday now. No! What was she thinking! She couldn't go out with him *any* night. She was Harry's girl. *This means you're mine now. You're my girl. I look after you, and you don't look at anyone else.* No, she couldn't risk it.

'You all right?'

So far away had she been in her thoughts that she hadn't heard them come in, but, staring expectantly back at her from the doorway was Liddy, with Flossie one step behind.

'Yes,' she said, flushing hot. For obvious reasons, she couldn't tell them what had just happened. Harry knew everyone. And if he even *thought* she'd spoken to another man about going out, well, there was no telling how he would react.

'Has he put you on a warning?'

She frowned. 'A warning? I don't understand.'

'If you do something wrong, they put you on a warning. Three warnings and you're out.'

'No,' she said, the realisation making her shiver. 'No, he just came by to see whether... well, whether we'd found anything.'

'The missing goods.'

'Yes.'

'And you aren't in trouble because we haven't? Only, that wouldn't seem fair.'

'Honestly,' she said, squirming at having to deceive the two of them. These days she seemed perpetually mired in deceit and, if nothing else, it was exhausting. 'He didn't tell me off. But it's plain he's not expecting the numbers to be off again this week.'

Evidently placated, Liddy shrugged and wandered away.

'See you in a bit for tea, then,' Flossie said, following on her heels.

Saints alive, what a pickle. The rather lovely Lieutenant Ross, of the Royal Canadian Navy, had asked her on a date. And with absolutely no thought whatsoever, and no right to even consider him, she had said yes. And now she would have to let him down. And she had about forty-eight hours to think of a kind way to do it.

★ ★ ★

The sky beyond Harry's heaving shoulder, Lou noticed, was turning the prettiest shade of pink. Rather less romantically, back down on the ground, something that felt like the corner of a jagged flint was sticking in her spine, a bumblebee droning in the heather sounded to be getting precariously close to her left ear and Harry's stubble was scratching back and forth against her cheek. She hadn't wanted to do this with him tonight but, when they'd left the pub and walked back to the van, and he'd reached in and produced the rug, rather than have him raise questions she might not be able to answer, she'd simply gone along with it. It wasn't as though it ever took long for him to be done.

'You liked that,' he said afterwards as he lit up a Craven 'A' and stretched out beside her on the rug.

Again, in the name of keeping things harmonious between them, she made a vague sound of agreement. 'Mm.'

'Thing is,' he went on, turning onto his side to look at her, 'I shan't be about for a couple of days.'

In her surprise, she raised her head to regard him. He wasn't going to be around for a couple of days? 'Oh?'

'But you needn't fret,' he went on, and with which she found herself studying the way he was clasping his cigarette. 'I'm not seeing anyone else.'

That he should imagine such a thing would be her first concern made her want to laugh.

'No?'

'Nah,' he said. 'I've just got some business to see to.'

Well there was a surprise.

'Oh.'

'Got to go up to Bristol for a couple of days to see about— well, no sense boring you with it.'

Deep inside, Lou felt a flicker of a realisation.

'So ... what are you saying? We won't be going out Saturday night?' Was it too much to hope for Friday, as well?

''Fraid not. Nor tomorrow. See, it's a fair old way to Bristol. So, I'll head up there Friday morning, stop over Friday night with someone I know up there, see about

198

these... bits of business Saturday, and be back down here some time on Sunday.'

Had he really, quite by chance, just gifted her an opportunity beyond her dreams? The timing of his absence would be perfect. Amazingly unbelievably perfect.

Sitting up from the rug, and reminding herself to act put out, she tidied her skirt. If he'd noticed she hadn't made much of an effort to dress up tonight, he hadn't said, her decision to spare her favourite red skirt the ordeal of Harry crushing it beneath him turning out to be even more far-sighted she'd thought. Now that she was actually going to be able to go out with Lieutenant Ross, it would still be clean and tidy for him. What a stroke of good fortune!

For effect, though, she exhaled heavily. 'That's a shame. I'd been hoping we might go back to the Starlight Lounge.'

'You liked that place.'

'I liked Cherry.' Borrowing one of Winnie's expressions, Lou went on, 'She's a laugh.'

'Remind me next week. I'll take you.'

She kept up her tone of disappointment. 'Mm.'

'In the meantime,' he said, reaching across for his jacket, finding his wallet and pulling it out. 'Treat yourself.' Pushing the hem of her skirt up her thigh, he poked a couple of bank notes into the top of her stocking. Not wanting to seem too cheaply bought off, she left them there, resisting the urge to look and see how much he'd given her. 'Maybe have a beauty treatment or something.'

A beauty treatment indeed. What a nerve.

Without replying, she pulled out the notes and slid her skirt back down her legs. 'You'll be back Sunday?'

'That's right.'

'Then I suppose I'll be having a couple of nights in.'

It wasn't a lie, she told herself, pulling her jacket more closely against the breeze. She would be having a night in Saturday and Sunday. Just not Friday, as he would naturally assume.

* * *

'You don't get car sick, do you?'

Seated alongside Lieutenant Douglas Ross in the shiny little black motorcar, Lou shook her head.

'Not ordinarily, no.'

It all felt so strange. For a start, she was out with someone other than Harry, which was both exciting and terrifying. Then there was the fact that Lieutenant Ross had collected her in a motorcar, which instantly made her feel more elegant and ladylike than she did in Harry's grocery delivery van. At her own suggestion, the lieutenant had picked her up at the bottom of Jubilee Street, which, she had explained, would be easier for him, but which was actually because she feared someone seeing what she was up to and feeling obliged to tell Harry. Even if, after tonight, she decided she didn't want to see Harry any more, she could do without having him accuse her of seeing someone else the moment his back was turned.

The other thing that felt strange was the fact that although she knew nothing about the man sitting next to her, she felt entirely at ease — even taking into account that she shouldn't really be there at all.

'Up here somewhere,' he said, stopping at a junction as though, in the absence of any road signs, to get his bearings, 'there's a little village called Merristowe. It's no more than a big old house and a few cottages but it's got

200

a quaint little inn called The Angler's Rest.'

Had she ever had cause to imagine how Canadians might sound, she reflected as she listened to him speaking, she would have thought them similar to the Americans she'd heard in films — either nasal and twangy or else a long and lazy drawl — but this voice was neither of those. If anything, it was English with a hint of Irish and Scottish, and just the slightest nod to American for good measure. Compared to Harry, Lieutenant Ross's speech was unhurried. He didn't keep fidgeting all the time, either.

A few miles further on, the roads grew narrower about the car, each bend a blind corner, twigs from the hedgerows scratching at the windows as they edged along.

'You won't get into trouble for getting the motorcar dirty, will you?' she asked as they sploshed through a puddle the width of the lane.

Looking briefly across at her, he grinned. 'It isn't booked out to me. I'm just borrowing it from someone else for a couple of hours. But seeing how narrow these roads are, it might be wise to allow plenty time to get back before it's completely dark.'

With that the road came to a dead end, ahead of them a low thatched building with a pretty front garden and a flat grassy area upon which was parked another vehicle. To the left, a wide and shallow stretch of river was wending its way slowly past dense woodland on the opposite bank. And when Lieutenant Ross came around to open her door for her, the thing that struck her first was the silence — evidence, she thought, accepting his hand and getting out, of how used she must have become to the constant clamour and kerfuffle of Devonport.

Smoothing a hand down her skirt, she looked around. It really was a tranquil spot.

'Do you think we might sit outside?' she said, noticing

201

that under the window were a couple of benches that looked as though they'd been hewn from fallen trees.

'I was hoping you might want to do that,' he replied. 'Peace like this is balm for the soul, don't you think?'

'I do. It reminds me of home.'

'Well,' he said, gesturing her across the grass towards the front of the inn, 'if you care to take a seat, then once I've got our drinks, you can tell me all about it. What would you like?'

Suddenly, the drinks she'd normally order with Harry felt inappropriate, brash even. She wondered what Esme would drink but found she had no idea. 'Do you think they would have ginger beer? Or if not, then lemonade?'

'I'll go and find out.'

Once he'd gone in through the porch, she made a quick check of the surface of the bench and sat down. The silence was pronounced, restful, soothing, so much so that even the illicit nature of her presence there was momentarily of no concern.

'Oh,' she said, when he returned moments later with two glasses, the cloudy contents an identical pale golden colour. 'Homemade by the look of it.'

'Brewed by the landlord's wife. He said to let him know if it's too fiery because apparently it turns out differently every time and this is the first of her latest batch.'

When he raised his glass towards her, she did the same. How nice that he knew better than to clink them!

'It tastes lovely,' she said, 'just like Nanny Edith makes.'

From there, their conversation continued in the same relaxed fashion. She explained about her family in Woodicombe — something she realised she had never done with Harry, probably because he had never shown the slightest interest — and, in turn, he told her about his two brothers, also in the navy, and his one sister who'd just had a baby. She learned how, at the encouragement of his elder brother, he'd joined the navy at eighteen *to see something of the world*, and how, had the war not started, he would have had just over two more years to serve until, if he chose, he could leave.

While he talked, she tried to work out his age. If pressed, she'd say he was in his late twenties, even though his fair hair and even skin tone made him look quite boyish. Where Harry's olive complexion often made him look much older — certainly beyond thirty — the lieutenant's colouring and general outdoorsy-ness gave him an air of youth and vitality. And she liked it rather a lot.

As the evening progressed, their conversation didn't falter, their topics wide-ranging.

'Not much,' she answered when he asked her whether North Devon was similar to the southern half of the county. 'It's more rugged and windswept on the north coast. And quieter and more old-fashioned. A bit stuck in the past, according to folk down here.'

'And was that what brought you here to work?'

She grinned. 'Is it that obvious?'

'Not until you just described home. I guess it's the same for country folk everywhere. For sure it is in Canada.'

'Mm.' There was much she would have liked to ask him about Canada but feared making a fool of herself, the only thing she could recall from a geography lesson at school being that in the forests there lived bears who went to the rivers and fished for salmon. It had sounded so unlikely she wondered even now whether it was true.

'People reach that point in their lives where, for the first time, they start to look to the future through adult eyes. And, well, some things look more attractive than others.' He was right of course. It was true of her own circumstances. 'But it doesn't always have to be a one-way move. Home will always be there.'

'Do you know what you'll do once you leave the navy?' she asked him at one point.

'Before I was drafted here, I had started to consider that very point. But now it rather depends upon what happens next, how things turn out with the war, I mean.'

'I suppose so, yes.'

'Say, do you like dancing, Miss Channer?'

She swallowed a gulp. 'I should like to know how to do it — properly, I mean — because it looks such fun. But the only dance I ever learned — sort of — was the waltz. And I only learned how to do *that* because our headmistress thought we should all be capable of waltzing at our own weddings.' Finding herself recounting such a daft thing, she laughed.

'Would you let me teach you something more modern?'

She glanced sideways at him. Was he asking her out again? Was he asking her to go dancing with him? The mere possibility made her well with happiness.

'I should like that.'

'And would you be free tomorrow evening? Or is that too soon?'

'No,' she whispered, unable to believe her good fortune. Harry wouldn't be back until Sunday; he'd said so. 'No, it would be perfect.'

'Then dust off your dancing shoes, Miss Channer, and I'll pick you up at seven.'

'All right. Thank you. But you're going to need the patience of a saint because I really don't know how to dance at all.'

'Then you're in luck because Patience is my middle name!' With that he put down his glass and glanced to the sky — what little of it was visible above the rising hills either side of this narrow little valley. 'But for now, I think we'd best head back into town.'

Moments later, when he had taken their empty glasses inside and they were driving back along the lanes, Lou realised she didn't want the evening to end. She had enjoyed every minute of it, the time flying as they got to know one another. But why put herself through the agony of going out with this lovely man again? She was seeing Harry. Actually, it wasn't just that she was *seeing* him; she was, as he took every opportunity to remind her, *Harry's girl*. And, by now, she knew enough about him to sense that he wouldn't just let her go. She belonged to him; he'd made that abundantly clear.

Staring out through the car window, she sighed heavily. Well, she wouldn't let thoughts of Harry ruin what had been a thoroughly enjoyable evening. Nor would she let it spoil tomorrow. After that, well, she would have to think seriously about what she was going to do. After all, it was more than possible that, after devoting a couple of hours to trying to teach her to dance, Lieutenant Douglas Ross would never want to see her again. And then she'd be glad she hadn't risked Harry's wrath by trying to break up with him.

* * *

Their tram was packed. And it was easy to tell, Lou thought, looking the length of it, which of the couples seated side-by-side were on their first date: giving it away were beads of perspiration on the foreheads of the young men in uniform and the high colour on the cheeks of the girls on their arms. And, just as she had been expecting, when the tram drew to a halt on the promenade, the couples in question all alighted to make their way along the pier to the ballroom at the end — to *the wedding cake* as it was known by the locals.

'I was told,' Lieutenant Ross said as they, too, alighted, and he offered her his arm, 'this is a good place for a beginner, by which,' he went on, 'I'm given to understand it gets crowded enough that no one is too concerned with watching anyone else.'

'Sounds just right, then,' she said. If the place was busy, presumably it also reduced the chances of anyone spotting her out with him. Nevertheless, concerned about drawing too much attention through her choice of dress and being spotted by any of Harry's friends, she'd struggled to decide what to wear. Her new black dress was far too showy, her red one better-suited but inextricably linked with Harry since it had been his money that had bought it. In the end, she'd worn it anyway, her ordinary summer frocks passable for a picnic but not for a dance. And she did want to look nice.

'So, what I thought we'd do,' Lieutenant Ross said, at the last minute steering her away from the entrance to the ballroom and on along the pier to the side of it instead, 'is see whether there's somewhere quiet out here where we can teach you your first steps.'

Oh, what a lovely man he was! So considerate. 'Very thoughtful of you.'

'Like just here,' he said as they came to a recess in the side of the building and the deck opened out into a square shape. 'So, this is what we're going to do.'

'Please,' she said, suddenly worried about making a hopeless mess of it, 'explain it slowly for me.'

'Don't worry. I'm told I'm good at showing people how to do things. Now, just while we get started, rest your hands on my forearms and I'll hold your waist. That

206

way, I can guide you. We're going to do the most basic step of all. Master this, and you can make it fit almost any type of music.'

Placing her hand on the sleeves of his jacket, she nodded. 'All right.'

'And you're going to start by going backwards. So, step back with your right foot and then sideways with your left.'

He was right about being able to guide her. The way he moved made it almost impossible for her to put her feet anywhere other than where he'd said. And when, following his instructions, they ended up back where they had started, she grinned.

'It's like the waltz,' she said at the end of the simple sequence of steps.

'Very similar. But once it's fixed in your mind, you can jazz it up to suit the mood of the music and yet still allow your partner to anticipate where you're going next.'

'Clever,' she remarked.

'So, let's do it again but, this time, keep going, repeat it over and over.'

'And now,' he said, once they had settled back into the rhythm, 'we'll take proper hold.'

'All right.' To her surprise, holding his hand and having his other pressing gently into her back felt entirely natural, the gap between their bodies sufficient not to make her feel uncomfortable.

'That's good,' he said, his continued hold of her meaning she had no choice but to keep going.

'What's next?'

'Next,' he said, 'you stop looking at your feet and look at your partner.'

'Oh! Yes. Sorry.'

'And then you try not to be so stiff. Lower your

shoulders, relax your arms. Feel the music, let it move you.'

At this last instruction, she burst into laughter. 'But we haven't got any music!' Her concentration broken, she fumbled her steps. 'Sorry!'

'It's all right,' he said. 'You missed my feet. So, what say you we go on in and give it a shot?'

Lightly breathless, she smiled. 'I'd like that.'

'Me too.'

After that, the evening passed far too quickly. They danced until the band took a break, when he bought her a lemonade and they eventually found a table at which to sit and catch their breath.

'This is fun,' she said.

He looked back at her. 'Isn't it?'

'Exhausting but fun.'

And when the band returned to play some more, they danced again, and she discovered that he was right: once you got the hang of it, you could sort of make it up as you went along; he could release his hold and she could twirl under his arm; and when the music was slower, he could draw her back against him and they need barely move. Above all, her fear of making a fool of herself evaporated and she found that she hadn't thought once — until that very moment — about the rights and wrongs of being there with him to start with.

'Do you have to be home by a certain time?' he asked a while later.

'Our landlady's curfew is half-past ten,' she said. 'But I have a key and she doesn't draw the bolt.'

'But we still have to make sure not to miss the last tram.'

Bother. Yes, of course, she'd forgotten they'd come by tram.

'That's true. After all this dancing, my feet would never forgive me if we had to walk.'

'Come on, then,' he said, drawing her towards the entrance, 'because I shouldn't want to have to be chivalrous and try to carry you, either.'

She laughed. In truth, she didn't think he'd have the least problem carrying her the entire distance. Compared to Harry, he looked so effortlessly athletic he could probably sweep her clean off her feet, carry her up the hill and not even break into a sweat.

Once aboard the tram towards Devonport, they sat in amiable contemplation.

'I've still got music in my head,' she said after a while. 'And my feet want to move to it.'

'Music gets you like that. Next time I'll have to teach you something else, something a little snazzier.'

Next time. He was talking about doing this again.

'Mm.'

When they alighted at her stop, he offered her his arm and she took it. And, when they started to walk, she deeply regretted that their date was at an end.

'So, how about—' But he didn't get any further because, almost directly above them, the air raid siren started up. 'Spot of luck,' he raised his voice to say and turned about. 'We're close to the dockyard. Come on. We can get in just along here.'

Having reached into his breast pocket for his identity card and shown it to the sentry on the gate, he led her along the side of a building, through a door and down a flight of stone steps lit by a succession of dim bulbs.

Holding onto his hand, Lou did her best to keep up. 'Where are we?' she asked as he opened a door, reached to flick on the light and then stood looking about.

'In one of the unofficial shelters. This far up from the

docks, these old buildings all have cellars. Rule is you seek shelter in whichever is closest. We'll be all right here, even if it's the dockyard they're after.'

Even if it's the dockyard they're after. Oddly, she'd never thought of her place of work as being a target for enemy bombers but, thinking about it now, it was obvious; the Germans would love to cripple the navy.

'We haven't had many raids, have we?' she said, watching him drag two chairs from the corner and dust them off with his hand.

'Here, sit down. I don't think it'll dirty your dress.' She did as he said, thinking that above them, the siren sounded really distant. 'And no, surprisingly few raids, though I have an idea that will change.'

'I hope not.'

'We all do.'

'Yes.' Silly thing to say, really. Who in their right mind hoped for air raids?

'I'd offer you a cigarette, but I don't smoke.'

She smiled. 'It's all right. Neither do I.'

'Though times like these I often think about taking it up.'

'Yes.'

'Look,' he said, putting the other chair down in front of her and sitting astride it. 'When I said we'll be all right down here, I meant it. These old buildings have been here for hundreds of years, some of them built to serve as gunpowder stores. So, you can imagine how thick they made these walls.'

'Yes.' But it wasn't the prospect of being bombed that had made her go quiet — though perhaps it should have been — it was that she'd had a lovely time and wanted to do it again. But she couldn't because of Harry.

'Tell me about Westward Quay,' he said. 'I have that

210

right, don't I?'

She nodded. He was trying to distract her, she knew that, but she told him about it anyway. 'I think it's the smells and the sounds I miss most,' she said, having described to him the harbour, the cobbled streets with their little shops, the railway station and the village green with its imposing gothic church. 'I miss the smell of woodsmoke. Here it's all dirty coal. I miss the birdsong at dawn and dusk. Here it's just screeching gulls and cawing crows. I miss the smell of mown hay and freshly dug carrots. Here, it's all hot tarmac and petrol fumes. Even the sea doesn't smell as clean.' She also missed the smell of her mother's Pears soap, and the scent of sawdust in her father's workshop but thought that an admission too far.

When she eventually looked up, it was to see that he was smiling.

'Homesickness gets you here, doesn't it?' He pressed a curled fist to the centre of his chest.

'I never thought of it as homesickness — just things I miss.'

'You could apply for some leave, you know. I could see to it that you got a few days to go home and see your folks, if that's what you wanted.'

She gave the tiniest of shrugs. 'I have been meaning to go and see Mum...'

'Well, the offer's there.'

'Thank you. It's very kind. What do *you* miss about home?' she asked, anxious to move the conversation away from subjects that might make her cry — especially given the way that she had begun to feel rather sorry for herself.

'The wide-open spaces. The cleanliness of the air. Sometimes, it's so fresh it almost hurts your lungs. And the colours. There's something about the light that makes them so sharp you find yourself squinting.'

Far above them, the All Clear sounded. 'Didn't last long tonight,' she observed.

'Most likely a false alarm. It will be safe to get you home now.'

But, turning the corner into Jubilee Street, she was gripped by a sense of panic. She didn't want to let him go — didn't want to let *this* go, this sense of calm, of everything being *all right*. But what to do? He'd mentioned going dancing again and it was something she wanted very much. But she wasn't free to just go out with him. She belonged to Harry.

At the doorstep to number eleven, she reached into her shoulder bag for her key. Then she slipped it into the lock, all the while struggling to work out what to say. And what to do if he moved to kiss her, wishing he would but hoping he didn't.

In the end, aware that neither of them was saying anything, she turned back to face him. 'I had a lovely time.'

He smiled warmly. 'Me too.'

'Thank you.'

'Would I be pushing my luck to ask if you'd like to do something similar next weekend?'

'You wouldn't be, no.' Good God, what was she doing? How on earth did she think she was going to avoid going out with Harry on a Saturday night? These last two evenings had been sheer fluke. Perfect timing.

'Then perhaps,' he said, standing with his hands behind his back, 'I could let you know on Friday where I've found for us to go?'

Trying to raise a smile to cover the fact that she felt like crying, she nodded. 'All right.'

'Well, goodnight, Miss Channer.'

'Goodnight, Lieutenant Ross. And thank you again for a lovely evening.'

'The pleasure was all mine.'

Having reluctantly taken her leave of him, she stepped inside and closed the door. Now she was in trouble. Now she had six days in which to work out how to let him down lightly — to come up with an excuse for why she wouldn't be able to go out with him again without giving away that she was already spoken for.

Bending to unfasten her shoes, she took them off and padded up the stairs. In her room, she unclipped her earrings, pulled the pins from her hair and then went to look at herself in the mirror above the basin. If she was quick, she could get undressed and be in bed before Jean came home and spotted that she'd been out; that woman had an uncanny knack for reading her mood and asking difficult questions, something she could really do without right now.

Unbuttoning her dress, she slipped it onto its hanger and hung it on the outside of the wardrobe to air. Then she unscrewed the lid of her tin of Crowes Cremine and started applying it to her face. Wiping away the excess, and with it her make-up, she stared at her reflection. Sometimes these days, she barely recognised herself — not her actual appearance, although she *was* beginning to wonder whether she might tone down the eyeliner and the lipstick — but the person she had become. She wouldn't deny how desperately she'd wanted to get out of Woodicombe and grow up. And she'd done that. Golly, she'd done that. But just who had she become — deceiving everyone around her without a second thought? She kept secrets from her parents. She kept secrets from Jean and the girls. She'd kept an almighty secret from Lieutenant Ross, and now she was going to have to keep one from Harry. She might only have let the lieutenant take her out for a drink, and then gone dancing with him — he hadn't even kissed her

— if Harry found out, he would explode into a rage. To be fair, what man wouldn't? She'd gone behind his back. And when he'd been so generous with her, as well.

Slipping off her underwear, and pulling on her night-dress in its place, she sighed wearily. Well, clearly, she couldn't breathe a word of this to Harry. She couldn't confess, tell him what she'd done and hope he'd forgive her. If it had just been a drink, she might have been able to say that a group of them from the dockyard had all gone out together. But the trouble with inventing something like that would be making it sound convincing. No, she thought, pulling back her eiderdown and getting into bed. Far better to say nothing and, when she felt guilty, remind herself of the trouble she risked by telling the truth.

Extinguishing the lamp, she lay staring up into the darkness. Ironic, really, she thought, that the man with whom she'd just behaved deceitfully should be the one with whom she'd been the most truthful: she did miss Woodicombe. She would never admit it to Mum and Dad but, for all the independence and the friendship and the glamour leaving there had given her, this new life didn't feel much like home. She wasn't even making a very good job of it; look at her, all tangled up with two men, the pair of them as different as chalk and cheese. And that was without reckoning on what she'd let Harry do on just their second date... and whenever the mood had taken him since. In truth, she probably didn't deserve someone as polite and considerate and wholesome as Lieutenant Ross, not any more, anyway.

Aware that she stood little chance of falling asleep, she nevertheless plumped her pillow and tried to get comfortable. If only she could start again. If only she could turn up here now, be diligent at her work and behave more like Nora and Liddy, content to go into town on Saturdays for tea and a bun, and dream about meeting 'her type' and then have him woo her chastely. Chastely. Huh. Bit late for that.

With a despairing sigh, she rolled onto her back. But *was* it too late? Granted, she couldn't reclaim her... her purity... but what if she did sort of start over? She didn't have to worry about her job; she was already competent at that. So, what if — carefully and discreetly, so as not to appear either desperate or insincere — she spent more time with the girls, made proper friends of them? And what if — and here was the hard part — she stopped seeing Harry and found a way to draw a veil over the last few weeks? Then she could let Lieutenant Ross court her like the gentleman he clearly was. Wouldn't that be more along the lines of the life she'd hoped to find here? The prospect of pulling it off certainly made her feel better. It wouldn't be an easy task but, in the morning, with a clear head, perhaps she could come up with a plan. What she could really do with, of course, was Esme; *she* would immediately see what had to be done. But Lou didn't even know where she was. Besides, she wasn't sure she'd want to be *completely* truthful about what she'd been doing, even with *Esme*. No, she'd got herself into this mess, and so she would have to be the one to get herself out of it.

In fact, when she awoke the next morning, it was with an even stronger sense that starting over was the right course of action. Finding a way out of her muddle might prove tricky but reaching a decision about the need to do so wasn't. She would end it with Harry. It was clear now that her attraction to him had only ever been based on him being like no one she'd known before; his forthright manner and way of going after what he wanted had felt thrilling. More recently she had come to see how, with that very unfamiliarity, with that drive of his, came down-

215

sides: he never asked her opinion or consulted her about anything, only ever telling her what was going to happen; he considered her less important than his business even when they were out on a supposed date. Oh, and he truly believed that giving her money to go and buy *something nice* smoothed over every little upset. Well, his ways were disrespectful. And, of late, growing irksome.

In fact, having now been in the company of a man who was about as different from him as it was possible to be, she recognised this morning that she'd grown weary of Harry Hinds and her role as his docile possession. That said, act in haste to remedy the situation and she risked jumping out of the fat and into the fire. In going out with Harry that first time, she had never expected to one day end up at his beck and call, which was, she could see know, what had happened. And it was a trap she had to avoid falling into with anyone else. So, although she was sure Lieutenant Ross was nothing like Harry Hinds, if she was going to throw over the one for the other, she had to be certain.

Either way, she thought, glancing across to Jean's sleeping form before folding back the bedcovers and getting out of bed, even if matters between her and Lieutenant Ross never went any further, she would always have him to thank for opening her eyes about Harry, for bringing her to realise what she wasn't prepared to tolerate from a boyfriend — from any boyfriend — from now on.

★ ★ ★

Unsurprisingly, Harry was full of himself.

'Go an' sit by the window and I'll bring you over a gin and orange,' he said as they went in through the doors of a pub called The Globe.

It was one evening that week, the couple of days that

had passed between her reaching her decision and Harry actually arriving to take her out only hardening Lou's resolve to be done with him. And, now, here she was, her opportunity before her.

Thankfully, the place to which he'd brought her was only a street or two away from The Hoe, which would at least mean she could get most of the way home by tram. She'd even planned ahead for that very eventuality and worn sensible shoes. But, golly, she was nervous. How would he react when she told him? She did hope he wouldn't cause a scene.

'All right,' she said wearily as he continued on towards the bar.

'Harry Hinds, as I live and breathe.'

If the reaction from the barman was anything to go by, give it a few moments and Harry would be deep in conversation about business. Even going three or four days without seeing her wasn't enough for him to put her first not for a moment. They'd barely exchanged a dozen words on the drive here. And, on the subject of the drive here, had his van always had a sort of damp vegetable smell about it? And if so, how was she only now noticing the fact? But then when it came to Harry Hinds, how had it taken her so long to notice a lot of things?

As he'd instructed, she went nonetheless to take a seat by the window, its grimy and obscured glass criss-crossed with tape, a measure supposed to prevent shards of it from flying everywhere in the event of a bomb exploding. A bomb would be a kindness to the dingy place, she thought as she took in the pretend leather chairs and grubby tables, the threadbare carpet and dusty glass lampshades. Anyone in their right mind would have to be pretty desperate to want to come and sit in here and drink. And if this was the lounge, then she could only imagine what the public bar and its clientele would be like.

Unusually, once Harry had been presented with their drinks, he came directly to join her. His business, whatever it was, clearly didn't involve the barman.

'So, how did you get on in Bristol?' she asked. She couldn't just dive in and tell him it was over between them not when he'd just bought her a gin and orange. Best work her way around to it. A suitable moment was bound to present itself.

'Worth making the trip. How's the dockyard? Still busy?'

Raising her glass, she took a sip of her drink. How typical that on the night she planned on dumping him, he should actually sit down with her and chat — show an interest in her work. But did they really have nothing better to talk about?

'Busier by the day. More operations getting going means more movement of goods. There's even talk of a night shift. And the week after next, we're getting another girl.'

'More hands make light work... and all that.'

'Yes.'

'Any news on your brother?'

And now he was even enquiring about Arthur! What the devil had brought this on — this unexpected cour-teousness? Tonight, of all nights, she could do without him showing concern for her well-being.

Fighting to keep a lid on her despair, she shook her head. 'Not yet. Our best hope now is that he will be on the list of men picked up and taken prisoner. But no one can tell us when the Germans will let our government have the names.'

'Your ma must be beside herself.'

218

'She is. I've been thinking about going home to see her.'

'Yeah? When?'

What did it matter to *him* when she went? It wasn't as though he would miss her even if she went for a fortnight. Not that she would.

'I don't know. I'm not even sure if I *will* go. It's only a thought I had.'

'Bet she'd be glad to see you.'

'Mm.' It was no good; she had to get on and do this before she lost her nerve. Much more of this sympathy from him and she'd change her mind. 'Harry...'

'Yep?'

Oh, dear God. Now her heart was beating so fast she was beginning to feel light-headed.

'Last week, a man asked me out.'

Looking back at him, she held her breath.

'Did he, now?'

That neither his tone nor his expression gave anything away made her wish she'd kept quiet.

'Yes.'

'Since you're sitting here with me now, I take it you turned him down.' Deep inside her head, a little voice was screaming at her to say that, actually, not only had she not turned him down, she'd already been out with him. Twice. Instead, unsurprisingly, she flushed. 'Who was he, then, this chancer who didn't know you were Harry's girl? Some cheeky blighter of a skate wanting to sweet-talk you up the pier for a dance and a quick grope behind the breakwaters afterwards?'

Christ he could be odious at times. Not all sailors were like that. Freddie wouldn't have been.

'Actually, it was one of the Canadians. A lieutenant, in fact.'

For a split second, he seemed taken aback. 'Yeah?'

'Uh-huh.'

'And you turned him down? A Canadian? In uniform? I'm surprised. According to most girls they're quite the catch.'

'If you say so.'

'Look,' he said, pausing to down the remainder of his drink and then get to his feet, 'don't let *me* stand in your way. If that's what you want, go ahead. Say yes to the man.'

'But —'

'Seriously, Lou. If your heart's not in this any more ...'

What was he saying? Was *he* dumping *her*?

'I didn't say that —'

'I mean, all good things come to an end, right?'

No, he couldn't do this! She wouldn't let him. After all she'd been through for him, *he* couldn't be the one to decide when this was over, to deny her that one little piece of satisfaction.

'Harry —'

'S'up to you, Lou. If you don't want to be Harry's girl no more, I'll find someone who does.' In his eyes was a steeliness she'd never seen before. And it frightened her. 'Now, what I'm going to do is pop upstairs and see someone. And while I'm up there, you think about what it is you want.'

With no control over the matter, she started to cry.

'H-how l-long will you be?'

'As long as it takes. So, you can either sit there nicely and wait for me to come back down, or you can leave. Like I say, it's up to you. But, *if* you leave, know this. There's no coming back. No second thoughts. And if you *do* decide to go, then that fox fur you're wearing, and that bracelet on your wrist? You can leave them with Larry behind the bar. The dress you can keep.'

With that, he turned away, crossed the room to a door in the far corner and disappeared through it without once looking back.

Wiping a hand across her cheeks, she stared down into her lap. How dare he? How dare he be the one to give the ultimatums? *She* was the one leaving *him*, not the other way around. Although, in a way, perhaps he'd just made her task easier.

Looking down at her bracelet, she twisted it around her wrist until she found the clasp, unfastened it and got to her feet. Walking towards the bar, she slid her beloved fox fur from her shoulders.

'Here,' the fellow behind it said to her, reaching for a glass, 'have another. On the 'ouse.'

'No, thank you,' she replied as evenly as her anger and her distress would allow. 'But when Harry comes back down, please give him these.' Onto the bar she put the stole and, on top of that, her bracelet. They might be the nicest things anyone had ever given her, but she could see now that they were nothing more than shackles, shackles that Harry Hinds could have back. She would make her fresh start free from the frippery that would otherwise only serve to remind her of her mistake.

Chapter 8

Out of the Blue

This, this was wonderful. In fact, as evenings went, she doubted it could be bettered. Here she was, in the splendid surroundings of the Princess Ballroom of The Majestic Hotel, dining and dancing with the kindest and most sincere of men, Lieutenant Douglas Ross, RCN. And she was enjoying every moment.

Yesterday evening, when they'd once again been sitting outside The Angler's Rest, and he'd told her that he'd arranged for them to go to a supper dance at The Majestic Hotel, she was pretty sure she'd gasped. And then, of course, she'd been thrown into a panic. Whatever was she going to wear to such a posh place? Her red dress was far too well worn. And the black one she'd had made up to a similar pattern was just too… well, to be blunt, too tarty. For a night at Ruby's with Harry it would have been fine but, for The Majestic with Lieutenant Ross, frighteningly unsuitable and, in any event, with all that exposed flesh, only ever intended to be worn with Harry's fox-fur stole.

So, this morning, shunning Marianne's little dress shop because she suspected there to be some sort of connection between Harry and Myrtle, the daughter of the proprietress, who had helped her last time, she had gone instead to Dingle's. She would have liked the company of one of the girls for a second opinion but didn't need the interrogation that would surely have ensued. *Ooh, hark at her — only gone and snagged herself a Canadian! What's his name? What's he like? Where's he taking you?* Admit that it was Lieutenant

Ross and she would never hear the end of it. And that was without what it might do to the friendship with Liddy and Flossie she was so tentatively rekindling.

Looking around the ballroom now at the dozens of elegant women, she felt she had chosen well. Guided by a knowledgeable assistant from the 'Occasions Wear' department — *No, Miss, definitely not red with your hair and complexion* — she had used every shilling she had been able to scrape together (a fair proportion of them Harry's) to buy a lovely rayon dress in a shade described by the assistant as *dark emerald.* A simple shift affair that fell to just below her knees, it was saved from being ordinary by a chiffon overlay from shoulder to waist. To raise the appearance further, stitched here and there upon the chiffon were tiny beads of crystal. It wasn't the showiest of outfits, nor was it of the latest styling, but wearing it made her feel both demure and classy. As Mum's gran, Nanny Mabel, would have said, *no one was going to stop a runaway horse to look at her,* but then she had no desire to be gawped at. Knowing that Douglas would be immaculate in his uniform, her main concern had been not to show him up. And she could sit here now, confident in the knowledge that she hadn't.

Playing this evening was a seventeen-piece big band, to the music of which Douglas had already taught her some new steps. Dancing with him proved as joyous as she remembered from the previous week. It was also thirsty work but, in her bid to consign all reminders of Harry to history, she had quelled the instinct to ask for a gin and orange and stuck instead to bitter lemon.

With Harry briefly on her mind, she found herself wondering whether he had already replaced her. Was he, at this moment, giving perfume to some other girl? Was someone else about to be given her sparkly bracelet and fox-fur stole? Apart from wishing she could warn the poor soul, what did it matter? She had left him. And for someone so very much nicer, too.

Later that evening, returned to the doorstep of number eleven with just the most chaste of kisses on her cheek, she felt as though she was walking on clouds. Nowhere about her body did she feel tense; nowhere in her head was there a little voice reminding her what to do or not do to keep anyone else happy. Being out with Douglas was simply joyous. Perfect. And yes, she *had* thought that once before but, this time, it was different. This time, she really did feel as though her dream of meeting a wonderful man and leading an interesting and grown-up life was coming true.

★ ★ ★

'Hullo? Hullo? Lou, is that you?'

'Yes? Hello? Who is this please?'

When Winnie had come upstairs to announce that there was a telephone call for her, and that the caller was a woman, Lou's first thought had been that it was her mother; no other women she could think of knew the number. Given the crackling on the line, though, she could barely tell that Winnie had been right about it being a woman, let alone who it was.

'Lou, it's Esme.' *Did that faint little voice just say Esme?* 'Lou, is that you? Are you there?'

'Esme! Good Lord, it *is* you! I wasn't sure. How on earth did you know to ring me *here*?'

'I rang Woodicombe. Your father answered. Told me you'd got fixed up with something in Plymouth. Something about the dockyard?'

With the static on their line seeming to settle, their

224

connection became a little clearer.

'That's right.' Golly, it really was Esme! 'I have a job as a clerk at the Royal Canadian Navy depot in Devonport Dockyard. I share a room in a house just up the road. Quite a few of us from there lodge here.'

'And are you enjoying it?'

'I am. I really like it. What about you? Where are you now? Mum mentioned being able to write to you care of somewhere in London.'

'That's right. I'm working for the government, but I can't talk about what I do nor where I do it. Not that I'd want to. It's terribly boring.'

Lou giggled. Knowing Esme, her work would be anything *but* boring, especially if, as she had just intimated, the nature of it was secret. Pound to a penny she wasn't writing entries into dusty ledgers. But then neither was she likely to be meeting nice men. Canadian men, at that.

'Top secret. Goodness. Do you like it?'

'I do. Has there been much bombing where you are?'

'Very little. You?' Picturing Douglas — Lieutenant Ross, as she was still calling him then — taking her down into that little basement the other night, she smiled.

'A lot of activity nearby but only the odd incident here. So far, at least.'

Now she'd forgotten what Esme was talking about! 'That's good.'

'Anyway, how are you?' Esme asked. 'Are you all right? I feel mean about being quiet for so long but with this job … well, you know how it is.'

'I'm fine,' she said. And she was, too — these last few days she'd felt bright and bubbly again, as though a great weight had been lifted from her. 'More than fine, to be honest. I was seeing this chap — my roommate's step-brother, actually — but that's ended now and… well, let's just say I'm seeing someone else, someone far nicer.'

'Lou Channer. You little minx! You'd better not let your father find out.'

'Don't worry. I don't tell Mum and Dad the half of what we get up to down here. It would send them grey. Anyway, what about you? Are you seeing anyone?'

'No time for it,' Esme replied succinctly. 'With everything being so secretive, I couldn't see anyone on a regular basis anyway, even if I wanted to.'

'No. Suppose not. Look, Esme,' she said, catching sight of Jess pulling a displeased face at her, 'I'm sorry to be rude, but I'm getting dirty looks from the girls queueing to use the telephone—'

'It's all right. I have somewhere to be too.'

'— but it's real lovely of you to call. And I'm so pleased you're all right. Truly I am.'

'And I'm pleased you've escaped from Woodicombe. It sounds as though you're having fun.'

'I am. Well, thanks again, Esme. Bye!'

'Bye Lou. Do take care.'

Putting down the receiver and walking away, Lou smiled warmly. Her dear cousin and friend, Esme, was happy: a lovely piece of news to end what was turning out to be a lovely week because, tonight, she was being taken out again by Lieutenant Ross — by *Douglas* — and she couldn't be happier.

★ ★ ★

'Lieutenant Ross.'

'Miss Channer. How are you this afternoon?'

'I'm fine… thank you. And you, Lieutenant?'

'Rather well, actually.'

It was the following Monday afternoon and, although

it was unusual for Lieutenant Ross to come by the warehouse so late in the day, Lou was thrilled that he had.

'Something you wanted to check in the ledgers?' she asked, aware that at the sound of a man's voice, Liddy's and Flossie's ears would have pricked up.

'If it's not too much trouble.'

With his back to the warehouse, he winked at her, and to which she did her best not to grin.

'It's no trouble at all. Won't you come in?'

When he followed her into the office, and took care to leave the door ajar, she pulled the current month's ledger from the shelf, put it on the desk and opened it at random.

'Just thought I'd drop by and say how much I enjoyed Saturday night,' he said, his voice lowered. 'And Friday, of course.'

Before replying, she glanced to the door. There was no reason for Liddy or Flossie to be suspicious and decide to eavesdrop but the two of them could be furtive when it suited them.

'I enjoyed it too. The orchestra was incredible.'

'Weren't they? Someone told me The Majestic was a stuffy place, but I liked it.'

'So did I. Very much.'

'You know, not so long ago, Duke Ellington and his orchestra played there.'

'Really? I should love to have seen them.'

'Perhaps we should go again. In a couple of weeks?'

She smiled warmly. 'I should like that.'

'But this Saturday, we'll do something else. Assuming you're up for going out again, that is.'

She could only hope that by smiling so much she wasn't making herself look simple. 'Oh, I think I could bear it.'

Drawing away from the table, he adopted a more formal tone. 'Well, keep up the good work, Miss

Channer. The three of you are doing a stellar job.'

'Thank you, Lieutenant Ross. We do our best.'

'What did *he* want?' Liddy poked her head around the door to ask the moment he'd left.

'We in trouble again?' Flossie wanted to know, arriving alongside her.

'Not at all,' Lou answered, hoping she didn't look as flushed as she felt. 'He just wanted to check up on something.'

Already, Flossie had lost interest. 'Ten minutes till we can push off.'

Lou glanced to the clock. 'You might as well go now. It's ten to six. Nothing's going to turn up this late in the day.'

Neither Flossie nor Liddy needed telling twice.

'See ya, then.'

'Yeah, see you in the morning, Lou,' Flossie responded before turning to accompany Liddy out.

Moving to the door and watching the two of them strolling together across the yard, Lou sighed. They'd be cross if they found out she'd been keeping a secret from them. But she couldn't tell them — wouldn't even dream of doing so without checking with Douglas first. While he'd never told her to keep their relationship quiet, merely mentioning that ratings and non-commissioned officers — whatever they were — were forbidden to date local girls, she didn't want to risk trouble for him.

Turning back to pack up for the night, she was surprised to hear the sound of engines. To her dismay, she then saw that coming down the ramp was a military lorry with a camouflage-painted cab and canvas roof over the load area. Puzzled, she watched it continue towards her. Behind it appeared a second identical lorry, and then a third. What was going on?

'Sorry to turn up so late, love.' Down from the cab of the first vehicle jumped a man who, to Lou's mind, looked as though he was the one in charge. 'Would have been here a couple of hours ago but one of the lorries burst a tyre and the blasted wheel nuts were seized. Pardon my language. It took us forever to get the ruddy spare on.'

Wondering how she'd missed being informed about an operation, Lou frowned at him. 'On your way over from where?' If she had been told there was a collection due this afternoon, she must have forgotten. But then, to be fair, her concentration had been a bit wayward today; when Miss Blatchford had come over this morning, she could easily have been daydreaming about Douglas and their evening at The Majestic and missed it.

'Pompey.' None the wiser, she stared back at him. '*Portsmuff*.'

'Heavens. How are you going to get back *there* tonight?' she asked, more through frustration at having to stay late than from any real interest.

He came towards her. 'Since there's some big operation on, as quick as we can.'

'Can I have your requisition?'

He reached into the cab of his lorry. 'Here. It's all in order.'

She ran her eyes over the paperwork. 'This is a long list.'

'Yeah. And urgent as hell. Hush-hush, too. So, any chance of a couple of lads to help us load up?'

She shook her head. How could she have known there was still a collection outstanding? 'I'm afraid they've gone home.'

'Good job there's three of us, then. Come on, lads, at the double. We're going to be in enough trouble when we get back as it is.'

229

And so, with the three drivers trotting back and forth without even pausing for breath, Lou directed them around the warehouse to the goods on the requisition, checking them off as they left the shelves.

'Well, that seems to be everything,' she eventually said, finally emerging from the warehouse to see them securing the covers to their trucks.

'Yeah. Sorry again for keeping you, Miss.'

'No matter. Here, these are your copies.'

'Oh. Yeah. Ta. Wouldn't want to get back without those!'

And then, one by one, the three lorries re-formed into their convoy and headed away up the ramp.

Thank goodness they'd been so quick, Lou thought as she watched them leave. If they'd been as slow as some of the drivers that turned up, she would have been there till nightfall.

Arriving back at Jubilee Street, she was grateful to find that Mrs Hannacott had kept a plate of tea for her. Exhausted, she sat down to eat.

'You don't seem to be out quite so much this last week,' her landlady said. 'Changed your fella?'

Lou grinned. Very little got past Mrs H unless she wanted it to.

'Happen I have.'

'Fed up with that other one?'

'Fed up with his ways,' she said, devouring the last mouthful of corned beef fritter and setting down her knife and fork.

'Good for you. You'll never change a wrong 'un, you know.' Leaning against the doorframe, Mrs Hannacott took a long pull on her cigarette. 'Try till you're blue in the face, you'll never change their ways. So, if you was fed up, then no doubt you done the right thing.'

230

'*I* think so,' Lou answered brightly. 'Though I doubt he would agree.'

Pleased to have avoided the need to relay the sorry details of her parting with Harry, Lou went up to her room, where she found Jean darning a stocking.

'You done with Harry then?' her roommate asked without even looking up.

Withholding a sigh, Lou turned to close the door. Clearly, everyone had put two and two together.

'I am.'

'Warned you, didn't I?' Jean said, bending to bite off the end of the length of cotton. 'I'm hoping that won't show under my skirt,' she went on, holding up the stocking to examine the darn. 'Caught it on a ruddy hangnail. My last pair as well.'

Lou squinted across. 'Put it on and I'll tell you if I can see it.'

'Thanks.'

'No, you're fine,' Lou said of the darn when Jean stood up.

'So, he dumped you, then.'

'Actually, no. *I* dumped *him*.'

Jean raised an eyebrow. 'Yeah? What was his crime?'

'Nothing especially — that I know of. He just made me feel... weary.'

'Hm. Got someone new?'

There was no point in lying. Everyone knew she was still getting dressed up and going out. But that didn't mean she had to tell all.

'Someone did ask me out... but it's a bit too soon to tell how it'll go.'

'Yeah, well, if Harry wants you back, and you don't want to go, stick to your guns. No matter what he tells you, he won't change his ways. Whatever you got fed up with first time around will still drive you mad. And I don't say that just about Harry, either. Trust me. I know. Not very good at taking my own advice, though.'

'Thanks,' Lou said, hoping that signalled an end to the matter. 'I'll bear that in mind.'

'Right then.' Getting to her feet, Jean smoothed a hand down her skirt. 'See you later.'

'Yes. Have a nice time.'

With Jean gone, Lou slumped onto the end of her bed. If no one was in the bathroom, she might go and have a bath — make the most of not having to get all dressed up on a weekday night only to then sit, ignored and growing bored out of her brains, while Harry went about his *business*. And what a relief not to have to worry about the mood he'd be in, either, or about accidentally upsetting him. In fact, she had to wonder now how it had taken her so long to call it a day. She still couldn't believe she'd said yes to Douglas that first time though. But, now that she'd found someone considerate and gentlemanly, she would work hard, make him proud of the way she went about her duties at work and enjoy every moment of their evenings together. And she might even tell her parents about him… but only when the moment felt completely right, of course.

★   ★   ★

'What the ruddy hell's with all the stuffed shirts?'

It was the following morning and, as Lou and Liddy walked towards the warehouse to start work, Lou found herself wondering the same thing. If the amount of gold braid on some of their uniforms was anything to go by, some very senior Canadian officials had taken it upon themselves to come across and open up the warehouse this morning.

'No idea,' Lou said, a sudden wariness causing her to slow her pace. 'But look, there's Flossie. Happen she'll know.'

With that, Flossie came scurrying towards them. 'Hey, you two,' she said, her eyes wide. 'You won't believe this! We've been burgled!'

Liddy and Lou exchanged glances. 'Burgled?'

'Some time last night. They've took a whole load of stuff. Ever so much.'

Realising the mistake, Lou laughed. 'No,' she said. 'We haven't been burgled. There was a late pick-up. Just after you two left, three trucks arrived from Portsmouth.'

'Then you best go an' tell the big wigs,' Flossie said, 'since they've only gone an' called the police.'

Scanning the gathering of uniformed officials, Lou spotted Douglas. 'I'll go and tell Lieutenant Ross. I can see him talking to Miss Blatchford.'

Seeing Lou approach and then wait nearby, Lieutenant Ross excused himself and came towards her. 'I imagine Miss Pascoe has told you the news.'

Lou couldn't help smiling; she'd never seen him look so worried. 'She told me we've been burgled. But it's all right, we haven't.'

His expression of concern turned to one of puzzlement. 'We haven't? I don't understand. The warehouse is almost half empty.'

'There was a late pick-up,' she said, 'three lorries from Portsmouth. Some big operation all in a rush. I've got the requisition. It's going to take hours to write up.'

'Come in and show me. But you should know that Commander Dutton is here.'

She understood what he meant; it was a warning to observe all of the usual proprieties. 'Of course.'

'Commander Dutton, sir, this is Miss Channer,' Douglas addressed his superior as they went into the office. 'Miss Channer is the clerk responsible for records and she's just informed me that late yesterday, a requisition from Portsmouth was fulfilled — a large one for an urgent operation. She says she has the papers.' Turning towards her, he went on, 'Go ahead, Miss Channer.'

'I've not written it up yet,' she explained, reaching into the tray labelled 'IN' and lifting out the sheets of the requisition document. 'The lorries didn't arrive until just before six o'clock. Luckily, they were real fast loading up and so I wasn't kept too late.' How funny that everyone's first thought should be to think they'd been burgled. Later, she and Douglas would have a good laugh about it. 'There you go, Lieutenant Ross, sir.'

Accepting the sheaf of papers from her, Douglas glanced the length of the uppermost sheet and then passed them to Commander Dutton. 'Miss Channer, you said these men mentioned there being a rush.'

She nodded. 'That's right. Said they'd be in trouble for being late back it was so urgent.'

'Thank you, Miss Channer. Please go and wait with the others while we look into this.'

'Was he cross?' Flossie wanted to know when Lou arrived back outside.

'Cross?'

'The top brass — at having egg on his face.'

She tried to picture the commander's expression. 'I wouldn't say cross, no. More flummoxed that no one had told him about such a big operation.'

''Spect it's top secret,' Flossie went on.

'Must be,' Lou said idly. 'But what I don't understand is why someone came over so early this morning to open up. Oftentimes, we're left standing here, waiting to make a start, and it's ages before anyone remembers to come over with the keys.'

'It was Miss Blatchford that came. I heard her telling one of the Canadians—'

'Heard her or *over*heard her?' Liddy butted in.

'All right, yes, I was eavesdropping. But don't you act all *holier than thou*, Liddy Knight. You do the same.'

'So, what did you overhear?' Lou pressed her friend. This whole business was beginning to feel peculiar. For certain, *something* wasn't what it seemed.

'I heard her say she'd come down here deliberately early to check up on us — see what time we all got here. She said it was just a routine check. And then she let herself in and couldn't believe her eyes.'

'And her first thought was that we'd been burgled?' To Lou's mind, it seemed a bit of an odd conclusion to leap to, especially if Miss Blatchford had needed to undo the padlock, there being no signs of anyone having broken in.

'Must have been, 'cause she sent someone for Lieutenant Ross, who sent for Commander Dutton.'

'And you know all this from listening in?' Lou said.

'From that and from asking Miss Blatchford. She was white as a sheet.'

'Then she must be relieved to find there hadn't been a burglary at all.'

Flossie shrugged. 'We're going to need to make sure we're on time for a while, though, that's for sure. Sneaky woman, coming down here to check up on us.'

'We're *always* here on time,' Liddy pointed out. 'Well *ahead of time* most days.'

With that, Miss Blatchford came towards them. To Lou's eyes, she still looked extraordinarily pale.

'Miss Pascoe, Miss Knight, since we might be a while yet with our enquiries, the two of you can run along to the canteen and get a cup of tea. We'll send for you when we're done here.'

Lou watched Liddy and Flossie exchange barely disguised looks of delight.

'Yes, Miss Blatchford.'

''Course, Miss Blatchford.'

'Miss Channer, you come with me to the office.'

'Of course, Miss Blatchford.' Watching Liddy and Flossie walk away, their heads bent together as they discussed this latest turn of events, Lou's uneasy feeling deepened. Why had those two been sent away and not her? 'Is there a problem?' she asked, following her supervisor into the warehouse.

'That's what we're hoping you can help us establish, Miss Channer. Please, come in.'

When she went in through the door, it was to see that Commander Dutton had left and that Douglas was now seated behind her desk. From out in the warehouse, an old chair had been put just inside the door.

'Please, Miss Channer,' Douglas said, gesturing towards it, 'take a seat.'

Lou forced herself to swallow. 'Thank you.'

'Would you mind describing exactly what happened with this pick-up last night?'

Describe what happened? Why did they want her to do that?

'Did I do something wrong?' she asked, looking between their two faces. Their expressions certainly looked serious.

'Just tell us what happened,' Miss Blatchford said.

At the sharpness of her tone, Lou thought she saw Douglas wince.

'If you could recount what happened, it would be a great help.'

236

'All right, well...' Trying to recall the exact sequence of events, Lou related how Liddy and Flossie had already set off when the three lorries arrived. She described the driver of the first vehicle to come down the ramp, and the bones of what he'd said to her. She recalled him recounting how they'd had a puncture that had been difficult to fix, which was why they were so late, and how they would now be late getting back to Portsmouth.

'They were in uniform, these men?' Douglas asked her.

She frowned. What a peculiar question. 'Of course, sir. The first man was, I would say, the most senior. I don't really understand all the different ranks ... but perhaps a Petty Officer. Anyway, he was the one with the requisition. And he was the one who asked if we had anyone who could help with the loading up. And directed the other two to make a start.'

'You see, the thing is, Miss Channer,' Douglas began. 'The requisition he gave you is almost certainly a forgery.'

In her disbelief, she stared back at him. 'I ... don't understand.'

'The whole thing,' Miss Blatchford elaborated, 'appears to have been an elaborate plan to relieve us of most of our goods.'

'No,' she said, trying to take in what Miss Blatchford had just suggested. 'No, that can't be right.'

'I assure you, Miss Channer,' her supervisor continued, 'Lieutenant Ross has checked. The base at Portsmouth raised no such requisition — from us or from anyone else. There is no *big operation*, rushed or otherwise.'

And then it came to her. 'Yes,' she said, 'yes, there is. The man in charge said it was secret. Yes, that's right. There's a rush on, was what he said. Urgent and hush-hush. So, maybe it's *so* secret, the person you spoke doesn't even know about it.' Feeling as though she was about to cry, she bit down hard on the side of her tongue. For that moment at least, the risk of tears receded. Crying would only make her look foolish. Besides, she'd done nothing wrong. This was all a mistake. It had to be.

'I'm afraid there's no doubt, Miss Channer.' Despite the kindliness of Douglas's tone — or, perhaps, because of it — she couldn't bring herself to look at him. Instead, she stared at her hands, screwed up in her lap. 'My counterpart at Portsmouth informed me that yesterday, no vehicles of any description were despatched to collect supplies, and none arrived back bearing any.'

'Perhaps he's mistaken,' she said, feebly.

'And, ordinarily, I concede that could be the case. But I know Lieutenant Bouchard personally and he said that had he been sending us a requisition of any sort — let alone one as large as this — he would have telephoned me beforehand. If nothing else, he would have taken the chance to catch up on old times.'

'So, what you're saying,' she began, the recognition slowly dawning, 'is that I was tricked ...'

'I'm afraid it would seem so, yes.'

Mortified, she continued to hang her head. Not only had she made an almighty mistake, but she'd made it in front of Douglas. What must he think of her? Probably that she was a gullible half-wit.

Eventually, she did raise her head but, unable to look him in the eye, she stared instead at the knot of his tie — the *immaculate* knot of his tie. 'I'm sorry.'

'All very well being sorry, Miss Channer.' At Miss Blatchford's tone, Lou turned sharply; the woman's expression was thunderous. 'Sorry isn't going to replace hundreds and hundreds of pounds' worth of stock, is it?'

Lou could see no option but to agree. 'No.'

'Miss Channer,' Douglas said rather more gently, 'since it would seem that a crime has been committed, more than likely one involving civilians, the police will be asked to investigate. The navy will hold its own enquiry — after an event like this they will want to look into procedures here — but, in the meantime, you will almost certainly be interviewed by the local constabulary. In light of that, I must ask you not to discuss with anyone what has happened.' Without looking directly at him, she nodded. 'To that end, I think it best we remove you to wait elsewhere while we talk to Miss Knight and Miss Pascoe.'

'But they w-weren't even here,' she pointed out.

'A fact we must establish with them directly,' Miss Blatchford replied.

'So, what I propose, Miss Blatchford,' Douglas said, getting to his feet, 'is that while you go and fetch our other two ladies, I will escort Miss Channer to wait in my office.'

'Very well, Lieutenant Ross.'

That told her, Lou thought as she got to her feet.

'Miss Channer, please,' Douglas said, gesturing her out of the office, 'follow me.'

Only when they were well away from the warehouse did she ask him the question eating away at her. 'Am I going to be in trouble for this?'

Examining his profile as he walked beside her, she noticed his expression soften ever so slightly. 'It would be grossly unfair if you were —'

'I mean, I know it's my fault for not spotting what was going on, that the documents weren't real ...'

'They're pretty good approximations. Someone, somewhere, has gone to a great deal of trouble to get the details right.'

Stepping ahead of her, he pushed open a door. She glanced up. She'd never been to this part of the dockyard before — hadn't even noticed the route they'd taken to get there.

'It never occurred to me the papers were anything other than real. I mean, why would it?'

'Up to the first floor,' he said, gesturing her ahead of him. Reaching the top of the stone staircase, she came to a halt. 'Through here.' Gloomily, she followed him along a dimly lit corridor and then through a door on the right. So, this was where he worked. 'Have a seat.'

'Thank you.'

Doing as he'd directed, she sat down and glanced about. His office was a very grey room with a square window that gave directly onto the side of another building. On the wall to her left were charts and documents, while to her other side stood a couple of filing cabinets and a bookcase stacked with box files. The only other furniture was a modern desk, either side of which stood a chair. Even the carpet was grey, she noticed as she looked down.

With a quick glance back to the closed door, Douglas perched on the corner of the desk. 'Louise, please forgive me for asking you this, but I'm sure we'd both rather nothing hung unsaid. There's nothing you want to tell me, is there?'

She stared back at him. 'I don't understand.'

'There's nothing you didn't want to say in front of Miss Blatchford. Such as if you had a suspicion about anyone from here and their involvement in this?'

Slowly, she shook her head. 'If only. Hard though it must be for you to believe, and mortified though I feel now, I really didn't suspect a thing. They were so ordinary, so... chatty. You know how these delivery men are — all

240

smooth talk.'

He smiled. 'I can imagine, yes.'

'To be honest, I was just grateful that they were getting on with it so quickly. When I first looked down all those pages of stock, all I could think was that I was going to be really late getting home.'

'Only natural.'

'But now you must think me dumb.'

When he held out his hand, she took it.

'I don't think any such thing. Why would I when I know differently? You're bright and lovely. And we'll put all this behind us, trust me.'

Still holding onto his hand, she exhaled heavily. 'You don't know what it means to hear you say that. This last hour or so I've been petrified that no one will believe me.'

'*I* believe you. I believe, as you say, that you made an innocent mistake. Considering you've been here barely two months, I think you do an excellent job.'

Once again, she felt tears welling. At least this time, she thought, reaching into the pocket of her skirt for a handkerchief, they were from relief. 'So, you'll still want to keep seeing me?'

'You bet I will. I don't deny things might get a little... rough for you. The police will want to talk to you, then someone from our side will want to look at your work here and how you go about it, but just tell everyone the truth. Keep nothing back. Although... maybe don't mention that you and I have been seeing one another. It might muddy the waters, lead someone to look for some sort of collusion between us when *we* both know nothing could be further from the truth.'

Feeling relief softening the tension from her limbs, she nodded. He was right; there was no need to worry. She had nothing to hide. Most importantly, he knew she'd simply made a mistake. No need to tell him that perhaps her mind had been elsewhere — that ever since the weekend, she'd been unable to concentrate fully for thinking about him.

'*You* won't be in trouble, will you?' she suddenly thought to ask. 'On account of being in charge here, I mean.'

'You can leave *me* to worry about *that*,' he said. 'But now, I'd better get back over there and talk to your cohorts.' When he laughed, she smiled. 'Poor choice of word. Colleagues, perhaps I should more properly call them.'

'Yes.'

'So, unless Miss Blatchford comes to tell you otherwise, wait here until I return. And, if the police arrive to talk to you before I get back, just remember, tell the truth and you'll be fine.'

She nodded. 'Tell the truth and I'll be fine. Yes.'

★ ★ ★

Detective Sergeant Milburn looked as though he would rather be somewhere else.

'Miss Louise Channer. That's you, is it?'

From the same chair in Douglas's office where she'd been sitting throughout, Lou nodded. 'That's right.'

'And you're employed here at the dockyard as a junior clerk.'

Again, she nodded. 'Yes.'

'Right. Then you can start by telling me what happened last night.'

By 'last night', she assumed he meant yesterday afternoon but nevertheless felt it best to make sure. 'Do you mean when the lorries arrived for the pick-up?'

'Why? Is there somewhere else we should start? Some other occurrence you think I should know about?'

Lou frowned. 'I'm sorry but I don't understand. You see, I haven't done this before.'

'Done what before, Miss Channer?'

Where on earth to begin with such a question? She'd never witnessed a burglary before. She'd never — inadvertently or otherwise — aided criminals before, never been interviewed by a police detective. At that precise moment, the list of things she'd never done until now was a frighteningly long one.

'Well … I've never had to describe a burglary, I suppose is what I meant. And so, I don't know how these things work.'

'How they work, Miss Channer,' the detective sergeant said, 'is that *I* ask you to tell me what you know, *you* furnish me with all the facts of the matter, and Detective Constable North, here, writes down what you say. So, tell me what happened, last night, when you were about to leave for the day.'

Blushing at the sharpness of his tone, Lou did as he said, recounting yet again how she'd told Liddy and Flossie to go on home, had checked the stock as it was loaded onto the three lorries, and had then gone home herself. 'Just as I told Miss Blatchford and Lieutenant Ross.'

'So, you're in charge of the two warehouse girls, then.'

'No,' she said, shaking her head in emphasis. 'We all report to Miss Blatchford.'

'Then what I don't understand, is why you would take it upon yourself to tell the other two girls, over whom you have no authority, to go home early.'

'It was only a *few minutes* early,' she clarified. Why, she wondered, out of everything she'd just told him, was he

243

most concerned about the others leaving early? 'The last lorries are normally gone by five. After that, we just deal with odds and ends. Liddy sorts the stock on the shelves, I write up as much of the ledgers as I can, Flossie sweeps up, that sort of thing. So, since we were already straight for the night, I just said they might as well go.'

'Long enough before the arrival of these three lorries you mention for neither of your colleagues to have seen them.'

Already, his tone was jarring her nerves. 'I couldn't rightly speak as to what they saw. They might have seen them coming in through the gates, I don't know. You'd have to ask them.'

'We will, Miss Channer.'

'Yes.'

'Now, you say the driver who appeared to be in charge presented the correct documentation to enable you to release all of the goods.'

'He did, yes.'

'Would you say you are thorough in the carrying out of your duties, miss?'

Struggling to follow the detective's line of thought, Lou once again frowned. Why couldn't he ask his questions in a more orderly fashion?

Tell the truth and you'll be fine.

'I would, yes. I've only ever made one mistake, and that was in my first week, when I was still learning the ropes. Since then, the totals in my ledgers have been correct every week. Miss Blatchford and Lieutenant Ross have both commented upon my diligence.'

'Then if you're so thorough and so diligent, how did this forged document get past you, hm?' From the desk in front of him, he picked up one of the pages of the requisition and held it up for her to see.

'I think,' she said, fearful now that her answers would be misconstrued, 'that might have been down to a lapse in my concentration. The warehouse is really busy at the moment, and there's only the three of us... and by the end of the day, we're all really tired. It was a bad time to have a big pick-up to deal with...'

'Especially since, for this particular pick-up, you were all on your own.'

'Well... yes.'

'You can see what I'm thinking, can't you, Miss Channer?'

Actually, she couldn't. She didn't have a clue what was going through the mind of this cantankerous man.

'No,' she said uncertainly. 'I'm afraid I can't.'

'The driver told you they'd come from Portsmouth. Is that right?'

'He did, yes.'

'Have you ever been to Portsmouth, Miss Channer?'

Why on earth was he asking her *that*? 'No.'

'Do you know where it is? Could you point to it on a map?'

In her puzzlement, she shook her head. 'No.'

'And yet it didn't strike you as odd that last night, three lorry loads of your stock should be going there?'

'All due respect, sir,' she said, forcing herself to remain polite, 'when it comes to the requisitions, I rarely look at anything other than the items of stock and their quantities. The ledgers I work with are set up by category of item. Where the stuff's come from, or for which vessel it's headed, is not something I trouble myself to look at. I've no need to know that sort of thing and too much else to concern myself with.'

'Are you aware of the nature of any of the items stolen?'

245

Stolen. It was such a horrible word. 'I remember a few of them, yes.'

Detective Sergeant Milburn looked at her. 'Go on.'

'Um ...' Her mind suddenly blank, she stared into her lap. *Think,* she told herself. What do you remember? 'Coffee. Yes, one of the items was coffee. Tinned salmon. Mackerel, too. Quite a lot of tinned goods.' Now she was beginning to remember. 'Ham, peaches, evaporated milk —'

'Beer, whisky —'

'Yes. Treacle —'

'Do you see any pattern, here, Miss Channer?'

She frowned. 'Pattern, sir?'

'Anything about those particular goods that strikes you as being of note?'

'Not... really.' In a bid to relieve the dryness of her throat, she swallowed. 'Do you think I might have a glass of water? Only, I've missed my break.'

'No, you may not have some water.' Behind the desk, the detective got to his feet. Then, squeezing past the constable scribbling in his notebook, he came to lean against the corner of the desk, much as Douglas had done. How she wished he was here now instead of this objectionable man. He was a portly great lump, the buttons on his jacket straining to stay done up across his belly. Not very nice at all, she decided. 'Do you have a boyfriend, Miss Channer?'

Thrown by the question, she found herself hoping he wasn't going to ask her out. Quelling the urge to giggle at her foolishness, she recalled Douglas's advice.

'Not at the moment.'

'See, here's what I think,' he said. This close, he reeked of cigarette smoke and BO. She pitied his wife. '*I* think, the only way these criminals could have known the sort of goods stored in your warehouse, would be to have someone on the inside. How else would they know to turn up last thing in the afternoon, when you would be on your own? I *also* think they would have needed someone to show them what a requisition document looked like… because how else would they be able to forge passable copies. *Now* do you see what I'm thinking?'

To her horror, she did. Which would be best though to say that yes, she understood what he was suggesting, or to say no, she still didn't understand? Which of the two possible responses made her look less guilty?

In her head, she heard something her brother, Arthur, had once said to her: *if in doubt, admit to nothing. If Mum and Dad think you're guilty of something, keep quiet and make them prove it.*

'No,' she said, meeting the sergeant's look and holding it. 'I don't. If you're asking me whether I think it possible they had someone *on the inside*, as you put it, then yes, considering the facts, I suppose that's possible. Apart from that, I can only repeat what I told you earlier about events as I saw them.'

'Miss Channer, I don't think it *possible* they had someone on the inside, I *know* they did. This whole thing was a put-up job. And I think *you* know more than you're letting on. I mean, look at it from my point of view for a moment. This gang of thieves would have to have known —' With that, he took the forefinger of his right hand to count across the fingers on his left. '— number one, that in this dockyard was a warehouse stuffed with goods that might easily be passed off without drawing too much attention. Number two, that the perpetrators were unlikely to be challenged or meet with any resistance. Number three, that the best time of day for that to be the case was late in the afternoon. And, last but not least, they would have to have known how to come and go without arousing suspicion — and by which I specifically mean the paperwork they would need to make their pickup look just like any other.'

Put like that, she had to concede the evidence looked damning. Damning enough to make her suddenly feel truly frightened.

'Hundreds of people work in the dockyard,' she said weakly. 'Hundreds and hundreds.'

'But none of them as well positioned as you, wouldn't you agree?'

Unable to help it, she started to cry. 'No... no, I don't agree. There are the caretakers who open up in the morning and... and lock up every evening. There are the guards who patrol the yard at night, or so I'm told. Then there are all the drivers who come in with deliveries, and the ratings who load it all onto the vessels. And that's without the... the... all the other people who work here... and who know just as much as we do.'

'So, you'd have me believe you had nothing to do with it.'

'I *did* have nothing to do with it.'

'You weren't the mastermind—'

Mastermind? Her? Had the man taken leave of his senses? Terrified by how this was turning out, she gave a funny little laugh. 'I'm a junior clerk with... with barely eight weeks' service. I wouldn't have the least clue where to start to arrange for lorries... and men and everything... I doubt I could even find my way from here to the railway station to go home without taking a wrong turn.'

'What you would do well to do, Miss Channer, is desist with the denials and think very carefully. If you're connected to this crime, we will find out and we will drag you into court to answer for it with the rest of them. Even the simple act of, say, leaving a door open for them to gain access, or deliberately leaving records on display for them to see, makes you guilty of aiding and abetting. Moreover, if we find that even a single item of these stolen goods has found its way onto the black market, not only will you be facing two years in prison and a fine of five hundred pounds, you will also be liable to pay three times the value of the goods sold. So, as I said to you just now, think very carefully.'

Five hundred pounds? Prison? Surely, they were just trying to frighten her. No one in their right mind would send her to prison... would they?

Terrified, she started to sob. 'But I did... none of those things...'

Saying nothing further on the matter, Detective Sergeant Milburn got to his feet. Then, with a heavy sigh and a shake of his head, he left the room. Seconds later, the door flew open again and he barked at his constable. 'North! With me!'

Leaping to his feet, the detective constable darted from the room.

Now what did she do? Presumably, even though she'd been left alone, she couldn't just get up and leave. On the other hand, how long could they expect her to just sit there? Bewildered, she looked about the room. She wished Douglas would come back. Had he — had anyone — asked to see her? And what about Liddy and Flossie? What was happening to them? And who would be seeing to the paperwork for the deliveries? She hoped it wouldn't be a mess when she got back; she hoped that someone would have properly checked it off and spotted any discrepancies, otherwise she would have the devil's own job balancing the ledgers come Friday.

Friday. Gosh. Would Douglas still want to take her to The Angler's Rest, as he had the last two Friday evenings? She supposed it would depend upon whether he was able to borrow the car again. He'd hinted that he wasn't really supposed to be using it. She did like that little pub. Last week, the tide in the river had been higher than on their last visit, and they'd sat watching swallows swooping down and plucking insects from just above the surface of the water. They'd discussed whether it was too late for the birds to still be feeding young somewhere — a second, late clutch of eggs. Soon now, come September, it would be too chilly to sit out for long in the evenings; already it was getting dark earlier. Once the nights drew in further still, she couldn't see Douglas wanting to negotiate those narrow lanes — not in someone else's car and with next to no lights by which to do so. Perhaps she should suggest they go again soon, before the chance was lost to them.

Growing uncomfortable on the hard little chair, she shifted her weight. Perhaps, rather than fantasise about going out with Douglas again, she would be better served thinking about her present predicament and how to convince the detective sergeant of her innocence.

Too agitated to remain seated, though, she got up and went to look out through the little glazed panel in the door, but the glass was of the reeded variety and she could tell nothing about what — or whom — was on the other side. Where on earth had they gone? What were they doing? Were they talking to someone else? And how long would it be before they came back? Dear God, this was taking on the feel of a nightmare.

Returning to the chair, she sat back down, her eyes falling upon her skirt. She really should think about getting a new one for the autumn. There wasn't much weight to this one, besides which, she'd noticed that the stitching along the edge of the pocket was becoming frayed. It would be unwise to wait too long to replace it; the assistant in Dingle's had said to expect clothes to go on the ration any day now. On the other hand, if that *was* going to happen, perhaps she shouldn't be too quick to demote this skirt to weekend wear just yet; perhaps she should just buy some contrasting piping and trim the pocket instead.

But why was she worrying about her skirt when, according to the detective, she could be going to prison? No, she wouldn't think like that. She had done nothing wrong. She was innocent. *Tell the truth and you'll be fine.*

When, without warning, the door burst open, she leapt to her feet. Disappointed to see that it was Detective Sergeant Milburn rather than Douglas, she sank back onto the chair.

'Still sticking to your story?' he demanded.

'It *isn't* a story,' she repeated wearily. 'It's what happened. I can't tell it any other way.'

With that, she saw him nod to the constable, who came towards the desk and, without saying anything, placed in front of her a pad of ruled paper and an ink pen.

'Write it down.'

She stared back at him. 'I'm sorry... write what down?'

'Write down everything you told me,' the detective sergeant said, 'from when you told the other two girls to go home to when you, yourself, left the yard. Write down the times the various events occurred. Describe the lorries, the drivers, the uniforms they wore. Write down the colours of their eyes and their hair, describe their voices, write down anything you overheard them saying while they were loading up. Everything you remember, write it down!'

When he slammed his fist down on the table, she

251

sprang away from him.

'Everything,' she said quietly. 'Yes.'

'Leave nothing out.'

'Leave nothing out,' she whispered under her breath.

'Well, go on then,' he chided. 'Unless you want to be here until gone six o'clock, you'd better make a start. Detective Constable North will stay here with you while you do it. And I will be back later to see what you've written. DO NOT LEAVE ANYTHING OUT!'

Her hand trembling uncontrollably, Lou reached for the pen. *Do not leave anything out.* Well, she'd do her best not to. But, first, she had to find a way to stop her hand shaking or she wouldn't be able to write a single word, let alone leave nothing out.

★　★　★

It took several hours for Lou to commit her recollection of events to paper. More than once, she remembered something she felt she should have included earlier and had to go back and write it in between the lines. A couple of times, remembering something she thought even more significant, she tore up the best part of a page of writing and started all over again. Eventually, her hand cramping from the effort, she pushed aside the pad, arched her back, and, to Detective Constable North, who had sat there throughout, said simply, 'That's it. All of it.' Then she waited while he went to find Detective Sergeant Milburn.

Eventually, the sergeant came through the door, picked up the sheets of paper and read aloud her account. Although wincing once or twice at her clumsy choice of words, she didn't interrupt him, simply sitting motionless until he reached the end.

'Nothing you want to add?' he demanded. She shook

252

her head. 'Nothing you'd like to change?' Again, she shook her head. 'Then sign your name here —' With a nicotine-stained finger, he stabbed at the bottom of the page, '— and write today's date.'

Dutifully, she obeyed, praying fervently that this brought her ordeal to an end.

'May I go now?' she looked briefly up at him to ask.

'No. Now you wait here until told otherwise.'

With that, he and his constable left the room.

She realised then that she didn't even know what time it was. But, with no other choice, she simply sat where she was, her shoulders aching, her eyelids feeling puffy, her head pounding.

To her relief, it wasn't long before the door opened, and Miss Blatchford came in. Despite her exhaustion, she shot to her feet.

'Now that the police have finished talking to you, you are to go home —'

'Please, Miss Blatchford, what time is it?'

Miss Blatchford looked at her wristwatch. 'Five and twenty minutes past two.'

'Then I should —'

'Miss Channer, you are to go home. And when you get there, if I were you, I should try to sleep for an hour or so.'

'But what about the deliveries? And the dockets and the ledgers?'

'*I'm* taking care of those. You are to go home. When the police tell us what they've decided to do, we will send word and you may come back to work.'

When the police tell us what they've decided to do? What did *that* mean?

'Tomorrow morning?' she ventured. 'Is that when you mean? Only, I'm more than happy to just go straight back now and get on with the ledgers. There must be loads of work piling up and I'd rather not get all behind. I hate to start the day with dockets left over from the day before, it's—'

'Miss Channer, go home. As soon as I receive the necessary clearance for you to return to the warehouse, I will let you know.'

'So… Liddy and Flossie have gone home, too?'

Momentarily, Miss Blatchford didn't reply. 'I see you have your handbag. Don't forget your jacket over there. Come on, I'll walk you to the gate. Wouldn't want you getting lost.'

Although Miss Blatchford was clearly trying to sound friendly, Lou knew she was keeping something back. The trouble was, she couldn't press her too hard; she *was* her supervisor, after all.

'Very well,' she said in a tone she hoped conveyed reluctance. 'But you'll let me know tomorrow.'

'As soon as I am able.'

'Then I'll go home and try and get some sleep so I'm fresh for the morning, ready to catch up on all those dockets.' And find out just what it is you're not telling me, she thought as she followed Miss Blatchford down the stairs and out through the doors into the blinding daylight.

In the meantime, all she could hope was that this evening, Douglas would come to Jubilee Street and reassure her that everything was going to be all right. Because if he didn't, it could only mean that… well, no, she wouldn't even think about it. This couldn't be how it ended between them — not when their relationship was just getting started. It simply couldn't.

Chapter 9

Home to Roost

'You all right?'

It was now several hours since Lou had been sent home by Miss Blatchford and, although she hadn't intended to, once she'd got up to her room, taken off her skirt and blouse and lain on the bed to think, she had immediately fallen asleep, waking only now that someone had just tapped at the door. By the looks of it, she hadn't even heard Jean come in and go out again.

With a quick glance to Liddy and the plate of shepherd's pie and marrowfat peas she was bearing, she beckoned her in. 'Not really,' she said, stretching her arms wide and yawning.

'Well, here, I brought you this.'

Accepting the plate, Lou stared down at the contents. Ordinarily, it would have looked quite appetising, but tonight she didn't fancy it. Since Liddy had gone to the trouble to bring it up to her, though, she would have to try and swallow at least a couple of mouthfuls.

'Thank you,' she said, perching on the corner of her bed, poking the fork into the mashed potato and lifting some of it to her mouth. Unfortunately, it was barely lukewarm.

'The others wanted to know what's wrong with you,' Liddy said. 'So, I told them you'd complained of a blinding headache and been sent home.'

Lou smiled gratefully. 'Thank you. And thank you for bringing me this but I'm afraid I can't eat it.'

'No matter. Here,' Liddy said, taking it from her. 'Put it there and I'll take it back down when I go.'

'So, what happened at the warehouse?'

'More important than that,' Liddy said, moving to perch beside her on the bed, 'what happened to *you*? Where did they take you? And did *they* send you home or did you just leave? Miss Blatchford refused point blank to tell us anything. Floss almost shouted at her she got so exasperated with it all.'

Realising the two of them were only concerned for her wellbeing, Lou wearily recounted what had happened that morning, in return for which, Liddy explained how she and Flossie had been questioned first by Lieutenant Ross and then by Detective Sergeant Milburn.

'I don't think that horrible man believed a word I said,' Lou remarked when Liddy had finished explaining.

'Why don't that surprise me? The fat bastard — 'scuse my language — kept *on* trying to get me to say I thought you had something to do with it. Same with Floss by all accounts. Shame we did as you said yesterday and pushed off early. If all three of us had been there, he would *have* to have believed us, wouldn't he?'

'Maybe,' said Lou. 'You didn't see the lorries at all, then?'

Liddy shook her head. 'We must have been out the gates by then. Either that or else when they drove down, we were in the alleyway. Wouldn't see or hear a thing along there.'

'No. So—'

'Lou? Are you there?' Recognising the voice calling from the landing as Nora's, Lou watched Liddy get up and open the door. 'Oh, hello, Lid. Is Lou there? Only, downstairs there's a Lieutenant Ross asking to see her.'

Instantly, Lou scrambled to her feet. Douglas? Here?

Oh, thank God. Now she might learn what was going on. 'Tell him I'll be down,' she called across to Nora. Dashing to the washbasin, she made a quick study of her appearance. 'Tell him two minutes. Christ almighty, look at me.'

'I wouldn't worry,' Liddy replied, picking up the plate of shepherd's pie as she moved to leave, 'I doubt he's come to ask you on a date.'

'I still don't want to look as though I've been dragged through a hedge backwards,' she called after her, ignoring what might well have been fishing on Liddy's part, and cursing under her breath as she rummaged about in her wash bag for her lipstick. *At least I didn't lie to her*, she thought, hastily scrunching some life into the side of her hair that had become flattened by having been slept on.

Arriving downstairs, she could see through the open front door that Douglas had chosen to wait outside. Did that mean he was here in his capacity as her superior or as her boyfriend? She supposed she was about to find out.

'Miss Channer, thank you for coming out to see me.'

Reaching to close the door behind her, Lou stepped down onto the pavement. Heavens, she was trembling.

'Lieutenant Ross, good evening.'

'I think perhaps we should walk,' Douglas said, his voice lowered.

She replied equally quietly. 'This way would be best then, up the hill rather than down.'

When he nodded, they started to walk, the distance between them respectable, neither of them speaking.

'I don't suppose there's a chance of finding somewhere to sit for a while,' he broke the silence to say as they reached the junction and stood looking left and right along the street.

Up ahead, Lou spotted the flint wall that bounded the cemetery and remembered seeing from Harry's van that halfway along there was a lychgate. 'There's always the churchyard,' she said. 'There's bound to be somewhere to sit in there.'

'Then shall we go and see?'

For Lou, the delay in finding out what had been going on that afternoon was excruciating, as was the need to walk so ordinarily by his side. At the very moment she craved reassurance from him, here she was, well within hand-holding distance but unable to touch him.

Reaching the gate and passing one behind the other into the churchyard beyond, they came to a halt and stood looking about.

'Perhaps in the porch,' he suggested and with which they set off along the gravel path towards it.

For her part, Lou didn't care where they sat just as long as she could ask him what had happened once she'd left. Oh, and where she could hear him say that tomorrow, she could go back to work.

Arriving under the porch, she sat down, the timber of the low bench worn to a satiny lustre by the centuries of people before her doing the same thing — although few of them, she thought, arranging her skirt, likely to have been doing so under suspicion of being involved in a burglary.

'I'm relieved you've come,' she said as he sat down beside her.

'How are you feeling?' he turned to her to ask. 'You look as though you've been crying.'

Since the last thing she wanted was for him to think her the sort of woman to wallow in self-pity, she took a moment to compose herself.

'I'll admit to getting a bit upset when Miss Blatchford

wouldn't let me go back to work. Was it awful busy this afternoon?'

'Actually,' he said, 'I couldn't say. Once I'd spoken to Miss Knight and Miss Pascoe, I went to brief Commander Dutton and—'

'Was he *very* cross?'

'I wouldn't say cross so much as frustrated by the inconvenience. The loss of the stock will delay the departure of at least two of our vessels, which in turn will reflect badly upon the whole base.'

'When Miss Blatchford came to fetch me from your office,' she said, her desire to get back to her own situation outweighing her concern for anything else, 'I got the impression she was keeping something from me.'

When she saw him angle his head, as though considering how to reply, she knew she was right. There *was* something Miss Blatchford had been keeping from her. Well, she would try not to press him to disclose anything he shouldn't. She would respect his position. On the other hand, if there *was* news — if, for example, the police investigations had uncovered something — then didn't she have a right to know?

Growing impatient at his continued silence, she wrapped her fingers around the edge of the bench and gripped it tightly.

To her relief, he eventually spoke.

'Miss Blatchford is in a difficult position. She wants to see you fairly treated… as do I… but, with this sort of matter, her hands are tied. Mine too.'

Having been staring down into her lap, she turned sharply. 'W-what do you mean, her hands are tied? I don't understand. Tied over what?'

'Well, like me, she's governed by official procedures. When something like this happens, she has no choice

259

but to follow the rules. And when it comes to employee transgressions, the rules are very clear.'

Employee transgressions? Rules? What was he building up to telling her?

'But I haven't... transgressed.'

'I know you haven't. I wouldn't be here with you now if I thought you had. And if Miss Blatchford wasn't of similar mind, she wouldn't have been reprimanded for speaking out of turn to the personnel officer.'

In the gloominess of the little porch, Lou frowned. 'Miss Blatchford was reprimanded? On *my* account?' Why, oh why, she thought, had she let Miss Blatchford talk her into going home? Had she demanded to be allowed to stay, she would been there to stand up for herself. Instead, while she had been moping at home, other people had been left trying to fight her corner. 'Only, if it was on my account, then—'

'Look, Louise.' Feeling him take hold of her hand and squeeze it tightly, she turned to examine his expression. He looked more serious than she'd ever seen him — more serious even than the day she'd had to admit to the warehouse being light of six boxes of stock. 'I think you know by now that I'm not one to beat about the bush. Even so, I've spent the last couple of hours trying to work out how to tell you something you're not going to be very happy about.'

Please don't let him be about to dump her. *Please*, God, she could deal with anything but that. 'Now you've got me *really* worried.'

Though she had tried to make her remark sound light-hearted, for a moment he didn't respond. Instead, from inside his jacket, he withdrew an envelope. And when he turned it over, the sight of her name written on the front made her gasp.

'This is a letter from the chief personnel officer for civilian employees. At my request, it was given to me to hand to you on the express understanding that I wait while you read it and answer any questions you might have.'

Wondering how fast it was possible for a human heart to beat without bursting under the strain, Lou took the envelope, jerked her forefinger under the sealed flap and withdrew from inside the single sheet of paper.

Dear Miss Channer, In light of events yesterday at HMC Dockyard —

Her eyes skipped down the page.

... and in accordance with Regulation 13.41.3, you are hereby informed that until such time as enquiries by ourselves and the police constabulary have been satisfactorily concluded, and we have been able to ascertain your part in the aforesaid events (or lack thereof), you are prohibited from returning to your place of work. With immediate effect, you may not enter onto any part of —

In her shock, she let out a little cry. Why was this letter saying she couldn't go back to work?

Trembling so badly that the sheet of paper was shaking in her hand, she turned to Douglas. 'What...?'

'Well, you see, in circumstances such as these...' Though his tone was kindly and his hand warm, his expression was terrifyingly serious. 'What I mean is, when an incident on this scale occurs, and remains unresolved, any staff member connected to it is automatically suspended pending further investigation.'

Suspended? From her job? But why? Everyone at the depot agreed that she was innocent. So rapidly was she

261

breathing that she could barely think. 'You mean... there's someone who thinks... I *did* do it?'

'No,' Douglas swiftly sought to reassure her, 'I give you my word. No conclusion had been reached either way—'

'But there's still doubt —'

'Louise, listen to me. There's not a person in the depot who thinks you had anything to do with it. Unfortunately, right now, what any of *us* thinks is neither here nor there. What matters at the moment is that all the while the police—'

'That blasted sergeant,' she muttered through gritted teeth. 'He took against me from the outset.'

'Louise, listen, I beg you.'

'It's true. I'd even go so far as to say that he doesn't like me because I'm a woman. Put a man in front of him and I guarantee you—'

'Louise, please!'

Her face burning with indignation, she turned sharply. 'Sorry,' she said, exhaling heavily. 'It's just that—'

Seemingly in despair, Douglas shook his head. 'Has anyone ever told you, Louise Channer, that you are your own worst enemy?'

She scoffed. 'More often than you might think.'

'I somehow doubt it. Now, are you ready to listen to me explaining why this has happened or will I be wasting my breath?' Afraid to open her mouth for fear of being tempted to pick up where she'd left off, Lou confined herself to nodding. She should know by now that raging never got her anywhere. Besides, none of this was Douglas's fault. In a moment, when he finished explaining, she would apologise sincerely for her outburst. 'Until the police find out who *was* behind it,' Douglas resumed, 'they don't rule anyone out. It's less about the facts of the matter in this instance and more about the way they do things.'

The reality of the situation sinking in, Lou simply stared back at him, eventually whispering, 'But I promise you, I had nothing to do with it.'

'I know you didn't. And, for what it's worth, Miss Blatchford agrees with me. And Commander Dutton actually laughed out loud when I told him of Detective Sergeant Milburn's supposition. His response went something along the lines of *the man must be a buffoon. It's clear to anyone with two eyes this was a professional job. That girl was no more involved than I was.*'

Listening to Douglas's impression of his commanding officer, Lou tried to raise a smile. Whilst it was reassuring to know that Commander Dutton thought her innocent, his opinion didn't seem to carry any weight.

'Suspended,' she whispered, shaking her head in wonder at how it could have come to this.

'It's not *so* bad,' Douglas whispered back, getting to his feet and pulling her up beside him.

Incredulous, she stared back at him. 'How on earth can you say that?'

'Well,' he said, putting an arm about her waist, 'for a start, you'll still be paid. No matter how long it takes for the truth to be uncovered, you'll still receive your wage and that's not true for everyone suspended from their employment.'

'Small consolation,' she said into his shoulder. 'I'd far rather not be under suspicion in the first place.'

'Of course.'

On any other occasion, she would have been overjoyed to be stood so close to him. Her heart would have brimmed with delight. As it was, she felt simply bereft.

'Is there *nothing* I can do to convince them I wasn't involved?' she asked, looking up to gauge his reaction. 'Or anything *you* can do?'

He shook his head. 'The best thing either of us can do is respect the rules and wait. Eventually, even if they never catch the actual perpetrators, it will become apparent that you were not one of them. The truth will always out.'

The smile she raised was an ironic one. 'That's what my Mum always says.'

'Then she's very sensible. Changing the subject, what have you told Miss Knight and Miss Pascoe?'

'Not much,' she said, picturing the concern on Liddy's face when she'd brought her the plate of supper. 'But they'll be cross when they know about *this*.' Leaning to pick up the letter from where she had tossed it onto the bench, she waved it in the air.

'I'll suggest Miss Blatchford talks to them. The news would be better coming from her.'

'I wish they didn't have to know at all,' she moaned.

'Better they hear the truth than piece two and two together for themselves.'

'And come up with five?'

'Quite. Anyway, come on. It's getting chilly. We should get you home.'

How was it possible, she thought as they stepped out from the protection of their little porch, to feel two such wildly different sets of emotions at the same time? On one hand, she felt hugely comforted by Douglas's belief in her — had a feeling it had even served to bring them closer. On the other hand, especially when she forced herself to think about the precariousness of her situation, she felt a kind of overwhelming terror. What if the police continued to insist she was involved? What if they never did catch the real perpetrators? What then? Would Douglas stand by her?

Would anyone?

Her heart racing, she turned to regard him. 'Douglas...'

'Yes?'

'With all of this going on, will you still want to see me? Only—'

'Just you try and stop me,' he said, pressing her to his side as they started back along the gravel path towards the lychgate. 'Although, for now, it might be wise to exercise a degree of caution, perhaps put our return visit to The Majestic on hold for a while.'

'The Angler's Rest instead?' she said, passing ahead of him through the gate. To her, it seemed the obvious choice. And, with the situation between them feeling so precarious, surely it was preferable to have him think her forward and secure their next date than to just leave matters hanging.

'Good idea. I'll pick you up Friday at seven.'

But to Lou, Friday felt like an eternity. 'You'll come and see me before, though, if there's news, I mean?'

'My dear Miss Louise Channer, you can take that as read. Now, go on home with you. I'll wait here to see that you get safely inside and then be on my way.'

'See you Friday then, if not before.'

'You can bank on it.'

Thank God for Douglas, she thought as she walked down the hill towards number eleven — both that he was there at all and for his belief in her innocence — because, without him, her situation would now be looking very bleak indeed.

★ ★ ★

'What's going on with you then?'

It was much later that same evening and, although Lou

had undressed, washed and got into bed, she'd had little expectation of falling asleep. Indeed, at almost midnight, and when, surprised to find the light still on, Jean had finally crept in, Lou had been sitting up in bed, deep in thought, her knees hugged to her chest.

'Nothing's going on with me.' Her tone, she realised as she answered Jean's question, had been rather abrupt.

'Really?' Having kicked off her shoes, Jean set about unfastening her earrings. Long and sparkly, they caught Lou's eye, something about the way Jean then carefully poked them back into a little jeweller's box making her think they were new.

'Those from Paul?' she asked, her enquiry made solely out of politeness.

'Nope. Just decided to treat myself,' Jean replied, angling the lid of the box for her to see. 'Got the necklace to match, too.'

It was only when Jean moved that Lou noticed the pendant glittering at her throat. It looked expensive — certainly more expensive than anyone could afford on dockyard wages. 'Must have taken you forever to save up enough for a treat like that,' she said, watching Jean carefully.

'I had to wait a while… yeah.'

Hm. Jean didn't strike her as a woman to wait for anything. Perhaps she had a new man and didn't want anyone to know yet.

'I wish I could save money like you. Mine always seems to slip *straight* through my fingers.'

'If you want something badly enough… Anyway,' Jean went on, 'this business of the break-in, you should know it's all round the dockyard.'

So what if it was? Gossip at the yard was the least of her worries. 'I suppose it would be.'

'Word is, it was an inside job. And now, here you are, skulking at home rather than back at work—'

'I am *not* skulking. If you must know,' she somewhat reluctantly decided to explain, 'and since you'll no doubt find out anyway, I've been suspended until the police decide I had nothing to do with it.'

Unbuttoning her blouse and slipping it off her shoulders, Jean looked disbelievingly back at her. 'You? They think *you* robbed the warehouse?'

In her despair to be going over this yet again, Lou exhaled wearily. 'I'll say to you what I said to them a hundred times over. I had nothing to do with it.'

'Never thought for a moment you did.'

Watching Jean roll her stockings into a ball and then slip them into the drawer where she kept her underwear, Lou frowned. 'You didn't?'

'Course not. Look at you. You could no more organise a robbery than you could climb up on a table in the canteen and do a striptease.'

Ignoring the picture conjured by Jean's rather crude comparison, Lou frowned. 'So... if *you* can see that, why can't *they*?'

'Does your supervisor believe you?'

'For what it's worth, she does. So does Lieutenant Ross.' Jean, she noticed, had started to grin.

'I saw him today. He came over to Personnel. Not much to dislike about *him*, is there? Put a big smile on any girl's face, he would.'

If Jean was fishing for something, she was going to be disappointed.

'But this Detective Sergeant Milburn accused me of masterminding the whole thing. And nothing I say will persuade him otherwise.'

'It's what coppers do,' Jean said, pulling her nightdress

over her head and going to the washbasin. 'They make out as though they're going to pin it on you in the hope that you'll be scared enough to spill the beans on someone else.'

'Truly?' To Lou, it seemed underhand.

'Well-known fact. Eventually, when it's plain you don't have anyone to give up, they'll leave you be.'

'You really think so?'

'I know so.'

'I hope to God you're right.' Watching Jean apply cold cream to her face and then wipe it away, Lou sighed. 'Because I don't have anyone to *give* up. The only people I even know are a few from the yard and everyone here at number eleven.'

'And eventually they'll see that.'

'Well, apart from Harry, of course. I know *him*. And the people I saw him with — not that he ever introduced me to any of them. Come to think of it, some of them didn't look as though *they'd* be above breaking the law if it suited them to.'

'You know, you might want to watch what you're saying.' When Lou looked up, it was to see that Jean was pointing her finger. 'Talk like that can land an innocent person in trouble.'

Astonished by this sudden change in her roommate's manner, Lou stiffened. 'I was only thinking of people I know.'

'Well when you do, don't think of Harry. I'm telling you now, put the name Harry Hinds into the mind of your sergeant fellow and he'll be like a dog with a bone. All right, Harry does the odd bit of business under the counter now and again, but that's all he does.'

If that was true, then what the devil was Jean getting so worked up about? It had been Jean, after all, who had told her to watch out for Harry in the first place — had warned her against getting involved with him. And she'd turned out to be right, too.

'I didn't say otherwise.'

'Well, just see you keep it that way. If he so much as gets a knock on the door one night, I shall make sure he knows who tipped them off.'

Tipped them off? Why would she do such a thing? As Jean herself had just said, Harry might not be above doing the odd bit of shady business, but he was hardly a criminal.

'Don't fret,' she said. 'I've no mind to mention him.'

Jean, though, wasn't placated. 'Harry's got his faults — as you came to see for yourself — but I promise you, any thoughts you might have of getting some sort of revenge for him dumping you, any thoughts you might have of landing him in it with the bobbies... well, let's just say you'll regret it.'

Despite being unsettled by a side to Jean she'd never seen before, Lou determined to stand up to her. 'I've *said* I won't *mention* him. And there's an end to it.'

Sadly, the following morning, Lou was to discover that, actually, it was far from the end of it. With nowhere to be that morning — or indeed, on any morning for the foreseeable future — she had stayed in bed until she'd heard each of the girls finish in the bathroom. Then she'd got up, dressed and gone downstairs, arriving just as they were all flying about, getting ready to leave.

'Any one of you seen my handbag?' wailed Winnie, darting from the kitchen through to the hallway.

Spotting a handbag on the floor, Lou pointed towards it. 'Is that it under the telephone stool?'

Without a word of thanks, Winnie bent down, snatched it up and rammed into the top of it her lighter and pack of cigarettes. 'You fit, Nora?' she yelled up the stairs.

Turning to see Nora thundering down towards her, Lou sent her a warm smile. 'Have a good day at work.'

But when Nora swept past without even acknowledging her presence, Lou was left to stand, bewildered. What was the matter with everyone this morning? Anyone could be forgiven for thinking she had become invisible.

'Wait for me, you two,' Liddy then arrived in the hallway to call after the others. 'I'll walk down with you.'

'I hope you get on all right with Miss Blatchford in the office today.'

But Liddy, too, ignored her. 'Bung me a fag, Win?'

Lastly, down the stairs traipsed Jess, muttering under her breath. 'Wrong, that's what it is,' she grumbled, her complaint clearly intended for Lou to hear, 'not having to go to work but still getting paid.'

And then, in from the lavatory came Jean, tucking her shirt into her slacks. 'Regret crossing me now, do you?' she drew level to whisper. 'Just imagine, if it took less than five minutes for me to turn this many people against you, think what havoc I could wreak in a couple of days.'

Startled, Lou was left to stand and watch as Jean stepped out through the front door and slammed it shut behind her. So *that* was it? *Jean* had set the others against her? But why? To what end? To prove that she could? To remind her to keep quiet about Harry? Most of the time, she couldn't wait to be rid of him. So, what had changed? It didn't make sense.

'That you, Lou?' Mrs Hannacott called from the kitchen. 'There's some tea left in the pot if you want it. And bread for toasting if you fancy.'

Telling herself that if she gave in to tears she would be letting Jean win, Lou drew a breath and went through to the kitchen. 'Good morning, Mrs H. Yes, please, tea and toast would be lovely.'

'Don't mind them others, duck,' Mrs Hannacott went on, reaching to cut a slice from the remains of the loaf. 'I don't know what's up, nor do I want to, but whatever started it all off, my advice would be to rise above it. Wait for it to blow over. These things usually do.'

With a quick glance to the bread toasting, Lou let out a sigh. How she wished now that she'd heeded Jean's advice and never got involved with Harry in the first place — had never been taken in by that smooth patter of his, had been wise enough to ignore the spark she'd felt when he'd asked her out. Thank goodness she'd eventually seen the light. Thank goodness that, by finding the courage to say yes to Douglas that first time, not only had she avoided wasting even more of her life on Harry Hinds, she'd been spared losing the remainder of her pride and her dignity in the process. In fact, had it not been for her spat with Jean this morning, she wouldn't even be thinking about him now; he would be where he belonged — firmly in her past. He *was* in her past. Yes. And once she was cleared of any involvement in this nightmarish mess surrounding the burglary, she would be free to look forward — to forget Harry Hinds altogether and to dream instead about what might lie in store for her with Douglas — who, by stark contrast, was turning out to be the most caring and lovely man she could ever have had the good fortune to meet.

★ ★ ★

'Lou? It's Dad.'

When, that evening, Lou had heard the telephone ringing and, in the absence of anyone else seeming about to answer it, had gone downstairs and picked up the

271

receiver, she hadn't been expecting to find herself talking to her father.

'Dad, hello. Yes, it's me.'

'How are you, love?'

'I'm ... fine.' From the flatness of her father's tone, she had the awful feeling that he was calling with news — and not the sort for which they'd all been hoping. In anticipation of that, she tightened her grip on the receiver. 'Has there been word of Arthur?'

For what felt like an eternity, all she could hear was static.

'There has, love, yes.' Unable to bring herself to ask, she simply stood there, her heart thudding. Oh, dear Lord, please don't let it be... please don't let it be... 'Captain Colborne telephoned. The list of survivors taken prisoner by the Germans has finally been received at the War Office.'

'And?'

'Arthur's not on it.'

She sank onto the stool. 'Oh, Dad...'

'Captain Colborne said he's checked it several times... in case, well, you know, in case they spelled his name wrong or something...'

'But there's no one that could be him.'

'Apparently not, no.'

Slumped on the stool, Lou exhaled a long and unsteady breath. 'But he could still be alive, though, couldn't he? Just because he wasn't captured... I mean, they haven't found his body, have they? So...'

'No, that's true. But if they didn't find it at the beginning, they're unlikely to do so now. Unless it washes ashore somewhere. But the ship was hundreds of miles out to sea—'

'And so they might never find it.'

272

'No, love.'

'So … what happens now? If they don't know for sure what happened to him—'

'He'll be pronounced *missing presumed dead in the service of the merchant marine fleet*, and they'll send us a note to that effect.'

'How's Mum?' she asked, her question pointless.

'Much as you'd expect. The only saving grace, I suppose, is that the longer it went on without us knowing either way, the more resigned she became to the fact that he wasn't coming back.'

'Same here,' she said, even though admitting it made her feel disloyal to Arthur. In truth, with so much going on around her, she'd chosen to ignore all the signs that pointed to him having been lost. 'Look, Dad—'

'Come home, Lou.' At her father's broken-sounding plea, tears came, rolling down her cheeks and dropping onto her blouse. 'Mum needs you now more than ever.'

Perhaps it *was* time to go home and see them. It wasn't as though she had to go to work at the moment. 'I'll see if I can get a couple of days' leave,' she said softly. 'I don't suppose I've earned any yet… but the lieutenant in charge doesn't seem like an unreasonable man… Is Vic able to come home?'

'I'm still trying to get through to him. Last we heard he was over on the Norfolk coast. But it's a while since we've heard from him, so…'

Hoping to spare her father the ordeal of hearing her crying, she stood stiffly. 'I can't promise, Dad, but I'll see what I can do.'

'Thanks, love. You're a good girl.'

No, she thought, replacing the receiver and then swiping at her tears, she wasn't a good girl. She wasn't a good girl at all.

* * *

God, she felt awful. Her head felt as though it had been replaced by a lead weight and her eyes felt swollen shut. After all that weeping last night, she must look a real sight. Not that it mattered. She had nowhere to go, nowhere to be. In fact, she might as well stay in bed. At least there, she could cry for Arthur — and for Mum and Dad — and no one would want to know what was wrong.

It was the morning after Lou's telephone call from her father, the dreadful news having opened the floodgates to tears that seemed beyond her to stop. Even now, every time she pictured her brother, fighting to keep his head above water on a sinking ship, they started all over again. She'd barely slept a wink and, even when she had, it had been the sleep of someone exhausted and drained and had done nothing to make her feel any better.

Raising her head and scanning the room, she saw that Jean was already up. Lifting her head further from the pillow, she listened: movement on the landing; the kettle whistling; the clipped tones of the man on the BBC Home Service as he read the news headlines.

Moving slowly, she got out of bed, went to the wash-basin, turned on the tap and splashed her face. Reaching for the towel, she purposely avoided looking in the mirror. In a minute, when everyone had gone to work, she might go and run herself the permitted five inches of bathwater and wash her hair. Sometimes, the act of scrubbing her scalp eased a headache. It was worth a try. But, before that — although only after she'd heard the front door slam the requisite number of times — she would go down and see if there was a cup of tea to be had. Piping hot, it was something else that often helped.

Dragging her dressing gown over her nightie, she went

274

to the door and eased it open. Apart from the wireless, everywhere seemed to have fallen still: it was probably safe to venture down.

As she set foot on the landing, though, she heard the front door being thrown open and someone thudding back up the stairs.

'Curse it!' she heard a voice complain. Swivelling about, she slipped back into her room and eased the door against the frame. Through just the tiniest of gaps, she peered out to see who it was. 'Ruddy cramps.' Jess. It was Jess. 'Better be able to find some ruddy sanitary towels.'

Carefully, Lou closed the door. She would wait for Jess to come back down and then she would— *Sanitary towels*. With a jolt, she swung about. When had *she* last needed any of those? Not in the last two weeks, that was for sure. With her heart pounding at the recognition, she lunged towards the stool and tossed aside the garments piled on top of her handbag. Seizing it up, and rummaging about inside, she pulled out her pocket diary and rifled through the pages. Early August it should have been; there should be a little note around about... Damn. Nothing. She must have forgotten to write it in. Never mind, she would go back to July and count from there. Hastily, she flicked back the pages, cursing when she came across several of them stuck together. Right. Here somewhere. July... But, as she scanned the days, a leaden sensation settled in her stomach. There was no note there, either. But then there wouldn't be, would there, because she was pretty certain there had been nothing to note. She had missed two months. Oh, dear God! She had missed two months. And, for the first time in her life, there was the very real possibility that the cause was something other than *everyone misses one now and again*. This time, she realised, doubling over and wrapping her arms about her waist, there was the very real possibility

275

that she was pregnant. And the only person who could be the father was Harry Hinds.

★ ★ ★

'Louise, though I've no wish to nag, you really must try to eat something.'

All the while Douglas had been talking, Lou had been staring down at the food he'd ordered for her. There was nothing wrong with it — it looked nice enough, on its cheery blue and white plate — the problem was that she hadn't the least appetite.

'I'm sorry,' she said.

'No need to apologise. But a body can't survive on air alone, especially not while in the thick of grief.'

Grief, huh. If only that was *all* it was.

It was later that same day and when, without warning, Douglas had arrived at number eleven to see how she was, Lou had simply stood on the doorstep, overcome with a mixture of relief and despair, his company something she both craved and dreaded: if she longed for anyone to help her through this ever-growing mess it was him; if there was anyone whose help she didn't deserve, it was his.

Apparently taken aback by her appearance, he had told her to go and fetch a jacket — he was taking her for something to eat and wasn't taking 'no' for an answer. And so, now, here they were in a little cafe, each of them with a plate of sausage and mash covered in a thick gravy. On any other day, she would have got stuck straight in.

'It looks nice,' she said, her eyes fixed firmly upon her plate. So far, she had managed to avoid looking directly at him. It wasn't that she didn't want to see his lovely warm eyes, it was just that meeting his look made her want to confess to everything. But she couldn't. Telling him only

276

that Arthur had now been pronounced *presumed dead* was as far as her conscience had let her go. Any mention of *the other thing* causing her grief would spell the end for them. And she wasn't ready to let him go. Not just yet.

'It *is* nice,' he replied to her observation. 'But I didn't buy it for you to admire, I bought it for you to eat, now, while it's still hot. And if you don't make a start on it this very minute,' he went on, reaching across the little table and jiggling her hand, 'then I shall come round there, cut it all up into little pieces and feed it to you as though you were two years old. And don't think I'm not serious.'

If only to stop him keep insisting, she picked up her knife and fork, cut through the sausage, stabbed the end with her fork and put it in her mouth. Across the table, she saw him pick up his cutlery and resume eating his own meal.

The sausage was actually delicious. It clearly contained a good helping of pork and less of the cereal that was all too common in sausages these days. For his sake, and so as not to appear ungrateful, she would eat as much of it as she could. At least here, in this little cafe, with the woman in the flowery apron looking on, she was less likely to dissolve into tears again.

Eventually, though, when she had eaten as much as she could, it was time for them to leave. And, just as she had feared, once back out on the pavement, she felt far less composed.

Desperate not to embarrass him by crying in public, she glanced about. 'Do you think there's somewhere we could sit for a while?'

Douglas too looked around. 'There's a park further along. I've walked past it a couple of times. We could try there if you like.'

She nodded. 'All right.'

'Come on then. Take my arm and we'll go and see if there's somewhere to sit.'

As it turned out, there was a seat close to where a group of young children were playing on the swings and a gaggle of older boys were playing football, mounds of jerseys serving as their goalposts.

Drawing level with the green-painted bench, they sat down.

'Thank you for supper,' she said.

'I would say it was my pleasure but, from the gauntness of your face, I could tell it was a while since you'd eaten and so it was more a case of necessity.'

'I ate as much as I could.'

'You ate *something*, that's all that matters.' Oh, dear God, he was so *kind*. And she was so *deceitful*. 'Even a little is better than nothing.'

'Yes,' she said.

'Now, would you like me to go in tomorrow and arrange for you to take some time off? I know you're currently suspended from duties, but if you want to be free to travel home and see your parents, we should really make it official leave.' When she didn't reply, he went on, 'Will there be a memorial service?'

Sat beside him, she shrugged. 'Dad never mentioned one. But I imagine it's too soon for them to have given it any thought. When I spoke to him, they hadn't even had the official confirmation from the ministry.'

'No, I suppose not.'

'So... perhaps I'll wait until I know about that before I go home.'

At the corner of her vision, she noticed him frown.

'I can arrange for you to go more than once, you know.'

What she wanted, was not to have to go at all — not because she didn't want to be with Mum and Dad

278

and share their grief but because… well, because how could she? In all conscience how could she, pregnant and with no prospect of being married, go home and keep such a thing from her parents, already grieving for the loss of their youngest son? She couldn't. She couldn't do it to them. Nor could she bring herself to tell the truth to Douglas. No, when the time came for her to stop seeing him, she would have to invent another reason. *Stop seeing him*. God, how cruel was that?

'There's been no word yet from the police, I suppose?' Although she had to ask, deep down she knew that if there had been he would already have told her.

'Not yet. But I know Commander Dutton is anxiousto have it all resolved and get things back to normal as soon as possible. Operations are really ramping up now and we need the depot at full strength.'

Was that a glimmer of hope among the shambles of her life? 'You mean, I could be back at work soon?'

'As far as I know, the police haven't asked anything further about you, or asked to see you again.'

'So … that has to be good, doesn't it?'

He squeezed her hand. 'I should like to think so.'

She exhaled heavily. 'Me too.'

What a relief that would be. Being able to go back to work would at least give her one less concern to stew over even if, right this moment, it wasn't the one causing her to lose the most sleep.

'Would you still like to go to The Angler's Rest tomorrow? I've arranged to borrow the car again but if it doesn't feel appropriate, I'll understand.'

'No,' she said, 'I'd like that.' Dear God, what was shedoing? She couldn't just keep going out with him as though nothing had changed. It was wrong. Horribly, horribly wrong. But, since he had offered, she would

279

allow herself to go for a drink with him. Then, as soon as she'd thought of a convincing reason to stop seeing him, she would do so. She would not lead him on any longer.

At the very thought, though, she started to cry.

'Hey.' Seeing her tears, he put his arm around her shoulders and pulled her towards him. If only *he* was the baby's father, she found herself thinking. Then everything would be all right. It wouldn't matter if she *never* got to go back to her job because he would take care of her. They would marry and go on to have a whole family. 'Time to get you home, I think,' he whispered into her hair. 'Come on. Sleep is a good healer.'

But, of course, back in her room, sleep didn't come. And the longer she lay in her bed staring up at the ceiling, the less likely it seemed it ever would. In her frustration, she turned onto her side. Then she returned to laying on her back. Then, pummelling some shape into her pillow, she turned onto her other side.

It wasn't supposed to be like this. For ages, her dream had been simply to get a job and earn herself a little bit of money. And it had all started so well. But now, here she was, her life in tatters. Worst of all, with the news that Arthur had now been officially declared missing presumed dead, she found herself desperate to go home and be with Mum and Dad. She wanted to console them, and to have them console her. All the time they'd been forced to wait she'd assumed that news, when it eventually came — even if it was of the worst kind — would provide some sort of relief, would bring an end to everyone's agony. How wrong she had been: if anything, her pain was deepening by the day. Making it worse was the fact that she had no idea how or when she was ever going to be able to see her parents. How could she see them now? How could she go home while there was so much she couldn't tell them?

Exhausted, she rolled onto her back and sighed. Well, one thing was clear: she couldn't carry on like this. She had to do something. If she wanted to go and see Mum and Dad, she had to accept that it would mean concealing her troubles from them. *All* of her troubles from them. No matter how badly she wanted to unburden herself, she would have to remind herself that wasn't why she was there. She would have to resolve that, no matter what it took, she would keep her worries to herself. And if she thought she could do that, then next time she saw Douglas, she would ask him to arrange for her to take a couple of days' leave.

That decided, she pulled up her eiderdown and tried to get comfortable. And then, what felt to be just moments later, she found herself waking to find the room filled with daylight and the sounds of Jean at the washbasin. Evidently, she'd been asleep. And now it was time to get up. Except that, as she threw back the bedcovers, the horror came flooding back to her: there was no point getting up; she was suspended. And pregnant. And Arthur was dead. For a few blissful seconds, she'd completely forgotten.

Flopping back onto her pillow, she tugged the eiderdown over her head. Why bother getting up at all when she had nowhere to go?

Eventually, though, with her fellow lodgers having left for work, she forced herself out of bed. Once dressed, she then braced herself to face the inevitable enquiries from her landlady about when she might be able to return to work. Then, a little after nine o'clock, while she was stood at the sink washing her smalls, Mrs Hannacott came through from dusting in the parlour to tell her there was a Lieutenant Ross at the door. Snatching the plug from the sink, she reached for the towel to dry her hands. What

281

was Douglas doing back here? And so early on a workday morning, too? Whatever his reason, she would ask him to arrange for her to take some leave.

Aware that Mrs H would probably be straining to hear, she kept her greeting formal. 'Good morning, Lieutenant Ross.'

'Miss Channer. Might I ask you to step outside for a moment? Only, I have some news.'

Was he *smiling*? He might be trying not to, but he was being given away by his eyes.

'Yes. Of course.' Closing the door, she stepped down onto the pavement. And, when he turned and started to walk slowly up the street, she fell into step beside him.

'This morning, Sergeant Milburn telephoned Commander Dutton to update him on progress with their investigation.'

'Yes?' God, she wished her heart wouldn't thunder so every time she felt panicky. One day it would beat so hard she would pass out.

'So far, they haven't been able to identify the perpetrators.'

She felt her shoulders sag. 'Oh.'

'But, neither, at this stage, do they propose arresting *you*.'

Reaching to a lamppost for support, she exhaled with relief. 'Truly?'

Coming to a halt beside her, he nodded. 'Yes.'

'Then thank God for that.' Turning to look at him, she saw him glance up ahead.

'Perhaps we could go and sit up in the churchyard again while I tell you the rest? I would have suggested we sit indoors but I didn't think you'd want your landlady eavesdropping.'

She smiled. He really was so considerate. 'The church-yard will be fine. I could do with the air.' Oh, what a relief! She wouldn't be going to prison! Everything was going to be all right. One way or another, she would climb out of this mess — she could feel it in her bones. Right this moment she might not have the least idea how but, she felt certain that once she returned to work, everything would once again fall into place.

'Unfortunately,' Douglas said, reaching for her hand as they arrived beneath the church porch and sat down, 'while the police no longer seem inclined to arrest you for the burglary, I'm afraid that's not an end to the matter.'

She almost didn't care. She could go back to work. That alone halved her worries. 'No?'

'From what I can gather, although they can find no conclusive proof of your involvement, all the while they have no one else under arrest for the crime, they still aren't prepared to rule you out.'

'Not rule me out? But I thought you said—'

'If I understand correctly, while they can't prove it was you, they aren't currently prepared to bring that part of their enquiries to a close.'

'So ...'

'So, for now, you remain *under suspicion*.'

'But *that's* not fair.'

'It's not. No. But it *is* the situation.'

'So, does that mean that if they *never* find out who did it, I will never be entirely free? That I shall have to live with this hanging over me for the rest of my days?'

He looked directly at her. 'I don't think it will come to that. Sooner or later, someone somewhere is bound to draw attention. The police are pretty hot now on black marketeering. Eventually, one of the burglars will slip up... be caught with the goods... or otherwise do something to give themselves away.'

'So —'

'The thing is, Louise, what I have come to tell you is that without you being exonerated, you can't continue to be employed in the warehouse.'

'*What?* You mean I *can't* go back to work? But for how long? And what am I supposed to do in the meantime?'

Staring disbelievingly back at him, she knew she was about to cry. Evidently recognising this, he moved closer.

'Dear Louise, I'm sorry to have to be the one to break this to you, but you can't go back at all. You're being dismissed.'

Dismissed? 'As in… given the sack?'

His grip on her hand tightened. 'I am afraid so.'

'No,' she said, hanging her head. 'I can't be dismissed. What will I do? How will I pay my rent?'

'Well, knowing how this would leave you, I went to see the head of civilian personnel. I thought at first to prevail upon him to change his mind and keep you on but, as Miss Blatchford pointed out, no one's going to break the rules—'

'Not for a junior clerk, you mean.'

'Not for anyone. But, credit where it's due, I *was* given a fair hearing. And since no one except the gossipmongers believe you had anything to do with it anyway, it's been agreed that you will receive two weeks' pay in lieu of notice. And I know it doesn't seem like it right now but that's incredibly generous. Usually in these circumstances, you would only be paid up to the last day you worked.'

'But what you're saying…' She paused. Dear God, this was a disaster. '…is that I'm going to need to find another job.' How much more bad luck was it possible to have? Just when she'd thought her problems were staring to ease, they'd actually got worse. Far worse.

'You will, yes.'

Then she would try to look on the bright side. In a place like the dockyard there had to be dozens of jobs she could do. These days, there were posters up everywhere urging women to do their bit.

'Then do you think you might ask around for me? I wouldn't normally ask... but you know all the people there... and how to go about it. And I don't mind too much what I do. I can type. I know shorthand. I can do bookkeeping and filing and so on. But I'll work anywhere in the canteen or in the kitchens if I have to. Please, Douglas, could you ask around for me?' When he was slow to respond, she tensed. '*Please?* I really think the dockyard's my best chance, with people there knowing what's happened, I mean.'

Eventually, to her relief, he nodded.

'Yes, of course. I'll go back to Personnel and enquire about vacancies.'

But just as she was sighing with relief, she felt as though she was going to be sick. 'Douglas...'

'Yes?'

'I ... don't feel very well.'

'All right. Then we'd best get you home. Did you have breakfast?'

'I had... toast.'

'Then if it's not hunger, I expect it's shock, especially coming on top of everything else.'

Everything else? Oh, he meant the news about Arthur. 'Yes,' she said weakly, closing her eyes against the swaying going on all around her. 'I expect so.'

'Do you feel able to stand up?'

Instinctively, she nodded, only to immediately regret it. Golly, she felt dizzy. 'I think so.'

When, with his assistance, she got to her feet, he stood

285

for a moment before asking, 'Feel able to walk slowly back with me?'

'Just about.'

'Good. Then we'll take it small stretches at a time. First, we'll concentrate on getting to the gate.'

With Douglas setting her little targets along the way — walk as far as the junction, get across the road, on to the next lamppost — they made their way back to the top of Jubilee Street and then on down the hill to number eleven. And when they finally arrived back at the doorstep, she turned towards him.

'Thank you for coming to see me. I'm sure you could have done without having to bring such news, but I'm grateful not to have heard it from anyone else.'

'That's why I came. Now, given all that you have to contend with, I'm going to suggest we don't go out this evening. But, if it's all right with you, I'd like to come back on Monday morning. By then I should be able to tell you what I've managed to find out about other possible jobs. And, of course, to see that you're all right.'

She cringed. She wasn't all right now and she wouldn't be by Monday. But she couldn't tell *him* that. His suggestion that they call off going to The Angler's Rest seemed sensible though.

'Thank you.'

'Monday morning then. I'd come sooner but I'm on duty all weekend.'

Feeling utterly wretched, she nodded. He was *so* nice — a complete gentleman. Nothing short of perfect, in fact. But the awful truth was that, somehow, when he came back on Monday, she was going to have to end it with him. Whether he'd found her a job or not, she really had no other choice.

Chapter 10

The Decision

The time had come. Despite it being her greatest hope that Douglas would return in the morning with news of a job, in her heart, Lou knew that even were he to have found her one, she was only putting off the inevitable. At best, she had less than three months before it would become obvious she was having a baby. At worst, barely two. And then what? When she was dismissed from yet another job, what would she do for money? Taking up new employment — even if there was some to be had could only buy her a few more weeks, during which she would simply grow more and more anxious. And so, the time had come to make a decision. The problem was, what was it to be?

In the quiet of the churchyard, where, by walking around, she had found a bench against a wall, she was at least able to sit and think without distraction. Here, in the warm sunshine of the late afternoon, listening to a nearby family of house sparrows bickering, her choices had become clear: she could go home, hope her parents would eventually forgive her, pray that she took to motherhood and, as an unmarried mother, resign herself to probably never having a husband. Or, she could put an end to the baby and go home as though nothing had ever happened — make Dad over the moon by apparently agreeing with him that, after the loss of Arthur, Mum's need was indeed greater than her own. But could she actually bring herself to do something like that? How would she even go about it? From the little she'd pieced together over the years, gin and hot baths were the most straightforward and least distressing way of taking care of the problem. She'd *also* heard it didn't always work. Her only other option on that front would be to find a woman in a backstreet somewhere. When it came down to it, though, would she really be able to go through with it — to risk what might happen?

Staring idly at the family of sparrows now bathing in the dust, she let out a long sigh. If neither of those options was palatable, her only other course of action was to go to Harry. On the surface, it did seem the most honest remedy, but it was also a very long-term one. Going back to Harry — if he'd even have her — would mean facing up to a lifetime with a man she didn't respect and didn't especially like. And for what? To save her reputation? To become Lou Hinds, wife to a grocer's son with big ideas? To raise a happy family? Somehow, she doubted it. And yet, because it lacked the deception and the upset that came with either of the other two choices, it was starting to feel like the right thing to do. And who knew presented with a baby, Harry might change. He would certainly be a good provider; neither she nor their child were likely to want for much. And life with him was unlikely to be dull; there was *that*. They had both liked each other once; perhaps they could do so again. Perhaps, if she made more of an effort — if they both did — it would work out all right. Louise Hinds. It didn't have the ring of Louise Ross, wife of a naval lieutenant — not that matters had progressed anywhere near far enough with Douglas for her to even entertain such thoughts! — but it didn't sound *so* bad.

Heaving another long sigh, she got wearily to her feet.

So, that was it decided, then. She would wait until Douglas called tomorrow morning, see whether he had been able to find her any work — better to go to Harry and be able to tell him she had a job for a while — thank Douglas for his time, and then explain that given the circumstances of her dismissal, it was only right that they brought things to an end. That done, she would ask Jean to tell Harry she wanted to see him.

After all, those who had committed the sin had to be the ones — and the only ones — to pay the price.

★ ★ ★

'Lou? It's Esme.'

Having returned from the churchyard and opened the front door to hear the telephone ringing, Lou had picked up the receiver and answered it. Discovering her cousin at the other end, her reaction had been to sigh: the last thing she needed right now was a chatty telephone call from someone whose life was no doubt going swimmingly.

'Oh, hello, Esme,' she said. 'How are you?'

As it happened, Esme herself didn't sound to be without woes.

'A bit up and down of late. I lost a couple of friends when a German bomb fell on their home and I don't seem able to quite get over it but otherwise, well, much the same. You know how it is. What about you?'

'Woeful, truth to tell.' While she regretted sounding so miserable, she didn't have it in her to pretend otherwise.

'There's been a... well, a bit of a to-do at work. I can't tell you over the telephone. And then there's been some bad news from home. But I don't want to talk about *that* because if I do, I'll cry. And I'd really rather not. Cry, that is.' If she started to explain what had hap-

289

pened to Arthur, she knew she would end up sobbing for everything else, too. And there was no earthly way she could risk letting slip to Esme that she was pregnant.

'I'm sorry to hear that, Lou. But you have friends there, don't you? People you can talk to?'

Bother. Already, Esme's kindly concern had her eyes brimming with tears.

'I *did* have. But since this business at work, everything's all turned upside down and... well...'

Oh, but this was hopeless! Here she was, desperate not to give in and confess the whole sorry mess and yet, of everyone, Esme was the person she trusted most. Despite her cousin's tendency to be impulsive, she was also mature and resourceful.

'Lou ...' She drew her attention back to Esme's voice. 'Can you get leave from work for a few days? Can we meet?' Oh, if only they could do that! But how? Damn. Now she was properly crying. 'Lou?'

Reaching into the pocket of her skirt for a handkerchief, she sniffed. 'Perhaps...'

'Then how about I book us a hotel somewhere? Could you get to Exeter for a couple of days? That wouldn't be too far for you to get a train, would it?'

'C-Can't,' she sobbed. 'N-No m-money.'

At the other end of the line she felt certain she heard Esme sigh.

'Right. Well, then I have another idea. I'm due some leave. And I also know someone who can organise things. So, how about we go to Aunt Diana's in Windsor? We can meet in town and travel out from there together. It might take me a couple of days to arrange, but how about next weekend? How about I get a rail warrant for you for Friday? And maybe one back for the Sunday evening? How does that sound?'

To Lou, it sounded like a lifesaver. In a few days' time, she would have someone to talk to. Of course, ideally, that person would be Mum — and part of her badly wanted it to be — but she simply couldn't bring herself to add to her mother's heartache. If nothing else, it would be selfish. At least face to face with Esme, she could be completely honest. She could certainly admit to more than she could over the telephone — standing as she was in the hallway of number eleven.

'N-Nice,' she replied to Esme's suggestion. 'That sounds n-nice.' Yes, this way, with Esme's help, she could decide what to do and, for now at least, not have to worry Mum.

'All right,' Esme said. 'And don't worry about money.'

Thank goodness her cousin was so level-headed — just the person to offer the impartial opinion and help she so badly needed. 'You're s-so kind, Esme.'

'Hm. Look, tell me your address and leave it all to me.'

Her details given, and Esme thanked yet again, Lou replaced the receiver and went upstairs. Jean, she knew from overhearing a conversation on the landing earlier, had been going to her Mum's for Sunday tea. And thank heavens for that: not only could she do without having to lie about why she had been crying but it was impossible to see that woman without thinking of Harry.

Harry. Golly, Lou thought, finding her handkerchief and blowing her nose. Marry him, and she and Jean would become related. Well, they would if there was such a thing as a stepsister-in-law. Either way, they would become inextricably linked. Christ, yet another depressing thought.

Bending down and unfastening her shoes, she eased them off her feet. Now that she was going to see Esme, she wouldn't rush to see Harry. She would still speak to

Douglas tomorrow but, just in case Esme came up with a way out of her mess that she'd failed to spot for herself, she would wait until she returned from Aunt Diana's to plead her case to Harry. No sense throwing herself on his mercy unless there truly was no alternative, even if, in her heart, she already knew it to be the case.

Mrs Harry Hinds. She supposed she had better start getting used to it.

* * *

'Good morning, Miss Channer.'

The following morning, staring back at Douglas, standing there on the doorstep looking immaculate in his uniform, Lou felt her fingers tremble on the door latch. Dear God, just look at what she was giving up.

'Good morning.' Her rather stiff little greeting was the best she could manage; better to keep it formal between them or she would lose her nerve. She hadn't slept a wink for worrying about this as it was. 'Would you like to come in?'

'Your fellow lodgers are all at work?'

She nodded. 'And Mrs H has gone over to her sister's in Stonehouse. She likes to do her shopping in the market over there.' Christ, now she was prattling.

When Douglas removed his cap and stepped into the hallway, Lou gestured him towards the parlour.

'How are you this morning?'

She followed him in. 'Better, thank you.' It wasn't true not in the least — but there was no need for him to know that. Preferable, in fact, that he didn't; she had to get this over and done with as quickly as possible. 'Would you like to sit down?'

She watched him glance about the tiny room and then

perch on the edge of the sofa. 'Thank you, yes.'

Was she imagining it or was he as nervous as she was? And if so, why? What did *he* have to be nervous about?

'I'd offer you tea or coffee, but the milkman is always late on Monday mornings. You'd have to have it black.'

'Don't worry,' he said and then, clearing his throat, went on, 'Over the weekend, I enquired regarding vacancies.'

Deciding her legs weren't to be trusted, Lou lowered herself onto the edge of the adjacent armchair.

'That was kind of you.'

'But what I had failed to realise is that once you have been dismissed from one part of the dockyard, you cannot be re-employed in it anywhere else.'

Ordinarily, her heart would have sunk at the news. This morning, though, she felt nothing. She felt nothing whatsoever because it didn't matter. Unbeknown to this caring man, her fate was already sealed. It would have been nice to earn some money for a few weeks, but to change her destiny now was going to take rather more than a new job.

'I see.'

'I'm sorry it couldn't be otherwise.'

She forced a swallow. 'Not your fault.'

'I… also have other news.'

She tried to raise a smile. Whatever he'd come up with to help her out, it wasn't going to alter the facts. She still had to be done with him.

'Yes?'

'Over the weekend, Commander Dutton made me privy to certain plans. Plans for Canada's role in this war, that is. And… well, for my own part in it too.'

Despite this particular piece of news appearing to have

nothing to do with her, she determined to show an interest. He was a good man. She should continue to be civil and polite.

'Are they going to put you in charge? They should do.'

He responded with a laugh. 'I admire your faith in me. And as it happens, you're not far wrong.'

Staring back at him, she felt her eyes widen. 'Really?' That she should be right about anything seemed unlikely. These days, she made a habit of being horribly wrong on just about every count.

'The British government has called upon Canada to take on a greater role in the war, in the North Atlantic in particular, which is going to require that we have better supply operations on both sides, here *and* back there. To that end, a new base will be required, and *I'm* being given the task of setting it up.'

Dare she believe what that meant? 'You're going back to Canada?'

'I am, yes.'

Then she was off the hook! She could wish him well and not be the villain of the piece. Oh, the relief!

'When do you leave?' Somehow, she would have to ignore that her heart felt to be breaking in two and remind herself that, where this lovely man was concerned, this turn of events would leave her with a clear conscience. She would be spared having to lie to him.

'No date to ship out just yet but, given there's the usual rush to get the thing operational, it's likely to be quite soon. Can't imagine I'll be here beyond the end of this month.'

By the end of September, he would be gone; she really couldn't have dreamt it any better.

'And you won't be coming back.'

'Not unless I one day get given command of Devon-

294

port… or somewhere else over here, no.'

As he told her, he laughed, and she knew that he was trying to make light of the situation. On the other hand, as a way of saying he was about to break up with her, he was being uncharacteristically blunt.

'I see. Well, congratulations —'

'Christ, Louise. Do you think you could come and sit over here a minute? You seem so far away.' Thinking it easier to move than make a fuss, she obliged, sitting down as far from him as the length of the settee would allow. 'Thank you. That's better.' Somewhat absently, he reached for her hand. Despite flinching, she didn't resist. Where was the harm? Any moment now he would be gone, and she would never see him again. 'Look, I might not have found a job for you, but I do have a suggestion.'

Something about the softening of his tone made her look directly at him. 'And that is?'

'Come to Canada with me.'

'What?'

'Come to Canada with me, Louise.'

Why was it suddenly so hard to breathe?

Pulling her hand from his, she stumbled to her feet, her eyes coming to rest upon the wall alongside the door. There. That exact spot could well be where Harry Hinds had got her pregnant. Had she summoned the wherewithal in that moment to resist him, her life might not now be ruined, and she might this very minute be leaping up with joy, rather than pulling away in distress.

'I can't… just go to Canada…'

'Well, no,' Douglas said, getting to his feet to join her. 'I wasn't suggesting you *just* come to Canada… I was going to ask that you come with me as my wife…'

★ ★ ★

295

The last few days had been torture, her face rarely free from tears. But then she deserved no less. She *wanted* to feel the despair, it seeming only proper that she suffer the punishment due to her for having been such a loose woman. And now, sitting here on the train to London to see Esme, Lou could feel tears welling yet again. Why couldn't she have met Douglas first? Why had she been so quick to leap at the chance to go out with Harry? Because he had seemed different to anyone she'd known before? Because he had seemed faintly dangerous? Because he had asked her?

Squashed next to the window in the cramped compartment, watching but not really seeing the countryside of south Devon as they trundled through it, she let out a sigh. More important than all her unanswerable questions about why she had gone out with Harry was why, when Douglas had explained what *he* was asking her, hadn't she turned him down flat? For Christ's sake, she was having another man's baby. She was in no position to even consider his proposal. But no, what had she done? Unable to bring herself to decline him outright, she had prevaricated, leading the poor man to apologise for the suddenness of his approach.

'I shouldn't have asked you yet,' he had rushed to say, his expression one of genuine regret. 'I overlooked that you're in mourning for your brother. I should have remembered that... and waited. So, please, take as long as you want to reflect upon my proposal... I'll wait.' And when she still hadn't replied, he'd gone on to explain further. 'We don't have to marry in a rush. Though I should like to take you back home with me when I go, I don't even know if that's possible. I've no idea how these things work. Besides, I'd quite understand if you wanted to wait until I'd got back there and got things organised first. I have to get permission to marry anyway, which would probably be best done here through Commander Dutton, and then I'd need to put in for accommodation at the new place. But whatever would make you feel comfortable, that's how we'll do it. All I ask, Louise, is that when you're thinking it over, you bear in mind that I don't want to be without you. I might not have known you very long, but I feel as though in you I've found my soulmate. And I can't bear the thought of leaving you behind, of just letting that go... of having to live on, always wondering what might have been...'

Even just recalling his sincerity made her insides ache, brought back the way he always smelled like fresh laundry, the way his lips curled when he smiled, how his hands always felt warm and soft. It was no wonder she had responded to him as she had. *She* couldn't bear the thought of being without *him*, either. And that had to be why, despite knowing that taking all the time in the world wouldn't enable her to say yes to him, she had promised him she would think about it. And so, here she was, travelling to see Esme, with no idea how much of her sorry circumstances she should disclose to her but horribly aware that when she got back on Sunday evening, Douglas was going to come to see her in the hope of getting the answer for which he would no doubt praying. Oh, what a nightmarish charade she had brought upon herself; what deceit she had spun. What a ghastly person she must be. The slippery and unreliable Harry Hinds was no more than she deserved.

'You all right there, love?'

Drawing her eyes back from the view beyond the window, she found the lady in the seat opposite leaning towards her.

'Oh. Yes, thank you, I'm fine. Just... a bit of bad news

the other day, that's all.'

'Here,' the woman said, prying the lid from a tin and holding it towards her, 'have a Mackintosh's. Can't go far wrong with a toffee. Mind you, they're as rare as hen's teeth, these days.' When Lou leant forward and helped herself to one, the woman grinned. 'Grandson gave them to me. *Here you go, Gran,* he says to me, *don't say I never give you nothing.*'

Lou smiled. 'Thank you.'

'Going all the way up to London?'

Lou nodded. 'Yes. I'm going to see my cousin. And you?' As travelling companions went, she wouldn't mind this woman's company for the next few hours. She looked the sort to have a sympathetic ear.

'Only as far as Exeter, love. Been down to see my daughter and her family in Plympton. Told her if the bombs start falling, she's to come up to mine. We'd be terrible cramped, but least I'd know they were safe.'

From there, their conversation continued in friendly vein, covering such innocuous topics as the weather (*wasn't much of a summer, was it?*) and rationing (*it's the restrictions on bacon my husband can't abide; breakfast ain't breakfast without it, he always says*) until, at Exeter, an older man, with a disapproving face and an annoying habit of clearing his throat, got into the carriage and took her companion's place. That was that, then, Lou thought, watching him open a book, find his place and start reading, her chance of some conversation to distract her from her thoughts at an end.

Left with nothing to do except watch the passing of the countryside, it didn't take her long to feel gloomy again — hardly surprising when she considered the tasks still ahead of her. Declining Douglas was just the start. After that, she was going to have to pluck up the courage to go to

Harry and tell him she was pregnant. Even then there remained the possibility he might not have her. He might, for instance, claim that the baby wasn't his. Then what would she do? She knew now that she couldn't go home, not with a baby on the way; there had been enough illegitimate babies in the family to last for centuries. Another one would be the final straw. Mum would be so disappointed in her. Dad would be heartbroken. And then there would be the shame of it. God, the shame of it. It was going to be hard enough when she had to tell them she was getting married. Harry might charm her mother, but her father would see *straight* through him — be in no doubt what was going on. *I thought we'd brought you up better than that*, he would lament.

Well, she would attach no blame to her parents. She had brought this on herself. She had thought she was being so grown-up, going out with Harry, wearing jewellery and perfume and furs, when, really, she could see now that all she had been was another country girl taken in by a smooth-talking opportunist. She had also come to realise that, if she was hoping for help from Esme, she would have to be completely truthful with her. Where was the point in travelling all of this way in the hope of getting some advice if she wasn't going to tell her the whole story? No, she must keep nothing back and pray that her dear cousin could find it in herself to set aside the urge to judge and, instead, to offer some help and support. Because, if she didn't, well, then she had no idea know how she was going to see this through. She really would be horribly on her own.

★ ★ ★

Waterloo station was chaotic. As she handed her ticket to the woman collector at the barrier and stepped out into

299

the clamour of the main concourse, it seemed to Lou as though every uniformed man in the country had chosen that moment to catch a train.

Glancing about, she saw from the station clock that she had about fifteen minutes until Esme was due to arrive. Thankfully, having been here just three months previously golly, was it only three months since the weekend of the wedding-that-never-was? — she could picture the news-agent's stand where her cousin had suggested they meet. All she had to do was find her way there through this swarming mass of khaki, navy and steel blue.

Pulling the strap of her handbag further onto her shoulder and then doing the same with the string for the box containing her gas mask, she gripped the handle of her overnight bag and set off.

Once at the newspaper stand, she chose a spot where she hoped Esme couldn't miss her and, setting her over-night case at her feet, exhaled with relief. She had got all the way here without incident — no small achievement in these days of delayed and overcrowded trains. All she had to do now was wait. In a moment, Esme would take over. She was good like that.

To distract herself, she turned to a stand of Penguin paperbacks and idly browsed the titles. But just as she was reaching to rotate the display, a violent cramp tore through her abdomen and made her bend double with the pain. Groaning softly, and shocked by the suddenness of it, she reached to the stand of books for support before slowly eas-ing herself upright. Golly, she could do without... But wait! Didn't that feel like the pains she sometimes got when her monthlies started? Yes. Yes, it did. Then dare she think ...?

Aware that her heart had begun to race, she looked wildly about. There. Over there was the ladies' cloakroom. Did she have time to go before Esme arrived? Just about. Not that she could wait: if this was what she thought it was, she had to know now, this instant. So very much hinged upon her knowing!

Grabbing her overnight case, she fled towards the Ladies', plunged down the steps, thrust her hand into the pocket of her jacket where she'd had the foresight earlier to put two pennies, searched for a cubicle showing as 'Vacant' and pushed one of her coins into the slot. Please, please, dear God, she willed, bolting the door behind her and quickly hanging the straps of her handbag and her gas mask over the hook on the back, please let this be what she hoped. Let this be… yes. Oh, God, yes! There was no baby! Precisely *why* there wasn't, she had no idea. In fact, she preferred not to dwell on why she was bleeding. All that mattered was that she was, and that she was saved. Praise the Lord, she was saved.

Light-headed with relief, she reached to the door and lowered her head. She wasn't pregnant. She didn't have to go cap in hand to Harry. Thank God. Oh, thank God. Feeling relief flooding her body, she even started to giggle. Ordinarily, being caught without any sanitary towels was a desperate inconvenience — as it was, she would have to fashion something out of her handkerchief, at least until Esme arrived and she could go in search of a chemist — but right this minute she couldn't care less. She wasn't having a baby. Everything was going to be all right!

Not only that, she reflected, making her way back to the newspaper stand a few minutes later, but no one need ever know how close she had come to disaster — not even Esme. She could even — joy of joys! — she could even consider Douglas's proposal.

No longer minding having to wait for Esme, and sighing yet again with relief, she closed her eyes and pictured Douglas's face. She did wish he wasn't leaving so soon, and that his proposal hadn't been made in such a rush, because, as much as she liked him, she barely knew him. And if the whole sorry mistake of getting involved with Harry Hinds had taught her one thing, it was that people weren't always what they seemed at first sight — that until you got to know them better, they didn't necessarily turn out to be who you imagined. And what was to say the same wasn't true of Douglas? She didn't *think* it was — in fact she was pretty certain it wasn't. But agreeing to marry him would mean plunging headlong into the unknown: not only would she have to go and live on the other side of an ocean, in a country she knew nothing about, but, if something was amiss, she would have no family or friends to go to for help. There could be no getting on a train and going home to see Mum; it would even be difficult to talk to Esme. And that by itself was enough to check her enthusiasm, the level of courage required to take such a step feeling beyond her to even contemplate.

Exhaling heavily, she glanced about for Esme. Still no sign. But she shouldn't be long now. Besides, having these moments to herself gave her the chance to think. In a way, the situation with Douglas was a shame because, from that very first evening at The Angler's Rest, she'd had a feeling he might actually be *the one*. But marry him, just like that, without really knowing him? It would be a huge gamble for both of them. Equally, without work and, ultimately, with nowhere to live, she was going to have to go *somewhere*. Yes, the other side of her head reasoned, but *Canada*? As the wife of a man she barely *knew*? Surely, better than leaping out of the fat and into the fire would be to just go back to Woodicombe, help her mother and father through their grief over Arthur and then, once this war was over, see what happened: take the chance that someone else — albeit someone more ordinary — would come along. Though she couldn't believe she was even thinking it, given that she'd recently proved to be such a terrible judge of character, it seemed by far the less risky option. Obviously, she would ask Esme what *she* thought but, in her heart, she was actually beginning to think there was quite a lot to be said for simply cutting her losses and going home.

★ ★ ★

'Darlings. How wonderful!'

The sight of Diana Lloyd sweeping down her grand staircase to greet them brought Lou to a halt and caused Esme to hurry on ahead.

'Aunt Diana. It's so lovely to see you. Thank you for allowing us to descend upon you like this.'

'Nonsense, my dear,' Aunt Diana replied. 'Always a joy to have you. And Louise, how grown-up you look now.'

Blushing, Lou submitted to an embrace. 'Hello, Mrs Lloyd.'

'For goodness sake dear, call me Diana — Aunt Diana if you prefer. Now, come on, both of you, come through to the conservatory and we'll take some tea. Which would you prefer — Assam or Ceylon? We don't have any Darjeeling — our usual man has shut up shop and gone *orf* to fight. Dreadful inconvenience. Tell me, are you finding this war as tedious as I am? Hopeless, isn't it? Did we not learn anything from that last debacle?'

As Lou and Esme followed Diana Lloyd through to the drawing room, Lou felt her cousin nudge her arm. 'It would seem that we learnt nothing at all from it, Aunt, no.'

Suddenly, Lou hoped that coming here wasn't going

to turn out to be a mistake. Esme's Great Aunt Diana wasknown to everyone as *something of a character*, a description that made her sound merely jolly, whereas Lou found her quite terrifying.

In the conservatory, over slabs of spiced raisin cake and cups of tea, the pair of them sat answering Aunt Diana's enquiries or, rather, nodding or shaking their heads as seemed appropriate. Yes, Lou answered on one occasion, she was keeping well, yes, she answered on another, she too was horrified by the terrible losses on both sides of the so-called Battle of Britain — but tried not to think about it and, yes, she also hoped those nasty little men Hitler and Goering got beaten back and taught a lesson. But when Aunt Diana then moved seamlessly on to regale them with the story of her ever diminishing household staff, Lou was horrified to find herself struggling to keep her eyes open.

Thankfully, seated next to her, Esme noticed. 'All right with you if we go and freshen up, Aunt? Only, poor Lou has spent the entire morning crammed into a railway carriage.'

'Dear me, child, yes, of course. Where are my manners? I asked Dolly to put you in the ladies' twin. You remember where that is, don't you?'

Getting to her feet, Esme nodded. 'Near enough.'

'Drinks at six then,' Diana said. 'I'm afraid I dine rather early nowadays.'

'Six it is.'

Upstairs, in a bedroom reminiscent of one of the drearier ones on the ladies' landing back at Woodicombe, Lou set about unpacking her overnight bag. 'Can you tell me where the bathroom is?' she looked across at Esme to ask.

'Down the landing, last door on the left.'

'Then I'll just take my things along and splash my face.'

However this couple of days turned out, Lou thought, examining her rather grey-looking complexion in the small bathroom mirror moments later, she had to make sure she spoke to Esme about Douglas and his proposal; she mustn't let herself miss the opportunity, either for wont of knowing where to start, or else because Esme took up the whole time with her own *great dilemma*. Whatever the nature of her cousin's problem, it couldn't, in any event, be either as significant or as pressing as her own. Having asked her to marry him, Douglas was about to be sent back to Canada. And, although he'd said she could take her time deciding, for her own sanity, she needed to make up her mind and tell him, one way or the other, before he left. She had to know where she stood.

Arriving back in the bedroom, she found her cousin holding aside the curtain and staring out through the window.

'Let's go for a walk,' Esme turned over her shoulder to say. 'If we go around past the church, we can pick up the footpath along the river. We *could* go down through the orchard, but the churchyard is usually less muddy. Come on, grab a sweater and we'll snatch an hour while it's sunny. While we're out, you can tell me what's upsetting you.'

Feeling utterly exhausted and wishing Esme had simply suggested going downstairs and finding somewhere quiet to sit, Lou tried to raise a smile. 'Yes. All right.'

Once out in the crisp air, Lou found herself racking her brains for where to start. She didn't want to just blurt out about Douglas; she wanted Esme to understand how she'd got into this mess and how desperate she was to avoid piling one mistake on top of another.

'Down here,' Esme said when a crumbling brick wall on their right gave way to a narrow lane. 'It brings us down to the river. So, tell me, what's happened to make you so glum?'

'Quite a lot,' Lou replied. 'And it's built up to the point of becoming one giant mess, a way out from which has unexpectedly presented itself… but which has left me floundering to know whether or not it's the right thing to do.'

Beside her, Esme nodded. 'Turn right here. This leads to the footpath. We'll find a bench and sit down. Sorry, go on, you were saying.'

It seeming as good a place to start as any, Lou chose to tell Esme first about Arthur, struggling to speak past the lump in her throat as she thought of her brother's body lying somewhere in that cold vast ocean.

'I didn't think he was old enough to go in the navy,' Esme observed when Lou had tearfully explained how long it had taken for the family to finally learn of his fate.

'He wasn't. That's why he joined the merchant service. Anyway,' she said, 'each day I feel as though I'm not crying quite so much for him — nor am I crying quite so much for Mum and Dad. I'm also coming to accept that *eventually* the grief will soften.'

'I wish I'd known,' Esme said, reaching for Lou's arm and giving it a squeeze. 'Poor you. Poor Aunt Kate and Uncle Luke. I must send a letter of condolence.'

'Please do. They'd like that.'

Her sorrow for Arthur out in the open, Lou was left trying to think how best to tell Esme about Harry. She didn't particularly *want* to tell her about him at all — and a good many of the details she had already decided to leave out — but for Esme to understand why she was so wary of making another mistake, she really did need to know about him.

'Why is it always the bad boys we get so drawn to?'

306

Esme remarked when Lou had recounted up to the point of leaving the bracelet and the fox-fur stole with the barman of The Globe and walking out. 'What is it about them that makes us take leave of our senses?'

Unprepared for such candour, Lou turned to see that her cousin's smile contained more than a hint of ruefulness. 'Don't tell me you've had a Harry as well.'

'In a sense, yes. Though largely because it's my job to get just such men to betray secrets.'

Betray secrets? 'Golly, Esme, just what sort of job do you have?' Looking both ways along the riverbank to make sure no one was coming, she lowered her voice. 'Are you a spy? And if you are, how on earth did you find *that* sort of job?'

'I didn't,' Esme said. '*They* found *me*. But we'll come to that later. Anyway, you dumped the odious Harry Hinds, so, what happened next?'

Next? Next was something she would never forget.

'There was a burglary — a huge one — at the warehouse where I work... and the police suspected me of masterminding it.'

When Esme stopped walking and turned towards her, her eyes were wide with disbelief. 'They did *what?*'

'I know it seems laughable now,' she said, 'but it wasn't at the time. It was truly terrifying. I tell you, I thought I was going to end up in prison.'

'Oh, Lou, dearest Lou. Look, just along here there's a bench. And it's in the sunshine. We'll sit down and you can tell me all about it.'

In silence, they walked on. The truth was, that of all the things weighing on Lou's mind, her job at the dockyard was no longer really one of them. What had happened there couldn't be undone. But she still needed to explain it to Esme in order to build up to the matter of Douglas's

307

proposal, her current lack of a job being a crucial part of the considerations.

'So, with the police being so convinced I'd had a hand in it,' Lou eventually wound up her explanation of events by saying, 'the powers-that-be had no choice but to suspend me from my job. And then, later, even though, just like that—' she snapped her fingers, '—the police lost interest in me, I was dismissed altogether.'

'You poor thing,' Esme said, reaching to pat Lou's shoulder. 'How absolutely dreadful for you. And have they caught anyone for it yet?'

Lou shook her head. 'Apparently not.'

'You don't suppose this Harry chap could have been behind it? Or one of his pals? Only, from what you've said, he does sound the type. And you did say he turned up there a couple of times when you weren't expecting him.'

For a split second, Lou felt as though she couldn't breathe. Harry. His pal Charlie. Harry in her office that day while she was getting changed. *If anyone's coming, Charlie will start whistling. It's a signal we have. All these bits of paper then, this your work?* Oh, dear God, she had even explained to him how things were done. *Those are requisition dockets waiting to be entered into the ledgers.* And it was all around the same time they'd been unable to account for those half a dozen boxes of stock, as well…

'Oh, God,' she said, feeling suddenly sick. 'I think you could be right. And I think I might unwittingly have helped him — allowed him to see how things worked. Oh, God, Essie, what do I do? *What do I do?*'

'What you do,' Esme said calmly, 'is go to the police and you tell them what you've just realised. After that, it's down to them to decide what they do about it. But these days, black marketeering on that scale falls into the same category as treason. After all, we can't send brave men off to risk their lives in enemy-occupied France if, back at home, we're turning a blind eye to profiteers. So, if Harry *was* involved, he should pay the price.'

Esme was right: she might not like the thought of going to the police, but to ignore her suspicions now would be wholly wrong. 'Yes. Yes, of course. I'll do that. I'll go on Monday.'

Dear God. How could she not have seen it before? How could it have taken Esme to point it out? Now, so many other things made sense, too, including why Jean had turned so nasty that evening when they'd been talking about her having been questioned by the police. And then there was that jewellery she'd suddenly been wearing. Christ, how could she have been so stupid not to see it? No wonder Jean had warned her against mentioning Harry's name; for heaven's sake, the woman was probably as much a part of the whole thing as her stepbrother. Perhaps, given her knowledge of the dockyard, *she* was even the mastermind. Well, she wouldn't let them get away with it; she would conquer her reluctance and tell the police, even if it did make her look gullible.

'Are you all right?' Esme enquired, bending to examine Lou's expression.

Slowly, Lou nodded. 'I will be. But you should know that Mum and Dad know nothing of this. And that's how I want it to stay. I couldn't bear to give Dad more reason to try and get me to go back... nor could I bear to have them think me a failure.'

'No,' Esme said. 'I see that. But without your job, what will you do for money? Is that chap — what was his name? – you know, the one who wanted you to wait for him. Is *he* still keen?'

At Esme's reference to Freddie, Lou stiffened. She'd

given the poor boy her word that she would write to him stay friends — and yet, the moment her head had been turned by someone else, she'd completely neglected him. The way she'd behaved still made her cringe, perhaps even more so now she knew what she did about Harry. In fact, the more she thought about it, the more she realised that taking up with Harry Hinds had made her do quite a lot of things she wasn't especially proud of, including the way she had taken to behaving towards her parents — avoiding them for fear that they would disapprove of how she was living, or that they would interfere and spoil things for her. Well, where her parents were concerned, it wasn't too late to change her ways and make things up to them. Freddie, on the other hand…

'He was killed,' she replied to Esme's question. 'A bomb was dropped on the base where he was training. He never even got to achieve his dream of going to sea.'

'Golly,' Esme replied. 'That's awful. I'm so sorry to hear that.'

'I felt real bad when I heard. Mainly because I let him go away believing something that was far from the truth.'

Reaching towards her, Esme squeezed Lou's hand. 'I'm so sorry,' she said. 'I feel truly terrible for not keeping in touch — for not knowing any of this.'

'No need to be sorry. *I* didn't write to *you*, either.'

'So, if you're not keen — understandably — to go home, what *are* you going to do?'

Finally, Lou realised, it was time to mention Douglas. And, once she started, she was surprised by how easy it was to speak of him. Unlike when she had explained about Harry, she didn't keep stopping and starting, wondering what best to leave out and how to paint herself as less of an idiot. Describing Douglas felt natural and easy and made her feel cosy and warm.

'The thing is,' she said, having described how he'd been so concerned for her wellbeing he'd taken her out, bought her a meal and made her eat it, 'everything was going along nicely until I lost my job. We were getting to know each other like... well, like ordinary couples do, I suppose. And then, the next thing I know, it's all going wrong. He's telling me he's being sent back to Canada to do something important for the war, and I'm wailing about what's going to become of me without a job, and then, without so much as a word of warning, he's asking me to go to Canada with him—'

'He wants you to go to Canada?'

'As his wife.'

Her cousin was wide-eyed. 'Heavens, Lou, you took your time getting around to *that* revelation! I rather think that's what *I* might have *started* with.'

'I thought to tell it all from the beginning, so that, well, so that—'

'Well, well. You dark horse. So, go on then. How did you answer him?'

This is where, Lou thought, it would be so much easier if she could simply tell Esme the truth: that she'd thought she was having a baby, and that she couldn't have accepted Douglas no matter what.

'I didn't say anything... least, not straight away. So that made him apologise for springing it on me so sudden, you know, when I was still getting over the shock of learning about Arthur—'

'And then what?'

From Esme's face, Lou read a mixture of concern and disbelief.

'Well, then he... apologised some more... said I didn't have to decide yet... and asked me to think about it... and to think of all the things I'd need to ask him before I could

311

be sure.' It was at that point she realised how pathetic her tale sounded when it lacked the crucial detail of the baby. In fact, Esme must now be thinking her *mazed*, as Mum would say.

'Dearest Lou,' Esme said wearily, 'if you're going to ask me what to do, I'm afraid you're in for a disappointment because it's not for *me* to sway you one way or the other. A decision of this nature is one only you can make. But what I *can* do is talk about life in general, especially as it seems at the moment.'

Esme was right. She was deeply disappointed. She really did want to know what, in her shoes, her cousin would do. But she would take any advice she could get — general or otherwise. 'Please, do tell me.'

'Well, with this war on, it seems to me that people are frightened to look too far ahead, or make too many plans, almost for fear of tempting fate. Instead, some of them do rather madcap things — the sort they wouldn't normally even entertain. They live for the day.' Listening to her cousin speaking, Lou wondered whether she was talking about something in her own circumstances — particularly if she really was involved with spies. 'Will they regret it? Without a doubt, some of them will. On the other hand, a great many other people, living in truly terrible circumstances, are somehow still finding love and do still dare to have hope. We can each of us only do what we feel is right for us.'

'Yes, I suppose so.'

'This charming Douglas — do you love him?'

Before answering, Lou paused. 'Left to its own devices, my heart says I do. But my head holds me back. Something in here—' With a finger, she tapped the side of her skull. '—wants me to be absolutely certain my thoughts aren't being clouded by how things have ended up—'

'That this isn't just love on the rebound, do you mean?'

'That I wouldn't just be drawn to anyone offering me kindness and sympathy — after losing Arthur, I mean. And Freddie, too. And maybe even after what happened with Harry.'

Esme, too, paused to think. 'That's not unreasonable. But going back to Douglas for a moment, if you were to take him home to your parents, would they like him?'

'They'd love him. *You'd* love him.' It was on the tip of her tongue to add *in some ways, he's not unlike Richard*.

'And at the thought of never seeing him again, how do you feel?'

'Honestly? Heartbroken.'

'Well, if there's one thing I've learned in the last three months,' Esme began again, 'it's that you're more likely to regret the things you *didn't* do than those you *did*. The other thing I've learned — the hard way, I might add — is that we all make mistakes. And that's never going to change. We're all only human beings doing our best. But what you mustn't do, is let your mistakes lead you to question your judgement. Learn from them, yes. Be wise after the event — this Harry, in your case — but don't let your mistakes stop you getting on with your life. I think all of us get our heads turned by the wrong man at some point, but the shrewd among us not only recognise that he's wrong, we move on and try again. Some of our best decisions are probably those we make on the back of surviving something frightening or uncomfortable. Bad men will always do bad things, but that doesn't mean there aren't some fine men out there as well. My advice? Get to know him better — really make it your mission, I mean. Ask him about himself — not just the bland things like how many siblings he has, and whether or not he likes dogs,

313

but the important stuff. Does he go to church? Does he gamble—'

'I can't ask him if he gambles!'

'You *should*. If he's asked you to marry him, there should be nothing he won't tell you. If you can't ask directly, you can always take a more roundabout approach. But ask him what he thinks about women going out to work. Ask how many children he wants. Would he want them to go away to boarding school? Would he want a nanny for them? Would he let you learn to drive? How many nights a week would he expect to go out with his chums? If you only have a few weeks with him, you really do need to get to know him as well as you can. Then, if your heart can satisfy your head that he's worth the risk — and let's face it, marriage is the biggest risk a woman can take — then take him home to meet your parents. And if, after all of that, you still believe you love the man, then for heaven's sake, marry him.'

Beside her, Lou laughed. 'Thank you, Essie.'

'Apologies if I started to sound like a schoolmarm there for a moment.'

She shook her head. 'It's exactly what I needed.'

'A kick up the backside? *Sorry*.'

'You've changed, Esme Colborne.'

'Actually, I go by Ward now.'

'Then you've changed, Esme Ward.'

'I'm not sure it's true to say *I've* changed as much as that *life* has changed *me*. But no, you're right. I have changed. And that's why I telephoned you to start with — to get your thoughts on something. But we'll leave that now until after dinner. I don't know about you but I'm starting to feel chilly sitting here. So, how about we wander back and investigate the contents of Aunt Diana's drinks' cabinet? She's not usually without a decent bottle of gin.'

'Yes, all right. And thank you, Essie,' Lou added as they got to their feet. 'I'm grateful to you for bringing me here.'

'No need to thank me. What's the point of knowing people who can grant you the odd privilege and then never calling upon them? Besides, my initial motivation was entirely selfish, and you can return the favour later by listening to *my* tale of woe.'

Lou smiled warmly. 'For what little my opinion's worth, you're welcome to it.'

'And truly, Lou, while I don't make light of what you've been through down there in Plymouth — as ordeals go, it sounds truly dreadful and I wish I'd known sooner — it's all behind you now. Choose to look at it that way, and I think you'll find many of the issues holding you back simply fade from consideration. The mists, if you like, will clear.'

At that precise moment, Lou reflected, smiling and tucking her arm through Esme's as they set off back along the towpath, she had a suspicion that her cousin was probably right.

★ ★ ★

What Lou craved more than anything was a bath. Travelling back on a train packed so tightly with passengers there was barely room to breathe, let alone move, she'd been dreaming of freeing herself from her itchy scalp and grimy skin. That way, when Douglas arrived to see her, she would be clean and fragrant and relaxed. Now, though, as the station taxi turned the corner into Jubilee Street, she was alarmed to see him already walking up the hill towards number eleven. How was it possible, especially given that she had come to a decision, for her heart to both leap with joy and sink with dismay all at the same time?

315

'Would you mind waiting a moment while I clean up?' she asked when Douglas drew alongside her just as she was paying the cab fare.

'And good evening to you, too, Louise.'

Realising how abrupt she must have sounded, she blushed. 'Sorry. Forgive me. Hello, Douglas. It's just that after being crammed into a filthy train for hours, I'm in desperate need of a good wash.'

When he then apologised profusely for being early and suggested coming back in an hour, she gratefully agreed and hurried indoors to get cleaned up. And now, here they were, by unspoken agreement walking up the hill towards the church.

'Well, you certainly seem brighter than the other day,' he remarked.

He hadn't, she noticed, presumed to offer her his arm. But then why would he; he had no idea how, having had the chance to reflect, she was going to respond to his proposal.

'I *feel* brighter,' she replied to his observation.

'How was your cousin? Only, if she's done you this much good in just two days then I like her already!'

Lou smiled. 'You'd like her anyway. She's kind and caring and doing something top secret for the government. She didn't say anything she shouldn't have, but I worked out for myself that it has to do with spies.'

'Spies?'

'Oh, and not only did she insist upon giving me the fare to get that taxi back from the station just now, but, despite my refusing it, she's given me the money to cover two more weeks' rent as well — so that I don't, as she put it, under the threat of homelessness, do anything rash. Of course, I fully intend paying her back.'

'She sounds incredibly thoughtful. I hope I get to meet

her one day.' When the two of them came to a somewhat awkward halt at the lychgate, he gestured towards the porch. 'Since we seem to have ended up here again, shall we go and sit down?'

'Let's. The quiet will be nice after that rattling old train.'

'So,' he said when they were once again seated under the ancient porch. 'Your trip was worthwhile.'

Despite her exhaustion, the long sigh she exhaled was one of relief. Barely forty-eight hours ago, she would have given anything to know she would be back here with him like this. 'In ways I could never have dreamed of,' she said.

'You helped her with her — what was the word you used? — her dilemma?'

Having forgotten she'd led him to believe her visit was in aid of Esme's problem rather than her own, she nodded. 'I did.'

'And you managed to find time to consider my proposal?'

It was on the tip of her tongue to say that, actually, barring the odd moment or two, she'd thought of little else. But, when she looked back at him and saw the earnestness of his expression, she appreciated what an agonising time he must have had; while *she* had been in charge of her own destiny — free to think about what he had proposed and decide either way — all *he* had been able to do was await her return, his fate out of his own hands.

'You'll be pleased to know that I did, yes.'

'And …?'

'And I've decided it's definitely worth finding out more about you, Lieutenant Douglas Ross.'

'Then how about,' he said, surprising her by leaping to his feet and rubbing his hands together, 'we go and find somewhere to get a drink and you commence your inquisition right now, without delay?'

317

His eagerness made her laugh. He truly was lovely. 'Good idea. Because believe me when I tell you that I intend leaving no stone unturned.'

'Nor should you, Miss Channer. Now as it happens,' he went on, '*I* also have some news for *you*.'

Turning towards him, she saw that he was still smiling. '*Good* news, I trust.'

'Late Friday afternoon, Commander Dutton had a telephone call from Sergeant Milburn.'

Feeling her heart speeding up, she looked directly at him. 'And...?'

'They have someone in their sights for the burglary.'

Well that was a relief! For a moment there, she'd feared what he was going to say. 'They have?'

'A local gang, apparently. Obviously, I'm not privy to the details — and for the moment, you can't breathe a word of this to anyone — but it looks as though they're close to making some arrests.'

Golly. It was almost too much to take in. Now she really could stop worrying. Now, she needn't even go to the police to share her suspicions about Harry and Jean — which also meant that once the police had the real burglars locked up, she could try and patch up her friendship with the girls. She certainly missed their company.

The news slowly sinking in, she sighed with relief. 'So, finally, I'm in the clear.'

'You are,' Douglas said. 'Completely. Although, in my eyes, you always were.' When he swiftly offered her his arm, she happily took it. 'So, how about we go and get that drink?'

As they set off along the path, Lou could still barely believe it. She was free — free from suspicion, free from Harry, free to go home and see Mum and Dad — which she would do just as soon as she could now. Most importantly, she was free to give proper consideration to marrying the wonderful man standing next to her.

As she went ahead of him through the gate, though, something dawned on her: she could ask him whatever she liked but nothing was going to change how she felt. The only thing stopping her accepting him the other day had been her belief that she was pregnant. With that obstacle now gone, and with the benefit of having spent a couple of days away from him, her head was in full agreement with her heart. While it was true that she still had reservations about going to live in Canada — and a hundred other things besides! — it was obvious now what she should do.

With a smile, she withdrew her arm from his and reached instead to take his hand. Clearly delighted, he turned to look at her.

'Actually,' she said, ''though there's still any number of things I want to ask you, I should perhaps tell you now that I intend saying yes.'

With her feet leaving the pavement as Douglas swept her up and whirled her around, she laughed out loud. What was it Esme had said at that family dinner in Clarence Square about finding the right man? *When you know, you just know?* At the time, it had seemed such a ridiculously unhelpful thing to say. But now, here, like this, with her heart fit to burst from happiness, she realised that it was true.

Epilogue

London
September 1940

'Are we *very* late?'

Trotting breathlessly up the steps to the town hall, Lou saw Douglas examine his wristwatch.

'At this precise moment,' he said calmly, 'we're not actually late at all. We have three whole minutes to spare.'

'Poor Essie,' she lamented, 'she'll be worried sick that we're not going to turn up.'

The entrance now in front of them, Douglas took hold of Lou's hand. 'Almost certainly she will be, yes,' he replied. 'But that's no reason for us to panic, too. So, let's you and I take just a moment to pause and gather our thoughts.'

Despite being terrified that Douglas's watch would turn out to be slow, and that they were, in fact, already late, Lou knew he was right. 'Gather our thoughts. Yes.'

At least they'd made it, she reflected, grateful for the chance to stand and recover her breath. What good fortune to have realised so quickly that when they'd left the station, they'd started to head in completely the wrong direction! What even greater good fortune to have found someone who knew where they were trying to reach!

Beginning to breathe more easily, she found herself thinking about Liddy and Flossie, and Winnie and Nora and Jess. It was a shame they couldn't be there — especially now they were all friends again. When, ahead of her return to Woodicombe, she and Douglas had told them about their engagement, they'd all begged her to get married in Plymouth: *only fair one of us catches your bouquet*, Winnie had grumbled, it taking Liddy to point out that since there was *a ruddy war on*, there was unlikely to be a bouquet for any of them *to* catch. But, despite their disappointment, Lou had stood firm, assuring them that this was what she wanted. So, when, the other day, she'd received a letter from them containing their love and good wishes, she'd shed more than a few tears. And as for their welcome — but not entirely surprising — news that Harry had been arrested for the burglary, and that Jean had been suspended from the dockyard, well, it had been just what she'd needed to finally draw a line under the whole sorry mess.

Feeling Douglas squeezing her hand, Lou looked up.

'Ready to go and do this?' he asked.

She didn't hesitate. 'I am.'

When Douglas pushed open the door and Lou stepped inside, it was to see Esme, standing in the middle of the vast foyer, her hands clasped tightly in front of her, her brow knitted with concern. Next to her, Richard looked equally vexed.

'Sorry!' she called, starting across the marble floor towards them. 'So terribly sorry, both of you...'

Instantly, Esme's expression softened. 'Well, you certainly cut *that* fine!'

'Yes, so sorry,' she said again, this time from within her cousin's embrace. 'We took a wrong turn leaving Waterloo.'

'Come on, then, quickly,' Esme urged, and with which Lou found herself being whisked along the corridor. 'I'm afraid the pleasantries will have to wait for now because the registrar's assistant has already warned us about holding things up. And trust me, I have absolutely no intention of missing

321

my wedding for a second time!'

Nor me for the first time, Lou reflected, turning over her shoulder to beam at Douglas and Richard, striding along behind them.

Hard to believe that any moment now, in this solemn little registry office, the four of them were about to start new lives, Esme long overdue to become Mrs Richard Trevannion, she, herself, by marrying *one of the Canadians* to become Mrs Douglas Ross. It simply couldn't be any more fitting.